SARAH,
SON OF GOD

Reviewers Praise Justine Saracen's Novels

Praise for *Mephisto Aria*

"Justine Saracen's latest thriller, *Mephisto Aria*, brims with delights for every sort of reader…delight at love's triumph, and at Saracen's queer reworkings of the Faust legend, are not this novel's only pleasures. Saracen's understanding of the world around opera is profound. She captures the sweat, fierce intelligence, terror and exultation that characterize singers' daily lives, in rehearsal and performance, she evokes well the camaraderie that a production's cast and crew share, and she brings to literary life the curious passions that bind people who make music together. Brilliantly fusing the insights of twenty years' worth of feminist and queer opera criticism to lesbian fantasy fiction, Saracen has written a passionate, action-packed thriller that sings—indeed, that sings the triumph of *Rosenkavalier*'s trio of lovers over Dr. Faustus' joyless composer. Brava! Brava! Brava!"—Suzanne G. Cusick, Professor of Music, New York University

"*Mephisto Aria* could well stand as a classic among gay and lesbian readers."—*ForeWord Reviews*

"Saracen's wonderfully descriptive writing is a joy to the eye and the ear, as scenes play out on the page, and almost audibly as well. The characters are extremely well drawn, with suave villains, and lovely heroines. There are also wonderful romances, a heart-stopping plot, and wonderful love scenes. *Mephisto Aria* is a great read."—*Just About Write*

Acclaim for *Sistene Heresy*

"Justine Saracen's *Sistine Heresy* is a well-written and surprisingly poignant romp through Renaissance Rome in the age of Michelangelo...The novel entertains and titillates while it challenges, warning of the mortal dangers of trespass in any theocracy (past or present) that polices same-sex desire."
—Professor Frederick Roden, University of Connecticut, Author of *Same-Sex Desire in Victorian Religious Culture*

"Historical fiction [is] a genre that must artfully blend historical accuracy with fanciful conjecture in order to succeed. And succeed Saracen does. A professor of German language and literature at such prestigious institutions as Stanford University and Rochester Institute of Technology, and the author of two previous theocentric novels, Saracen is a self-proclaimed amateur historian who nevertheless renders accepted period details with a robust physicality. And while the rapid-fire pacing of the tale spins on the dangers inherent in succumbing to homosexual temptation, its gay/lesbian characterizations are handled with a discerning degree of restraint. Casting such an iconic artistic and historic figure as Michelangelo in a controversial new light is risky business—some would say a heresy unto itself. But Saracen portrays Michelangelo and his cohorts as anything but corrupt, endowing them with an absolute sensitivity and absolute humanity."—*ForeWord Reviews*

Praise for *The 100ᵗʰ Generation*

"[T]he lesbian equivalent of Indiana Jones...Saracen has sprinkled cliffhangers throughout this tale...If you enjoy the History Channel presentations about ancient Egypt, you will love this book. If you haven't ever indulged, it will be a wonderful introduction to the land of the Pharaohs. If you're a *Raiders of the Lost Ark*–type adventure fan, you'll love reading a woman in the hero's role."—*Just About Write*

Visit us at www.boldstrokesbooks.com

By the Author

The 100th Generation

Vulture's Kiss

Sistine Heresy

Mephisto Aria

Sarah, Son of God

SARAH,
SON OF GOD

by
Justine Saracen

A Division of Bold Strokes Books

2011

SARAH, SON OF GOD
© 2011 By Justine Saracen. All Rights Reserved.

ISBN 10: 1-60282-212-3
ISBN 13: 978-1-60282-212-2

This Trade Paperback Original Is Published By
Bold Strokes Books, Inc.
P.O. Box 249
Valley Falls, NY 12185

First Edition: March 2011

CREDITS
EDITOR: SHELLEY THRASHER
PRODUCTION DESIGN: STACIA SEAMAN
COVER DESIGN BY SHERI (GRAPHICARTIST2020@HOTMAIL.COM)

Acknowledgments

For starters, I want to thank Georgi Badakhshan for introducing me to the strange and wonderful phenomenon of Eddie Izzard, whose images in full girl mode became the inspiration for one of the main characters. I am also grateful for her later assistance in finding visual representations of the sailing vessels called carracks.

On the sensitive subject of gender change, transgendered author Iolanthe Woulff was not only an invaluable source of information, but is also a friend. Any misinformation here comes from my not paying enough attention to her candid explanations.

Nicolo' Giacomuzzi-Moore and Mercedes Binda, whom good luck granted me as neighbors, were a regular reference point for Italian terms. *Mille grazie.* Thanks also to Tiziana Plebani, librarian at the National Library in Venice, who assisted me while both of us struggled in French, our only common language. *Merci beaucoup pour les informations*, Tiziana, though I might not have mentioned that it was (ahem) for a lesbian novel.

Thanks also to Ellen Isaacs for being clever enough to arrange the fabulous apartment that forms the model for Joanna and Sara's accommodations while in Venice.

Another wave to Storm, for the occasional bit of trivia about Italian life.

I want to express my gratitude in general to the people of Venice, who were always patient and polite to me in the face of considerable language obstacles, and of the never-ending tsunami of tourists.

My deep gratitude ever and always to Shelley Thrasher, my editor and trusted friend who helped turn a stream of consciousness into a lucid story. I don't know what I'd do if we couldn't have our ongoing dialogue.

Thanks also to Stacia, who brings sensitivity and craft to the final polish to create this nice book you are holding, and to Sheri for yet another of her delicious covers, which she seems to conjure out of her endlessly rich internal inventory.

Radclyffe, if you've read this manuscript, you'll know this whole book is a tribute to you.

Dedication

This book is dedicated to Eddie Izzard.

PROLOGUE

Venice, June 1560

"Mother of God!"

Massimo screamed as he dropped to the end of the rope and the *strappado* dislocated his shoulders. He sobbed as he hung, swaying in a small arc.

The Dominican inquisitor rose from his chair and braced his hands on the table, his long sleeves slipping like eels from under his satin *mozzetta*. Their whiteness contrasted sharply with the filth around him. Not only had lice made a home in the brocade cover of his table, but the room reeked of sweat and urine from countless accused men who had pissed themselves during torture.

He studied the face of the agonized Massimo for a moment, then came around in front of the table. He took care not to touch the prisoner but shook his head slowly. He spoke gently, a loving shepherd. "Take care to not add another blasphemy to your sins, my son. Answer the question truthfully and all will be well."

Massimo whimpered incoherently.

The inquisitor signaled the torturer at the winch to reel the moaning man back up onto the high platform. "Once more, my son. Clear your troubled conscience before God and end your suffering. Where are the books?"

Massimo knelt panting at the edge of the platform, his bound wrists drawn up high behind his back. "I swear, my lord," he moaned. "On my soul. I know not. He who ordered them claimed them of an evening."

"And whither brought them? Who was he, by name and origin?"

The inquisitor repeated his questions for the third time, gesturing to the torturer to haul the man to his feet.

"I told you. It was a Turk or Jew named Hakim. He fetched the books away anon they were printed. I know not where."

The inquisitor took his time, glancing first at the notary to assure that the response was recorded, then at the doge, who could bear witness to his attempt at mercy. Finally he nodded to the torturer on the high platform. Obeying the signal, the masked man shoved the prisoner from the platform so that he fell, jerking to a halt in midair. As the muscles of his back tore again, he released a raw, rasping scream.

In the wooden cell adjacent to the torture chamber, Leonora Barotti cowered, her stomach churning at her brother-in-law's torture. Massimo was telling the truth. He did not know the fate of the heretical books, but she *did*, and she trembled, knowing that they would torture her next. How long could she hold out against the strappado, or any of the other horrors they used on women? Not long, she feared.

Poor courageous Massimo. Tortured first, simply because the inquisitors assumed he was master of the printing house. In truth, he was, though in name only. Upon her husband's death, his brother Massimo had taken on the business, ineptly as it turned out. Had they been thriving, as before, he would ne'er have insisted on printing the strange translation. And now his last bad decision would cost them both their lives.

Thank the Virgin that Anne was safe. At least that.

Finally the screaming stopped and Leonora fell into troubled sleep on the straw pallet. An hour later, she jerked back to wakefulness at the sound of the jailor's key. She cowered again, her heart pounding. Was this her time on the rope?

But no. By the light of the jailor's lantern, she could see he was smiling. Even better, she saw no attending priest. A good sign. He came into the cell, swaying slightly. He held something wide and flat. As he lurched, it dropped from his hand and fell against the cell wall.

"How goes the lady on such a Carnival night? A great spectacle we're missing." He leaned against the doorjamb to steady himself.

"Well enough. What will you at this hour?" Leonora answered coolly, waiting for him to explain why he had disturbed her. Then she saw the object he had brought. "What's that?"

"A gift, from your brother," the jailor said, slurring his words slightly. "Will you have it? A favor for a favor, eh?" He stepped toward her on uncertain feet and laid a hand on her breast.

Leonora recoiled, brushing his hand away, and was about to say, "I don't have a brother," then caught herself.

"This is no place for airs, lady, and no hour for prudery. All of Venice is sunk in wine. Yet here we be, in a quiet, private place. And I've a present, two in truth. But one of them is here." He stroked his crotch. "What say you, lady, we make a carnival of our own?" He pulled her toward him, his breath foul.

"What's going on here?" Another voice spoke from the cell doorway. The jailor sprang back as if stung. "Nothing, Captain. A gentleman left a kindness for the prisoner and I've just delivered it."

"Then be done with it." The jail captain continued down the corridor.

The jailor muttered something unintelligible and slid the object toward Leonora. "A picture of the Savior," he grumbled. "Your brother said to keep the image by your head that you see him when you wake."

What cruel jest was this? Had they set a trap for her? Silence seemed the wisest.

"He further said to search the image well, for if redemption come, it will spring forth from this place." The jailor burped wetly. "He also paid for an extra candle."

"Thank you," she said, lowering her gaze as she accepted the gifts, not moving from the spot until the jailor had left and locked the door behind him. Then, still puzzled, she placed the candle inside the cell lantern and set it by the head of her pallet. Following the instructions of her mysterious "brother," she propped the picture against the wall. "Search the image," he'd said. How could she do that in the dim light? As she adjusted the frame, something sharp scraped her palm. She held the lantern to the bottom left corner of it to see what had pricked her. A piece of metal protruded from a split in the wood, and when she pried it out, she saw it was a small serrated blade. What was she supposed to do with it? The window bars were iron.

And what did "Redemption from this place" mean? She pressed her ear against the floor and heard a faint scrabbling noise. She flinched, thinking it was rats. But, no, she also detected the low rumble of a man's voice. She tapped with her knuckle on the floor once and immediately received an answering tap. She tapped again, twice, and it was echoed back to her. Now she understood. Someone was chipping the wood from the other side, and she was to cut away at it from her side. It seemed that the grinding was coming from a spot a hand's breadth away from the two adjoining walls. Fortunately, when she knelt and bent over the corner, the jailor would be able to see only her feet through the opening in the cell door. If she prayed, loudly and fervently as her "brother" had suggested, she might be able to conceal the sound of scraping away the wood.

So, redemption *was* coming after all. She set to work.

❖

After eight hours and hundreds of prayers, her fingers were swollen and bleeding, but the ring she had marked out on the floor was now cut deep. She could even see light through a small spot on one side of the disk. But the hole she was cutting from the top was misaligned to the one below and, worse, was too small to slip through. She would need another night to enlarge it.

Too late. It was daylight. The jailors were moving about and she dared not draw their attention, so she positioned the picture over the hole and sat far away from it, dozing slightly.

The hours passed, and by noon she could hear the dull sound of the crowds on the San Marco Piazzetta below celebrating another day of Carnival. She dozed again, dreaming she was in Carnival mask and disguise in the great piazza. Miraculously, Anne was by her side, brightly costumed in something elaborate and silken. Seizing her hand, Leonora tried to run, but it was as if she were lame and all she could do was drag herself forward one laborious step at a time.

The iron key turning in the lock awakened her and she lurched to her feet. It was a different jailor this time, and behind him stood a Dominican, tonsured and grim. "It is time, signora," the jailor said.

Wordlessly she went to the doorway, not daring to look back for fear they would discover the hole behind the picture. Then she realized it made no difference. Broken by the strappado, she would be sentenced to death immediately. She was lost.

With the jailor in front and the priest behind her, she descended the narrow wooden staircase to the torture chamber. Her legs were so weak from kneeling, and now from sheer terror at the sight of the rope, she collapsed at the doorway.

The jailor took one of her arms and a guard the other, and together they stood her up on a low platform. In front of her, three men sat behind a long table under a painted crucifix. The crucified man seemed a reminder of the suffering to come. She recognized two of the three men: the inquisitor, in the white robe and red mozzetta of a Dominican, and the doge, Girolamo Priuli. The man on the left, she assumed, was another member of the Council. At an adjacent table, a scribe sat with parchment, quill, and ink.

A winch creaked high overhead and something brushed against her back. The strappado rope. She trembled violently and closed her eyes to fight off nausea.

The voice of the inquisitor drew her attention as he dictated to the scribe. "You may begin. This day, the eighth June, anno Domini 1560. Called before the Sacred Tribunal of the Holy Office, the widow Leonora Barotti, residing in the parish of S. Samuel."

He turned to the prisoner. "What is your name?"

"Leonora Barotti," she managed, through chattering teeth.

"Note that, being asked her name and surname, she replied correctly."

"What is your profession?" His voice was cool and businesslike.

She took a deep breath. "A printer of books, my lord."

"Know you the reasons you have been called here?"

They were trying to get her to implicate herself. Should she pretend innocence and risk their wrath?

"I think I am accused of publishing a heretical book."

"Do you confess it?"

Her heartbeat roared in her ears and she could scarcely hear him, but she knew what he had asked. What was the right thing to say? "I confess I knew it not as heresy, only as a jest. A slight blasphemy like the songs the bravos sing in the streets. Such is my guilt, my lords." She took another deep breath to fight off the dizziness. If she had a gram of courage, this was the last moment to show it.

"But I am the only one, signori. I alone made compact with the stranger and took him at his word. I alone knew the text and deemed it profitable to print. My printers, journeymen, all others in my employ were innocent of this knowledge." Curiously, she felt a sense of relief, knowing that she might still save Lucca and the others. Maybe even the foolish Massimo. If her hour had come, then so be it.

"How many copies did you print?"

"Two hundred, my lord."

"And what befell those books? I warn you, do not perjure."

"A Jew named Hakim Yaakub fetched them erewhile they were completed. By cart, my lords. He asked the travel time and state of road of the highway to Milan."

The doge snorted. "Selling to the Milanese. Of course. That scum will feed off anything for amusement."

Leonora was lying. During the long night of scratching a hole in her cell floor, she had brooded on who her rescuer might be. Only one person was likely, and if she was right, Hakim was surely fleeing the same way she was supposed to—by sea.

The inquisitor looked into her eyes and she knew he saw the lie. He signaled to someone behind her, and, with a few deft strokes, strong hands tied her elbows together.

"Be you sure of this? Bethink you long and hard, my daughter," the doge said.

Her breathing became fast as she anticipated the pain. "Yes, my lord. I am sure."

The creak of the winch came first, then the odd sensation of her arms being raised behind her, and finally the searing pain in her shoulders and ribs as she was slowly lifted off her feet. She writhed, trying uselessly to lift herself in the air, and cried out. The pain spread downward to her hips and back, then to her neck and up around her ears. Her shoulders were on fire. She dropped her head forward and drew up her knees, but the agony continued. Her head pounded with every heartbeat.

The inquisitor's hand went up and suddenly Leonora's feet touched the platform again. Her shoulders still throbbed, but the unbearable fire had ebbed, and she gulped for air.

"Reflect again, Leonora Barotti, and remember you are a Christian. Whither did the Jew transport the books?"

"To Milan, my lord," she forced herself to say again, though it came out a murmur.

The inquisitor shook his head slowly in disappointment, as if before an incorrigible child, and the rope behind her tightened again. This time she was lifted more quickly, and the muscles in her shoulders and neck threatened to rip. A jolt of intolerable pain shot through her, like sheet lightning, and she blacked out.

❖

Leonora awoke in her cell on her pallet. Her arms stretched out on both sides of her were aching, and her fingers were numb. She clenched and unclenched her hands, trying to restore sensation. She was certain they had left her alone because they knew that fear of the same torture the next day would cause her to confess. They were right. Her courage was spent.

She pulled herself up with effort, trying not to put weight on her arms. It was still day, for though her window looked onto a corridor, afternoon light still spilled through an outside window farther down the hall.

A plate of dark bread and a flask of water were nearby on the floor, and when she could control her hands, she lifted the flask and drank gratefully. She used her chamber pot and set it at the opposite end of the cell. Turning back to her pallet, she noted that the picture of the Savior was undisturbed.

She sat down again and rested against the cell wall, waiting for darkness and for strength to return to her hands.

Oh! Leonora awoke with a start. She must have fallen asleep, for it was full night. Her arms ached less now, and she was able to fumble toward the painting and uncover the hole. She felt its ragged edges with her fingertips, then groped along the picture's frame to retrieve the tiny blade.

This was her only chance for life. Ignoring the pain in her fingertips, her ravaged back, and, increasingly, in her knees, she worked furiously, scoring an ever-deepening cut in the floor. Soon a whisper came from below, then the brief flash of a lantern. "Only a little more, signora. Over here." Fingers guided her to a jagged piece of wood that they hacked at, from both above and below.

"Push now," the stranger whispered, and she put all her weight on one knee at the center of the carved ring. Finally, with a frighteningly loud rip, the wooden disk gave way.

"Wait," someone growled, and she heard the breaking of splinters around the periphery of the hole.

"Now," he ordered. She gathered her skirt and plunged feet first in the darkness through the hole, the jagged wood tearing her clothing and bruising her hips. The circle they had cut was still smaller than it needed to be, but nothing could stop her now. She would have broken bones to get through.

Finally, with a soft grunt, she forced her hips past the cutting rim, and rough hands caught her as she dropped into a cell on the lower level. She did not recognize the lantern-lit face. "Who be you?" she whispered.

"Shh," he hissed, then added, barely audibly, "Piero."

The empty cell opened to a corridor that led to the same stairwell she had walked that morning. She shuddered as they passed the torture chamber and descended to a floor below.

Her rescuer had a black cloth wrapped around his hand and held a tiny lantern. Something scrabbled in the wall and he dropped the cloth over the light, leaving them in darkness. But their alarm proved unnecessary; it was probably a mouse. He uncovered the lantern, and they crept along a second corridor to another hall.

It was cavernous, and their little light did not reach to the far end. Only the gilt on the ceiling directly overhead revealed where they were. Leonora gasped softly. It was the majestic Council Chamber where the thousand nobles of the *Gran Consiglio* gathered to rule Venice. She sensed the residue of their power as she groped along the wall toward the door.

A moment later they were in the palace courtyard, and as they approached the gateway that opened to the piazzetta, Piero drew her back behind a column. From the darkness, she saw four officers of the Council marching past. Two of them carried a ladder.

Soon the men were out of sight, and she and her rescuer slipped through the gate, turning left to flee under the arcaded walkway toward the water. The sun was just rising; its first rays shone along the water of the bay and into the arcade, shooting a glistening path between the horizon and themselves. When they reached the end of the arcade, Leonora glanced to the right, toward the first pillar, and stumbled in shock. Now she understood the presence of the Council officers and their ladder.

At the top of the pillar stood the familiar winged lion of Saint Mark, but on a gibbet at its foot hung the body of Massimo, a lesson to heretics.

Leonora followed blindly now, with the single thought of escape. She stepped heavily into the shallow *sàndolo* behind its oars and crouched, shivering as Piero shoved off from the bank. The rising sun afforded light for them to navigate to the center of the canal, and though they would be visible from shore, as yet, no one was looking for them.

Dread slowly left her as they moved eastward to the creaking of the oarlocks and the screeching of the first gulls coming from the lagoon. A gondola passed them, its gondolier rowing drunkenly with long lethargic pulls on his oar. His passengers were a man in a tricorne hat with a wide black tabarro around his shoulders and a woman wearing an elaborately ruffled blue costume with puff sleeves and deep décolleté.

Both were masked, he in a chalk white face with a menacing chin, and she in a feathered eye mask, yet they managed nonetheless to exchange intimacies. His hand draped over her shoulder had hold of her breast, while her hand rested between his spread thighs.

Leonora looked away and watched the palazzi of the Genovese and the Barbarigi slide by. She could identify all the great homes of the old nobility, but now their names rang hollow. Her days in Venice under their rule were over. That is, if her "savior" could manage her escape from them. The authorities would certainly be watching for her throughout the city and at every exit from it. Her life depended on the skill and will of her rescuer to evade them.

She had an idea who Piero's master might be, and though she was too spent to ask, it soon became apparent she was right. As the Grand Canal curved north, crossing first the Rio di Trovaso and then the Rio Malpaga, Piero brought the boat gradually closer to the left bank. Then, just before the corner where the Rio Foscari flowed into the Grand Canal, Piero swung the craft alongside a wide water entrance to a palazzo. In the half-light of dawn she could see it was majestic, with a double row of balconies, each with an arcade of carved stone. She recognized the huge iron lamp that hung over the water at the corner where the large and the small canal intersected.

"The Ca' Foscari," she said, unnecessarily, as the iron water gates swung open.

Inside the corridor, where dank water plashed softly against stone, the dull morning light was augmented by a torch thrust into an iron loop on the wall. Under the torch, a stone platform received boat passengers and led to several doorways, presumably to storerooms. Piero tied the sàndolo to the mooring pole inside, and as the gates swung shut behind them, a man strode down the stone steps to meet them. He helped Leonora to her feet, and in a moment, she stood on the platform beside him.

"Maffeo Foscari. I thought it might be you."

By the flickering torchlight his features were rendered stark and two-toned, bronze where lit and black in the hollows. Yet she knew he was a vigorously handsome man.

"Yes, but forgive me if I do not waste precious time on greetings. None of my house know of you but these two good men, Piero and Rico. They will bring you food whilst you stay sequestered." He guided her into a room just off the water entrance where building materials, tools, and miscellaneous bales and boxes were piled. Behind a wall of crates was a bed and some candles.

"Yes, thank you, but what then?"

"The *Grazie Dei* sets sail in two days. You must forthwith make a list of goods, urgent for your travel, that will fit into a single crate. Lucca will bring them hence. I will see to your passage."

"Signor Foscari, you have plundered the doge's prison of me at your peril, for which I am grateful. But how think you to abscond with me? There is no place to hide a woman on shipboard."

"With those." He pointed to a bundle at the foot of her bed. "There's a looking glass, as well. You do well to begin today to craft your newer person. And now I beg your pardon, lady. I have a visitor who already puzzles at my absence. Be assured you are safe for now. None but Piero or Rico will disturb you in this place. Rico will be back shortly with water for your ablutions." With that he strode back the way he had come, with the two men behind him.

Leonora sat down on the makeshift bed, more a padded platform, but blissful compared to her jail-cell pallet. She was exhausted, both physically and emotionally, but the excitement of escape and the sounds of morning activity outside the high window, kept her nervously awake. She lit a second candle and examined what lay folded on her bed.

She held up a woolen outer garment, a cassock in the English style. Lined with fur, it had clearly belonged to someone prosperous. Under it were doublet, breeches, hose, and hat. Now she understood. She was to travel as a young Englishman.

After a moment's consternation, she saw the logic of it. Dressing in the clothing of the opposite sex was punishable, she knew, but the best way to guarantee her safety while in the company of men. Fortunately, she was tall for a woman; perhaps she could pull it off.

"By your leave, madama." It was Piero again, with a basin of steaming water and a tailor's shears. He set the basin down on one of the crates. Rico followed him with a wooden bowl of bread and cheese and a ewer of wine. "The signor said this is for your preparations. I will leave you now and lock both the water gates and the door from the house. None shall enter here and you may rest safely. At day's end, one of us will bring you supper."

Holding up her candle, she studied Piero for the first time. He was slightly stooped, but robust, his forearms knotty with muscles. A powerful oarsman. His thin dark hair was long and tied behind his neck.

The sparse beard that covered his cheeks and neck made it difficult to tell his age, but she guessed him to be older than his master. "Thank you, Piero. And thank you for all your labor last night. I hope God in heaven rewards you for it."

"My reward is to serve a man like Maffeo Foscari, signora. I will leave you to your labor now."

Then he was gone, and the sound of the door locking at the top of the stairs relieved her. Feeling safe, she set about undressing. She could barely lift her arms for the damage she still felt in her back from the strappado. Her whole body ached, and her fingertips were swollen and rubbed raw. But the quiet joy that came over her at being free and in trusted hands lent her strength to finally pull off her dress. After a week in prison it was torn and rank, and she was happy to be rid of it. She washed luxuriously with the warm water and looked down at herself. She was pale, from so many days without sunlight, but nothing took away from her stature as a tall, still-robust woman who had just passed her fortieth year. Her breasts were still firm, her legs strong, and her arms, unbroken by the torture, would soon be strong again too. She could work as many hours as a man. But could she pass for one?

The men's undergarments were clean and soft against her skin. The linen shirt was wide and long, and did much to conceal her breasts. The breeches also were a trifle long, but she folded them at the waist and improved the fit. The hose looked quite smart as she gartered them at the knee under the breeches. As she expected, the shoes were too large, but she could stuff a bit of straw into the toes. The ochre-colored doublet fit remarkably well, even after she attached the sleeves, and when it was fully buttoned, it flattened the swell of her breasts to suggest a wide male chest.

She stepped before the mirror and, with some amusement, saw a rather handsome, fine-boned English gentleman. Only one thing was still amiss, and she understood now why Foscari had sent a tailor's shears. With a sigh, she took them up and began to cut her hair. While she did so, she ran men's names through her mind, pronouncing each one to see if it suited her. As she lopped off the last hank of hair, she finally settled on one.

Standing with her hands on her hips before the mirror, she addressed her image, uttering the few English phrases she had learned from Anne.

"Good day to you. I am Lawrence Bolde, merchant from London. Thank you very much."

CHAPTER ONE

New York City, June 1969

Mozart's *Marriage of Figaro* played on the stereo as Tadzio Falier prepared for a night out. The mezzo-soprano was just singing Cherubino's entrance, and Tadzio sang with her an octave lower in Italian.

He pulled on his favorite green shirt and ran his hands over his breasts, wishing they were larger. They lay like warm apples in his palms and stood out nicely under the silk fabric, but they weren't quite full enough to produce cleavage. Nonetheless, years of electrolysis had made his face and neck hairless, and the estrogen had cushioned his skin, so his opened shirt revealed a softly feminized upper body.

"Non so più cosa son, cosa faccio…" He sang the long-familiar words along with the mezzo-soprano, bemoaning Cherubino's amorous confusion and his feverous hunger for all the women in the palace.

Bending toward the mirror, he examined his carefully plucked eyebrows and applied a hint of pencil to emphasize their curve. He needed only a thin layer of foundation and the faintest hint of blush to add warmth to his cheeks. With equal delicacy, he added a touch of iridescent blue-green shadow to his upper lids. A curve of eyeliner along his eyelids and a quick swipe of the mascara brush over the lashes drew attention to his already-intense blue eyes.

"Un desìo ch'io non posso spiegar," Cherubino's "desire that I cannot explain" seemed to comment lyrically.

Tadzio chose a soft pink shade of lipstick, blotted it on a tissue, then tested a slightly open-mouthed smile. Yes, that was the look he wanted.

His frosted gold-blond hair curled nicely over his ears and neck but was still not quite long enough to be womanly, so even with his two small gold earrings, he left people uncertain of his sex. "Renaissance princeling," he muttered to himself. In fact, he did rather look like some of the beautiful lads he'd seen in sixteenth-century Italian paintings. Donatello's slender boys and the young men of Bellini and Titian. Except for the breasts, of course.

Cherubino ended his aria as Tadzio stood up from the table and surveyed himself in profile. His leather pants, which stretched over well-muscled buttocks and legs, said "male," while the high heels that jutted out below them said "female." He was a bundle of erotic contradictions. On the inside too.

❖

Tadzio knocked on the door of the "private club" and saw the eye of the bouncer scrutinizing him. Apparently he passed muster because the door opened and he paid his three dollars for entrance and drink tickets. "Sign the book," the bouncer growled, indicating the volume of scarcely legible scrawls that maintained the fiction that the place wasn't a public bar. Tadzio chose Alessandro Botticelli out of the air, scribbled it down beneath Richard Nixon and the dozens of other ludicrously invented names, and strolled inside.

It was disco dark, though pulsing ultraviolet lights flashed regularly so he could weave his way to the bar. As far as he could see, the crowd was mixed and very young—white, black, and Hispanic young men milling around in jeans and T-shirts, holding drinks. Several looked up as he passed, then looked away. Well, he'd give it an hour and use his two drink tickets, then go home. He held one up and pointed to the ice bath of beer bottles behind the bar.

As he accepted his bottle, a soft bump at his elbow told him someone had discovered him. Another trannie, a young black man, who hadn't quite gotten his look right. Makeup was a bit on the heavy side, and he wore a cheap wig.

"Haven't seen you here before," the young man shouted through the pounding music.

"I don't go out much. Once or twice to the Checkerboard, till it closed. But then I heard of the Stonewall, so I thought I'd stop in. Maybe get to know the regulars."

"No one more regular than me." The young man offered his

hand—slender, manicured, hung with bracelets. "They call me Satin. A good name for a singer, don't you think?"

"Name's Tad," Tadzio half lied. Not that it mattered. "Satin. Hmm. Reminds me of fifties rhythm and blues. Didn't a group called Satin record 'Tonite, Tonite'?"

Satin smiled knowledgeably and brushed back a strand of artificial hair, bracelets tinkling. "That was the Mello-Kings. You're thinking of the Five Satins. They did 'In the Still of the Night.' Remember?" He began softly. "In the stillll, uuvvvv the naaaaight…doo wop, doo wah."

"Yeah, you're right. I remember the 'doo-wop' part. I heard it on the radio, on one of those music-revival stations. Kind of a nice sound."

"If you like rhythm and blues, there's a room in the back where they play oldies. It's sort of 'our' place, if you know what I mean. Want to take a look?"

"Sure, why not?" Rhythm and blues would be quieter than the pounding music of the front bar.

The rear bar was smaller, and Tadzio saw at once what "our place" meant. Unlike the leather or Levi's boys in the front, who were largely indistinguishable from each other or from all the other young men in Greenwich Village, the back-room patrons all wore makeup and had teased hair. One or two were in full drag. Tadzio took another swallow of beer, trying to fend off depression.

Was this as close as he would ever get to acceptance? He faced the same dilemma every weekend—go out among strangers looking for quick intimacy, a compliment or two, a fleeting sense of "our place," or stay home alone. He had no particular sexual attraction to Satin, or for men in general, but these were the only people who didn't consider him a freak. And now, having ventured out, he couldn't bear the thought of going home to an empty apartment.

Tadzio resumed their conversation. "So, you're a singer."

Satin hesitated, blinking false eyelashes. "Well, I used to be in the New Jersey Baptist Boys Choir, but now I just sing for myself. I haven't actually had any auditions yet, but I practice."

"Oh," Tadzio said blandly. "It's too bad, then, that no one ever hears you."

Satin hesitated again, seeming to decide how much more information to give. "I sometimes sing to my patients."

"Patients? You're in medicine?" Health care and drag seemed incongruous.

"Kind of. I'm a male nurse. In a hospice."

"And they let you sing there?"

"Oh, not in a concert or anything like that. But to the patients by their beds. The ones close to the end. I hold their hands, talk really soft to them, and put on earrings that I keep in my pocket. Sometimes I even put on a little eye glitter for them, but of course it's also for me. Makes me feel pretty. Know what I mean?"

"I definitely do. But the patients like that?"

"Oh, yes. They don't laugh. They sort of relax. Then I sing a gospel song or a little 'Somewhere Over the Rainbow,' whatever I think they'll like."

"Actually, that sounds really beautiful." Tadzio tried to imagine the grim sickroom and Satin's strange comfort.

"It is. Last week a man died while he was holding my hand. He called me 'sweetheart.' For those last minutes of his life, he wanted to be with the woman he loved, not with a male nurse, so I called him 'handsome' and 'studly man,' whatever I could think of that maybe his wife or his girlfriend once called him. And you know, he just sighed and then he was gone. I swear he was smiling when his heart stopped."

Tadzio focused fully on Satin's face and saw deep kindness. "We all need that, don't we? To be loved. It never goes away."

"No, never." Satin dropped his eyes and leaned against the bar, his fingertips brushing along Tadzio's thigh. "So, what do you think? About us, I mean."

A faint buzz of arousal began and Tadzio wondered if he should push the hand away and wait for someone subtler. He took a long drink from his beer bottle while he decided.

The lights flickered, then went on full. Someone shouted, "What the fuck!" Burly men in suits burst in from the main bar, followed by uniformed police with nightsticks.

"Police! We're taking the place. Everyone move against the wall. I said, move AGAINST THE WALL!" The plainclothesman in charge began shoving men off the dance floor toward the wall. "IDs out and ready. Anyone without, goes into the wagon."

On all sides, patrons tried to flee, but the windows were boarded and the police blocked the only door to the front. A nightstick pressed against his shoulders shoved Tadzio along with the others. Then someone seized him by the arm and dragged him to a corner of the room. A female officer.

"You, girly face. Come with me to the ladies' room. We're gonna do a little sex check."

"No, you can't." That was all Tadzio could think to say. Horrifying enough to be caught in a raid. The thought of being undressed by force made him nauseous.

The officer laughed. "A queen. Just like I thought." She unhooked one of several sets of handcuffs from her belt and clipped them over his wrists. Tadzio stared down at his own hands, horrified, as if they were alien creatures. Then she pushed him through the front room of the bar into the street.

Outside a crowd had already gathered, and Tadzio cringed, but a moment later he realized it was the bar patrons, the ones who had shown IDs and been released. Strangely, they hadn't fled, but stayed, watching, and passersby were streaming in to join them.

Tadzio was pressed against the outside wall of the bar with a couple of the other transvestites, as the raid seemed to stall. The police were having a problem with radio communication and the wagons hadn't arrived. The crowd radiated an odd mixture of moods: anger, mockery, and, from the curious outsiders, good humor. But it increased rapidly in size until it seemed ten times the number of people who were arrested. When the first patrol wagon arrived, everyone suddenly became quiet.

First, the police escorted the bar owner to the wagon. Someone shouted, "Mafia," and the crowd cheered. Then they loaded the bar employees, and someone else shouted, "Gay Power!"

An officer burst from the doorway of the bar dragging one of the other transvestites by the arm. Though she was handcuffed, she still held a purse and swung it against the officer's face. The policeman yanked her by the elbow and shoved her into the wagon, and the crowd began to boo. Tadzio sensed that the atmosphere was changing, and the police seemed to sense it too. A plainclothesman, who appeared to be the detective in charge, signaled a patrolman to bring up more of the arrestees, and the officer took hold of Satin.

"Take your hands off me," Satin hissed, and wrenched herself away from him. Ignoring the handcuffs, she strode back toward the bar as if refusing to acknowledge the entire raid. The officer seized her again, but she twisted away and he shoved her against the wall. Unable to raise her hands, she spat at the officer, and he struck her across the face with his club. Blood gushed suddenly from Satin's nose. She slid to the sidewalk, kicking with high heels at the legs of the two policemen who tried to haul her to her feet. As she thrashed, she shouted to the crowd, "Why are you letting them treat me like this? Why don't you guys *do* something?"

When the officers picked her up bodily and forced her into the wagon, the crowd finally edged forward.

Someone called out, "Whatsa matter? Payoff not big enough this time?" and others echoed the jeer. "You want more payoff? Here's your fucking payoff!" Pennies flew through the air at the police. The game caught on and soon a barrage of coins was pelting the officers and rattling against the metal of the patrol-wagon door. A beer bottle sailed overhead, then another, and smashed against the wall.

The tide of power had turned. Angry men jumped onto the patrol wagon and started rocking it back and forth, trying to overturn it. The shouting grew louder, and other objects sailed through the air along with the beer cans, bottles, and coins.

"Take this one, and barricade the rest of them inside," one of the detectives shouted, pointing at Tadzio. A bright light flashed in Tadzio's face as two officers grabbed him by his elbows and lifted him inside the patrol wagon.

As it rolled off, he heard the muffled noise of the growing riot outside.

❖

Tadzio braced himself for a meeting with the curator to whom he would have to explain why he'd missed a day of work. Obviously he couldn't say he'd spent two nights in jail. He'd just been released and had time only to rush home to shower and change into office clothes. Too late, he'd glanced down at his hands, resting on his knees in the taxi, and seen that he still wore nail polish.

As Tadzio entered George Hudson's office, the curator was already standing and his expression was grim. He motioned Tadzio to take a seat, but remained standing, looming over his assistant while he spoke.

"I'm assuming you can explain this," Hudson said, reaching behind him for a newspaper. It was the *New York Daily News*, folded open to a photo in the center section that showed three patrolmen and a detective facing an angry crowd. The caption was straightforward: STONEWALL RIOTERS ARRESTED. Three faces in the crowd were clearly visible: two dark-haired men shouting, and the third, conspicuous by his blond-streaked hair, his makeup, and the fact that an officer was seizing him by the shoulder, was Tadzio.

Tadzio's mouth went dry. He had no explanation. All he had was the memory of shame and fear, of being pressed, helpless, against the brick wall of the Stonewall Inn. The whole humiliating evening flashed through his mind: the jeering, the snarling contempt of the raid squad, the shower of coins, and the bleeding face of Satin, who sang to the dying. That explanation certainly wouldn't satisfy Hudson, and Tadzio knew what the outcome of the conversation would be. His job and his career at the museum were finished.

But since the first night in the jail cell, another emotion had begun to smolder beneath the shame, like a tiny coal under ashes. Anger. He saw his supervisor's lips moving, perceived the disdain in his expression, but no he longer heard the words. The hot nugget of resentment deep inside grew with every pounding heartbeat. He recalled Satin, bloodied but unwilling to be shamed, fighting back.

Tadzio stood up. "I wasn't hurting anyone. No one in that bar was hurting anyone."

"It was indecent, disgusting, a public nuisance. Those are not the kind of people we want to employ at the museum. We have a public image to maintain."

"To hell with your public image. I don't have to answer to you for what I do at night in my private life." Tadzio didn't bother to listen to Hudson's reply. He didn't need to. The man was already holding the door open and motioning him out. All he heard behind him was, "You have ten minutes to collect your things and get out."

CHAPTER TWO

Tadzio slouched in the armchair of his living room and brooded. Was this what the bottom was like? A beating, two days in jail, being fired, and coming home to an empty house. He felt like he was drowning. No, he corrected himself, drowning was much worse.

But the whole disaster, from arrest to joblessness, was just more evidence that he didn't belong. He would never belong. He had learned that in childhood when his parents had taken him from school and friends and familiar streets, and set him down in a new country where he couldn't talk to anyone.

It made no difference that within a year he had made the transition, from Italian to English and from immigrant to American; he was still a misfit. His father, on the other hand, had a clear idea of what it meant to be American and had enlisted in the army to show it. Worse, he had insisted that Tadzio be a little soldier as well.

Just when it seemed things couldn't get worse, his mother, his only bulwark against Silvio Falier's hypermasculinity, died of a stroke. In stoic silence, Silvio came home on leave, buried his wife, and put his slight, timid son into a military boarding school. Tadzio was ten years old.

Though he spoke English perfectly by then, he grasped that he wasn't like the other boys at school, and if he wasn't part of their rough world, what was left for him? By the age of twelve, he was beginning to guess.

He knew no girls and had no access to girls' things, but once, on a trip into town, he shoplifted mascara and lipstick from the town drugstore. Later that night, in the secrecy of the bathroom, he explored being a girl. It was a revelation.

The face that looked back at him from the mirror was beautiful. Like his mother, but with blue eyes of movie-star intensity. He rolled up socks, stuffed them under his pajama top, and studied himself in profile. He liked what he saw. Because he understood the danger, he carefully washed the makeup off, but now he knew who he was. He was the "other."

A distant car horn drew Tadzio back to his present misery. He slumped in his chair, morose and craving comfort, and only one woman could give that to him now. He strode into the bathroom, rummaged through the medicine cabinet, and in a few minutes he had on his full female face. His favorite gold-hoop earrings provided the finishing touch. He was She, a handsome, no-nonsense woman who obviously had her life together. A woman who looked like that took crap from no one.

The fantasy lasted only for a moment before reality seeped back into his consciousness. She and He oscillated in the mirror and tears began to pour from the mascara-rimmed eyes, ruining the image.

Maybe sleep would help. He dragged himself to the bedroom and was about to unlace his shoes when he heard the fluttering of wings. Two steps took him to the window where he saw the bird that had just lit on the fire escape. Not a pigeon, but a huge crow, that stared at him fearlessly through the glass before ripping at the scrap of roadkill it held in its claws. He tapped loudly on the window, causing the bird to lift off again with another loud fluttering. Tadzio thought, absurdly, of the opera *Salome*, in which the fluttering of wings heralded the angel of death. Great, Tadzio muttered to himself; now he was getting morbid. He had to talk to someone.

He yanked open the door of his apartment, strode down the hall to the last doorway, and knocked.

"Tony. It's me, Tadzio. I need to talk."

Tadzio heard the multiple clacks of locks turning and bolts sliding, and when the door finally opened, the seventy-eight-year-old Tony Foscari stood narrow-shouldered and paunchy in front of him. Only his full head of white hair and carefully trimmed Vandyke beard saved him from looking pathetic.

"Mother of God, what happened to you? You look like hell!"

Tadzio sniffed. "Yeah, I feel like hell too. I lost my job."

"Come in, kiddo. Sit down and tell me about it. I'll get us some wine." Tony walked ahead of him into the living room and turned off the television set. In a minute he was back with a half-drunk bottle of Chianti and two juice glasses.

"Talk to me," he commanded gently. "The guys at work find out about the arrest?"

"What? How did you know?"

"C'mon. I read the papers, same as everybody. Your picture was all over. Lousy luck, eh?" He poured two full glasses of the wine, handed one over to Tadzio and took a long swallow from his own. "How long did they keep you in the can?"

"Two nights. I just had time to shower this morning and rush to work, but of course that picture ruined me. I also forgot about these." He held up his hands, displaying bright red fingernails.

"Poor kid. But you had to know it would catch up with you."

Tadzio took a gulp of the wine and stared absentmindedly at the glass. No lip print, he noted, thanks to smear-proof lipstick. "Christ, I'm tired of hiding, or being treated like a freak. I think of all the 'real' men who are idiots, cheaters, racists, wife-beaters, or just plain selfish jerks. But as long as they do the man thing, they get respect. I've been a good person, hard-working, but I have to live like a fugitive just to be accepted. It's making me crazy."

"Hey, go easy on yourself. Things'll get better. You'll see. Here, have a saltine." Tony held out the wax-paper column of soda crackers he'd obviously been nibbling in front of the television. "Tomorrow you'll feel better. You'll put on the man-face, as you call it, and go look for another job. And you'll forget all about this."

Tadzio waved the crackers away. "No, Tony. I don't think I'll forget. You know, I met a really beautiful person the other night. A kind, gentle man, who helped dying people feel at peace at the end. And you know what the cops did? They smashed his face."

"Yeah, I know. The cops can be bastards, but you were in the wrong place. You shouldn't oughtta go to those bars anyhow."

"It's the only place I can go to be with people who don't treat me like dirt. Why can't we get together and be ourselves, just like truckers do, or businessmen? We don't hurt anyone."

"Taddy, you know I think you're a great kid, but I just don't understand. Why you gotta dress in women's clothes?"

"They're not women's clothes. They're *my* clothes."

"You know what I mean. What about the tits? You wanna be a woman, or what?"

"I don't know. Can't I at least try it out? Why do I have to choose?"

"Because you got a dick. Nature chose for you."

"My brain's not in my penis. I don't care about my penis, for God's sake."

"Okay, so let's leave out the anatomy lesson. But why cause yourself so much grief by wearing makeup? In public, I mean."

"For the same reason you wear a Vandyke beard."

"Heh? That's to attract chicks."

Tadzio chuckled. "Well, in my case, it's just to look attractive."

"And you think mascara and tits make you look good?"

"Yeah. I do. When I look in the mirror, I like what I see."

"So, who you looking to attract, men or women?" Tony bit into a Saltine.

"I don't know. Maybe both, or none."

"You ever even been with a woman?"

Tadzio took a long drink of wine, then sighed. "Yeah. My father took me to a brothel when I was fifteen. Nice intro, right?"

"Poor kid. Maybe that's what screwed things up for you."

"Stop saying 'poor kid.' Besides, it's not about who I want to fuck. It's what I want to *be*, and people who don't like what I am can stay away. But they shouldn't beat me up for it."

"No, they shouldn't, but if you can't stop wearing makeup and growing tits, you're gonna have to live with that. People are scared of things they don't understand, especially things that have to do with sex." He poured more wine into Tadzio's glass.

"I don't know. I think it's more the surprise factor. Maybe if people got used to seeing men in makeup, they'd stop worrying about it."

"Yeah, maybe. In a hundred years."

"I don't think it'll take that long. This is New York City, after all. Full of radicals, hippies, and—considering the riots the papers are talking about—a lot of gays too. Shit. It's time we stopped trying to be invisible and let people see who we are." He frowned, enjoying the feel of the unfamiliar expression, finding outrage much more satisfying than humiliation.

"You mean you wanna walk around in makeup and dresses all the time?"

"Well, I don't have the courage to do all of it at once. Maybe I'll just start with the makeup." Tadzio downed the rest of his wine, as if it would give him courage.

"Well, good luck to you, bambino. In the meantime…" Tony took the newspaper from the coffee table. "It so happens I don't just read crap like the *Daily News*. I also have *The New York Times*."

He opened it to the back pages, then folded the entire paper into a quarter section. "So, bambino, have another glass of wine and start looking for a job. I suggest something in the Village."

CHAPTER THREE

Stony Brook, New York, January 1970

Joanna Valois raised her glass of champagne for the first toast of the evening. "To the Venice Project!" she said, and the room full of her colleagues echoed it back. "To the Venice Project!"

Joanna generally didn't much care for champagne, especially not the cheap stuff her chairman had purchased for the party, but tonight it was delicious. Tonight, everything was delicious. It had been a hard year, formulating proposals and work plans, presenting and justifying to various committees, then waiting white-knuckled as the proposal made the first cut, then the second, and finally was accepted. Ten months to the day after she had conceived the project, she received the grant.

She felt the same calm euphoria that she'd experienced the day Stanford awarded her the Ph.D., only this time she stood at the beginning of an undertaking, not at the end. And this time a roomful of friends and colleagues were celebrating with her. She could allow herself one giddy evening of merriment.

Giulio Giglioti, who was clearly far ahead of her in merriment, raised his glass a second time. "Stony Brook University is very proud of you, Joanna. But you have to tell everyone how you got started."

"You mean how I was born in a log cabin and split logs to get to college?"

Soft laughter at the cliché rippled through the crowd of academics.

"No, but seriously. In a nutshell, a British friend of mine, may he rest in peace, came across a packet of letters that had been hidden for centuries in the wall of his study in Kent. They were his last gift to me. The letters were in old Italian, that is, Venetian, and he never bothered to have them translated. When I began working at Stony Brook last fall, I engaged Professor Giglioti to read and summarize them, at least the legible ones. We soon realized that a woman fleeing the Inquisition in Venice on a merchant ship had written them and knew we had a major story on our hands."

"Like an opera," Giglioti said. "There's torture, a prison escape, a shipboard murder, pirates, Jesuits. I'm telling you, we could make a movie."

"Yes, but we're missing lots of details," Joanna said. "So this…" She held up the letter from the Grants Committee. "This will enable our interdisciplinary collaboration. Dr. Giglioti, from Economics, and I, from History, will spend three weeks in the libraries and archives of Venice tracking down those details."

Giglioti cleared his throat. "Fortunately, I have a friend at the University of Venice, so I was able to pave the way a little." He glanced toward Joanna for confirmation of his importance.

Obligingly, she lifted her glass again. "A toast to Giulio for reading and summarizing ten pages of sixteenth-century Venetian dialect. All handwritten, of course. Hear! Hear!" She sipped from her glass while Giulio drained his, obviously pleased to be the focus of attention.

The fifty-year-old Italian was lean and handsome, with a full head of thick peppery hair and obviously successful with women. But that success had made him arrogant and slightly contemptuous of female intellectuals. As the attention of the group dwindled and private conversations began again, Joanna watched him migrate toward one of the new assistant professors. Before long, he had his hand on the young woman's back, in a manner that was beyond collegial.

Joanna wouldn't have chosen him, but no one else on the faculty knew Renaissance Italian, specifically the Venetian dialect. That, plus his Venetian connection, made him invaluable. She'd just have to put up with him.

She began mingling again, going around the room, touching elbows, making small talk, being careful not to overlook anyone.

Ah, there was one of her favorites, Dottie Mandelbaum. Gray-haired and frumpy, she was probably the liveliest woman in the Liberal Arts faculty. Though she had emigrated from England immediately after WWII, she never lost her British accent, and Joanna laughingly accused her of rehearsing it in private to keep it fresh. Joanna let herself drop down next to the senior professor who clinked glasses with her.

"Well done, Joanna. I wish like hell you needed a specialist in

Semitic languages rather than old Italian. I haven't seen Venice since I
was a child."

"That's odd. I got the same offer from Michel in the French
Department and from Sergei in Slavic Languages. I'd choose you in a
minute over all of them, Dottie. You'd be much more fun to room with
than any of those guys. Unfortunately, my letters are in Venetian, not
Hebrew."

"Well, I also do Arabic, Aramaic, Phoenician, and, if pressed,
Akkadian."

"Uh, I'll remember that, Dottie. Maybe on my next research
project to the Middle East." She finished her glass of champagne
and glanced down at her watch. Damn, it was already after midnight.
Not that the hour was anything magical and she was Cinderella. But
the sparkle of the evening had worn off. She had to make important
preparations. Not the least of which would be a very delicately worded
letter to Monique. Joanna didn't believe in signs, but she did believe
in obligations. A travel grant to Europe gave her the opportunity to
repair some of the damage she'd caused in Paris, or at least properly
apologize for it.

She looked around for the secretary who had given her a lift to the
party, but she and her husband had already left. Joanna cursed the fact
that on that day of all days, her own car had broken down, and debated
whether she should ask a colleague for a ride or simply telephone for
a taxi.

Giulio Giglioti was suddenly at her side. "I'm about ready to leave
too. Can I give you a lift?" His face was redder than usual, and his eyes
somewhat glassy, but he seemed steady on his feet.

"Are you sure you can drive?"

He laughed warmly. "This old Italian's blood has always been half
wine. It's what keeps me young and sexy. Don't worry. I hold it well
and I'm a very careful driver." He was already sauntering toward the
bedroom where the coats were piled on the bed.

❖

As they careened around the last uphill corner and Joanna's house
appeared among the trees, she exhaled relief. Giglioti was far drunker
than he'd seemed at the party. During the trip his speech had become
slurred and, in the confined interior of the car, he seemed to exude the

smell of alcohol. Worse, his conversation had veered toward a clumsy attempt at seduction and was getting on her nerves.

"You know how romantic Italians are. Wine and pretty women go right to our heads. Passion. It's in our blood. There's no telling *what* might happen when this old Italian boy gets into a gondola."

"I don't plan on any gondola rides. We'll be working in libraries all day, remember?"

"Oh, come *on*. We've got three weeks. That's twenty-one nights, twenty-one dinners, twenty-one bottles of wine. You can't tell me you haven't thought about that. Remember, we'll be sharing an apartment. An *apartment in Venice*, for God's sake, the most romantic city in the world. We'd have to be robots not to have that heat up our blood."

Giglioti stopped the car with a slight lurch just before her house and turned off the motor.

"My blood will be just fine, and so will yours," Joanna said and turned to let herself out of the car. As she bent toward the handle, however, Giglioti's hand fell on her shoulder and pulled her back toward him. His face was inches from her own, and the smell of alcohol and cigarettes on his breath revolted her.

"I've seen the way you've been looking at me. You've been thinking the same thing I have, haven't you? You and me, in Venice. You set it all up. But, hey, it's a great idea. I just think we should stop playing games and get down to what we both want." Suddenly his other hand was on her breast.

She slapped it away. "Listen to me. For the sake of the project, I'll overlook this little assault, because you're obviously drunk. I'll also assume this will never happen again. So I suggest you turn the motor on again and go straight home. I'll accept your apologies tomorrow." She yanked the car door open, stepped out, then bent down for a last word. "And never bring up the subject of romance again." She slammed the door.

Obviously insulted, Giglioti gunned the engine and started away with a screech. Accelerating rapidly, he careened down the hill away from her house and disappeared around a curve. Before she had climbed the steps to her front door, she heard the crash.

CHAPTER FOUR

Joanna spread out the curriculum vitae and letter of application in front of the campus gardener. "Thanks for taking off an hour to help me out today, Bruno."

"It's my pleasure, Dr. Valois," he said in heavily accented English. "There's not so much landscaping to do in the winter anyhow, and I'd rather be in here with a lady than outside spreading compost." He glanced down at the single application. "This is the only person you're interviewing?"

"He's the only one we could find. Not many people can take off three weeks from a real job to work for a pittance. A couple of graduate students in music are interested, but they're not native speakers. I need someone not only for conversation with librarians and so forth, but also for translation. You can see by his CV—master's degree in Renaissance art, native proficiency in Italian—this guy's perfect for the job. All you have to do is make sure he really *can* speak Italian."

Bruno read down the page. "Yeah, he does look good. Almost too good to be true."

"That's what I'm afraid of. Anyhow, don't bother asking him about Renaissance art. Just make him speak Italian, about anything." Joanna heard the rap at the door and sat down at the far end of the table, as the secretary entered the room.

As the candidate appeared a moment later, a single word zipped through Joanna's mind: *elf.* The man, in his late twenties or early thirties, was wearing a dark suit jacket over ordinary corduroy pants, but that was where the "ordinary" ended. His ample hair, an artful mixture of yellow and gold shades, and carefully groomed to look tousled, touched his collar and curled up slightly at the end. Tufts of it were brushed forward over his ears, which held gold earrings. His riveting blue eyes were ringed by mascara and he wore a pale shade of lipstick. For all that, he comported himself with a certain aloof dignity, and she amended her first impression. An elf crossed with a baroness.

Bruno was also momentarily speechless, but quickly recovered and offered his hand. The young man shook hands first with him, then with Joanna. His grip was soft, but not limp, and his nails were painted dark pink. Joanna maintained her equanimity as all three sat down, but Bruno's darting eyes showed he was thrown.

After some hesitation, Bruno began, scarcely looking up from the page of questions he had prepared. Joanna could follow most of the Italian conversation, though it went quickly. The young man was explaining that, as the child of immigrants, he had spoken Italian at home and learned English only after starting school in the U.S. His master's degree in Renaissance art also required him to read and write Italian.

Bruno kept his eyes glued to the curriculum vitae in his hands, never making eye contact with the candidate, but he dutifully kept up his end of the interview.

"I see you worked at the Met Museum. Must have been a good job. Why did you leave?"

"A difference of opinion. It had nothing to do with my work per se."

"Uh-huh." Bruno didn't conceal his skepticism. "And where are you working now?" He studied the CV again. "Ah, I see, the Greenwich Village Theater. What do you do?"

The young man glanced toward Joanna, presumably wondering why she was silent, but otherwise answered without hesitation. "I'm assistant stage manager."

"What does an assistant stage manager do?" Bruno kept him talking.

"I help coordinate the physical aspects of the production. Organize the rental or creation of costumes and the building of stage sets, and help the director plan the rehearsal schedules. I make sure the light manager's notes jibe with the staging, and during the run of a play, I check that the props are on hand and everything is in place."

"Do you like your job?"

The candidate shrugged faintly. "I've only been there six or seven months, but it's a nice group of people. Talented, imaginative, accepting."

"Ah, yes. I can see how that would be a place you'd want to work," Bruno said, half to the candidate, half to himself.

"About your degree in Italian art, what did you do there?"

The candidate leaned back comfortably and crossed his legs, a feminine, though not effeminate, gesture. "As an undergraduate, I studied Italian art and music in general, but my graduate specialty was in Renaissance painting. We began with the precursors: Giotto and Cimabue, then of course moved on to Ghiberti, Uccello, Masaccio. My master's thesis was on the High Renaissance, specifically, the Sistine Chapel ceiling. But I also did a lot of research on Raphael, Bellini, Veronese. Others too, but—"

"Have you been to Italy as an adult?" Bruno asked abruptly.

"Not recently."

"I see," Bruno let the word "see" trail off, as if to leave unspoken, "of course you haven't. Not looking like that." Then, as if he could no longer contain himself, he blurted, "Do you always wear makeup and those earrings?"

The candidate was unfazed. "No, not always. Sometimes I wear dangling rubies. These are my 'interview' earrings. More conservative."

Nonplussed at the response, Bruno seemed to run out of steam. "I see. Well, I guess that's all, then." He looked toward Joanna.

She spoke for the first time, returning the conversation to English. "Yes, that about covers it. I'll continue talking to Mr. Falier now. Thank you very much for your help, Bruno. I'll check back with you later," she said, making it clear that he was to leave.

Bruno stood, apparently relieved. He offered his hand again, his glance sliding quickly over the candidate's face and body, then slipped from the room.

Joanna moved into the vacated seat. Though the candidate was unsuitable and she saw little point in continuing the interview, she didn't want to dismiss him without posing a question or two, if only out of courtesy.

"Tadzio isn't an Italian name, is it?"

"No. My mother apparently named me after a character in a novel."

"Ah, interesting. Well, I'm sorry if Mr. Libretti was a bit abrupt there at the end. All he was supposed to do was determine how good your Italian is. But his question about the makeup and earrings was legitimate. Should I assume your slightly sarcastic reply meant that you *do* always wear makeup?"

"Yes, you should. Yes, I do." He studied her face for a moment and added almost sweetly, "As *you* do, I imagine."

"Of course, but I..." She caught herself, grasping his meaning. "Well, of course you have the right to wear what you like, and, I admit, you manage to pull it off quite well. 'Interview earrings' was a good comeback. You seem like a reasonable and self-confident person, so I won't beat about the bush. There is no way I can hire you."

"Why not? I don't fill your requirements?" His voice was still soft, but a slight stiffening of his back revealed he was affronted.

"You do, you fill them very well. But, you see, I'll be working with the Venetian authorities, men I don't know and who tolerate me only because my deceased colleague obtained their cooperation. I'll have a very short time in which to find what I need and I'll be focused only on research. Please forgive me if I'm blunt, but if you walked around like that in Italy, there would certainly be...incidents."

"Incidents? You mean that people might accost me or refuse me admittance to a library or something?"

"Mr. Falier, please try to appreciate my position. As an American rummaging around in Italian archives by special permission, I barely have credibility as it is. You may be accepted in a Greenwich Village theater, and by a few artsy New York academics, but not in the world in general. The attention you would attract could potentially derail the entire project. Unless you're willing to forgo the makeup and nail polish, I'm afraid I can't afford to hire a...a person so visibly confrontational."

Tadzio looked down at his nails, coincidently the same color he'd worn the day he was fired. But this time he made no effort to hide his hands.

"Thank you for your candor, Dr. Valois. At least you're up front, and not pretending it's something else. The problem, obviously, is that I am a transvestite. I believe that's the word you're looking for. An Italian-speaking Renaissance art–expert transvestite." He held up the fingers of one hand. "Fuchsia. My favorite nail color. I sat for two days in a jail cell for this color. And a friend of mine had his nose broken for a similar offense. Surely that counts as an injustice, don't you think? There comes a time when you just have to stand up."

"I'm sure you're right, and I respect you for doing that, for taking a stand, I mean. We all are who we are. Though I've never gone to jail for who I am, I've had to work doubly hard to be taken seriously in my field. I support you philosophically, I really do, but I can't jeopardize my project for your identity."

There was a long moment of silence. Then Joanna dropped her eyes to the aimless scribbling she had begun on her notepad. "I'm sorry."

❖

The next morning, tapping her pencil on her desk, Joanna read through the applications once again, hoping she had overlooked some promising talent. But no. She had judged correctly the first time; they were all rather pathetic. Graduate students in second-year Italian classes keen on a free trip to Venice. Even if they were exceptionally gifted, she doubted they could read four-hundred-year-old Venetian writing any better than she could. And if they couldn't do that, they'd merely be traveling companions, the last thing she needed. No, only Tadzio was anywhere near being qualified, but he was a liability. It would be much more difficult now, but she had all but concluded that she would have to go alone.

After a brisk knock, the secretary poked her head through the doorway. "A woman's waiting in the office who'd like to talk to you."

"A student?"

"I don't think so. A bit older than that. I said I'd check to see if you were in. Are you?"

"Thanks for shielding me from the world, but I'm winding up here anyhow. Send her in." Smiling at the idea of being shielded, she squared the thin pile of applications and put them back into their folder.

A moment later the door opened again and Joanna looked up, astonished.

A beautiful woman stood in the doorway. Not magazine cover–beautiful, but soul-beautiful. Superbly, yet inconspicuously made up, with delicately mascaraed blue eyes that shone like beacons. Perfect skin with a hint of youthful vitality in the cheeks. Well-formed, lightly tinted lips that hinted at a smile. A face full of character and complexity and sensuality. Under a charcoal-gray blazer, she wore a form-fitting décolleté black tee tucked into a tailored knee-length skirt, dark hose, and low-cut suede boots. Everything about her whispered quality, seriousness, and class.

Whatever this woman wanted to talk about, Joanna wanted to talk about it too. As long as possible. But something was familiar…

"I was wondering if we could readdress your research project," a familiar contralto voice said.

"Tadzio?" That was all that Joanna could manage.

"Sara is my female name. Uh, can I come in?"

Speechless, Joanna gestured toward a chair and, after slipping off her jacket, Sara sat down gracefully. Joanna searched for words. "I didn't recognize you." She stated the obvious.

"That was the point. Sara is a different persona. Do you like her? Me?"

"You'll have to let me get used to her." Joanna studied the new person called Sara who sat in the same sort of relaxed pose she herself had taken. Sara seemed perfectly at home in her role, feminine but not effeminate. Nothing about her was exaggerated or false, or "drag." She had only a slight habit of licking her lower lip, subtly, unobtrusively. Joanna had stopped wearing lipstick years before, but she remembered having had the same urge to constantly check if it was still there.

Sara's tousled and longish gold hair now seemed absolutely fitting. Joanna glanced from the ruby earrings to Sara's décolleté and the swell of breasts beneath. Small and youthful; were they real? She forced her eyes back to Sara's face. Her jaw was a trifle large for a woman, but not excessively so, more strong-willed than masculine. It wouldn't give her away. Nor would the handsome mouth or the nicely curved lips that drew attention by their color, a shade between natural and warm red. "Is this the persona you assume most of the time?"

"No, the one you saw yesterday was closer to who I am. And Sara doesn't usually wear skirts. They're not really in fashion anymore." The voice was the same as the day before, but softer. A Marlene Dietrich or Greta Garbo voice, without the mannerisms.

Joanna had a flash of confusion. Was this some sort of test of her liberal principles? A niggling voice at the back of her mind reminded her of her own outsider status, and that her advancement in the academic world owed much to the pressures of feminism. But this was different. This was an invitation to put her own project in jeopardy for…for what? A social misfit.

Sara broke the silence. "I think the questions you should be asking are, 'Does Sara pass?' and, if so, 'Can she keep it up for three weeks?' You did say three weeks, didn't you?"

"Thank you for covering my side of the interview as well, but I hadn't gotten to that point yet." Joanna smiled softly to take the sting out of the remark.

Sara was unperturbed. "Well, the answer to both questions is yes. She's more than a mask. She's really another part of me. Maybe the main part of me. So I think you should interview her for the job."

Joanna scratched the side of her jaw although it didn't itch. "I certainly have to give you credit for persistence. All right. Tell me about your knowledge of Renaissance Venetian, the language, I mean."

Sara relaxed and looked off into space for a moment, apparently formulating her answer. "My family left Venice when I was six, so the language I spoke as a very young child was the Venetian dialect. It has changed, of course, since the *quattrocento*, but when I was studying it at the university, I could navigate through it pretty well."

Joanna smiled at Sara's use of the Italian term for fifteenth-century Italy. "Do you know the city itself?"

"No. To be frank, I always associated it with my father's family, who were wheelers and dealers, and none of them very nice, so I never had any interest in going back. I know a lot about the city from books, but I have only a few memories, the odd things a child recalls. Nothing to be nostalgic about. For me, as it is for you, Venice is the *Serenissima* of the art and history books." Sara stopped, as if fearing she had said too much. "Is knowledge of the current city critical to your research?"

"Not particularly. The project has to do with a sixteenth-century book publisher."

"You mean Aldus Manutius? I wrote a paper on him."

"Ah, you do know your quattrocento. No, I'm not interested in the Aldine Press, but rather in a much smaller publisher who was arrested for printing a heretical book."

"Heretical book? Ah, then we're talking about the Italian Inquisition. A brutal time."

"Less brutal than in the rest of Italy, I think. A tension always existed between the Roman Church and Venice, and, as I understand it, Venice never executed any witches."

Sara seemed to study her for a moment, assessing her more than Joanna liked. "No witches, perhaps, but sodomites, homosexuals. They burned them alive."

"Really? I hadn't read that."

"Yes, in the 1400s. Though, in the 1500s, the Council of Ten went soft on crime and allowed the condemned to be throttled first."

Joanna stared back now from her side. Sara was knowledgeable beyond all expectations. But then, what good would her knowledge do them if they became the laughingstock of Renaissance Studies? Abruptly, she returned to the more dangerous subject.

"Do you go out like this very often in public?"

"No, but when I do, I usually pass, especially when my hair's longer. At least I get a lot of male attention. If you don't believe me, why don't we go walk around a bit, and you can see for yourself." Sara's eyes brightened. "What about lunch?"

Joanna looked at her watch. "You know, that's not a bad suggestion. There's a small dining hall across the quad. Nothing fancy, just student food, but at this time of day, both students and faculty will be there. Let's see what happens. I'll let you do all the talking."

❖

The January air was crisp and Joanna put on her hat. Sara noticed it immediately.

"I like your fedora. It suits you."

"Thank you. An English friend gave it to me, just before he died. You don't wear a hat?"

"Rarely. I like to feel the wind in my hair." Pulling up her jacket collar, Sara fell in step with Joanna with a graceful ambling gait. One hand held a canvas shoulder bag and the other hand was shoved into the pocket of her jacket. Subtly elegant, she was the model for the successful professional female.

Joanna wondered where a transvestite bought clothing. "Do you like to shop?" she asked suddenly.

Sara pursed her lips slightly. "No. Not so much for clothes. Once I've found something that suits me, I buy three of them and have done with it. I do enjoy farmers' markets, but that could be because I'm a vegetarian."

"Why's that?" Another eccentricity, Joanna thought. Small alarm flags went up. "You don't eat meat? Is it the killing-animals thing?"

"Not just the killing, but all the torture before. Feed-lot farms, slaughterhouse terror, tiny cages for chickens, beaks cut off."

"They cut off the chickens' beaks?"

"Yes, it's a cruel industry. What about you?"

"I never much thought about it."

They were in the cafeteria now, which was rather quiet. A handful of girls ate in one corner and, diagonally from them, two boys sat laughing about something. At the food counter, Sara ordered spinach lasagna. Joanna would have preferred a steak sandwich but didn't dare order one. "Make that two," she said.

When they were sitting, Sara began the conversation. "Valois is French, of course. Do you speak the language?"

Joanna hadn't expected to be the one quizzed, but it was a reasonable question. "Enough to ask for information but not enough to understand the responses. I took a total-immersion course last summer in Paris, but I don't think it stuck. I'm better in Italian. My father was French-Canadian, my mother was Italian, and she's the reason I studied it."

"I'm sure you know about the important Valois in sixteenth-century Venice. Henry of Valois's visit was the cause of one of the biggest celebrations of the century."

"I read about that. The whole city turned out to welcome him. But a lot of Valois in France aren't royal. In Canada too. By the way, thanks for pronouncing it 'Val*wa*.' You have no idea how often I hear 'Valoize.'"

"Well, you can't really blame people. If the French don't want us pronouncing all those letters, they should jolly well remove them."

Joanna chuckled softly and set about eating, leaving space for Sara to talk while she herself watched. And between small bites, Sara kept up a flow of lighthearted information, about Italian shoes (well-crafted), Italian men (egotistical and vain), and Italian wine (reliable). Her hands were always in motion, and though they were graceful, they were more muscular than the hands of most women. Sara noticed Joanna's scrutiny and held up one hand, as if to clear the air of secrets.

"Yes, I know. My hands are the giveaway. That's why I wear polish. Not much else I can do."

"Some women have large, strong hands. But I guess you'd want to be careful of handshakes. However, the makeup is good. Does it take you a long time to put on?"

"No longer than some women."

"What about your beard?"

"Electrolysis took care of most of it. What's left here and there is blond."

"A blond Italian."

"Yes, it's not that uncommon in the north. I was a towhead as a baby and naturally blond through most of my—"

"Well, hello, ladies."

In the second it took Joanna to refocus her attention upward, toward the bulky form at her side, she was already annoyed.

It was Ted Loomis. Today of all days. Narrow-hipped and broad-shouldered, he'd been a football hero in his youth and seemed never to have gotten over it. When he walked, he swung his shoulders, as if plowing his way through hostile, resistant air, and when he stood still, he squinted condescension at his shorter colleagues.

"I heard about Giulio's car accident. What a terrible tragedy. A man thinks everything is going his way and then fate strikes him down." He was speaking to Joanna, but his gaze kept returning to Sara.

"Yes, very…tragic." Joanna couldn't think of anything else to say that wouldn't elicit a longer conversation.

"But you're going anyhow, aren't you? I wouldn't mind a trip to Venice myself. Only about seven hours from New York, right?"

"I don't know. I'm flying to Paris for other business first. Then I'll train to Venice."

"Paris *and* Venice. *Quelle horreur!*" Loomis quipped. "Well, it's a dirty job, but—" He interrupted himself in the middle of the old joke and turned toward Sara. "Oh, I'm sorry." He held out his hand. "Ted Loomis, Department of English. Down the hall from Professor Valois. And you are?"

Sara laid her hand gently in his. "Sara Falier. Nice to meet you."

"Are you just visiting campus or a new faculty member I've somehow missed?" His hand tightened around Sara's.

Sara looked toward Joanna, then replied, "No, just a visitor."

"Ms. Falier will be my assistant on my research trip. Giulio's replacement, in fact," Joanna announced, and glanced over at Sara, whose eyes just then seemed to lighten to an even brighter shade of blue.

"The two of you traveling together. I don't know who to be more jealous of," Loomis said, dropping his voice a tone. Neither Joanna nor Sara reacted and the moment of silence grew too long. "Well, then I guess I'll leave you both to discuss things." He finally released Sara's hand, which slid gracefully out of his grip.

"So nice to meet you, Dr. Loomy," she said with perfectly calibrated gentility.

Joanna was certain the error was intentional and decided that Sara was going to be much more fun than Giulio Giglioti, may he rest in peace.

CHAPTER FIVE

Paris, January 1970

There it was, 22 Quai d'Orleans, an elegant Parisian apartment building in the old style, overlooking the Seine. Handsome in its simplicity, a discreet display of old Parisian wealth, it had appeared in at least one Catherine Deneuve movie Joanna had seen. The breeze coming off the river was freezing, and her fedora did little to keep her ears warm. Where the devil was Monique?

Joanna had prepared a little speech for their meeting, though in the dialogue in the back of her mind, one voice asked her why she bothered. Of course she knew the answer. Monique had been her first romance. Their two and a half months together the previous summer were a revelation. But she had come to Paris, after all, to learn French, and for all the giddy fun they'd had, Joanna had always hungered for learning rather than love. And that, in the end, had been the problem.

It was her family background, she decided. The desire to rise above her dreary working-class childhood had fueled her early ambitions. Her single-mindedness, not to say obsession, through all her school years had paid off in the nearly unfathomable prize of a full graduate fellowship to Stanford. But that achievement had its costs. She never had, and never looked for, romantic attachments.

She was attractive by anyone's standards. In college, people told her she looked like the folk singer Joan Baez (whom she hadn't yet heard of). But the adolescent fever for boys had passed her by. While other students were learning the joys of copulation, or at least its foreplay, lust remained foreign to her. When it erupted playfully that summer with Monique, she was like a child with a new toy.

But for all their frolicking, their intellectual differences soon became apparent. When Joanna had left childhood, she had outgrown religion too, while Monique was devoutly Catholic. Their first quarrel was about evolution, the second about the Problem of Evil, and each time the gap between them widened. When the flame of simple lust began to burn low, and when the French-study project was over, Joanna was ready to leave. Worse, she departed three days earlier than planned, to visit the dying Nigel in England on the way home. She grasped only in hindsight that Monique had still thought of herself as "in love" and that Joanna's walking away calmly on a Sunday afternoon counted as abandonment.

Joanna's punishment, she supposed, was a year of intense academic labor and celibacy.

Ah, finally. Monique appeared in front of the portal in a thick coat and fur hat, and after a brief wave, she hurried across the street. Her greeting kiss was perfunctory and, instead of linking arms, she simply touched Joanna's elbow. "Let's go where it's warm and we can talk," she said, drawing Joanna along the embankment.

"Is there a quiet restaurant nearby?" Joanna studied the woman she once thought sexy and saw only a round, somewhat plump face with cheeks reddened by the cold. The long black hair she had loved to stroke had been severely cut.

"No, I was thinking more of going there." Monique nodded farther up the Seine, where Notre Dame hulked, its tall apse and flying buttresses suggesting an enormous insect. "So, how are you?" she asked in a monotone as bland as her greeting had been. "And what brings you to Paris?"

Disappointed, Joanna fell into the same noncommittal tone. "I'm fine. Busy. As I wrote you, we're just on the way to Venice, but I decided to detour through Paris so I could see you."

Monique looked straight ahead. "I was surprised to hear from you, after a whole year." The remark held a hint of reproach.

Joanna resisted apologizing. After all, Monique could have initiated contact as well. "I wanted to see if you were okay."

"Okay? Yeah, I'm okay now. But a lot has changed. I'll tell you about it when we're inside."

"Why did you refuse to have dinner with us?"

"'Us?' You mean the woman you were with? I saw you from the window. Is that your new girlfriend?"

"Absolutely not. That's my research partner. The grant covers travel for two, and when I told her I was making a side trip to Paris, she came along. We'll take the overnight train from here."

Annoyed at Monique's assumption about Sara, Joanna changed the subject. "Why do you want to sit in a church?" She nodded toward Notre Dame. "How will we be able to talk in the middle of thousands of tourists?"

"There won't be so many. This time of year, they stay along the outside aisles. You'll see."

They were at the cathedral entrance now and filed in behind a cluster of Japanese. Once they were inside, it was clear that Monique was right. Along with the murmurs of admiration and occasional flash of camera light along the periphery, the great cathedral held an oasis of quiet at its center.

Joanna sat down and waited for the cold of the wooden chair under her bottom to dissipate. Thousands of votive candles twinkled from stands all around them, suggesting heat even if they didn't furnish it. "I'd forgotten how beautiful Notre Dame is," she said, genuinely impressed. Monique smiled approval. They sat in silence for a few minutes, then something fluttered at the edge of her vision and Joanna glanced upward. "Looks like a pigeon has gotten into the church."

"No, look closer. It's a crow. Nasty things. My grandmother always said when a crow lands nearby, someone's going to die. It's nonsense, I know, but they *are* a symbol of death for a lot of people."

"Really? I never heard that. You'd think they'd symbolize survival. They're one of the toughest bird species in the world. They're supposed to be smart too, although this one maybe not so much." She chuckled.

The crow fluttered past them again and disappeared into one of the chapels, but the air between them now seemed warmer. It was the right moment to get to the point of the meeting.

"I'm sorry it all ended so abruptly. I should at least have contacted you. But…well, I have no excuse. I didn't know what I could say from so far away. And then, of course, academic pressure just took over."

Joanna waited for a reaction, but none came. The murmuring of the tourists seemed to only amplify the silence. "But you look content," she tried again. "Are you? What have you been doing?" Joanna shifted to sitting on one buttock, minimizing contact with the chair.

"Content? Yes, very much. I told you, a lot has changed. My family has helped me find peace."

"I could use a little of that." Joanna winced inwardly at the sarcasm that had crept into her voice, but she was already annoyed to be sitting in a cold church. Still, she didn't need to be rude. Joanna tried again. "Have you met someone?"

"In a manner of speaking. I've renewed my relationship with God."

"Ah, so that's what this is all about." Joanna let her eyes roam around the edifice, to the columns leading up to the breathtakingly high vault, then to the south rose window. "You dragged me here to tell me you were saved."

"You're so crass, to sit in this place filled with the divine spirit and not be affected."

"If God created the universe, then there's no more God here than anywhere else in His creation. I've already told you I find it beautiful. But you're not satisfied. You want the beauty to be some kind of proof of the supernatural. But it's not."

"How easily you toss off those certainties, without humility or gratitude. You're a heartless rationalist who doesn't believe anything that isn't in front of her nose. If you'd been less certain of things and a little more willing to believe, you might have been better at love." She paused for breath. "I don't think you've ever loved anyone."

The remark stung. "How did this end up being about me?" Joanna asked. "But, all right, if that's what you want to talk about, I admit, love is uncertain. We had a wonderful time, you and I, but when the summer term was over, well…"

"I don't want to be loved with uncertainty ever again. I want love that won't go away."

"I don't think anyone can offer that."

"You're wrong. There is someone who *can*."

Joanna looked quizzically at her, then realization dawned. "You have an announcement, don't you?"

Monique fidgeted, fingering the buttons of her coat. "Yes. I've joined the Soeurs de la Visitation. As a lay sister. I'll stay, at least for a while, at the convent in Metz."

"I don't think convents accept lesbians. They're quite fussy about that."

"I'm not a lesbian."

"You could have fooled me."

"Look, I don't want to get into another argument. I'm done with all that. I have my service to God, and now my family is the Soeurs de la Visitation. You have neither love nor God. I pity you." Monique planted a quick, gentle kiss on Joanna's cheek, then got up and walked away.

Silenced by the remark, Joanna sat staring at the rose window. Monique was right. She *had* lost God, and she even remembered when. On the last day of school, upon arriving home, she learned that Rex, the German shepherd belonging to a family at the end of her street, had been found chained to the fence behind their home, starved to death. For weeks Joanna cringed when she passed the house, as if the ghost of the tormented animal haunted it. It sickened her that she'd passed it every day on her way to school, could have brought food at any time, while it grew emaciated, ravening hunger gnawing its stomach. She could have saved it, *so easily*, if fate hadn't blocked her from knowing about it. God knew all things, her religion had told her. But if that was true, God had not only not saved Rex, God had prevented her from hearing his whimpering and going to his aid.

On that day, the notion of a higher benevolence crumbled under the heart-crushing weight of Rex's death. "All things happen for a reason," one of the neighbors had said. "Free will," someone else explained, and proclaimed that tragedy taught us the consequences of our sins. But Joanna rejected the impossible logic. What lesson was there in the days and nights of suffering of a helpless beast, incapable of either sin or free will?

No, she hadn't *lost* God, Joanna thought as she wandered lethargically along the aisle to the narthex. God had simply withered and died inside her like a starving dog.

"That didn't look good," someone said gently.

Glancing up from her morose reverie, Joanna, saw a familiar face. "Just some unfinished business."

"And now?"

Joanna pulled up her collar and slid her arm around Sara's elbow. "Now it's finished."

CHAPTER SIX

It was already dark when they reached the Gare de Lyon, and Joanna stopped for a moment to study its Italianate clock tower. Though she knew the station had been built in 1900, she could easily imagine brightly liveried sixteenth-century heralds lined up on the balcony of the tower blowing a fanfare on long brass horns. The interior of the station, an elaborate network of steel covering a vast field of tracks, brought her back to the realities of the industrial age.

The 19:48 train to Venice was already on the track and open, so they boarded immediately, locating their compartment in the fourth car.

Sara looked around the two-bed couchette they shared. "First class, very nice." She hefted her suitcase onto the overhead shelf and brushed dust off her slacks before sitting down. "Very Agatha Christie. Do you suppose a mysterious murder will occur somewhere on the train tonight?"

Joanna tossed her luggage up on her side of the cabin but left her rucksack by the window. "And a prissy Belgian detective will solve it? You're thinking of the Orient Express. Out of our league, I'm afraid."

They both stared awhile out the train window, watching the station platform and then the industrial cityscape slide past with ever greater speed until they were in the suburbs of Paris.

Sara settled back against her seat. "So, you want to fill me in on more of the details of this project? What made you decide to do it?"

Joanna took off her fedora and set it carefully next to her on the seat. "I sort of inherited it. Not the project, but the artifact that inspired it. It really should have been the brainchild of an old friend, but he was too sick to pursue it."

"Who was that?"

"Nigel Worthington. He lived in what was left of Windhurst Castle, a structure in Kent built in the 1500s. The castle belongs to the National Trust, but when his family sold it to the Trust, they included a provision that Nigel could continue to live there until his death."

"How did you know someone in Kent?"

"I met him years ago when I began studying Tudor England and took a tour of the castle. He chatted me up and we talked for an hour. After that, we corresponded a lot and I visited him whenever I was in the U.K. I suppose he thought of me as a sort of intellectual granddaughter. He liked that I was studying the English Renaissance and was always sending me articles and books from his library."

"A dream grandfather."

"Yes, I suppose so. Anyhow, last summer, he got sick with leukemia, not unusual for a man of eighty-six, and he asked me to visit him. I was in Paris at the time, so I left a few days earlier than planned and went to pay my respects. When I arrived he was desperately ill and his family was just about to take him to the hospital where we all knew he would die. I spent only an hour with him, but he presented me with two things. His favorite fedora—and this." She reached into her rucksack and drew out a sort of large leather wallet, obviously very old, and tied together with a rawhide cord.

"He told me that when he first got sick, he spent a lot of time just sitting by the fireplace in the library, staring at the walls. One day, he noticed a couple of slightly mismatched bricks on the outside of it. Imagine, after living for fifty years in that house, he finally noticed those bricks. He poked at them and they slid right out, and behind them was this bundle. If he'd found it a year earlier, he'd have had it translated, but at that moment, he had no heart for it. I suppose he sensed that things were coming to a close. In any case, a few months later, he really was at the end and when I visited him, he presented it to me, more or less as a mission. In any case, I took it as that."

Joanna undid the cord and slipped out some dozen pieces of paper, folded into thirds.

"Who else has seen these?" Sara asked.

"Other than Nigel, only Giulio Giglioti, the colleague who was supposed to travel with me until he was killed in an accident. He read and summarized them for me, so I know they were penned between June and July 1560, to someone living in England named Anne. Obviously we'll ultimately want someone to translate them precisely, but for now, I'm interested in the historical events and the people that surround them."

"Do the letters give the name of the author?"

"Only her first name, Leonora. She was a widow who wrote them while on a merchant ship sailing from Venice to Flanders. She wasn't just sailing *from* Venice, but apparently fleeing for her life. And you'll love this. She was traveling disguised as a man."

Delicately, Joanna unfolded the packet. The outer two pages in which the bundle was wrapped were brown and partially disintegrated.

"They've held up remarkably well, considering their age. Part of it is the high quality of the paper, and part of it, I think, is that the whole bundle was inside the brick wall. The leather wrapping would have kept the paper from drying out completely while the indirect heat from the fireplace would have kept it just dry enough to prevent mold. Only the outer pages are more or less ruined."

Sara's eyebrows went up. "Is that brown stuff all over them what I think it is?"

"If you're thinking it's blood, then yes. The writer says so. The first legible letter, which is really number three, explains what happened to the first two."

Sara took one of the unstained pages gingerly by the edges and tilted it toward the light. "I should be able to manage sixteenth-century Venetian." She peered at it for several moments, frowning in concentration, then began to read out loud.

15 June 1560
Cara mia,

Pray God this letter reaches you, even if perchance I do not. I wrote ere we sailed of Massimo's reckless agreement to print a heretical book, and of our arrest by the Inquisition. I lamented the closing and confiscation of C.A., of the torture and hanging of poor Massimo, of my interrogation on the rope, and of my escape at dawn through the hole I scratched in the floor of my cell. But those letters are soaked in blood now, and I have not the will to rewrite them.

Hakim, the author of the book, boarded the ship as I did, under a false name, though he as an Italian and I an Englishman. When anon the G.D. set sail,

I rejoiced we both were saved, but then the Hand
of God did strike. Two Jesuits, brothers of the family
Bracco, boarded on their way to found a school in
Alexandria. In their company was a churlish, red-
beard lay brother with more airs than a duke. With
them came their sponsor, the nobleman Vettor
Morosini. They sup with us at the captain's table and
glower righteously. I live in fear they will nose out
my deceit, for they are ever watchful of me, holding,
I suppose, that English Christians are tainted by
their Protestant queen. I thank God none of them
speaks English or I would be undone. I glower back
at them, with as much masculine condescension as
I can muster, and—so far—am left in peace. For
Hakim, the supper hour was more precarious.

Though he booked passage and registered cargo
under the name Leon Negri, by accent and garment,
he was marked as a Jew. The officers treated with
him as any other merchant from the Rialto, but
the Jesuits were affronted and dogged him without
mercy. One of them demanded to know what cargo
he carried. "Venetian glass," he said, but the lay
brother—Barbieri, he is called—would not have it.
"Nor silver? Nor gold? God's wounds! If that be so,
then you're the first Jew I've met who does not have
a fortune."

The captain minded the table of other matters,
and the quarrel passed, to my relief, for I too
smuggle cargo, but still the Jesuits would not leave
off bleating of infidels and apostates. Even the young
Morosini had much to say of Lutheran heresy and
the Jews. One of the Jesuits, with much brawn and
the face of a brute, offered to baptize Hakim, to
the chaplain's grand amusement. But before the jest
could go far, the captain spoke. "You mistake, sir.
Venice does business with Lutheran, Moor, and Jew
alike." Clearly, he spends his wit keeping things calm
until we reach Corfu, where the quarreling parties
were to disembark, the Jesuits to attend a vessel to

Alexandria and Hakim to travel with his dreadful cargo on to Constantinople.

The second night was e'er as evil, with Barbieri grumbling that Jews were as infidel as Saracens, for both slandered Christ's divinity. Finally, after the third night, Hakim came to my cabin, affright. Someone had broken into one of his crates and pilfered some of the volumes. It were good, he said, if I would hide the crates in my cabin where no one would think to look. I was unwilling, minding him that his accursed book had already caused the death of an honest printer. But he would not leave and, seeing what I had written—for the paper lay open under the lantern—he accused me of exposing him to mortal danger.

"Nonsense," I said. "It was I who was denounced for printing your filthy book, and was thus arrested, while you fled unscathed. These letters do not concern you." I pushed him from my cabin and closed the door in his face. For all that, he was an honest man and I never thought him moved by malice to slander the doctrines of the Church. And I had not begrudged him bringing his opus to Italy and to the North. But the codex he translated could not but bring the charge of heresy, and we were fools to not have seen it.

The next night, he was absent from the supper and the Jesuits asked mockingly, "Where's our Jew?" I knew not, but when I regained my cabin, my letters to you were gone and I was certain he'd purloined them. Seized with outrage, I went below to track the thief myself, but ere I came to the lower cargo deck, I heard them.

Rude shouting, anon a scream, and it was the voice of Hakim. I clambered down and on the ladder passed two men who bore Hakim's crates upon their backs, and with them was Barbieri. I knew calamity had struck.

I came upon him, grievously harmed, blood

pumping from his throat. I laid my hand upon him, to press the mortal wound. Alas, it was too late. He whispered, "Naomi...my children..." then fell still. Under my wrist I felt paper, and there, beneath his blood-drenched shirt, were my two letters. I reclaimed them, useless though they were, and then, o'ercome with fear, I fled.

On deck all was confusion. Barbieri stood o'er the crates, now broken all asunder. The Jesuits joined him, crying out, "Drown the blasphemy," and together they flung the books one by one into the sea. I pondered how they knew the contents of the book, and then recalled the pilfering the night before.

The captain appeared upon the moment and fired his arquebus into the air, halting the mayhem. For a single moment, it did seem that every man held a book in hand, everyone but me. Thereupon, the mate arrived to report the murdered man below. Appalled, the captain ordered the offenders seized and put in irons.

I kept a timid distance till order was restored. Anon, tranquility returned, and the moon shone a brilliant trail on the calm night sea that had swallowed up the books, as if two men had not been slain for them.

Sara laid down the letter and said with quiet awe, "Wow. Starts with a bang, doesn't it? Did you know all this?"

Joanna returned the letter to the half dozen others and folded them back into their wallet. "Only the basic facts from Giulio's summary. But I never imagined it would all sound so…Shakespearean."

"I'm trying to translate literally, so of course it comes across a little archaic. I can render it into colloquial English if you'd like."

"Oh, no. I like hearing Leonora in her own idiom, if not in her own language. She seems much more present, don't you think?"

"Yes, I suppose so, but tell me, if we have the story here, what are we looking for?"

"We're looking for the stories around the story, the historical context. Why was she fleeing? Who was Hakim? Who was Anne? Who was the captain and why was he so cooperative? And, most important of all, what was in the book that was so terrible that it destroyed this woman's livelihood and Hakim's life?"

Sara studied the sweep and flow of the script she'd just read. "I'm going to love working on this. What's the plan once we're in Venice?"

Joanna tucked the wallet back into her rucksack. "Giulio not only summarized the letters, he also put me in contact with Antonio Alvise, a historian at the University of Venice. We have an appointment to meet with him tomorrow afternoon and he will hopefully help us gain entry to both the National Library and the State Archives. Step one will be to find a record of the voyage in the archives."

"Anything I should be doing to prepare for this?"

"No. For the time being, just remember your name, and get a good night's sleep."

For all her lightheartedness, Joanna found sharing quarters with Sara a bit awkward. While the steward came by to make up their beds she went to brush her teeth in the bathroom at the end of the car. She had worn her loose "travel jeans" and planned to sleep in them. When she returned to the couchette, Sara had changed out of her day clothes into a black sweatsuit. "Oh, you brought sleepwear. Very smart."

"Yes, girl clothes look terrible when they wrinkle."

"Do you want me to give you some privacy while you take off your makeup?"

"No, it's all right. Not many people see me that way, but we'll be roommates for three weeks, right? So I guess I'll make allowances."

"Well, as long as I'm allowed to watch, maybe you can give me a few makeup hints. For example, regarding mascara: liquid or pencil?"

Sara rubbed a coating of cold cream on her cheeks and around her eyes. "Liquid. The pencil is quicker, but it smears all over your eyelids in a couple of hours, sooner if you sweat. The liquid stuff dries on and stays put." She wiped her face clean with a handful of tissues, revealing the face Joanna remembered from the first interview. It was Tadzio's face, now softened by the personality of Sara. The sight was confusing, but somehow pleasing, like seeing a bird smile.

Shrugging internally, Joanna lay down on her bunk and turned off her bed light. A moment later, Sara flicked off the overhead light as well and they were in darkness. An occasional flash of light along the edges of the window shade punctuated the soothing *reddeddet reddeddet* of the train wheels, reassurances that while they slept, activity went on in the world outside.

Joanna lay awake, considering Sara's wardrobe. At one time she might have vaguely disapproved of someone focusing so much attention on appearance. But now she thought of the other men she knew, whose casual clothing were a declaration of not caring.

Sara obviously did care. In Paris she had worn a long belted wool coat with epaulets. With its wide sleeves and side pockets, the coat had a distinct 1940s Garbo look. The classic slacks were Garboesque too, as was the ivory silk shirt. Even without knowing the contents of Sara's suitcase, Joanna was confident that everything would be tasteful and chic. It had to be. A transvestite either looked good or freakish. She wouldn't wear any overlarge T-shirts or baggy pants, none of the sloppy throw-on clothes that men—and some lesbians—allowed themselves. No golfer's jackets, hooded sweatshirts, and, almost certainly, no sports jerseys.

Joanna considered her own wardrobe and decided to pick up a few new things. It couldn't hurt.

Gradually the familiar syrupy sensation of pre-sleep settled over her. She briefly wondered if her cabin mate would snore, then remembered with faint chagrin that she herself did.

CHAPTER SEVEN

Joanna strode through the exit of the Santa Lucia Station and stopped. Under a too blue sky, a line of impossibly beautiful edifices extended along the Grand Canal. The series of palazzi with pillared balconies, narrow arched windows, pediments, and terra-cotta roofs was interrupted by a domed church, then continued like an oil painting as far as she could see.

Sara came up behind her. "So, what do you think?"

"I'm trying to find a word that millions of tourists before me haven't used."

"Don't. You won't come up with anything new. Best to settle for speechless admiration."

"Yeah, for what human beings can build. Pyramids, cathedrals, then this." She stretched out her hand. "Palaces on a swamp. Gives you hope for the human race."

"At least for its architects." Sara was clearly less overwhelmed and glanced past Joanna toward the vaporetto. "Look, there's the Number One ready to go. That's convenient."

They allowed themselves to be swept along with the mass of people that swarmed onto the vessel. Unable to move, they stood in the middle of the crowd on the deck between the passenger cabin and the engine room. The breeze blowing from the canal was cold, but the bodies surrounding them provided a certain warmth while they gazed out at the fairy-tale buildings.

At the Rialto stop, dozens more passengers crowded onto the vaporetto. Joanna and Sara were forced to the far side of the deck and pressed against the railing. The metal ceiling amplified the cacophony of voices, the fragments of conversations in various languages, as well as the thudding of the ferry's motor. Joanna felt pressure against her side and glanced down to see a child clutching a large doll to her chest with one hand and gripping her mother's coat with the other. Seemingly oblivious to the child, the mother rummaged energetically through a handbag, muttering to herself.

"What *sestiere* are we going to?" Sara asked, looking in the other direction.

"Cannaregio, the Ponte dei Greci neighborhood. We'll get off at San Marco and walk the rest of the way."

Joanna could see nothing but shoulders, but the shift of the vaporetto motor to a low growl signaled that they were pulling over to another stop. The ferry thumped against the floating transit dock and yet more passengers squeezed on. Everyone shifted back a step to accommodate them.

Suddenly, people called out in alarm in several languages. "What's that? *Guardate! Mein Gott!*"

Joanna twisted sideways to spot the cause and caught her breath. A man leaned over the railing, pointing with his entire arm and, with nauseous horror, she saw a tiny pale head disappear beneath the water of the canal. Half a dozen voices called for help, and for a second, she thought of leaping after the drowning child. Then she heard a little voice whining to her mother. A second later the mother called out in Italian to the crowd, *"Era soltanto la bambola!"*

It was the doll. Joanna's sudden relief was mixed with slight irritation at the child's whining. "What a drama," she started to say, then stopped.

Next to her, Sara clutched the railing, ashen.

Joanna laid her hand on the still-tense wrist and said, "It's all right. It was only the doll."

"Yes, yes. I know. I just thought…for a moment…"

"We all did. Relax. I'm sure people drop things into the canal all the time. It's no big deal."

Sara nodded agreement and looked away.

Some twenty minutes later, they entered the final curve, which brought them within sight of the Piazzetta San Marco. The square was exactly as she had seen it on countless calendars and postcards and commercial advertisements. A wide plaza with two columns in the foreground, the doge's palace on the right side, the corner of the basilica and the clock tower at the far end, and, on the left, the endless row of capitals of the National Library. Joanna allowed herself another moment of speechless admiration. This would be their "neighborhood" for the next three weeks.

The vaporetto disgorged its passengers in a steady stream. Joanna and Sara waited patiently at the rear, then hefted their baggage and strode out onto the wide Riva degli Schiavoni. Joanna noted the tourist kiosks, all filled with nearly identical souvenir trinkets, scarves, handbags, T-shirts, all stamped with Venetian scenes, plastic copies of the gondolas or the doge's ceremonial galley, the *Bucintoro*, and thousands of ornamented plaster masks.

They walked along the embankment, too tired to circle around the cluster of tourists and the lake of birds they were feeding. Pigeons, sparrows, one crow. The birds scattered momentarily as they passed through them, all but the defiant crow, but most returned unfazed a moment later.

They turned left through an underpass to a network of streets that would bring them finally to their apartment. The restaurants along the way were already filled with breakfast crowds, giving them the sense they were joining an ongoing party. As they wound along the *calli* toward the Ponte dei Greci, Joanna memorized the shop names at each turn so she could find her way back later without a map. Some of the *trattorias* looked like good lunch possibilities as well. She laughed inwardly at herself for preparing the archetypal tourist agenda: look, buy, eat.

Finally they arrived. Their apartment building was on the embankment near the Ponte dei Greci bridge. An iron gate at the street held the building number. Behind the gate was a corridor leading to a two-story house with a massive double oak door. Several apartments took up the ground floor; theirs was the one at the back.

Once inside, they faced an L-shaped corridor that led on the long side to the living room and kitchen, and on the short side to the bathroom and bedroom. "I had no idea it would be so big," Joanna said, surveying the exposed beams over the living room.

"Look, we've got a fireplace," Sara said. "One of those gas ones. Very elegant with the bookshelves on both sides."

"A nice reading selection too." Joanna ran her finger along the backs of some of the books. "*A History of Venice, Venice through the Ages, Venetian Baroque Art, Lives of the Doges*, also biographies of Giorgione, Titian, Tintoretto, Veronese. Here's a Bible, and a booklet on flora and fauna of the lagoon. Well chosen. For nights when there's nothing good on television."

"If I remember correctly, there's *always* nothing good on television," Sara said, wandering back down the corridor to the bedroom.

Joanna drew back the drapes and discovered a wide window opening to a small private garden with a lunch table and chairs. In the morning light, it looked inviting.

Sara called from the bedroom. "Hey, come look. It's huge. Closets you could park a sports car in."

Joanna followed the voice toward the bedroom and stood in the doorway. "Oh, nice. I like the carnival masks on the walls too. Very, um, Venetian."

"I love costume masks. They're one of the few things I remember from my childhood."

"Since you're in your element here, why don't you take the bedroom? I'll sleep on the sofa," Joanna said.

Sara acquiesced with a cheerful shrug. "Bedroom's fine."

They both migrated to the kitchen and discovered the rental agent had left coffee and a small welcome package of cheese and pastry. "Why don't I make us a pot while you unpack?" Sara suggested.

"Spontaneous domesticity. I'm going to like living with you," Joanna said as she returned to deal with her rucksack.

"Yeah, but I don't do windows," Sara called after her.

Unpacking went quickly, and soon they were seated at the table in the garden having their first Venetian meal. The sugary pastry and potent Italian coffee enlivened both of them, and Joanna saw no reason not to begin work. She fetched the packet of letters and her notebook and carried them to the table where Sara still sat.

"Do you feel up to doing a little more translating? We have a meeting with this Professor Alvise after lunch and I'd like to be well prepared."

"Good idea. I also want to know as much as possible at the start." Sara set aside her cup and cleared a space on the table. "Letter three tells us about the murder of Hakim. Let's see what the fourth one says. Would be nice if it mentioned the name of the captain. That would certainly help."

Sara pulled her chair alongside Joanna and, after carefully unfolding the centuries-old paper, she began to read again.

Tuesday, 17 June 1560

Cara mia,

The sun has set and I lie here in this stinking cabin, where odors penetrate but ne'er the ocean air. O'erhead, the calls of seamen about their duties, and those below, rude in their banter. Yet sailing is cruel labor, and I begrudge them not their brutishness if they but carry me to you.

I bethink myself how bless'd I am to have your love, and I summon memories of our sweet nights together and that you crept into my chamber when the household was asleep. What strange and secret love we had, rendered the more secret by the darkness that we dared not light, and the silence, which we dared not break. How much of our love-talk was in the language of hands and lips and flesh. Yet your soft moan into my neck when I brought you to the summit was all the speech I ever needed.

Would that I could send a dove ahead to London, to forewarn you that I come. The thought of you is all that sustains me on this murderous voyage.

The ship's physician carried out his office and after scrutiny of Hakim's body made official declaration of the cause of death. We were nigh to Durazzo and scarcely a day from Corfu. But the body was corrupting in the heat and the men made much of the odor it gave forth. Upon the wisdom of the physician (and to keep the peace, I'll warrant) the captain commanded he be given to the sea.

Hakim, may his soul find the peace that mine has lost, was wrapped in canvas and given to the water with brief ceremony. The chaplain was loath to offer pious words o'er an unbaptized man, and Hakim himself would have mocked them. But the captain declared it behooved us all to pray for the salvation of a murdered man, and that God Himself would decide whether to receive his soul.

After the mortal part of Hakim was cast into the sea, the chaplain saw fit to insult him yet again, saying, "The fool was offered baptism in water, but he refused, and now he's drowned in it."

Reflecting on the man himself, I recalled the last words he breathed, of wife and children. He had ne'er spoken of his family 'til that moment, nor, with such a wall 'tween Christian and Jew, had I ever thought to ask. In my indifference, I saw but a short, wiry man who played with his beard when he thought. Though his translation was a heresy, which brought us only woe, there was no malice in him, and in our conversations, I found him thoughtful. Now, somewhere in Constantinople a woman named Naomi and her children wait for one who will never return. Nor will they ever know why.

The ship's scribe has recorded the events and taken testimony from witnesses, excluding myself, who is deemed all but mute. The Jesuits are confined to quarters until Corfu, and their man, who has confessed to the murder, is held in irons. He justifies his act as defense of the faith, an argument that may carry weight if the smooth-talking Jesuits deliver it. Whate'er the outcome, I pray God I am in England, with you, by the time he hangs or is acquitted. I wager it will be the latter.

At eventime, we supped again, now seven of us at table. Only Morosini still attends. The pilot spoke everyone's thoughts but mine: "Of what did the blasphemy consist, I wonder?"

"Heretical writings worse than Lutheranism," Morosini said.

The navigator joined in. "What was it, then? Calvinism? Catharism? Anabaptism? The ravings of Socinius? Some Jewish perversion of scripture?" His tone was mocking. "There are so many possibilities for error, are there not? The mind reels."

The chaplain squinted menace. "You know much about heresies, sir."

"Yes, I do, and I know that the Inquisition is efficient at trying them. It does not need our assistance." The navigator chewed his bread,

unperturbed. "Did you see the contents of the book,
Signor Morosini?"

"A portion of it. It was of unfathomable
depravity."

I glanced at the captain and saw his grim
expression. I fear that he has claimed one of the
books, and woe to him if he should read it.

Sara laid the letter back down on the table. "Amazing. The Counter-
Reformation in microcosm. I'd always imagined it as something
abstract, decrees from Church councils and autos-da-fé for the poor
sods who fell afoul of them. But here it's part of the everyday mentality
of fear—of differences in general."

Joanna folded the letter carefully back into the leather wallet with
the others. "You also see that it's not monolithic. People had different
levels of tolerance, like they do today. The captain seems supportive,
the ship's chaplain hostile, the navigator skeptical. People don't seem
to change much."

"No, but institutions do. I'm curious to know what part the Jesuits
played here."

Joanna set the wallet carefully aside. "The Jesuits are an interesting
phenomenon. They were the best and the brightest at the time, and they
became the teachers and scholars, the church's version of modernization.
It makes complete sense that they'd go to Alexandria to found a school.
What puzzles me is that they'd soil their hands with murder."

"The lay brother apparently committed the murder, though. Sort of
their hit man who could do what their high principles wouldn't permit
them."

"Or maybe red-beard was more of a fanatic than they were and
less open to theological coexistence."

"Theological coexistence? Ha. Good one. Not a term I'd associate
with the Counter-Reformation. In any case, we have no idea what got
him so riled up that he was willing to stab a man to death. Even Luther
had the right to be heard in the court at Worms."

"They obviously thought it was something worse than Lutheranism.
I suppose we'll never know, not unless a copy of Hakim's book survived.
But without a title, or even the name of the publisher, how would we
ever track it down?"

"We might still come up with that information." Sara went back
into the kitchen to pour a second coffee. When she returned to the table,

Joanna had moved on to another concern. "Today, on the vaporetto. You seemed very upset."

"Yeah, a little. I thought the doll falling into the canal was a child."

"We all thought that. It was a moment of horror for everyone."

"Maybe a little more for me." She toyed with a spoon, seemingly reluctant to pursue the subject. Then, abruptly, "I nearly drowned when I was young and I'm terrified of deep water. I still don't know how to swim."

"Oh, I'm sorry. Then Venice must not be your favorite place."

"Of course I would have preferred it if Leonora had been from a village in the Alps and had fled the bad guys on a horse heading north." She chortled nervously. "But don't worry about it. I'll just make sure not to fall into a canal."

"So what happened?" Joanna asked. "I mean when you almost drowned? Or is that something you don't want to talk about?"

"It wasn't the brightest period of my life. Just after my mother died when I was eight and my father put me into a military boarding school."

"Oh, it must have been terrible for you. So young and so alone."

"The other boys were having their problems too. In a sense, they'd also been put out of their families, or at least felt like it. But they sort of worked things out among themselves, the way boys do, fighting, competing in sports. You know, the whole power hierarchy. But me…I just couldn't compete. I was small for my age, and I was pretty timid. I seemed to have a sign over my head that said, 'Weakest link. Take out your frustrations on me.'"

"So, what happened?" Joanna studied Sara's blue eyes, which dulled as she stared off into space, reminiscing.

"An outing, at a local pond. The first day we'd been let out of the school and everyone was a little wild. The boys were on a long raft, in shallow water on one side and in deep water on the other. Of course I stayed on the shallow end and tried to keep away from the roughhousing, especially when the contests began. The usual boy stuff. Who could jump the farthest, stay down the longest, swim the fastest. When they finally noticed skinny little Tadzio, they dragged me to the deep end and insisted that with just a little effort I could swim. Then they threw me in. It was as simple as that. No ill will, really."

"Oh, my God. It must have been awful."

Sara shrugged. "Yeah, it sort of was. Mostly I remember

swallowing water, then I blacked out. When I came to, I was on my back on the beach and the headmaster was furious. He ended the outing immediately, of course. The boys blamed me for ruining their holiday, and after that I was a pariah."

"Hell. No wonder you never felt like 'one of the guys.' They nearly killed you."

"I don't think of myself as a victim. That near drowning was a sort of baptism for me."

"Baptism?" Odd way to look at something so awful."

"I know. But something changed in me just then. When we got back to the school, I was somebody else. I knew I would never be in that brotherhood and I stopped trying to be. Not that I especially wanted to be a girl, but from that moment, I didn't want to be a boy. That same weekend, I went into town and shoplifted makeup." Sara tapped her coffee spoon softly on the table, musing. "Baptized into a new life. A born-again trannie."

Joanna gently took the spoon from Sara's nervous hand. "I suppose that's what baptism is, fundamentally. Dying and being reborn into something new. In your case, it simply gave you a clearer vision of who you already were."

"You mean, what doesn't kill us makes us stronger, or at least smarter," Sara quipped.

"Yeah. That's exactly what I mean." Joanna checked her watch and stood up from the table. "I hate to end this conversation when we were *so* close to discovering the meaning of life, but it's getting late. We have a meeting with Professor Alvise, and I'm eager to find out how good Giulio Giglioti's academic connection really is."

CHAPTER EIGHT

"Thank you, Rosso. That's all we'll need today," a male voice said.

Joanna and Sara entered the top-floor office just as an electrician or maintenance man was folding up a tall ladder under a ceiling lamp. The worker was elderly and the ladder long and unwieldy. As he tilted it downward, one of the legs hit the corner of a desk, knocking over a pile of papers.

"Look what you've done, Rosso." A man in professorial tweed knelt down and gathered up the papers. Seeing them enter, he dropped the loose pile at the center of the desk and held out a hand of welcome.

"Ah, the American ladies. Please come in. I apologize for this disturbance." He pointed toward the ceiling. "A burnt-out bulb. The maintenance man will be out of our way in just a moment."

The hapless worker tried to thread the ladder through the desks and cabinets that filled the office. As he struggled, his cap fell off and his suddenly exposed face revealed a crimson birthmark, a long and narrow red patch, vaguely triangular, with its apex at his chin. With both hands occupied, he could not retrieve the cap and so stood for a moment, nonplussed.

Passing him, Sara knelt down and swept up the cap and, without a word, placed it back on the man's head. *"Grazie, signorina,"* he said, his rheumy gaze lingering on his benefactor's face. Then, with a final clatter, he was out and the office door closed behind him.

"Ah, you must be Signorina Valois." The man in the tweed jacket took Joanna's hand and shook it warmly. "Antonio Alvise at your service. And your colleague is…?"

"Sara Falier," Joanna replied, and there was another handshake.

"I'm sorry for the interruption, ladies. But to make up for it, come have a look at the city from up here." He motioned them to the window on the top floor of the Università Ca' Foscari Venezia, opened the vertical panes, and thrust his hand out into the air over the canal.

The pose he struck allowed Joanna to study him for a moment before stepping toward the window. He was a handsome man, in a smooth, Italian sort of way. He had a long nose and square jaw, thick hair graying at the temples but full and black at the top. It was clear why he and Giglioti had become friends. They had the same suave, flirtatious Ezio Pinza voice DNA.

Following his invitation, she leaned out the high window and gazed down at the busy Grand Canal. The midday sun had burned away the morning fog, and the line of churches, scuoli, and palazzi snaking its way up the canal to the Rialto was as fantastical and painterly as the sight that had greeted them at the station. Joanna absorbed it, marveled at it. "Do you ever grow bored with this view?" she asked, turning back toward her host.

"No, never." Alvise also did an about-face toward the room. "What I do grow tired of is this." He swept his arm in a wide arc, indicating the general disorder on his desk and bookshelves. "Preparing lectures that simplify Venetian economic history for foreign students, writing reports for the higher authorities."

Sara was still at the window studying the ornamental columns between the windows. "The Ca' Foscari is almost as much an icon of Venice as the Rialto. It's a pity nothing's left of its original interior. Do you know the history of the building?"

"Oh, yes. The Palazzo Foscari was built in 1452. A splendid example of the Venetian Byzantine-Gothic architecture. You might have noticed that the tracery of its columns and arches resembles that of the Doge's Palace."

"It never hurts to look like the people in power, does it?" Joanna said.

"The Foscari *were* the power. There was a Foscari doge, wasn't there?" Sara added. "Fifteenth century, as I recall."

Alvise nodded, though his voice took on the monotone of someone who had told the story many times. "Oh, yes, from an ancient and noble family. Francesco Foscari, who built this palazzo, was doge in 1423, though he had a son accused of corruption. His son's exile and death unhinged the doge to the extent he was forced to resign and, shortly after, he died as well. The family seems to have consistently produced its renegades. 'Loose cannons,' I believe you call them in English."

"I have a neighbor in New York called Foscari," Sara said. "I wonder if he's a descendant."

"Very likely. The family was…is…large."

"I'll be sure to tell him he has ducal blood, and a palazzo that he missed living in by a few centuries."

Alvise looked around the cluttered office. "Alas, the magnificent palace disintegrated over the centuries, and the Austrians even used it as a barracks."

"When did it become a university?" Joanna asked.

"Only two years ago, and that's when I met our dear friend Dr. Giglioti, who came as a guest lecturer. My condolences, by the way, for the loss of your colleague. I had looked forward to seeing him again." Alvise tilted his head toward Sara. "Not to detract in any way from the pleasure of meeting you, signorina," he said, his smile stopping just short of a leer. Sara's return smile was cool.

"So, ladies, perhaps you can tell me in greater detail than he did, how I can help you."

"I understood that Dr. Giglioti told you about the letters we're investigating," Joanna replied. "He informed me that you had generously consented to assist us in gaining access to various documents from around 1560."

"The word 'assist' is perhaps a bit overstated. As a historical economist, I am poorly equipped to guide you in your research. However, I *can* introduce you to the new head of our history department, who is bound to be of far greater help than I could be. I have already told him of your arrival. His name is Vincent Morosini."

Sara's eyebrows went up. "Morosini? That's an old Venetian name, isn't it?"

Alvise frowned for the briefest instant. "I see you know your Venetian history. Yes. Dr. Morosini is quite proud of his family. Doges, senators, and no end of cardinals. The rest of us are immigrants by comparison." There was faint sarcasm in his voice as he guided them toward the door. "I'll take you to our nobleman now. He said he'd be available all morning."

They descended two flights. At the foot of the stairs, Joanna stopped and glanced around at the functional lobby and partitioned offices. "This would have been the *piano nobile,* the 'noble' floor of the palace designed for public reception. Am I right?"

"Yes, quite right. Five hundred years ago. Alas, very few Venetian houses have been able to retain their banquet rooms in their original glory. This way, if you please." He led them to one of the doors at the end of a row of large photographs, presumably of the university's prominent figures.

"Dr. Morosini just moved into this office a few weeks ago, upon his promotion to department chairmanship. Before that, it was my office." Alvise's voice was emotionless as he reached past them to open the door.

The office in question was noticeably larger than the one Alvise currently inhabited, though it had the same expanse of windows opening to the Grand Canal. Another handsome man, well over sixty, but with a full head of snow-white hair, stood up from his desk as they entered. "Ah, our two American scholars have arrived," he said, in halting, thickly accented English, as he came around to meet them and offered his hand.

"It's a pleasure to meet you, Signor Morosini," Joanna replied in Italian, to his obvious relief. Sara repeated the greeting, making it clear he could continue the conversation in his own language.

Morosini directed them to chairs already drawn up close to his desk. "Dr. Alvise tells me you are doing research on a heretical book from the sixteenth century. An intriguing subject."

Alvise stood off to the side for a moment. Then, apparently satisfied that he had adroitly passed off his guests, he shook hands with them again, perhaps a moment longer with Sara, and exited discreetly.

"It's not really about the book, although that's part of the mystery." Joanna returned to Morosini's remark. "Mainly we have a series of letters written by a woman bound for England. It appears she fled Venice after a charge of heresy. There is frustratingly little information about the escape, not to mention the names of the individuals, or even the ship she was escaping on. We hope to uncover much more here in Venice, even after four centuries."

"Your hope is justified, signorina, and that is the difference between the Americans and the Italians. You build your rocket ships and land on the moon, while we cultivate our past. Venice is obsessive about holding onto its historical documents, particularly from the *Rinascimento*. We'll get you your answers, I'm sure."

Noting his use of the word "we," Joanna smiled. "An obsession for which we can only be thankful. Unfortunately, we have rather little to go on other than the year, 1560, and the fact that the ship was bound for Flanders carrying commercial cargo."

"I take it you have the letter-writer's name."

"Only her first name, Leonora. And that the charge against her was heresy. Given Venice's historical lack of enthusiasm for the Inquisition, we thought we'd find some commentary here. In the records of the Council of Ten, for example."

Morosini raised one hand, as a teacher might before correcting a student. "Let me tell you first that the Inquisition and the Council were not separate entities. If this Leonora was condemned, it was by a tribunal that would have held both secular Venetians and agents of the Holy Office. A warrant could not be issued without Venetian authority. As for the names of the ship and the press, I am sure you can obtain useful preliminary information in the National Library, that is, the Libreria Marciana in the Piazza San Marco. The librarian, Tiziana, is my niece, and I have already informed her that you will be coming. She will be glad to direct you to books that provide an overview of the legal and commercial activity occurring at that time. The library is closed on Sundays, but she will assist you first thing on Monday morning."

"That was very kind of you, Dr. Morosini." Joanna smiled genuine gratitude at him.

"It should not be too difficult to ascertain the names of the offending press and the ship, for example, and then you can then go to the State Archives to find the record and cargo manifest for that voyage. The Republic was extremely thorough about recording its commerce."

"An appointment on Monday is perfect," Joanna said. "That will give us tomorrow to be tourists."

"Oh, yes. Do spend some time enjoying our lovely city." He paused. "You know, some of the places you will want to visit might be closed to tourists. I can reduce some of the bureaucratic obstacles by writing you a general letter of introduction. The university letterhead usually carries enough weight to overcome them."

"That would help us enormously, I'm sure," Joanna replied.

"I'll dictate one to my secretary this afternoon and you can pick it up tomorrow."

Joanna had a sudden twinge of guilt toward the ghost of Giulio Giglioti. Vain and obnoxious as he was, he really had found excellent support for the project.

"In the meantime, would you like to see a diagram of a ship of that period? I don't know how much it can advance your research, but the subject interests me greatly."

Joanna was delighted. "Of course. It would be helpful for us to have a clearer image of our heroine's surroundings."

Morosini turned toward the bookshelf behind his desk and withdrew a heavy volume half a meter in height. "This gives you a close look at the typical merchant vessels of the time. Many rowed galleys were still operating through the sixteenth century, but, increasingly, fully sail-rigged boats took care of the mercantile trade. Let's see." He turned the large pages with a careful sweep of the hand. "Here it is." He laid the book out flat to a cross-section of a two-masted ship that covered both pages.

"As you can see, every meter of the ship is utilized. The hold is filled with the sturdiest items that will travel the farthest, while the lower cargo deck is also packed from floor to ceiling with barrels, crates, and sacks of hardtack for the crew. Most likely also bales of fabric from Venetian weavers. Above that is the gun deck."

"Did all the merchant ships carry cannon?" Sara asked.

"For the most part, yes. The high seas were crawling with pirates, corsairs, Turks, ships from rival cities."

"But this deck also has cabins." Joanna tapped the relevant part of the drawing with a fingertip.

"Yes, cargo stalls reserved by the larger merchant houses. The seamen slept here, in the corridor between the two masts, on straw mattresses that they rolled up in the morning. The livestock would have been kept here, around the mainmast. Farther forward are the kitchen and the cook's and purser's quarters. Here at the stern is the quarterdeck, where the captain and his officers were quartered."

"And the passengers?"

Morosini slid his finger back to the bow of the ship. "Over here, in the forecastle. The tiny cabins held particularly valuable cargo or sleeping quarters for passengers who could afford to pay. As you can imagine, they would have been terribly uncomfortable. No toilet, no daylight. Damp, airless, hot in summer, freezing in winter."

Joanna stared at the forecastle, trying to visualize what life must have been like for Leonora. A single image came to her. The creaking of wet wood, a dark chamber. At its center, a figure hunched over a tiny table, writing in the dull sphere of lantern light.

Morosini closed the book. "I'm not sure how much a ship's cutaway will help you discover the authenticity of your story, especially since it would have been nearly impossible for a woman to travel alone. The possibility of a woman 'escaping,' as you say, alone and unassisted by husband or father, is remote, and points to the letters being a flight of imagination."

Joanna had already considered the possibility, but the blood on the letters alone suggested otherwise. "Well, that's exactly why we're here, Dr. Morosini. A few days' research in Venice's archives should tell us whether we have history or fiction."

"Yes, indeed. Forgive me for casting any doubt on your search. As I've pointed out, my niece will be at your disposal on Monday. In the meantime, you have a day to yourselves. Do you have any special places you want to visit?"

"The doge's prison, of course. Our mysterious Leonora writes about being imprisoned there."

"In the 'wells' or in the 'leads'?"

"She wrote 'under the roof.' What does that mean?"

"Ah, she was fortunate. The cells under the lead roof are tiny wooden cubicles, very hot in summer, but they're dry and have no rats. Unlike the 'wells' beneath the palace, where there's always flooding, especially during the *acqua alta*. Usually privileged prisoners were kept in the 'leads.' It was also slightly less secure, apparently. Our famous Casanova was imprisoned there, and escaped."

"It seems our Leonora did also, and we hope to find out how."

"The dungeon tour should give you some insights. In any case, you will be entertained. Everyone seems to enjoy a little shiver at the sight of the torturer's rope." He guided them toward the door. "If you don't mind, I'll escort you to the main hall. I have a meeting there in a few minutes."

They descended the several flights of stairs to the entry hall where students were coming and going, their demeanor and dress the same as at Joanna's own university. If they felt any awe at the thought of being schooled in a Renaissance palazzo, they gave no evidence of it.

Sara, on the other hand, seemed reluctant to leave. At the foot of the staircase, she left Joanna engaged with Morosini and went to examine the two paintings that hung on one of the walls. A moment later, they joined her.

"Ah, I see you have discovered our Foscari wall," Morosini said.

"Interesting paintings," Sara remarked.

Joanna took a step toward the larger one. Under a portico, a young man knelt, his hands raised in supplication to a patriarchal figure. To the right, women looked on the scene as children gathered at their knees. Behind them, the tracery of the columns and the high balustrade showed they were on the portico of the doge's palace.

"Isn't that Hayez's *Farewell of Jacopo Foscari*?" Sara asked. She peered at the signature on the lower right corner. "Yes, Hayez. I was right."

Morosini seemed impressed. "Not many know him outside of Italy. I rather like the sentiment, myself. The penitent son, begging forgiveness on his knees, the father refusing to look at him. A great tragedy, to reject a son."

"Even more of a tragedy to *be* rejected," Sara murmured.

Sensing Sara's aversion, Joanna directed attention away from the scene and stepped farther along the wall. "Who is this one?"

A gray-haired man with a trim beard was seated against the backdrop of a harbor. In one hand he held a Bible, with chapter and verse visible on the cover, and in the other hand, a carnival mask that seemed to stare eyelessly out at the viewer. Behind him, in the middle distance, several figures stood about in carnival costumes.

Morosini shrugged faintly. "Another Foscari, Maffeo, who came along a century or so later. The Salome mask suggests it was posed during Carnival. The original is in the British Museum."

"Looks a bit like Anthony Quinn," Joanna said.

"I'm sure Anthony Quinn would be amused, seeing as how he's Mexican." Sara laughed, turning away.

Joanna and Morosini remained a moment longer before the portrait. "I quite like Venetian portraiture," Morosini said. "It shows the Venetians in their finery. It may not tell of the hardship of their daily lives, but it reveals their ideals."

Behind him, Sara had wandered away toward the maintenance man who was folding up his ladder from another repair, and the two were chatting amiably. Joanna watched, puzzled at their interaction, until Sara broke away and came toward them. "I think we've bothered you long enough," Joanna said, turning to their host. "We won't keep you from your meeting. Thank you so much for your help."

Morosini executed an abbreviated military bow and saw them to the exit.

"You have a new admirer?" Joanna asked, once they were out in the Venetian sunlight.

"If you mean the maintenance man, uh, not exactly. Remember, I said I lived here as a small child? A friend of my father, someone he used to get drunk with, had a hardware store near our house. Although I was only five or six, I remember being afraid of him because he had that red spot on his face and my father told me it was the mark of the devil. Stupid thing to say to a child, but you see I remember it after all these years. Anyhow, the man was called Roberto, but everyone called him Rosso, because of the birthmark. That electrician with the ladder was him. I guess his drinking finally cost him his hardware shop and now he's a maintenance man."

"Did he remember you?" Joanna asked.

"He remembered my father and a little boy called Tadzio. He even asked about him. I said it was my older brother."

"What a bizarre coincidence, that you'd run into him again here."

"Not so bizarre. Venice is a small city and many of the old families know each other. He's really fallen apart, though. He seemed affected when I told him my father had died. He said to tell my brother to come back to Venice someday and visit him. He had some good stories to tell him."

"That must have been strange. He had stories for your 'brother,' but not for you."

"Well, if he met Tadzio, he probably wouldn't want to sit down and reminisce with him either. Most people get a picture in their minds of the way things should be and don't like being surprised."

"Or being wrong," Joanna said, recalling her initial dismissal of Tadzio. "I apologize for us all."

❖

Weary from a poor sleep the previous night on the train followed by a longish first day in Venice, Sara removed her makeup and slid into the freshly made bed. She relaxed into the creamy state of pre-sleep, then into unconsciousness.

At first she slept, deeply and restfully. But then she began to dream. She was on shipboard. Below deck was a schoolroom, and class had just been dismissed. The other boys crowded past, going up on deck to do their rough sailor's work—climbing rigging, hauling anchor, all with noise and energy. She was swept along with them, though she wasn't a sailor but a woman disguised as a man. When she emerged on deck, she saw a chest lying open before the mast. The others boys were clawing out books and throwing them into the sea. One of them pointed at her and shouted, "He's the one," and hands seized her from all directions. They lifted her off her feet and threw her over the gunwale, amidst a hail of books. She flailed for a while in the water, surrounded by the floating books. Then she sank, gulping ice-cold water.

Sara awoke with a wrench and sat up in the dark room, befuddled.

Where was she? *When* was she? Then the dark blurs on the wall coalesced to Carnival masks and she remembered it was Venice. She was where she wanted to be, and she was safe. Taking a deep breath, she settled down again, knowing she wasn't alone. Joanna was in the living room. Tomorrow they would begin their work together, and all would be well.

CHAPTER NINE

The morning sun was just beginning to warm the air when Joanna and Sara started along the Ponte dei Greci embankment. The waterfront restaurants had not yet opened, but all along the way, waiters were setting tables for the breakfast business. The clinking of their plates and silverware and their lighthearted banter were soothingly homelike.

At the end of the embankment, a tiny stone bridge crossed the canal. Five steps up, five paces across, five steps down. On the other side, a gondolier waited in a striped jersey and straw boater, though he made no effort to attract the attention of the passing tourists. He was propped against the stone wall of the bridge reading a paperback novel. Joanna saw with amusement that it was an Italian translation of a James Bond novel, *Goldfinger*. He glanced up briefly, acknowledged them with a nod, and returned to his book.

"Funny that he's reading James Bond, isn't it?" Joanna remarked. "Like Venice isn't exciting enough." She chuckled. Suddenly something colorful flashed in front of her and she halted. A flyer, held out by a young man in the costume of an eighteenth-century gentleman. She took it and perused it idly as they turned right and continued along the new embankment of the canal they had just crossed.

THE ORCHESTRA COLLEGIUM DUCALE PLAYS VIVALDI FOUR SEASONS AND BACH BWV 1041, it announced in five European languages. Obviously something for the tourists. She looked around for a place to discard it but saw no bin, so handed it to Sara, who glanced at it and slipped it into her shoulder bag.

Joanna slowed her pace to gaze, half-distracted, into one of the shop windows. Scores of colored masks in dozens of shapes and ornamentations gazed back at her. She scarcely noticed. "I'm wondering now if we should have told Morosini that one of his ancestors was on the ship we're looking for. That could help us find the name in the records."

Half a head taller, Sara stood behind her, reflected with her in the glass window. "No. I think you were right not to mention it."

"Really? It seems a little dishonest. I mean, it's not like Leonora's letter indicts Vittor Morosini for anything. He was simply part of the Jesuit group."

"Yes, but he defended the attack on Hakim. In modern terms, that would make him an accomplice to murder, morally if not legally. Scions of noble lineages don't like to have the crimes of their ancestors pointed out to them."

"If it were my ancestor, I might find it amusing."

"That's because we're Americans and have no concept of nobility. You carry the family name of Henry of Valois, for God's sake, and you toss it out as if it were a lineage of shoemakers."

"Electricians, actually." Joanna laughed. "I see what you mean. I suppose I don't want him to know that we're dealing with love letters to a woman. I'd rather not give him an opportunity to say something rude about lesbians."

"I agree. Some of the nicest people turn to ice when they meet someone with an 'alternate' sexuality. On the other hand, support sometimes comes from unexpected quarters."

"Which category do you think Morosini falls into?"

"I'd say the category of 'I don't want to know about it.'"

Joanna sighed. "Like most of the world."

The guide finished her iteration of the history of the Great Council chamber, including its hanging ceiling, gold veneer, and panoramic artwork. She raised her notebook to signal that the first part of the tour was over and guided her flock back toward the door.

Joanna took a final glance around the vast hall at the gold molding and gargantuan murals that covered every inch of walls and ceiling. "A bit busy," she mumbled as they followed the throng back through the corridors.

"Philistine." Sara mumbled back the accusation.

"Well, I did like the one with the battle scene, showing all the galleys and the zillion sailors with pikes."

"Yeah, Veronese's *Battle of Lepanto*."

"Who was fighting whom?"

"Renaissance historian? Shame on you. Venetians versus Turks." Sara hinted at a sideward smile.

"*English* Renaissance. I could take you any day on the Tudors or the Stewarts."

"I'm sure you could. But here, you have to know about Lepanto. It comes up at all the Renaissance-historian cocktail parties."

"Shhh," one of the other tourists hissed. The guide was talking again at the head of the group. "And here we are in the inquisitors' room. This is where the inquisitors read the secret denunciations and decided whom to arrest."

The pleasantly lit chamber with its honey-colored polished wood paneling looked innocent enough. Except for a table and three large chairs situated at one end, the only furnishings were two enormous wardrobes at opposite corners. At some mysterious triggering by the guide, one of the wardrobes swung out away from the wall, revealing the entrance to a narrow, dark staircase.

"And here is where the terror begins," she said, leading their small group up the stairs.

"What did they do for plumbing?" one of the other tourists asked.

"The same as everyone else in Venice. Chamber pot. Presumably it was emptied at intervals."

A collective murmur of disgust filled the narrow enclosure.

"And meals?"

"Prison food was gruel and apparently dreadful. If you were lucky, you could pay your jailor to bring you something better. At least up here. But the disadvantage of being imprisoned here is that it was right next to the room where the prisoners were 'put to the question.'" She paused for effect. "The torture room."

She guided the group into a chamber that formed a sort of silo between two floors of cells. Far overhead was an iron ring that held a rope that must have been some twenty feet in length. Its lower end hung over a slightly elevated platform.

"The strappado." The guide answered their unasked question. "It was considerably less gruesome than the horrors inflicted with hot iron in the dungeons of the North. However, that concession was less out of mercy than out of fear of fire breaking out and destroying the entire palace. But the rope did its work, nonetheless. Jailors' records from the period show that dislocated shoulders were agonizing enough to get confessions, almost always."

"By the innocent too, of course. I wonder why no one ever got that," the talkative tourist observed.

"Faith. The torturers believed God would not allow an innocent man to suffer."

"No comment," Sara muttered as they trailed along another narrow stairwell to the cells that flanked the torturer's rope. As they filed into one of them, the guide resumed her recitation.

"Compared with the dungeons of northern Europe at the time, these cells are less than horrifying, but you will note that they are not very high. If you were lucky, and short, you could pace your cell, but the average man would not be able to do so. Thus you could spend months, even years, never being able to stand up." She touched the wooden ceiling about an inch from the top of her head. "The cells were tolerably warm in winter, but stifling in summer, for this," she rested her hand on the single window that was crisscrossed with thick cast-iron bars, "only opened to the interior."

She led them across a narrow corridor to an adjacent cell. "And here is the 'confessor's cell,' so called because one side overlooked the torture room and the inmate could hear the sobs and screams of the person being interrogated. That alone was usually enough to make him confess without having to apply the rope."

"Do you suppose this is the cell Leonora was in?" Sara whispered.

"It's possible. I wonder if there's still any sign of a hole."

"Only one way to know." Sara tapped the guide gently on the shoulder. "Excuse me, but could you shine your light on the corner over there?"

"Uhh, if you wish." Perplexed, the young woman swept the circle of light over the floor and the two adjoining walls. There was nothing to see.

"Maybe the other corner?" Sara pointed to the other side.

"Did you lose something, miss?" The guide was losing patience and the other tourists were beginning to shuffle. Nonetheless, she redirected the flashlight beam.

Sara knelt and traced her finger over the floor. Hovering over her, Joanna could just make out the faintest of lines. Age and a layer of wood varnish all but concealed the circle where a hole had been masterfully filled in with nearly identical wood. Only the difference in the direction of the wood grain revealed that it was a later addition.

"That's it. Where she escaped," Joanna said with quiet excitement. "Nice work, you."

"I'm sorry to disappoint you, but no one has ever escaped from these cells except the famous Casanova in the seventeenth century, and he was in another cell. That is just a repair to the floor."

Joanna opened her mouth to reply, but saw no point in arguing. "Yes, of course," she said with quiet deference, and scrambled to her feet. But as the young lady led the group from the cell back down the stairwell, Joanna whispered into Sara's ear. "Brava. This deserves a bottle of wine at dinner."

"At least."

❖

Joanna halted just before the footbridge leading to their embankment. The gondolier was still there, this time sitting and smoking a cigarette. His empty gondola was tied up nearby. "No business today?" she asked pleasantly.

"Lots of business. A good day," he replied cheerfully. "And you?"

"Superb," Joanna said with a wave of the hand, then continued along the sidewalk that fronted the canal. "Nice man," she observed, catching up with Sara. "I wonder how he feels about living in a costume every day."

Sara shrugged. "Everyone puts on costume when they go out. People are just more colorful about it here."

"Mmm. Interesting way of looking at things, except outside of Venice, or Disneyland, people don't do it consciously." Joanna threw a quick sideways look at Sara's carefully chosen young-professional-woman outfit for the day and added, "Well, *most* people don't."

They arrived just then at the restaurant and the focus turned to food. "Good choice," Sara said as they sat down. "The red-checkered tablecloths are a bit kitschy, but the smells are wonderful. I like it that it's quiet and we can talk."

The wine came immediately and, after the ritual sampling and pouring, Joanna held up her glass. "To more wonderful finds like the one you made this morning. Brava!"

"It *was* a good beginning, wasn't it?" Sara tapped the lip of her glass against Joanna's. "But also a little grim. I couldn't help but think of what it must have been like, sitting in that cell, eating gruel, waiting to be tortured. And then *being* tortured. I wonder how she managed to dig that hole?"

"She must have had help of some kind. Which of course brings up still more questions. Who? How? Why? More details that we'll want to look for."

Sara raised her glass again. "To Leonora."

"To Leonora, her friends and enemies." Joanna reached for the menu. "All that talk about prison gruel has made me hungry." She ran her eye over the red-meat dishes, then remembered Sara's report of the "industry of cruelty." "I guess I'll go for the eggplant parmesan."

"Good choice. I'll have that too."

They chatted lightly as they ate, about cooking (Sara did, Joanna did not), boiling lobster (Joanna did, Sara did not), favoring Belgian chocolate (both did), and foie gras (both agreed it was torture food).

Joanna found it amusing that Sara's table manners were better than her own, that her forkfuls of food were small and that she never spoke when she chewed. She could probably draw a lesson from that, maybe several.

Finally, Joanna pushed her plate aside and leaned forward on her elbows. "You're right about Leonora. She's like a friend who's disappeared and we urgently have to find out what happened to her. I want to go over the letters again. When can you look at the next one?"

Sara emptied her wineglass. "Why not right now? I've gotten used to her language and her writing, and can translate almost directly. Do you have them with you?"

"It so happens, yes, here in my rucksack." After a quick rummage, Joanna lifted out the leather wallet while Sara moved the dishes to the end of the table.

"Here's the two we've already read, and here's the next one in chronological order." Joanna peeled out the fifth page and handed it over. Sara unfolded it only partially, so as not to break the crease, and Joanna slid her chair around the table to read over her shoulder.

20 June 1560
Cara mia,

Though I had scant comfort from his company
Hakim was, at least, an ally, and I mourn him now
he's dead. The days pass dully and I have nothing
left but my hope of you. I pray God you are well and
that I find you.

Staring at the sea, I pluck from memory the
day you came to us, newly widowed of that brute of
a husband. How your father could have contracted
for such a marriage appalled but did not surprise
me. We are the chattel of our men until benevolent
fate takes them away. It was the beginning of my
happiness when the condottiere left you in our care
and hired himself off again to warring. And yet, we
had so little time, scarcely a year to discover our
strange love and then to conceal it. Though Venice
is lost to me now, I think it may have been the hand
of fate that drove me out, westward, and to you.

But who would have thought it would be so
cruel? Massimo hanged and Hakim left abutchered.
His murderers have been taken off the ship at Corfu
and incarcerated by the Venetian authorities. The
hearing is tomorrow, but if they are to stand trial, the
argumentations will take no end of time. The villains
will have Vittor Morosini to plead for them, and no
doubt he will use the weight of his family name to
free them. He too makes the case that the murder
was a defense of the faith. But to do that, he must
give the book as evidence, and I cannot but wonder
if he dares to do so.

I care not about the outcome, what ere it be,
and am only grateful to have escaped discovery
through the whole tragedy. The captain protects me
by ignoring me, for he speaks no English, and I
feign to speak no Italian. This dissembling leaves
me lonely, for he is my only friend and prodigal in his
generosity. 'Twas he who hid me in his palazzo when
I escaped, and I trust him, not only with my life, but

with the happiness of Lucca, my sweet apprentice. I
see the nobility in his face when he strides past me
on the deck, and I hear the wisdom in his voice at
supper when he turns the subject away from hateful
dogma.

Silence weighs heavily upon me and your image
is my only companion, in sleep and waking. How
shall you look at me when I walk through your
door? I pray only that you do not marry in despair,
thinking you have lost me, the while I am rushing
toward you.

Corfu harbor is Venice in miniature. We were but
one of the big-masted ships when we dropped anchor
beside a Venetian galley bound for the Aegean.
Splendid crafts, the galleys. What Venetian does not
love their majestic size and the rhythmic motion
of their oars? Their swiftness suits them for rapid
trade down the Adriatic, but they are ill-suited for
winter. Nor would I wish to be a passenger housed
among hundreds of woeful prisoners chained to their
benches.

We unloaded cargo from the upper deck, took on
fresh food, and the scribe made note of all transfers.
Chatter of Hakim's death and the destruction of
his cargo is on the wind through the harbor, though
naught will come of it. I will never know what moved
him to bring his translation to me. That he was a
scholar and loved the truth, I do not doubt, nor that
his book was honest meant, but how could he, or we,
not have sniffed the poison in it?

But that is past evil now. The while, I am
growing comfortable in my new guise. While the ship
lay at anchor, I betook me through Corfu and to
its marketplace. As a woman, I would ne'er have
ventured alone through a strange city. But as a man,
I marched uncontested where I chose. I marvel
that clothing has such power to separate man from
woman, noble from yeoman, yeoman from slave. I
also puzzle at the way we alter inwardly with our

garments. Is there something of the man in me that only needed breeches? Something of the woman, perhaps, in all men?

Though I dared not speak myself, I heard Venetian everywhere. Venetian bankers are active in the marketplace and Venetian laws apply.

There are pilgrims aplenty here, attending passage on vessels to Tripoli and Beirut. They wear one or another sign of the Holy Cross, drawing attention to themselves. When, perchance, I pass one on the street, I shudder a little and think, "If e'er they knew..."

"And that's it." Sara carefully folded the letter and slipped it back into its folder.

"'If e'er they knew.' Charmingly Elizabethan the way you say that. But 'if e'er *we* knew' too. I swear I'm going to find out if it kills me. For starters, what do we know about Corfu? It was a Venetian colony then, but would there have been a trial there?"

Sara poured more wine for both of them. "I think so. Corfu's government was Venetian, and so it was quite logical that the captain—whoever he was—would leave the prisoners there to be heard in what were essentially Venetian courts."

"So you think the ship would not have been delayed for the trial?"

"A day or two perhaps, but no longer, I'm sure. A trial could take weeks to unfold, and time was money. If maritime Venice was at all like Tudor England, we're talking about a commercial venture worth a fortune, dependent on powerful investors and clients. I think the captain would have been able to leave testimony of some sort and continue. Besides, the assassin had already confessed."

Joanna calculated. "That means we'll want to look for a manifest, or ship's log, or scribe's report, whatever it was called. Of course we have to identify the ship, carrack or galleon, and hope that its log has survived the centuries."

"Those nautical terms roll so easily off your tongue."

"I've done a little reading since finding these letters," Joanna said. "And I like to imagine life at sea. From the safety of a warm, dry living room, of course."

Sara swirled the last of the wine in her glass. "It never appealed to me. Never wanted to be a sailor or a pirate, or even go fishing. It's the water, of course."

"Ah, yes. That's right. Listen, I'll make a pledge to you. We'll minimize the vaporetto trips, and when we do make them, I'll stay by you and jump in if necessary."

Sara smiled and emptied the wine bottle into their two glasses. "Let's drink to never having that baptism."

CHAPTER TEN

So this is La Serenissima, Joanna thought as she wandered through the still-quiet Piazzetta San Marco toward the waterfront. She congratulated herself for arriving a half hour early, simply to see the sun rise, while Sara prepared for the day in more leisurely fashion.

Joanna faced the doge's palace across the piazzetta and studied the rounded columns of its ground-floor arcade, their capitals curving gradually into arches. The first-floor gallery held another row of columns with delicate stone tracery. On top of it, the rest of the palace was a monotonous block of marble broken only by a few windows. Slightly silhouetted against the slowly lightening sky, the whole edifice seemed top-heavy and ghostly.

It had rained during the night; a morning mist dulled the light of the rising sun and the entire piazzetta was still wet. Joanna shifted her position a few paces so she could watch the burning orb rise under the arches at the corner of the palace. While she gazed, hypnotized, the mist began to burn away. Suddenly the sun flashed in undimmed whiteness and shot a sparkling path through the archway along the flooded walk.

How many others through the ages had seen the same spectacle through the doge's archway? Hundreds of thousands, probably, though a more somber thought came to her. Just in front of her at the corner of the palace was the pillar of San Marco, with its winged lion at the top. Right below it, for centuries, criminals had been hanged at dawn, by the light of the rising sun.

"It takes your breath away, doesn't it?"

Joanna jumped slightly as she heard Sara's voice behind her. "Oh, you're here. Good, you didn't miss sunrise. I'm trying to enjoy the light show, but I keep thinking of the executions that took place right here, at just this time of day."

"You're thinking of Massimo, from Leonora's letters. Yeah, I know what you mean. It makes that golden glow suddenly poignant, doesn't it?"

Joanna nodded, trying to imagine how it might have felt, to stand before death and darkness just at the moment the sky brought awakening light.

"It's almost eight," Sara reminded her. "We'd better go meet Tiziana Morosini." They made an about-face and approached the stately glass doors of the national library. "Tiziana. Such a nice name. Like the painter, I assume. Do you suppose she'll look voluptuous and languid, like Titian's women? You know, like the Venus of Urbino, naked on a couch?"

Joanna glanced sideways at her. "You've been spending way too much time reading art books, Sara. You need to get out more."

❖

Tiziana Morosini was, in fact, neither voluptuous nor languid. An attractive woman in her forties, with thick black hair drawn loosely into a chignon, she was energetic, businesslike, and completely clothed. Large brown eyes shone with guarded intelligence from an immaculately made-up face, while full Mediterranean lips suggested a sensuality at odds with the image of a librarian. After a cool handshake, she explained briefly the rules of the library—no food, no drink, no noise—then guided them to the stairs.

"I thought, before you started work, you might like to look at the staterooms of the library. We're rather proud of them."

Joanna had hoped to begin immediately, but one did not offend one's host. "Yes, of course. Very kind of you to offer."

They entered a hall in white and cream marble, full of classical statues and busts. Glass cases at the corners held massive globes revealing the Venetian understanding of the charted world. The checkered floor had a clean, modern look that discouraged lingering. "I will spare you a description of the sculptures, although several of them come from the collection of Cardinal Bessarion, the original donor of the library," Tiziana said, and led them to the entrance of the next room.

"This is the salon," Tiziana announced, ushering them ahead of her. She let them appreciate the opulence of the hall for a moment, then pointed to the wooden ceiling that held a grid work of plaster frames, carved in Baroque filigree and painted in gold. "As you can see, the ceiling contains twenty-one murals, all from the cinquecento."

The onslaught of sixteenth-century allegorical paintings gave Joanna a headache, but apparently they did not intimidate Sara. "That one's Veronese," she said, pointing directly overhead, "and those two by the portal. But I don't recognize the others."

"Brava. I see you know our art as well as I do," Tiziana said, though it was not clear whether she was amused or annoyed at being upstaged.

"What's in the display cases?" Joanna asked.

"Opera scores by Cavalli, sonatas by Domenico Scarlatti, the so-called Codex Marcianus. Shall I go on?"

"Well, actually…" Joanna searched for words to forestall any such listing, but Tiziana was already walking ahead of then.

"Let me show you the main reading room."

Hardly a room, the space hinted more at imperial courtyard. Daylight streamed through the glass ceiling, so that one had the sense of open sky. The surrounding walls rose in three tiers, their architecture neoclassical and robust. The two lower levels were arcades, and between the levels, a handsome balustrade circled the entire space. Behind them all, visible through glass, countless bookshelves stood discreetly. The enclosed space was vast, the effect powerful. One could imagine mustering a battalion in the hall, were it not for the tables and low bookshelves that quietly suggested reading.

Tiziana guided them to a table close to the door. "Dr. Morosini tells me you both speak excellent Italian, so of course our main collection is available to you. Over there at the far end of the hall is our card catalog, from which you can locate anything in the library."

At the door to the catalog room Joanna stopped, awestruck. Not one room, but two, with card drawers from floor to ceiling on all eight walls.

"The cards on this side are by subject, while those over there are by author's name, and those at the far end are by title," Tiziana said blithely, as if she swept through them every day for casual reading. "After you find what you're looking for, give me the call numbers and I'll have them brought from the shelves to your table in groups of five."

Joanna glanced over at Sara and almost laughed at her slack-jawed expression. It was true, the thought of hunting through hundreds of drawers on a poorly defined search for which they had no reference point other than year was a bit daunting. But she also felt a certain euphoria at standing before such a vast amount of knowledge. She recalled suddenly how rich she'd felt as a child each time she came home from the library with a dozen new books. Even before she started them, she anticipated the pleasure of turning the pages, letting the characters and events flow into her mind, a pastime infinitely more satisfying than "hanging out" with school friends.

Tiziana spoke from the doorway. "I know. It's frightening the first time you face these. But don't worry. After a while, you get the hang of it." Then, with an ambiguous smile, which could have been either condolence or schadenfreude, she left them to their labor.

Sara cautiously circled the first room, peering at the labels on the drawers. "Sure. We can do this. No problem," she said weakly, obviously summoning courage.

"Of course we can. It's what we came for." Joanna unconsciously rubbed her hands in a little circular motion. "Think that we're in the company of the thousands of world scholars who thought those ideas. Imagine them as phantoms swirling around us while we read."

"Swirling phantoms. If you say so. So how about I look under Printing presses, sixteenth century, and you search under Commercial shipping or Merchant ships." Sara stared up again at the cliffs of card drawers. "Piece of cake."

Joanna began methodically, reading opening paragraphs to every relevant chapter, giving each volume a chance to yield its secrets. She savored the feel and sound of parchment as she turned each heavy page. The musty smell that came from them was evocative of monasteries and scriptoria, even when the book was an early print, and, just as she had in her study of the Tudors at the Bodleian Library, she imagined the scribe who penned the pages she read.

But soon she appreciated the number of books piled up in front of her and she forced herself to digest each one more quickly.

By noon they had perused some fifty books, skimmed whole chapters of nineteen, and photocopied excerpts from eight. After lunch in the Piazza San Marco, they began the labor again.

At four o'clock in the afternoon, Sara rubbed her eyes. "I'm completely burnt out, but I've located several independent sources that more or less agree. Apparently two presses in Venice in the mid-1500s had the initials T.A. One of them is a music press named Tomás Adorno, and the other is Tratti Audaci, a much smaller one that printed popular works."

Joanna took off her reading glasses and rubbed her face. "Hmm. Neither one sounds promising, but if that's all that shows up with those letters, one of them has to be ours."

"It's a start. If the State Archives has any evidence of the authorities closing either one in 1560, we'll know that's it."

"Good point. We can check there tomorrow. But, look, I've got something too."

Joanna slid one of her open books across the table. "Three merchant ships were sailing the Adriatic at that time with the initials G.D. The *Ghianna Dore*, the *Gloria d'Venezia*, and the *Grazie Dei*. The first one was a galley, the second one a galleon, and the third a carrack."

"Didn't Dr. Morosini say that only a carrack would have been able to make the trip to Flanders?"

"Yes, he did, and according to, uh, that pile of books over there, the carracks were large galleons, originally Spanish or Portuguese, but then showed up more in the Venetian fleet too. They were all-sail, that is, no rowers."

"Wait, one of Leonora's letters said something about 'galleys being no good for winter travel, and she would not like to live among hundreds of prisoners chained to their benches.' So she was definitely not on a ship with rowers." Sara wrote out *Tratti Audaci* and *Grazie Dei* on a separate page of her notes, underlining both names with a solid stroke of the pen. "I think we're onto something in both cases."

Joanna was about to reply when Tiziana approached along the center aisle. "How is the research coming?"

"Very well. We've got some good leads," Sara said.

Tiziana directed her reply to Joanna. "Good for you. You've scarcely come up for air all day and deserve some success. It must be very satisfying."

Joanna studied the librarian's handsome face. "It will be more satisfying when we've cross-checked everything with the State Archives, but otherwise, I think we're finished here." Joanna stood up from the table. "Thank you for your help."

"You're quite welcome. Are you sure the Libreria Marciana can't do anything else for you?"

Joanna pondered for a moment, but Sara replied. "You can answer a question. What are the main collections in the historical part of the library? I mean, before the eighteenth century."

Tiziana turned her attention back to Sara. "We have quite a large number, but that information is available in the introductory brochure. I'll get you one." She strode toward a bronze bust on a table where a box held pamphlets, and in a moment she was back with one in hand.

"You can read a summary of our entire history here. I'm sure you already know about the original endowment of the library of Cardinal Bessarion to the city of Venice in 1468."

The pamphlet seemed to trigger a recitation that Tiziana had learned by heart and that Joanna had no desire to hear. "May we keep this brochure and study it at home?"

"Of course. It's public information." She pressed the booklet into Joanna's hand. Was it Joanna's imagination, or did Tiziana's fingers brush against hers a bit longer than necessary?

"Thank you for all your help, Signora Morosini," she repeated.

"Oh, you're most welcome. Please let me know if I can assist you in any other way," Tiziana replied with warmth.

"We certainly will," Joanna answered automatically and moved toward the library door. In the reflection of the glass exit door, Joanna could see two things: Tiziana still watching them and Sara's sudden frown.

Well, that added an interesting new wrinkle to the project.

CHAPTER ELEVEN

Joanna threw the apartment key on the table in the entry. "It's probably not good to spend eight hours staring at small print and then have three glasses of wine. I thought the dinner would energize me, but it's done just the opposite." She glanced at her watch. "It's only nine thirty and I'm dragging."

"I am too, and I've got a headache, but I'm not ready to go to bed. I'll just wake up at four and stare at the ceiling."

"What about television?"

"Have you *seen* Italian television? I was thinking we could discuss the letters a bit more." Sara ran her hand over the folder that contained them on the sofa end table. "The summaries that Giglioti wrote are so superficial, I think we shouldn't bother with them, now that we can refer to the letters directly."

"They're that bad, eh?" Joanna passed by her to go into the kitchen and set water on the stove. "What's missing?" she asked from the kitchen doorway.

"Giglioti presents the letters as a simple narrative of events, but they're above all a collection of love letters, full of fear and longing."

"How fortunate that you read the language well enough to get all of that."

Sara ignited the gas fireplace, kicked off her low-heeled shoes, and padded over to the sofa. "It's not just the language. It's easy to put myself in Leonora's place. Just imagine. All her bridges are destroyed and she has no way back." Sara drew her knees up and let her thoughts drift. "She's a woman alone, amidst rough and dangerous men. And even the nobles and clergy, who presumably wouldn't molest her, were a threat to her life, since they'd return her to prison in Venice. Not to mention that the simple act of cross-dressing was a crime."

Joanna came in with the tea mugs and an aspirin capsule for Sara and sat down at the other end of the sofa. "You're right. She was in danger every minute. What kept her going?"

"She was in love. You can't forget that. She had something precious to live for. Rough seas, sex-starved sailors, fanatical Jesuits, quarrels, murder, smashing of cargo, all that swirled around her, and she never lost her hope of reaching Anne. At least not in the letters I've read so far." Sara tossed back the aspirin with a sip of tea, then studied her steaming cup. "Were you ever in love?"

Joanna thought for a moment. "I was in a relationship, but I think it was not so much love as the excitement of finding something foreign and forbidden."

"And the other...person?" Sara asked delicately. They'd never discussed sexual preferences.

"I don't really know what she felt. I can't imagine it was love in her case either, but whatever it was, I got over it more quickly. It was pretty obvious that she felt cheated when I left. Maybe she *was* cheated. I don't know any more. What about you? Have *you* ever been in love?"

"Not the way I imagine love should be."

"How *do* you imagine it to be?"

Sara sipped her tea again. "Good question. It keeps changing. When I was young, I pined after anyone who came along, but I was looking for the kind of love I lost when my mother died. Then, when puberty hit, it was just a physical longing, usually for movie stars. You know when you see movies with love scenes between men and women? Usually you imagine yourself as one of them. I always wanted to be both. The beautiful woman who stirs love and the dashing hero who arrives and saves her. I guess I should have been a lipstick lesbian, eh?"

The half-humorous, half-serious remark seemed an invitation to more specific questions. Joanna studied her own cup for a moment, then ventured, "When did you start doing it? Dressing up, I mean?"

Sara hesitated, perhaps deciding how much to reveal. "I had a slight interest in it very early on, but I had no sister and, after the age of eight, no mother either, so I had no access to female stuff. I pushed it to the back of my mind until boarding school, when I had that 'baptism' at the pond. I came out of it with a different sense of myself."

"Ah, yes. You told me the beginning. How did you get a hold of makeup?"

"I shoplifted things, lipstick, mascara. The first night, when everyone was asleep, I tried the lipstick and eye makeup. I just stared at myself in the mirror, hypnotized. The face that looked back at me was this person living inside me. The one I had been feeling all along. Then at some point when I was home on vacation and had my own room, I shoplifted a blouse too, a very fru-fru one, with ruffles and all. It was a revelation. I walked around my room for a while feeling wonderful, then took everything off and hid it again. I must have been about ten."

"Did you wish you'd been born a girl?"

"Not completely. I liked some of the things boys could do. I even did sports. Well, track. It was the only time my father ever said anything good about me."

"Ah, the father. Maybe you should tell me about him."

Sara gave a little puff of disdain. "You could write a psychology textbook about him. I think he'd heard that in America, anything was possible, and he must have been deeply disappointed by how hard everything actually was for a foreigner. But when the Korean War started, he joined the army. Four years of service brought him long-term employment, and at the end of it he could apply for citizenship."

"That doesn't sound so bad."

"For him it wasn't. Soldiering suited his personality. It just didn't suit mine. But when he came home on leave, he took me to a range to teach me how to use a gun. You know, 'in case the communists came.' That was bad enough, but then he took me to the country and forced me to fire at rabbits. Of course I missed every single one of them. Finally he'd had enough. He stood me in front of a chicken and held me by the collar until I shot it. Do you know how hard it is to kill a chicken with a rifle? I shot it three times and still it ran around. Finally he took out his pocket knife and cut its head off." Sara brooded for a moment.

"I even remember the clothes he forced me to wear when we went on those bloody escapades. Little fatigues, made especially for children. I was supposed to be a miniature copy of him, but, well, you can see how *that* worked out."

"You identified with your mother, then?"

"I don't know. Mostly I knew I *didn't* want to be like him."

"But what's your sexual preference? Sorry. You don't have to answer that, if you don't want. But I'm gay myself, so you'll get no homophobia from me."

Sara played unconsciously with an earring. "Well, I like pretty clothes and opera. Does that make me gay? I don't know. I've never done romance, but I've been with men at various places along the transgender spectrum."

"Theirs, or yours?"

"Theirs. There's a whole range, you know, from straight male cross-dressers to drag queens, to…well, there are as many variations as there are men. I liked being courted, having someone be interested, but the sex part was never anything special."

"And women? You don't care for women?"

"Oh, I do. I like women best of all, but straight women don't want boyfriends with breasts, and the stealth technique doesn't work either. Girls don't like finding out their girlfriends are guys. And that's not even addressing the…uh…dynamic in bed."

Arriving at the subjects of breasts and sex, the conversation came to a halt. They were topics Joanna wasn't ready to pursue. She cleared her throat. "We seem to have gotten sidetracked. You started by suggesting that we work more on the letters since Giglioti's summaries were insufficient."

Sara also seemed relieved to change the subject. "Yes, I'd like to do that. The letters are pretty emotional, don't you think? The Italian is elegant too. I would have loved to hear them in the author's own voice."

Joanna took up her notebook and the leather folder and slid out the next letter. "Well, short of Leonora's voice, let's hear it in yours."

Sara drew her knees up on the sofa and settled in for a long read.

23 June 1560
Cara mia,

Will I ne'er be free of this book? I thought the tragedy was finished when they were thrown into the sea, but it seems the blasphemy has o'erlived the drowning. Yesterday, the captain led the vesper prayer, and whilst heads were bowed, he made known to me that I should visit him in his quarters. To guard the fiction of the Englishman, I tarried 'til the late night hours when we could speak unheard.

Scarcely had I closed the cabin door when I saw the book lay open on his table, mocking me. And by his somber countenance I knew that he had read it.

"I have always thought it counterfeit. A

blasphemy, though little more than drunkards sing at Carnival," I ventured. But my words rang hollow.

The captain shook his head. "Leon Negri seemed an honest man. Why would he spend his coin and wit to spread a lie?"

"His real name was Hakim Yaakub, a scholar from Constantinople," I said, and I confessed I knew not why he would want to lie. Mayhap he was himself beguiled and translated what he thought was real. But the captain would have none of it.

"I am sure the Jesuits make the selfsame claim. And the young Morosini too. It is an easy thing to decry the work as forgery. But I know the Jews of Constantinople, serious men of trade. What have they to gain from counterfeit but the wrath of Christendom? They've had well enough of that. You know yourself, the book is half made up of proofs. Descriptions of where the codex was found, who witnessed the finding, how long it had been buried."

The while he spoke, he reached into an ivory chest at his elbow. "And there is this," he said, and laid an object on the table that shattered my defense. A clay cylinder, the length of a man's boot, with curious writing along the side of it." It was at the bottom of the crate under the books," he said. He unstoppered it, retrieved a scroll on vellum, without unrolling it. "I've looked at it. The writing is in the language of the Jews, and I'll wager it is the codex he translated."

I stared, appalled, as at a venomous snake." What will you do with it?" I asked.

"I do not know. I wish I did not have it, for it is a terrible tale."

The ground seemed to drop from under me and I could scarcely bring forth words. "If this be true, it has made a mockery of sacrifice, crusade, and martyrdom. Rivers of blood have been shed for naught."

Both of us were silent, dwelling on the chasm opened up before us. Then he seized the book and cached it in a cabinet. "I am not innocent to doubt," he said. "On all my voyages, the chaplain leads the crew in prayer to bring ship and cargo unscathed to port, to weather storm and piracy. But we use charts and navigation books, and carry cannon. No ship in Venice would venture forth unguided and unprotected but by prayer. Yet I know that infidels, whose god is false, also pray and use their charts. If so, mayhap it is the navigation that saves us both, and not the prayers."

My heart was already wounded by my loss of home, and now so was my soul. With nothing more to say, I fled the captain and his heresy.

Oh, Anne. If only you were here with me to weather this. The captain is brave and honorable, but he ventures into deadly waters and takes me with him.

Do you remember him? I have not named him lest these letters fall one day into malicious hands, but he stopped by T.A. once before you left for England. A handsome man of some forty years. He came often after you were gone, always with some good reason or other. But once, near midnight, fear that I had left a candle burning drew me from my bed back down to the print shop. I saw them there, the captain and Lucca, in an embrace. I left undetected, but on the morrow I confronted Lucca for surety he was not forced. But the poor terrified lad confessed the two of them were lovers and did entreat me to keep silent, lest the older man pay with his life. I understood their love and kept their secret. In the end, my discretion was rewarded, for it was that man who rescued me from the doge's prison and hid me in his house.

It was also he who "made a man" of me and rowed me in new attire to the harbor just before dawn and embarkation. You must imagine me with my precious cargo, about to board. The Serenissima in all her mystery lay behind me scarcely visible in the dark. Only a few specks of light shone in the sleeping city. Before me, the prow of the *G.D.* jutted black and fearsome. I wanted to weep for all that I had lost, but the captain forbade me tears. "Henceforth, you are a man, and a man does not weep. You go to join your love, and this should be your only thought."

And so you are. Each night I call up the memory of how I did caress you that you cried with happiness. And more sweetly, I remember our "wedding" on Ascension Day. E'en now I can see the Bucintoro, the Doge's floating palace, gilded o'er, its forty oars rising and falling as one, carrying him into the lagoon for his Wedding with the Sea. We stood amidst the cheering crowd on the embankment, and heard the gun salute as he rendered the ring unto the water invoking God's witness to his fidelity. As Venice thus plied its troth to the sea, you and I, in stealth, exchanged our widow's rings in a wedding of our own. Then, as the ceremony ended and the Bucintoro swept past us again in stately rhythm, the sunlight sparkling off the golden statue on its prow did bathe us in its glow. That moment, when Venus blessed us, was our nuptial. In my thoughts of you, forever is the Bucintoro our wedding barge and ne'er has doge nor prince had greater joy of it.

This morning, donning these rough clothes, I wondered if they would provoke your mirth or your desire. Would you like me to make love to you in travesty? For I do long to be with you, as man or woman, I care not. We are already wed.

Sara's voice had grown soft as she spoke the final phrases of the letter, and Joanna watched the wide, expressive mouth form the ardent words. Passionate words that Sara had never uttered on her own, but only now, reading Leonora's. Suddenly there was too much longing in the room.

Joanna stood up and marched toward the gas fireplace. She adjusted the metal grating that needed no adjusting and focused on the row of flames. Even the flames couldn't decide how they should look—blue at the bottom of the cast-iron burner, then yellow as they leapt from the concrete logs.

"How's the headache?" she asked over her shoulder.

"Still there, but the aspirin took the edge off. Sorry to be the simpering damsel tonight. I get this sometimes. It's the hormones. I'll just go lie down now and wait for it to pass. It always does."

Joanna watched her disappear into the bedroom, concerned but uncertain. Should she take in more tea? Another aspirin? Comforting small talk? No. Following Sara into the bedroom, her private space, would be an intrusion.

She turned down the flame in the fireplace and made up her own bed on the sofa. They could talk more in the coming days, if Sara wanted to. Curious, that while they worked together to penetrate the mysteries of the letters, the mystery of Sara's world still separated them. Yet something also seemed to tie the three of them together: Leonora, herself, and Sara. Was it the fact of being an outcast? Of being *other*?

Surely people who fitted no mold, who refused the identity their world put upon them had always existed. Dynasties had risen and fallen on gender expectations, yet some hardy souls had defied them successfully. Interestingly, the women who crossed over into the opposite sexual territory were applauded, while men were shamed. But surely a fraternity, a sense of shared resistance to the rules, was possible.

Joanna smiled inwardly, recalling Elizabeth the First's famous remark, though of course she voiced the reverse complaint: "Had I, my lords, been born crested and not cloven, you had not treated me thus!"

She dozed off thinking that Sara, who wanted to be cloven and not crested, would be pleased to know that greater women than she had lamented the prisons of their bodies.

CHAPTER TWELVE

State Archives

The early morning rain had tapered off when they stepped from the vaporetto at the Sant Tomà stop and wound along the labyrinth of *calli*, that took them finally to the side wall of an enormous red-brick church.

"So that's the dei Frari church," Joanna announced.

"Yes. Santa Maria Gloriosa dei Frari Basilica, to be exact. Full of monuments. It's also part of the monastery that houses the archives. We should take a look inside later."

They walked along the flank of the church to its austere Gothic front. To the left of the church portal stood an anonymous two-story building. One of its two doors bore a discreet sign: *Archivio di Stato*.

"What a disappointment," Joanna said. "No columns, no lions, nothing. If you didn't know what you were looking for, you'd go right past it."

"Maybe they'd just as soon have tourists stay away. That reminds me. Did you bring our letter of introduction?"

"Got it right here." She patted the side pocket of her jacket as they entered. "Um, cheerful place," she added under her breath. The reception space was little more than a poorly lit stone hall, as unornamented as the exterior. The round reception counter on one side was the only furniture. An electric heater buzzed near the knees of the receptionist, though the rest of the hall was cold and damp.

"Must have been loads of fun to be a monk here," Joanna murmured.

A clerk came out to meet them, perused their letter of introduction, and led them along a circuitous route to the reading room. It was a purely functional, high-ceilinged room with columns and tables that could have been in any prewar building in Europe. But a few paces away a glass doorway revealed the well-manicured garden and ambulatory. "Now that's more like a monastery," Joanna remarked, then heard the footfall of the librarian behind her.

He was muscular and hirsute, with a brutish face that was in no way improved by a narrow goatee. Dark curls peeked up from the open collar of his shirt, and his forearms were heavily haired. Even the backs of his hands had tufts of hair. He didn't introduce himself but held a clipboard with what appeared to be the list of books she'd requested by telephone the day before.

"The signora has asked to see the ship's manifests of the *Grazie Dei* and the orders of the Council of Ten from the year 1560. Is that correct?" His eyes darted back and forth between them.

"Yes, and also any material available on the two presses, Tomás Adorno and the Tratti Audaci." Joanna was becoming excited. Speaking the names out loud seemed to add to their reality and to the likelihood that at least one of them was correct.

Her excitement was dampened slightly when the librarian's assistant unloaded a cart of huge tomes onto the counter in front of them. Both the manifest and the Council record were handwritten in florid script, some of the pages in both volumes water-stained and nearly illegible. Worse, the amount of material on the Tomás Adorno press was vast.

Sara took a deep breath. "Want to flip a coin for the ship's manifest? At least it has drawings."

"You mean the company logos?" Joanna turned a few pages, noting with pleasure the column of clever designs, all built around the forms of crosses or anchors. "Yes, these are nice. Unfortunately, I need you to glance through the decrees looking for heresy denunciations. You can read much faster than I can. But on the lighter side, you'll have only two volumes to work through this time."

"Mmm." Sara acquiesced blandly.

"In the meantime, I'll peruse the ship's manifest. That should give me consigners of cargo, destination, ports of embarkation for passengers, and so forth. Maybe one of the passenger names will ring a bell or someone's cargo will sound suspicious. I think the material on the two presses can wait until later."

Joanna took the cargo manifest of the *Grazie Dei*, inwardly praying that it was the ship they were looking for, and carried it to a table near the window. Sara installed herself on the other side of the table, opening the first volume of the *Decrees of the Council of Ten 1560–1561*.

❖

At the reception counter, the hirsute librarian dialed the phone and waited for someone to pick up at the other end of the line.

"It's happened. Someone is nosing around about the Book," he said to the one who answered. "Two women asked for the ship's manifest and the Council of Ten decrees. I couldn't tell them no. They're looking at them now. We need to talk. All right. By six this evening."

He hung up, his excitement dulled by the lack of enthusiasm at the other end of the line. After all the preparation, he had imagined more drama, an arrest perhaps, or an attempted escape that he would of course thwart. Surely there would be more to come. He watched the two women through the doorway, fantasizing wildly.

❖

At one in the afternoon, Joanna closed the manifest of the *Grazie Dei* with a satisfying thud. She gathered up her notes, tapped them upright on the table to square them, and then announced, "I've got them."

Sara looked up from the decrees, obviously relieved to have an excuse to stop. "Them? Who?"

"All of them, I think. For starters, the passenger list shows a Vettor Morosini, two Jesuits named Bracco, and a lay brother named Barbieri."

"Oh, well done."

"Not only that. It also lists one Leon Negri with a very small cargo declaration, porcelain and glassware. His merchant's insignia is suspicious too. It looks like most of the others, but it doesn't show up in the Council's registry of Venetian mercantile businesses."

"What about Leonora?" Any sign of an English merchant?"

"I think so. After Morosini and our Jesuits, four passengers remain, and one of them is 'Lawrence Bolde.' Also with very little cargo: only one crate identified as 'ceramic tiles.' If that's our Leonora, I wonder what she was carrying."

"More books, maybe," Sara said without conviction.

"Well, her letters don't mention any more books, so we've got nothing to go on. But here's the best part. I have the name of the captain, and you'll love this."

"Who was it? Out with it."

Joanna paused a beat to savor the pleasure of the discovery, then announced, "Maffeo Foscari. And that means that the palazzo Leonora hid in before going on board was the Ca' Foscari, where his portrait hangs."

"Oh, you're right. I do love it. Tony will love it too."

"Tony?"

"My Italian neighbor. He'll be thrilled to know his family was a bunch of renegades. I'll be sure to also mention that one of them was a Sodomite."

"Okay, that's my news. So, what have *you* got?"

Sara smiled. "I've found something really great too. Thank God, since I couldn't take much more reading. My eyes are dripping blood."

"Stop being such a drama queen and tell me what it is."

"I've got…the Council of Ten's accusation against Leonora. Look here." She rotated the manuscript 180 degrees and slid it gently across the table. "It's the entire record of the Tribunal for the Inquisition of Heresy. Am I good, or what?"

"Oh, you *are* good."

This day, the eighth June 1560. The Sacred Tribunal of the Holy Office convened to question the widow Leonora Barotti, residing in the parish of S. Samuel, and being asked her name and surname, replied as stated. The prisoner was put to the question on the rope as here described.

The tribunal: "What is your profession?"

Accused: "A printer of books."

Tribunal: "Know you the reasons you have been called here?"

Accused: "I think I am accused of publishing a heretical book."

Tribunal: "Do you confess it?"

Accused: "I confess I knew it not as heresy."

The accused claimed to have misjudged the work as jest and confessed to a lesser charge of careless blasphemy. She also confessed that the number of copies was two hundred and that she accepted sole guilt, without accomplice. In this matter, she was found to be lying due to the contrary confession of her brother-in-law, Massimo Barotti.

The tribunal attempted to question the prisoner further, but she passed out and the hearing was postponed until the next day.

"My God, is that chilling," Joanna said. "The tone of a modern court stenographer. But now we also know who Massimo was. It looks like he was executed first because he was the owner of the press."

"Probably." Sara swept her hand over the table. "So, where do we go from here?"

"We'll order photocopies, of course. I'd also like a little more documentation from the ship, if it exists. I'll request it before we go for lunch."

They set the several manuscripts aside under their name and approached the front desk. The hairy man was there, along with a younger librarian in glasses. Slender and pale, in clothes that seemed too big for him, he fit the popular image of the light-starved, slightly effeminate bookworm, the polar opposite to his brutish looking colleague. The new man smiled at both of them, then seemed to not take his eyes off Sara.

Sara stepped up to the counter first. "I believe most ships of this period carried a scribe to keep a log or record of events. A report separate from the initial manifest. Is it possible to obtain such a record for the voyage of the *Grazie Dei* in 1560?"

"I'll be happy to look for you, signorina," the bookworm said.

The other man held up a hairy hand. "Don't bother, Marco. I asked for that already, when I called up the ship's manifest, but it doesn't exist."

Young Marco looked timidly at the older man, then back at Sara, apparently enraptured. "I'm sure Signor Bracco is correct. He knows the archives inside and out," he said haltingly. "Still…" He drew out the word, and the older man's expression darkened at being contradicted.

Marco took a breath. "I don't mind checking again, signorina. It would be very unusual for a voyage to take place without a scribe to keep the log. It might simply have been misshelved. That happens sometimes. Give me an hour to go into the vault. If I locate the record, I'll put it with your other books, all right?"

"Oh, that would be so good of you." Sara's slightly open-lipped smile sent warmth and gratitude toward him. In response, the young librarian looked like he would have undertaken any service for her.

❖

Seated at the café in the piazza, Joanna finished her sandwich. "You're really getting good at that flirt thing, you know. In three seconds flat that poor librarian was smitten."

"Was that flirting? I was just trying to get him to like us. Isn't that what women do?"

"Not usually in such doses. You might want to reduce the temperature a bit for the rest of the week. Otherwise we'll have men following us home." They exited the café and migrated spontaneously toward the gelato window next door. Nothing seemed more normal in a sunny Italian piazza than to eat gelato, so they wandered back with their cones toward the front of the dei Frari church and crossed the footbridge in a leisurely stroll.

Sara stepped down first onto the campo while Joanna was distracted by some sound to her right. Glancing to the left, Sara was startled by the sight of a bicyclist speeding toward them only a few feet away. She stopped in mid-step to keep from being hit and instinctively reached sideways toward Joanna. "Look out!" she called, her eyes locked on the oncoming vehicle. Her hand struck Joanna's elbow, halting her, and only when the bicycle was safely past did Sara look back.

For a second, she was horrified.

Joanna stood, paralyzed with astonishment, a red ball of ice cream impaled on her nose and rivulets of raspberry trickling down both sides of her mouth.

"Oh, I'm *so* sorry." Sara covered her mouth for the two seconds it took for alarm to evolve into hilarity. Finally exploding into giggles, she choked out, "You look like a reindeer."

Joanna remained expressionless.

"I was trying to keep you from getting hit." Sara held out her hand to catch the gelato ball as it slid off Joanna's nose. "I swear it. How could I know…" Sara's voice rose in pitch from giggle to uncontrollable laughter.

"Couldn't you have just said, 'Stop'? That would've worked," Joanna replied with mock severity, but Sara's strangled sounds were infectious and Joanna too began snickering. Soon they were both hysterical and gasping.

When they regained composure Sara found a tissue to wipe the remaining gelato from Joanna's nose, and they leaned exhausted against the balustrade, in the glow of shared silliness.

Eventually, something moving on the *rio* caught Joanna's eye and she turned to see a gondola drifting toward them with four elderly tourists snapping pictures.

"Look," Joanna said, her voice returned to normal. "It's *our* gondolier. The one we see every morning." As he passed under the bridge, she waved down at him, then crossed to the other wall of the bridge to watch him emerge. The black prow of the gondola appeared, then the heads and snapping cameras of the passengers. Last of all, the gondolier flowed into sight, and glanced back at them.

"When will you come and ride with me, signoras?" he called up to them.

Joanna bent over the stone wall. "Soon. I promise," she called, waving again, then wondered why she'd made such a pledge. She had absolutely no intention of riding in a gondola.

"Looks like you have a fan of your own," Sara said.

"Well, it's about time. Anyhow, we've been out for an hour. Let's go find out if your good looks have gotten us our ship's log."

❖

At the archives desk, Marco was beaming. "I found it, signora," he said softly as he came around to the other side of the counter and delivered the volume personally into Sara's hands. "Would you believe it? Someone simply put it on a higher shelf. Unforgivable for an archivist."

For a brief moment, both Marco and Sara grasped the book, as if an electric charge held them together. Then the young librarian surrendered the volume. Sara thanked him with one of her most engaging smiles and carried the book to the work table.

She and Joanna leaned shoulder to shoulder over the manuscript while Joanna turned the pages slowly. Sara read the title page sotto voce, and with obvious satisfaction. "'Account of the Voyage of the *Grazie Dei*, departing from Venice Anno Domini 1560 as recorded by Pietro Arnoldi, scribe appointed by His Serenity, Doge Girolamo Priuli.'"

"There it is, a list of all the officers on board." Sara continued reading. "'Captained by Maffeo Foscari, with Tomasso Torcelli as mate,

Stefano Brignani the navigator, and Ludovico Stentor as chaplain.' And so on and so forth. If they had brought us this first, I never would have had to spend all that time trying to make sense of the manifest." She slid back the page. "'We set sail on the morning of June 11 in good weather and after morning prayers.' Then he goes on to list the passengers, the condition of the crew. Everything."

"Any sign of our Leonora?"

"Yes, here she is. He, rather. 'An English merchant named Lawrence Bolde, who speaks no Italian.'" Joanna ran her finger down the list of names. "And here's Hakim, 'Leon Negri, of Constantinople, who transports porcelain and glass.'"

"Fantastic. Everything falls right into place. Anything about the Jesuits?"

Sara and turned the page. "Those are named here too, Signors Bracco and Barbieri, along with Vettor Morosini. This is really fascinating. All the details of shipboard life. I wish we had the time to read it all."

"Of course there's a lot of nautical data too. 'Moderate winds NW to SE, we added topsail.' Then, the next day: 'Gales from NW all day with much rain and thunder. Ship taking on water and four men sent below to pump.' Can't you just picture it?"

"Yes, but I'm more interested in corroborating Leonora's accounts of the dinner-table confrontations. You can translate faster than I can. Can you read while I take notes?" Joanna opened her own notebook while Sara studied the new text for a moment.

"'SE course continuing, aft pump put in service too, though storm is abating.' Ah, here's something. 'Captain Foscari feeds his men well and keeps a good table for his officers and passengers. Some unpleasantness from Ser Bracco and Ser Barbieri, a lay brother who does not care to share his dinner with the Jew Negri. The others at table changed the subject. The Englishman never spoke.'"

"Amazing. Her whole account is accurate. Go on. I'm dying to see what happens."

Sara was already reading. "It's more ordinary ship's business. 'We passed the *Magdalena*, returning from Malta. They came alongside and we exchanged fresh food for coin. They've bypassed Corfu and, though close to Venice, are depleted of fresh meat.'"

"Jump ahead." Joanna was impatient. "There's got to be something about the murder."

"I'm sure you're right. But this scribe is really thorough. More weather reporting, depth soundings, and so forth." Sara's voice dropped to a murmur as she translated bits and pieces of the nautical notations, "'Wind blowing now W to E. Topsail down, mizzen sail up.' Oh, here it gets interesting. 'The Jesuits have joined the chaplain leading the morning prayers in place of the captain. The crew seems much inspired. Only Ser Negri is absent, and the men have noticed. They grumble about rich Jews while 'good Christian sailors' work like dogs.'"

"Hmm, Leonora never mentioned that the crew was hostile. That could explain why they were so easily provoked to smash open Hakim's crates. Keep reading," Joanna urged her.

"'Fresh gales from due west. Ship tacking all morning to keep SSW. Some seasickness among the crew. Cook will not light the fire while the wind is heavy. Finally we tacked and stood in, and sat down to dinner two hours late. More quarreling at table about Jews and infidels, though Capt. Foscari maintained calm and good manners. Sparked by the Jesuits, suspicion of the Jew has spread among the seamen. They whisper that he does Hebrew prayers and rituals in his cabin, that he is in the service of the Caliph, and smuggles Christian gold to the Turks at Constantinople.'"

"The poor man. They'd already condemned him as an Islamic Jew, of all things, and were ready to cut his throat long before they saw the books." Sara read while Joanna leaned against her arm and peered from the side.

"Let's see. Next day. More weather, depth sounding, wind direction, course correction, etc. Ah, here it is."

"'Some of the crew have been hounding the merchant Leon Negri, imputing to him the evil eye. Two of them, Andretti and Dallo, under pretext he had practiced Jewish rituals, took it upon themselves to examine his cargo. They brought his crates on deck and forced them open, though it were an act of mutiny. In truth, the crates contained no gold, nor held they the registered glassware. Instead there were books and therein lay the condemnation. One of the Jesuits held up a copy and called out, "Behold, this is the vilest heresy." Thereupon the men set to throwing the books into the sea, all but those snatched up by the captain, and a few others. The captain halted the mutiny with his firearm and ordered the seamen put in irons. Nor but a moment later, Ser Negri was found with his throat cut in the cargo hold. The captain confined the Jesuits to quarters and ordered the confessed assassin into chains until Corfu.'"

Sara turned the page. "Damn. That's all there is. Then he goes back to wind and weather."

"Skip to the next day." Joanna rested on both elbows, engrossed. "There's got to be more to it."

"Yes, he does go back to it on June 16. 'The unseasonable warmth makes it dangerous to keep the body longer. Though we are close to Corfu, Captain Foscari called for the merchant Leon Negri to be buried at sea, there being unanimous agreement as to his manner of death. The magistrate at Corfu will decide upon the charges of mutiny and murder, though the matter is now clouded by the claim of heresy.'"

"That corresponds almost exactly to what Leonora writes. Does he say what happened in Corfu?"

Sara skimmed through the next several entries. "No, the next notations are about meeting a galleon that had run aground, the galleon captain's name. Looks like the *Grazie Dei* helped them, then sailed on under a wind from the northwest with full mainsails."

"Nothing about Corfu?"

Sara read on. "Not much. Only that they arrived in the harbor on June 18 and that they 'hove to.' Here he reports, 'the case is remanded to the Venetian court. We are held in harbor, waiting for word from authorities to embark again. Empty passenger berths turned over to new cargo of citron.' Nothing more about the murderers. Strange, huh?"

She skipped ahead several pages. "Now this is really strange. All the entries after Corfu are in a different hand. Another person is keeping the log." She read out loud.

"'Further Account of the Voyage of the *Grazie Dei*, departing from Corfu 21 June, Anno Domini 1560, as recorded by Stefano Brignani, navigator of said vessel, having been appointed by Captain Maffeo Foscari.'"

"Just like that? The scribe disappears without explanation? Go back to the last page in his writing. What does he say?"

Sara turned back and studied the rambling last page in Arnoldi's clearly identifiable handwriting. She sat upright. "Oh, my god."

"What is it? What's he saying?" Joanna tried to peer at the text from the side.

"He read the Book. He must have grabbed a copy during the brief mutiny."

"Great. Does he say what it was about?"

"No, only his reaction to it. The last page says, 'I can do this no longer and I have been asked to be put off at Corfu. The book has poisoned everything.' The last line is barely legible."

"Try to make it out. We have to know what's so awful in the book that it drives these men to bizarre behavior."

Sara brought her face close to the scribe's final entry and tried to piece it out.

"Well, that's strange. I think it says, 'A curse upon them all.'"

❖

When the archives closed its doors at five, Joanna and Sara gathered their notes and left in animated conversation. Behind them, their stalker followed at a cautious distance. It was difficult at first, to keep sight of them among the twisting calli, but after they had made a few predicable turns, he determined that they were simply going to the vaporetto stop, and so was able to take an alternate route and remain out of sight. At the dock his luck improved. A crowd of workers was going home, so he boarded undetected behind the women and remained concealed during the entire trip. When they edged toward the exit as the vessel approached the San Zaccharia stop, he dropped behind the crowd that departed with them.

Despite the density of people on the streets around the restaurants he kept sight of them. He stopped just before the Ponte dei Greci, noting the number on the iron gateway where the women had finally entered.

Pleased and slightly excited by his success, he left them for the night. But he knew now where they lived and was confident he could get closer. Much closer.

❖

At roughly the same time, Benito Bracco jogged past the San Zaccaria church and made a sharp left toward the administrative headquarters of the Carabinieri Provincial Command. The sun had already set behind him with a magnificent pink and orange display, but Bracco had not noticed. Major Barbieri had not expected his call and, obviously not sharing his excitement, had insisted the meeting be before six, when he left for the day. Thus Bracco had to hurry, which he found annoying. To be sure, they could have discussed the matter by telephone, but the news seemed to require a face-to-face, if only to mark the fact that the thing they had decided was impossible, was in fact happening.

Did anyone know what they were supposed to do now? Bracco was a man of action, but, for him, action meant physical "persuasion" of some sort, or at least the threat of it. Subtle interference, especially when it was supposed to be coordinated with the Church, was not really in his inventory.

He announced himself to the sergeant on duty and was immediately admitted to the second-floor office. Orazio Barbieri leaned over his desk, reading a report, his bowed head revealing the bald spot at the center of his thinning red hair. A cigarette burned in a full ashtray next to him, and the pall of smoke that filled the room revealed the quantity of cigarettes he had consumed that day. Bracco had the habit too, but the smell of old sour smoke that filled the room and that was always on Barbieri's clothes made him wish he could kick it.

Barbieri glanced up. "To what do I owe the pleasure?" He appeared bored, and when he was bored, his chin receded greatly and lost itself in the folds of skin between his jowls and neck.

"It's happening. Two Americans are here looking for it. Women." Bracco dropped down on the chair that stood at the side of the desk and crossed his arms, as if waiting for a reaction.

Barbieri took a puff from his cigarette and laid it back among the remains of a dozen others. "What the hell are you talking about?"

"I told you on the phone. It's about the book we're supposed to be protecting. For chrissake, Orazio. Why else would I come here like this? Someone at the university set the whole thing up, and now two women are nosing around in the archives and God knows where else. When I got the call ordering the books, I deliberately misplaced some of them so they'd hit a dead end, but my goddamned efficient assistant went and found them again. This was never supposed to happen. What's the plan now?"

Barbieri sat back in his chair, revealing the wrinkled part of his uniform shirt that was usually tucked under his belt. "I don't think we need a plan because they won't find anything. Didn't we decide there was nothing left?"

"Not exactly. We just decided that no one was bothering to look anymore. But now someone's looking again. So what do we do if they find it? Shouldn't we contact someone at the Congregation for the Doctrine?"

"Why are you so panicked? Shit, Benito, I thought you were the smart one. If two foreigners arrive and start rummaging around, we just keep an eye on them. Either they go home empty-handed, in which case we smile and wave good-bye, or they dredge up something, in which case I confiscate it. It's what this place is all about, after all." He pointed with his thumb toward the door where *National Heritage Command* was painted in large gold letters. Painted under it, in small black ones, was *Major Orazio Barbieri*.

"You think it's that simple? Just keep an eye on them?"

"Yes, it's that simple. There's only one problem." The major stubbed out the last of the cigarette and felt his pockets for another. He frowned, noting that he'd run out.

"What problem?" Bracco asked, noting with relief the end of the cigarette chain. "It can't be that difficult to monitor two women in a library."

"If you know what they look like. Do you have a picture?"

"Uh, no, but I'm sure I can get one."

"That would be good. It would be even better if I could see them in person." The policeman drummed his fingers for a moment. "You think you can find a way for me to see them without them seeing me?"

Bracco imagined the major on his knees peering through a keyhole. "I don't know..." he said slowly. Then he remembered that it was Carnival week. "Maybe I can. Let me talk to the others about it."

❖

Antonio Alvise was waiting for them when they arrived at the Naval Museum on the Riva degli Schiavoni. The wind blowing in from the lagoon was cold, but Sara wore a high-neck cashmere sweater and Joanna, in a blazer, made good use of her fedora.

"Thank you for offering to show us around the museum, Dr. Alvise. Even beyond our research, I'm very much interested in knowing more about Venice's maritime history."

"I have a great fondness for it myself," he said, holding the door open for them. "One has a vicarious thrill at seeing the excitement without the danger or discomfort, don't you think?"

Joanna nodded agreement. "Though I suppose that may be why we all study history."

Without responding, he gestured toward the staircase. "The period you are interested in is on the first floor," Alvise said, leading them up the main staircase. "They have very fine ship's models from the fourteenth century onward. Of course, Venice's specialty was always the galley, and there are several nice models of those."

They strolled past glass cabinets of wooden scale-models, from miniatures that one could carry, to elaborate reconstructions fifteen feet in length. Shipboard life intrigued Joanna, but thinking of Leonora in each case kept her from romanticizing it. "The galleys are beautiful," she said, "though it must have gotten awfully cold on those rowing benches out at sea."

"I can assure you it did. I was never a galley rower, of course," Alvise chortled, "but I was in the Italian navy as a young man and rowed a few skiffs in my day. Sailors wear heavy wool coats for a reason."

Joanna glanced at him from the side, judged him to be at least fifty, and did a quick calculation. He would have been old enough to fight during the last years of World War II. She wondered where he served and how he'd felt about Mussolini.

"The military is a young man's game," he added. "My son's in the forces and seems to quite like it."

"You have children," Joanna commented politely.

"Yes, two sons. The older one works for a petroleum company in Libya. I'm very proud of them both, and their mother would have been too, but I lost her some years ago."

"Oh, I'm sorry," Joanna said, wondering why he was revealing so much about himself. It seemed very un-Italian.

Sara waved them over to a cabinet at the far end of the room. "Is this a carrack? It has the right date, and two masts, but there's no notation here." They joined her and Alvise studied the five-foot model.

"No, that's a galleon. But you're close. The carrack would have a set of cabins high on the stern, like that over there." He led them to a display mounted on the wall of what looked like a long shed.

"That's where passengers would have slept?"

"Yes, high off the water. The crew, on the other hand, would have been much lower down, and slept either on deck or just below."

They wandered through the remainder of the display room, studying galleys and sailing ships from the Middle Ages through the nineteenth century, but none of them was a carrack, Alvise apologized for the deficiency. "I regret we cannot provide you with a model that meets your specifications, but perhaps this next item will make your visit here worthwhile."

He led them to a corridor that contained a single display case, which filled it almost completely. "*Eccolo.* A vessel to which Venice has sole claim."

"The Bucintoro!" Joanna exclaimed as they arrived before a twelve-foot glass cabinet containing a scale-model replication of the gaudy Venetian-Baroque galley of the doge. "I'd forgotten that Venice had made a scale-model. Oh, it's magnificent." She started at the rear and made a slow half circle around the vessel.

"*A* Bucintoro," Alvise corrected her amiably. "There were four of them, in the fourteenth, sixteenth, seventeenth, and eighteenth centuries, each larger than the previous one. The basic pattern didn't change much, though. There were always two decks, the lower one for the rowers and the upper one for the doge and his retinue. He had a little platform at the rear for the Wedding with the Sea ceremony. You're familiar with that, I assume."

Joanna came around to the front. "Yes, the *Sposalizio del Mare,* every year on Ascension Day." She studied the gilded lady on the ship's prow. "So this is Venus dressed as Justice, with the sword and scales. Good advertising."

"To my knowledge, other than for the Wedding with the Sea, it wasn't used except on the rarest occasions, coronation ceremonies, or royal visits," Alvise droned on.

Sara had come around the other side of the display and stood next to Joanna in front of the gilded Venus. "So this is the Venus that blessed them," Sara murmured, and Joanna knew at once she referred to the "wedding" of Leonora and Anne.

"Yeah. She seems like an old friend, doesn't she?" Joanna murmured back.

"Now that's a ceremony I'd have gone out on the water to attend," Sara remarked.

Alvise gave an avuncular smile. "You have a fondness for that era, don't you?"

"Oh, I do. Of course I know that life then was difficult, disease-ridden, and brutal. But for all that, I can't help but romanticize it just a little in my imagination. An elaborately dressed doge and his captains and senators, surrounded by conspiratorial cardinals and princesses, everyone in silk and velvet. I can so easily imagine myself aboard the Bucintoro, in long brocade skirts, my hair wrapped in pearls, and a big fat gaudy crucifix of rubies on my bodice."

"Do you like to dress in costumes, Signorina Falier? I thought I saw a sparkle in your eye just then," Alvise said.

Joanna stifled laughter. "Sparkle" was hardly the word.

Sara's glance swept over the Bucintoro again. "Yes, I do. I've always regretted having no talent for acting. There are so many roles one could dress up for: Scarlett, Cleopatra, Queen Christina." Her voice grew wistful.

"Well, you've come to the right city and at the right time. You're no doubt aware that we're in Carnival season. And, quite by coincidence, Dr. Morosini has recently suggested that we have a Carnival party at my palazzo. In costume, of course."

"You live in a palazzo?" Joanna was impressed.

Alvise nodded demurely. "In part of one. Though its original glory is severely diminished. Still, it is a good setting for a masquerade. I told him it would be a fine idea, as long as it could be in your honor. If you accept now, you can save me the expense of written invitations."

Though the invitation was obviously extended to both of them, Alvise had spoken almost exclusively to Sara. Standing behind him, Joanna asked, "Where could we get costumes?"

Almost reluctantly, he drew his attention away from Sara and turned sideways to reply. "Costumes will be no problem at all. You'll find shops all over Venice. Where are you staying?"

"Near the Ponte dei Greci bridge."

"Oh, there are two shops just past the restaurants at the end of the embankment. If you can find something suitable, the party will be in two days." He was talking to Sara again. "How do you plan to appear?"

"I don't know. As something princessy, I would think. Isabella d'Este or Lucrezia Borgia—feminine and a little diabolical."

"And you, signorina?" He again focused on Joanna.

"Something more subtle, perhaps. We'll see. And you?" she added politely.

"I don't know, though surely something risqué. Carnival is, after all, a time for adventure and excess. Don't you agree?"

"A chance to explore other identities and fulfill fantasies. How wonderful is that?" Sara did agree.

Alvise beamed. "Well, then, it's settled. Two nights hence, at eight. I'll send a boat to pick you up."

Sara glanced past Alvise toward Joanna, who gave a slight shrug as if to say, *Why not?* "That sounds lovely, Dr. Alvise. We look forward to it."

"As do I," he replied in his Ezio Pinza voice, "and I shall be most interested in seeing what personas you choose for yourselves."

With a last glance at the Bucintoro, Venice's most extravagant flight of maritime fancy, he led them on to the exhibit of armaments.

❖

Antonio Alvise accompanied the two women along the Riva degli Schiavoni to their street, then continued on alone to the Piazza San Marco, very pleased with himself. When Morosini had first suggested the masquerade, he had at first balked at the thought of the trouble and expense. He was also more than slightly annoyed that he was being asked to provide the location, when Morosini himself lived in even nicer accommodations. Typical of the man to have a big idea, then to foist the work onto another person, as if a nobility still existed and he claimed its privileges.

But very quickly Alvise saw the advantages. As host, he could impress the guests of honor with his Venetian décor and hospitality, whereas at Morosini's house he would have been just another guest. Sara—he always thought of the lovely blond American by her first name—would be quite taken, he was sure, by the atmosphere he intended to create. Morosini could play the patrician all he wanted; he would still be one guest among others, and all would be in costume.

He imagined Sara in his own piano nobile, in décolleté gown and sitting next to him on his sofa. The light would be subdued and they'd perhaps be a bit tipsy. "A chance to fulfill fantasies," she'd said. And a woman like Sara would definitely have lively fantasies. "Feminine and diabolical," she'd said. Did she mean diabolical fantasies? Did they involve Italian men? The thought aroused him.

The other guests? He didn't care. Morosini had already drawn up a list of his friends and could take care of the telephone calls. What costume should he choose for himself? Alvise was tired of the typical ruffled shirt, waistcoat, and hose of the seventeenth-century dandy, and was certain that Americans found it unappealing anyhow. Why not something more daring? Something more "diabolical."

Yes, Sara would like diabolical.

CHAPTER THIRTEEN

While they waited at the foot of the Ponte dei Greci, Joanna tested for range of vision through the eyeholes of her mask. Its field of vision was limited and she was sorry now she'd chosen the heavy Bauta mask. She could peer upward—noting the eerie aura that the evening mist formed around the street lamp—but not downward, and so risked tripping. She adjusted the mask, setting it lower, and refitted her tricorne hat over it. The knee pants and hose were a better choice and she rather liked the way they made her swagger, but the black tabarro cape was cumbersome.

"It's hard to imagine how people walked around in all this," she said, her voice muffled by the mouthless mask. "I feel like I'm wearing a tent."

"Oh, not me," Sara said. "I'd *die* to own a dress like this. Look at all this gold trim." She drew out the folds of her skirt on both sides of her, displaying the abundance of crimson velvet. "And I especially love the slashed sleeves and the ornamental buttons. Magnificent, isn't it?"

Joanna had to agree. A dress of the sort that Sara wore required height, which she had, and with the help of a tight bra, the square-cut gold-trimmed décolleté exposed a pleasing hint of cleavage. Her hair was also done up in a sort of roll, with an inserted spray of feathers in lieu of a hat. Sara was, in fact, a knockout, at least until she put the mask on. Then she was a knockout in a mask.

Joanna checked her watch. "Sending a water taxi was a nice touch, but we could just as easily have walked to Alvise's place."

"I'm guessing he wants to show off the water entrance to his house. You can't really blame him. I'm already impressed, aren't—"

A gondola drawing alongside of the canal wall interrupted her.

"Oh, look what he sent instead of a taxi. How very Carnivalesque."

Sara stepped into the rocking boat first and reached back to help Joanna in after her. Joanna accepted the hand, noting once again that it held more strength than expected from a woman. They sat side by side in the gondola, the fabric of their costumes filling half the passenger space with black wool and crimson velvet.

"Is this the height of coolness or the biggest of all clichés?" Sara asked.

"I'd say the latter, but we might as well enjoy it. I can't imagine we'll ever do this again." Joanna relaxed against the cushioned seat and studied the lantern-lit stairways and balconies as the boat slid along the winding rio. The mist overhead dissipated at intervals, revealing stars, then closed over them again.

"It's so easy to forget what century we're in," she said softly. "We could be noble ladies of the Renaissance and everything around us would be exactly the same."

Sara chuckled softly. "Yes, except for the fact that women like us wouldn't have existed."

At that moment, they swung around a curve at the intersection of two canals and passed under a footbridge. The gondolier brought them toward the water entrance of what had once been a palazzo. The façade was poorly visible in the darkness, but the shutters on the upper-story windows, from which light and music poured, were slightly dilapidated, and the stone foundation of the building was dark with moss. The smell of algae was strong under the covered waterway where the gondola came to rest.

Joanna shifted her attention to the stone landing steps which they would have to negotiate in their costumes. As she gathered the folds of her voluminous tabarro to climb onto the slippery surface, the iron-grill gate at the top of the steps opened. A butler or hired man in a dark suit descended and helped them from the gondola. At the back of the landing platform where he led them, a double door opened to a staircase that had obviously been recently renovated, for its wood was fresh and unwarped.

At the top of the stairs, they found themselves before a second, more ornate oak door. It opened suddenly and the Devil welcomed them with a flourish. Someone in a bright red doublet and hose and a red leather eye mask with tiny horns over each eyebrow bowed from the waist.

"Dr. Alvise?" Joanna asked, surprised less by the flamboyance of the costume than by the realization that Antonio Alvise thought of the Devil as his alter ego.

"Indeed it is. Welcome, ladies," the demonic host said, sweeping them into what Joanna recognized as the piano nobile, the central banquet hall. She halted momentarily, absorbing the scene, until she felt hands on her shoulders helping her off with her tabarro.

"I see you are wearing the Bauta costume, Signorina Valois, complete with the tricorne. Brava. It suits you." As Alvise handed the cloak to the butler and turned his attention to Sara, Joanna let her gaze return to the hall.

With its high ceiling beams and large windows opening at one end to the Grand Canal, the central banquet hall was majestic and mysterious. Three-armed, candle-filled sconces hung from the paneled walls over velvet sofas, and blue goblet-like lustres stood flickering on consoles strategically arranged throughout the room. The banquet table, which ran down the center of the room and was set for a buffet rather than for dinner, was lit by two spectacular candelabra. The wavering candle flames were dizzyingly multiplied on both sides of the hall by two large mirrors, framed in scrolling gilt foliage. Though there was a faint smell of food and dusty fabric, the fragrance of candle wax and perfume dominated. The entire effect was of a shimmering, fairy-tale theatricality, the dark indoor version of the cityscape along the Grand Canal.

As Joanna and Sara stepped farther into the room, a landscape of masks suddenly turned toward them.

"Dear friends," the Devil announced loudly. "With apologies for violating the first rule of the Carnival masquerade, I must present to you our guests of honor: Signorina Falier and Signorina Valois."

Light applause and a murmur of greeting welcomed them.

Joanna nodded thanks toward the spectacle in front of her and tried to orient herself to the strange experience. Amidst the ponderous and opulent décor of the banquet room, the masked, painted, feathered, gilded, horned, and bejeweled party guests seemed not so much fellow revelers as a witches' sabbath of fantasies. It was like walking into a Hieronymus Bosch painting.

Unintimidated, Sara lifted her Lucrezia Borgia skirts and wafted toward a group of people gathered near a painted screen with a Persian motif. Joanna remained standing, still a bit bewildered, when the demon beside her explained, "By the rules of Carnival anonymity, we will not exchange names this evening, although, alas, as our guests of honor, you and Signorina Falier must be the exceptions."

"How should I address your other guests, then?" Joanna asked.

"By their mask names, of course. Do you know them?"

"No, I'm sorry. I don't."

"I will be delighted to tell you." He pointed with a red velvet glove to the guests seated around the room, ticking off their mask names from left to right.

"Over there, our friend Sara is conversing with Farfalla, the butterfly. Next to them is Gato, the cat. Then Arlecchino, Colombina, Zanni, Dottore, Pulcinella, and Volo, the bird. From the *Commedia dell'arte*, of course. There are more fantastical costumes as well, and some interpretations of mythical and biblical figures which you will recognize." His arm made a series of little starts across the room like the second hand of a clock. The only ones she was familiar with were Arlecchino, the famous buffoon harlequin in diamond-patterned smock and tights, and the coquettish Colombina. The others she would simply ask.

Alvise was still talking. "Signorina Falier's mask is slightly different. As you might not know, it is called the Dama, or Salome, and comes from the *cinquecento*, when the ladies covered themselves in jewels and elaborate coifs."

"No, I didn't know that. But it does suit her well, doesn't it?"

"Oh, it does indeed," Alvise replied, and his Devil role lent the remark a certain lasciviousness. "As for the other guests, you've already met some of them in your peregrinations, though I won't reveal which ones. Mystery is, after all, the whole point of a masquerade."

"An interesting challenge," Joanna said, studying the guests. From a distance, she recognized only one. A woman stood in conversation with Sara in a rich green silk gown, similar in cut to Sara's but with rings of blue and green iridescent material down each sleeve. The wide and shimmering blue-green butterfly mask left visible a familiar thick chignon and the full Mediterranean lips of Tiziana.

From her vantage point, Joanna studied the two women. Though both wore luxurious gowns, they were a contrast in styles. Tiziana was dark, womanly. Though still sexually attractive, her body was no longer youthful, and one knew immediately she had grown children. Standing next to the earthy librarian, the slender Sara seemed of a different species. She had a grace and dignity equal to that of her dark companion, but Joanna decided her initial assessment was accurate.

Even in an opulent velvet gown, and by flickering candlelight, Sara was ever a cross between an elf and a baroness.

Joanna threaded her way across the room to join them, arriving just as the Tiziana butterfly was saying, "All you needed was the slightest nudge. Millions of wonderful things are hidden in our libraries and archives if you know how to find them." Tiziana greeted Joanna, touching her lightly on the forearm, her voice sultry and sincere. Joanna couldn't tell if she was flirting, or merely affable, but the sensation was very pleasant. After a year of celibacy, she missed being touched.

From out of the darkness, a man approached them in chain mail, a cross-emblazoned tabard, gauntlets, cape, and a sword strapped to his back. He lacked only the crusader's helmet, wearing instead a silver mask that covered only his eyes and upper cheeks.

Joanna thought she recognized his mouth, and when he spoke she was certain. "Dr. Morosini, how nice to see you." She hesitated a moment. "Unless it's not you."

He chuckled. "It is me. But you are required to address me as 'Knight.' Do you think it suits me?"

"I surely hope it doesn't," Joanna replied. "It's not the jousting-type knight, but a serious slaughter-the-infidel type knight. Is that the inner you?"

"Only when called upon, signorina. At the moment, I am off duty." He took a glass of wine from a passing waiter and started to offer it to her. "Oh, I see we have a problem, don't we?"

Joanna's hand went to the mouthless chin of the white mask. "Yes, Sara—sorry, Lucrezia—and I thought we'd wear the masks that were hanging in our apartment and only now realize that with these you can't eat or drink. Everyone else here has a half-mask. Stupid of us not to think of that."

"An easy mistake. Those were designed more for street wear and state balls, not for dinner among friends. Your Bauta mask and costume, for example, was the standard disguise for gentlemen out for no good and wishing complete anonymity. But since we know who you are, there's no need to be so thorough. It's such a harsh mask too. Please, allow me to relieve you of it," he said, and untied the mask while Tiziana helped Sara detach the Salome face.

Sara attached the retired mask to her waist while Joanna wore hers hanging on her back where it felt like a cowboy hat.

Relieved of the weight on her face, Joanna took her first drink of wine of the evening and began to warm to the party atmosphere.

"Venice is famous for Carnival. Why did they stop having the public spectacles?" she asked the Butterfly.

"Interest in Carnival grew and faded for centuries, but when Mussolini's fascists came to power, they made it illegal to wear a mask," Tiziana said, the metallic threads in her costume shining with reflected candlelight. "Those laws are gone now, but the city hasn't gotten around to making it a big public event again. They're probably afraid of the drunkenness."

Two men had migrated closer and seemed to have followed the conversation. One of them, in the Arlecchino costume, interjected, "The *fascisti* were right. Public Carnival just meant a lot of immoral behavior." The man's voice and goatee seemed familiar, but Joanna couldn't place them. Then she saw the hairy hands. Ah, yes. Arlecchino was Bracco, the rude librarian.

"Surely people don't need masks to be immoral, Signor Arlecchino," she said, getting the hang of calling people by their masks.

"That's true, but wearing masks seemed to bring out the worst in men." Support came from his companion, in a long-nosed white mask over a floor-length black robe.

"Even one such as yours?" Joanna couldn't help but reply.

"You're quite right," the man said. "Plague doctor masks might have been the exception, seeing as how they stood for something benevolent. These long noses, filled with herbs, and this total covering made possible the only medical attention people got during the plague. Of course the sight of 'plague doctor' ought to have been pretty terrifying to the sick."

Arlecchino would not be contradicted. "Benevolent associations or not, masks permitted a sexual free-for-all."

Joanna was skeptical. "Didn't they have prostitutes and courtesans in the city all year round? What was so forbidden that they had to save it until Carnival?"

"Frankly, boys." Plague Doctor, unhampered by his long proboscis, lit a cigarette and inhaled deeply. "Carnival made sexual perversion possible, even encouraged it."

"Perversion?" Sara asked innocently. "What do you mean?"

Plague Doctor blew smoke out to the side, then squinted, his eyes visible in the eyeholes of the mask. He seemed to be studying both her and Sara. "I mean that people dressed as the opposite sex and…eh… engaged in perverted behavior."

Joanna found it hard not to laugh. The outdated attitude fit well with the long-snouted doctor's mask—which drew attention to his receding chin—and made him appear as if he were reciting lines in a comedy.

A waiter appeared with another tray of drinks, and Joanna refreshed her glass and returned to the subject. "That doesn't sound so terrible. After all, the Baroque dramas and operas involved women dressed as boys and vice versa. People had a huge appetite for that."

"Yes, but that was art." Arlecchino raised an index finger to make a point, and Joanna could not help but focus on the black hairs on the knuckles. "I know it's not polite to discuss in front of ladies," he warned, "but I'm talking about common buggery, which in other times was punishable by death. I'm not saying I support that, but my point is that Carnival disguise brought out all the hidden sexual depravity. And Venice was rife with it."

"Rife," Joanna murmured. "Imagine that." She took another sip of wine.

The waiters circulated now with trays of decorative hors d'oeuvres of fish and meat.

Laying his hand on his own Holy Cross–covered chain-mail chest, Morosini's Knight joined the disapproving side. "The government also sanctioned mass brawls across bridges with broken noses and sometimes even deaths. Sex and violence were all of a piece. The fascists were right to make it all illegal."

Sara weighed in. "I think it's a shame that it all stopped. A little public dressing up now and then frees the spirit. And if there is a little sexual misbehaving, consensual, of course, then who does it harm?"

"Are you advocating sexual anarchy, signorina?" the Devil asked.

Sara chuckled. "A remark one might expect from the Devil. Sorry, Lucifer. Don't get your hopes up. I only meant freedom of imagination."

The Devil laughed, but Arlecchino continued the debate. "I believe what my colleagues are trying to say is that disguise brings a breakdown in the social order. Society either functions in a right way or a wrong way, and we know the difference."

The conversation seemed to become tense, so the Devil host signaled the musicians with his red leather glove. In a moment the string quartet began to play.

Joanna took advantage of the interruption to step away from the somewhat disagreeable Arlecchino and Dottore and felt only slightly guilty for leaving Sara to contend with them. Still clear-headed, but relaxed now from the wine, she drifted slowly to the far end of the banquet room. There a carved screen extended halfway across the floor, and behind it was a corner with only a single candelabra. Was it a place to store things out of sight? If so, why was it illuminated at all, and so romantically? Upon reflection, she decided it was a corner for intimate conversation, or intimate anything.

Suddenly Arlecchino's observation that Carnival brought out socially unacceptable urges seemed more convincing. No one had taken advantage of the little nook, but the night was still young, so Joanna wandered back to the group she had just abandoned. A few others had joined in: the Zanni mask and Colombina. The string quartet was playing something vaguely familiar, though she couldn't name it. "Is that Vivaldi?" she asked the Devil.

"Of course. Our 'red-haired priest,'" the Devil replied. "Clever of you to recognize it too. Most people know only his *Four Seasons*. I've asked them to play some of his sonatas."

"Curious, isn't it, that Vivaldi left the church right after he was ordained and began to compose secular music," Sara said.

"Yes, to work in the *ospedale*, teaching music to orphan girls." The Zanni mask chuckled. "Of course *ospedali* were also places where noblemen met their mistresses, so it wasn't quite the same as church."

"Does anyone know why Vivaldi traded the sanctuary for such a place?" Sara asked.

Zanni shrugged. "Some say he was too sick to hold mass. But other rumors have it that he lost his faith."

"Well, in the early eighteenth century, there were plenty of dangerous ideas around to make him lose it," Joanna said.

The Knight at Joanna's side offered her an hors d'oeuvre. Something with fish and lemon peels, and delicious. "Speaking of dangerous ideas," he said, "I'm curious to learn what you've found in our libraries."

"Quite a lot," Joanna said. "We know everyone's name now. We found not only the manifest, but also the record of the ship's scribe— the ship's log, in effect. All confirm the information we have in our original letters."

"Ah, yes. The letters. Of course, that's where it started. I'd love to see them some time," the Knight said.

Tiziana the Butterfly had broken away from a trio of dandies in waistcoats and in approaching overheard Joanna's last remark. "The ship's scribe, how interesting. Did you find his name too?"

Joanna warmed at the voice. "Yes. Pietro Arnoldi."

"Arnoldi?" The Knight shook his head as if in regret. "If that's your main evidence, Dr, Valois, I fear you've wasted a great deal of time." He sighed, a man forced to impart some difficult truth to the innocent. "You couldn't have stumbled upon a more dubious source."

"What do you mean?" Joanna suddenly felt a surge of dread.

The Knight continued gently. "You see, the family is infamous. One of my ancestors wrote an account of the fortunes of the Arnoldi. An old Venetian family, which fell into degeneracy. Very sad."

"Degeneracy? What does that mean?" Sara asked calmly. "Can you direct us to a biography of Pietro Arnoldi?"

"I have one of the whole dynasty, though the book does dedicate several chapters to Pietro. As I recall, he suffered from delusions and returned to Venice abruptly after his first voyage. He was suspected of blasphemy but under torture was found to be mad, so the Council merely exiled him. He died alone and in squalor. Syphilis, probably. So, as you can see, one cannot rely on the accuracy of anything the man wrote."

"I know that book," the Butterfly mask said. "I remember coming across it when I was organizing your library. Yes, the Arnoldi are a very tragic family."

"Would it be possible for me to see it?" Joanna asked.

The Knight spent a long moment adjusting the cross-strap that held his sword on his back. "I'm terribly sorry, signorina. I'm leaving tomorrow before daylight to catch a plane to Madrid for a conference. I'll be pleased to look for the volume when I return in a few days."

Joanna imagined all their research suddenly thrown into question. She couldn't afford to wait "a few days" before finding out just how far off they were. Unconsciously, she was wringing her hands.

Suddenly the Butterfly took the Knight's arm, the silk of her gown rustling. "Uncle Vincent, these women have flown all the way from America to investigate this story. If the book is so important, why can't you give it to them tonight? I organized your library and know where the book is located. You don't even need to come with us. We'll call a water taxi and pick it up and be back in twenty minutes."

Joanna glanced back at her gratefully, then turned to Morosini. "It would be enormously helpful if we could have it to read tomorrow."

The Knight patted his niece's hand. "If it's that important, then of course you can."

Joanna addressed her demonic host. "Please don't think me rude, Signor Alvise, uh, sorry, Satan, but we have such limited time, and that information could be crucial."

The Devil raised a red glove in mild protest. "Dear Lady, it would not inconvenience me in the slightest, provided the lovely Signorina Falier stays here with us. You are our guests of honor and we cannot spare both of you."

"I'll be happy to stay," Sara said woodenly.

"Well, then, it's decided. Off you go then. But hurry back. We will have far too many men at this party, and you know how dreary that is." The Knight's jocular tone seemed strange coming from a crusader with an enormous sword on his back.

In the meantime, the Devil was already leading Sara toward a sofa and he spoke over his red velvet shoulder. "Be careful on the canal at night. And please don't feel you have to rush."

❖

Vincent Morosini's library was like a Norman Rockwell painting of a study, but Catholic. Three of its four walls supported floor-to-ceiling bookshelves, and the fourth wall held a crucifix. Below it were a neatly organized desk, an office chair with well-worn cushions, an armchair against the wall, and a floor lamp that cast a warm yellow light below it. Joanna could easily imagine the old man spending long evenings there squinting over manuscripts.

"Ah, here it is, right where I remember it being." Tiziana reached over her head to withdraw a leather-bound book from the corner of a high shelf. She had removed her Butterfly mask, and now, in her scintillating gown, she appeared a sort of fairy godmother, wise and slightly enticing.

They sat down at the corner of the desk where the light cast by the solitary lamp created a sphere of intimacy that Joanna found pleasant. Joanna smoothed her hand over the book, then set it aside. She made the opening gambit.

"I was hoping to meet your husband this evening."

Tiziana touched an earring. "I'm sorry to disappoint you. He lives in Genoa. We are separated. That is why I use my maiden name professionally."

"Oh, I'm sorry."

"No need to be. The arrangement is amicable. And you?"

Joanna hesitated. "I'm single. Married to my work, I suppose. The dark side of ambition."

"And the bright side?"

"Meaningful work, new places, discoveries."

"You never get lonely?" Tiziana's voice dropped a notch in volume. Her dark eyes held Joanna's gaze.

"No, not often. The discoveries, the new things, people. They're very satisfying."

"They can also be rather frightening, don't you think? New things, I mean. They disrupt the normal flow of life and stop you in your tracks." Tiziana looked away for a moment and seemed to meditate while she turned a pencil between thumb and forefinger. "Sometimes a new idea appears in your life, and at first you just ignore it. It's too different. Then it begins to come into focus, and the more you see it, the more it changes your perspective on everything else. Has that ever happened to you?"

Whatever are you talking about? Joanna wanted to ask, but didn't. Was Tiziana flirting with her, about to confess something, or were they just discussing the psychology of learning? Best to keep things vague.

"It seems to me that absorbing new information and experiences is what learning is all about. Discovery is how you grow, isn't it?"

"And what have you discovered in Venice so far?" Tiziana tapped the book that lay between them. "Besides the fact that the Arnoldi are prone to mental illness?"

"I told you. We know the names of our players and a little bit about the heretical book."

"What was it about? Lutheranism? That was a big threat in 1560."

"No. We don't know exactly. Judging by the murderous reactions it caused, I would think it contradicts the established dogma. If it was authentic, just imagine—"

"I *can't* imagine. I would have to assume such an account was fraudulent."

"Why is that? Even if you're a believer, I should think you'd be hungry to have new information that might fill out the areas of uncertainty."

"Authoritative men whom the Church has canonized have decided what information and interpretations are authentic. These form the basis for the doctrines that have held the Christian world together for millennia. Even if you aren't Catholic, if you understood Venice, if you understood Italy, you'd know the power of that catechism."

"But what if you were to find something new, an eyewitness report that was more authoritative than the gospels. What if—"

"There can't be any 'what if.' There's no room for 'new things' in the doctrines of the Church."

"But I thought you were just talking about a new idea that had come into your life, that was changing your perspective on everything."

"I was referring to something personal, not religious."

Joanna was confused again. It was difficult to mix flirtation and intellectual discussion. She could do only one of them at a time. She chose the discussion.

"But humor me, just for a moment," she said, holding up the book as if it were evidence. "Let's just say in a hypothetical, abstract situation, if you'd made a discovery that questioned the doctrines of the Church in some way, what would you do?"

"How can anything that has inspired devotion and beauty for almost two thousand years not be true?"

"Even if—"

"I'm sorry." Tiziana stood and checked her watch. "It's getting late and we shouldn't keep our host waiting any longer." She gestured toward the staircase leading down to the water portal. As they left the study, she flicked off the light behind them, plunging them again into the murky light of the stairwell.

❖

Some fifteen minutes later, the water taxi drew up to Alvise's palazzo and, by the lantern over the landing steps. Joanna looked at her watch.

"Looks like it took longer than we thought," Tiziana said, "but I doubt we've missed much. With this group, the more wine, the more talk."

They reached the entry door at the top of the stairs and knocked. One of the hired waiters admitted them and returned to the kitchen without comment.

The atmosphere of the party seemed to have passed into a less festive and more intimate phase. The string quartet still quietly played—

this time Bach—but the dining table had been cleared except for a few trays of sweets and a cluster of wine bottles. The number of guests had also dwindled. Some seven or eight of them were clustered around the sofa where Morosini's Knight appeared to be holding court, his sword now on the floor at his feet. Others, in twos and threes, were scattered about the room speaking softly.

The Knight glanced up as they came in and rose to greet them. "Did you find the book?"

"Yes, everything's sorted." Tiziana put on her mask, becoming Butterfly again.

"Oh, very good. I look forward to discussing it with you after you've read it. In the meantime, please come join our little discussion. We were just talking about the value of faith."

"Sounds interesting," Butterfly said without conviction, and sat down in the place he made for her on the sofa.

Joanna perused the little circle of masks and was relieved to see that neither the obnoxious Arlecchino nor the mysterious Plague Doctor was among them. But a closer approach revealed that Sara wasn't there either. Curiously, neither was Satan.

"Thank you. I'll be along in just a moment," she said, and turned toward the table as if to take another glass of wine. But she passed the table and moved toward the more somber part of the banquet room behind the Persian screen. She heard giggling, and just as she reached the screen, a figure emerged suddenly in front of her, startling her. It was Jester, in a cap sporting two provocatively erect silk horns wound in pearls. His varicolored costume was slightly rumpled, as if he had been wrestling in it. He dragged with him an obviously drunken Gato, whose gold and long whiskered cat-mask was also askew. As Gato staggered past, she bumped into Joanna, mumbled "Scusi," and began giggling again.

Behind them, in the alcove created by the screen, four of the six candles in the candelabra had burned down and the remaining two sputtered.

Joanna halted for the second time. In the dim and wavering light, a single masked figure stood, inexplicably, in a costume made up of a series of veils, each one of a different color. But it was her headgear that had startled Joanna. Tilted sideways, and held in place with a ribbon under the woman's chin, was a silver platter—or the imitation of one—and at its center was a cheerfully painted wooden head.

Joanna backed away from the appalling sight without speaking and returned to the more populated part of the room. Now she was doubly baffled. What had gone on at the party in her absence, and where was Sara?

The bathroom, perhaps? Joanna knew it was across from the kitchen. A light tap on the bathroom door was met with silence.

Feeling increasingly awkward and annoyed, she noted another door farther along the corridor. A bedroom, most likely. She hesitated, stepped nervously toward the living room, then back again to the door, and opened it just a crack.

In the dim light of a single candle, Joanna could see them. Sara and the Devil were on the bed in an embrace.

CHAPTER FOURTEEN

Joanna felt a sudden sense of betrayal. Sara had seemed so close, so allied with her against foolish Italian men. How could she do this?

For a brief, deeply wounded moment Joanna backed away again, then saw Sara's arm hanging from the side of the bed.

She burst into the room.

"What the hell is going on?"

Alvise bolted upright and Joanna saw immediately that it wasn't an embrace at all, but a molestation. Sara lay limp against the pillow, her head thrown back. Both their masks lay on the floor.

Joanna stormed over to the bed and grasped Alvise by his red sleeve, shoving him aside. "What have you done to her?" She sat beside the dazed woman and tapped her lightly on one cheek.

"Sara, are you all right? Can you hear me?"

"Your friend's had a bit too much to drink." On his feet, Alvise straightened his doublet and wiped his mouth with the back of his hand. "I brought her here to lie down for a few minutes, and we both succumbed to the moment. No harm done."

Sara seemed to wrench herself into partial lucidity. "Not drunk," she mumbled. "Something in the wine."

Joanna helped her up into a sitting position. "Are you sick?"

"No. Got dizzy, all of a sudden." Sara rubbed her forehead. Her carefully coiffed hair had become undone and hung loosely over her hands. "Help me home."

Joanna spun around to Alvise, who had moved toward the door. "Sara never drinks that much. Did you drug her? What a disgusting thing to do."

"Of course not! What do you imagine?" He looked slightly ridiculous bending over and snatching up both their masks, more clown than demon.

Morosini's Knight stood in the doorway now. "Is something wrong?"

Joanna helped Sara to her feet and urged her to walk. She staggered a few feet, holding her head in her hands.

Alvise took a different tack. "The signorina has reacted adversely to the wine and has taken sick. Perhaps we should call a doctor."

"No. No doctor," Sara babbled, and Joanna knew why. They couldn't risk an examination unless it was something serious. She hoped it wasn't.

"Are you sure?" she whispered.

"Yes. Just need air, coffee, get home."

Joanna debated whether to accuse Alvise in front of witnesses. But it would sever their relationship with the university and possibly jeopardize the project. She had no real proof, anyhow.

"Please, just call a water taxi. I'll take her home and everything will be fine." She took Sara's mask from Alvise's hand, but he looked away.

❖

The cold air over the canal seemed to clear Sara's head, and by the time they reached the Ponte dei Greci embankment, she could walk again without assistance. They had collected their cloaks, though Sara now wore the warmer tabarro and clutched it across her chest while Joanna opened the iron gate to their apartment building.

"Does your head still hurt?"

"Yes, like someone's hammering on it."

"*Could* it be an allergic reaction?" Joanna still held Sara by the arm, more to comfort than to physically support her. She guided her into the apartment and toward the sofa.

"No, I don't have any allergies. How can you even ask? I know he put something in the wine. I had only two glasses, the same as you. He brought me a third in a new glass when you left, and a little after that I got dizzy. He 'helped' me to the bedroom and then was all over me, the bastard."

Joanna went to the kitchen and came back with a glass of water.

"Despicable, I agree. But, you have to admit, colorful. Poisoned wine is very Renaissance Venetian."

"It's not funny. The guy's a creep and you left me alone with him while you went off on a little tête-à-tête with Tiziana."

"We didn't have a tête-à-tête," Johanna half lied. "Besides, I can't protect you from men like Alvise. Welcome to the world of women. You have to learn to read the signs of trouble and get around it somehow."

"If I hadn't been half-unconscious, I'd have clocked him."

"I wish you had. Did he grope anything...dangerous?"

"I don't think so, but he sure as hell tried. Bastard. And now I've got a raging headache. I can't even focus my eyes enough to remove my makeup."

"I'll do it for you, but first take this." She handed Sara the water and two aspirin capsules. "These will take the edge off the headache without harming you. The water will do you good too."

Sara dropped the capsules in her mouth and drank the glass of water in three swallows.

"Now go take off your nice dress and put on your pajamas. I'll come in shortly."

Joanna removed her own costume and packed the trousers, tabarro, and tricorne for return. She prepared the box for Sara's costume, made up the sofa bed, then ventured into the bedroom.

Sara was in bed, propped up against her pillows. The velvet gown lay over a chair and the Salome mask was on the wall over the bed again.

Sitting on the edge of the bed, Joanna went to work with lotion and tissues. "Close your eyes now, so I can take off the mascara."

Sara obeyed, but continued talking. "Pretty clever the way she lured you away."

"What are you talking about? Oh, Tiziana? Please, stop harping on Tiziana. Nothing's going on. And if there were, what business would it be of yours?"

"You're right." Sara's lips drooped to a sulk. "None."

Joanna felt a twinge of guilt that she had indeed been sidetracked by the librarian, but then had become enraged to think that Sara had betrayed *her* with Alvise. It was all so schoolgirlish and confusing. They both were too mature and too serious for such nonsense.

She made another pass with the tissue under Sara's eyes and

changed the subject. "Didn't you find it bizarre to spend an evening with people in masks and costume? It's true we knew a couple of them, but the rest were like phantoms."

"That was the part of the evening I enjoyed. Disguise gives people a chance to reinvent themselves. How could I not like that?"

"I see your point. It would be more convincing if people could change personalities too. But Arlecchino, who was arguing with you about Carnival 'perversion,' turned out to be just as big a jerk in a mask as he was without it. Did you recognize him? He was one of the archivists. Bracco was his name, I think."

"Ah, right. I thought he seemed familiar. Bracco. Isn't that also the name of the two Jesuits on the *Grazie Dei*?"

Joanna stopped wiping, her hand suspended in midair for a moment. "You're right. Interesting coincidence." They looked at each other, exchanging glances that seemed hold the same questions. Could it be more than a coincidence? Probably not. But still…

Finally, Joanna gathered up the makeup-stained tissues and tossed them into the waste-paper bin. Suddenly tender, she took Sara's hand where it lay across her stomach. "I'm really sorry about leaving you in Alvise's clutches. I couldn't avoid it, but I'm still sorry. How's the headache?"

"Better, thanks. I think I can sleep now."

"Well, then, I'll let you do that." Joanna rose from the bed and made her way from the room, extinguishing the overhead light at the doorway. Behind her, Sara said softly, "Good night, Joanna. Thanks for saving me."

"You're welcome. Maybe you can return the favor some time."

Joanna showered leisurely, turning the evening's events over in her mind. The constellation of allies was changing and they would have to adjust with it. Alvise had proved himself obnoxious and would have to be avoided. Fortunately, he seemed to have less to offer the project than Morosini.

Tiziana, on the other hand… On the other hand, what? Was that avenue worth going down? Another religious woman from a foreign culture. Monique in middle age.

Coming out of the bathroom, she passed the door to Sara's bedroom and glanced inside. The small table lamp was still on and, on the pillow below the Salome mask, Sara was breathing the slow deep breaths of unconsciousness.

Standing in the doorway, Joanna watched her for a moment and felt a sudden pathos for the little boy who had spent almost an entire childhood longing to be loved. She tiptoed toward the bed, resisted the urge to pull up the covers, but clicked off the bedside lamp before creeping from the room.

❖

Around eleven the next day, Joanna was at the garden table with the Arnoldi book still open in front of her. She glanced up as Sara came into the garden with two cups of coffee. "You look much better. I guess ten hours' sleep will do the trick. Did you hear the siren last night?"

"Siren? No. What siren?" She set one cup down in front of Joanna.

"The *acqua alta* siren warning of a high tide around midnight. You didn't hear it?"

"No. I didn't hear a thing. Did you check the news to see if San Marco is flooded?"

"Yes. I watched it on the television this morning. The tide wasn't so bad, but tomorrow is a full moon, so they're predicting an even higher one at about the same time."

"They seem to be happening more often now than when I was a child." Sara sat down, warming her hands on both sides of her coffee mug. "So what's the story about our ship's scribe? Should we believe Morosini's report?"

"I don't know. This account is really damning. The author"—Joanna tapped the leather cover where the author's name was embossed—"Benedetto Morosini clearly discredits the whole lineage. Primarily he damns Pietro for being demented, but he also implies that the entire family goes crazy. What's more, I checked the Venetian history books on the shelf, and they support that idea."

"What do you mean by 'goes crazy'?"

"Keep in mind that the Arnoldi family was one of the Old Families, that were expected to represent the true Venetian virtues. But in a single year, 1561, not only is Pietro himself declared demented and sent into exile, but his brother is charged with theft from the church and sentenced to prison, his oldest son defrauds an investor, and the year after that, the youngest son is charged with murder. The family just suddenly falls apart, in a single generation. Comparing the dates with the ship's log, I'd say the deterioration started with the voyage of the *Grazie Dei*."

"Well, we already saw in the log that something happened to Pietro during that voyage." Sara stirred sugar into her coffee. "But you think Pietro's shipboard breakdown is what caused the damage to his family?"

"If it did, reading Leonora's book was the start of it all. He says so outright, remember?"

"Yeah?" Sara drew out the word, wanting to hear more. "Where is this line of thinking taking us?"

"Stay with me here." Joanna tapped the book again. "The author talks about 'other heresies,' not just Lutheranism, so I'm wondering now if Leonora's book might have found its way into other hands after this voyage. *A lot* of other hands. I'm even wondering if it might not also be a contributing cause of the Counter-Reformation."

Sara frowned. "That's pushing it a little, isn't it? We should collect a lot more information before we go that far."

"Fair enough. At least let's read the rest of the letters. Maybe we'll find some clues as to what everyone was so excited about." Joanna got up from the garden table and fetched the leather wallet and notebook from the living room.

"We have only these two left."

"Let's finish them now and have all of Leonora's story on the table. I'll read while you take notes."

28 June 1560
Cara mia,

Had you but been by my side yesterday, we could have seen this wonder together. As we left Palermo, the heavens darkened suddenly and a black disk passed o'er the face of the sun. Could you see it in England? Some of the crew proclaimed it God's Wrath (though for what they could not say) despite the common wisdom that the event is natural. Yet e'en for me, it seemed ominous, for Hakim's book also spoke of such an eclipse in the heavens over Palestine. Mayhap it was Wrath after all, on both those fateful days, at the creation of the Confession and upon its destruction.

As the disk slid away and the light returned, I bethought me of the day you came to me, when your husband died and your condottiere father departed to fight one more of Venice's battles. Had I known John Falke would retire from the field a year later and take you back to England, I would have guarded my heart better. But how could I resist you, newly widowed and wanting. You said I was a better husband to you in a single night than that brute who married you was in four years. Were you here now, what might you think of me as a husband?

For I have become a strange thing, neither man nor woman, but something there between that has no name. I perceive with new eyes that much of "manliness" is manner. Yet manner itself is stirred by dress. A man in a rich garment wins admiration, which then feeds his importance. He grows comfortable with authority and soon the world defers to him. All for an expensive weskit and hose.

Now, both speak in me, the woman that is within and the man I wear and act. Surely this knowledge is forbidden, for if all women knew it, there'd be no wives. For disobeying God, Adam was given to see the difference between men and women. But I too have disobeyed, and I see how they are the same.

Alas, I have another knowledge, which has more cruelly undone my faith. Its symbol stands in the Baptistery of San Marco, carrying a mask. The mask that was a lie that unmasked the truth.

Some, like the Jesuits and the pilgrims, wear a cross, but it is my fate to wear the mask.

Joanna still scribbled the final phrases. "I like her more and more. She says nothing about Arnoldi, of course, though he must have also been at the captain's table. But she doesn't talk much about the book anymore either. I guess, for her, it's over."

Sara folded the letter and handed it back. "Well, she's spot-on about identity having so much to do with display. In some ways, we become the mask we put on."

Joanna tucked the precious pages back into their wallet. "I suppose so. But what I'd like to find out now is—who in the San Marco baptistery is holding a mask? Maybe that discovery can shed some light on this mystery."

"What about the last letter?"

"Let's do that one later tonight." She looked at her watch. "We've still got plenty of time. Let's go to church."

❖

Though the acqua alta had fully subsided with the low tide, an elevated walkway still ran the width of the San Marco piazza, and they had to climb over it to reach the entrance of the church.

Sara gazed up at the glittering façade of the Basilica of San Marco. "I can't decide if it's gorgeous or kitschy."

"Both, I'd say," Joanna remarked. "With all those mosaics, columns, towers, statuary, and glitter, it's more like a fairy castle than a church, but that's what I like about it."

"'Fairy castle' is a good image, though you might want to combine it with 'stage set.' The cupolas are fake, you know."

"Fake? They look real to me."

"The original ones are still underneath. A wooden superstructure was added to make them look more impressive and match the doge's palace in height. Sort of architectural falsies. Just goes to show you that for churches too, it's all in the presentation."

"I suppose they have the usual relics?"

"One great big one, in fact. The bones of Saint Mark the Evangelist that were stolen from Egypt. They were in the crypt until the nineteenth century, when someone decided the flood risk to the bones was too great, so they were moved up to the altar."

"A holy skeleton. Mmm. It doesn't get much better than that."

"The Venetians apparently agree. Venetian merchants supposedly 'rescued' it from Mark's sepulchre in Alexandria in the ninth century and smuggled it out in a barrel of pork. There's even a mosaic in the church that illustrates the tale."

"Pork?" Joanna giggled. "Ah, yes. That would have kept the Muslim inspectors away. A little humiliating for the saint, though. I mean, if he knew about it. Has anyone seen the skeleton?"

"Well, there's a great story connected with that. After a

conflagration in 1063, when the Venetians were constructing a new basilica over the remains of the old one, they couldn't find the relics. But, *miraculously*, an arm appeared sticking out of a pillar and pointed to where the bones had been moved."

"The saint himself?"

"But of course. Who else could hide inside a pillar? In any case, the bones were placed in a sarcophagus in the crypt of the new basilica."

Joanna was slightly bored yet impressed. "I'm amazed you know so much about this church, things that aren't in the guidebooks."

"I have a soft spot for San Marco. I was baptized here."

"What?" Joanna halted at the entrance. "You never mentioned that. I didn't even know they still did baptisms here."

"They did thirty years ago. My parents were not only good Catholics, they were snobs about it. It had to be San Marco holy water they dunked me in."

"Doesn't seem to have done you any good, though," Joanna teased as they passed the souvenir counter and arrived at the foot of the central aisle. They stood shoulder to shoulder for a moment, studying the vast interior. The high central dome drew their eyes upward, toward the scant light shining through the ring of windows at its base. Illumination also came from electric bulbs along the walls, but even in the subdued artificial light, the entire interior shimmered.

"Now I know why it costs so much to get a gold tooth. The Italians have half the world's supply locked up right here."

Sara nodded. "Thousands of square meters of it. The flashiest, goldiest part of the sanctuary is the *Pala d'Oro* altarpiece. Not to mention all the other treasures, mostly booty taken from the East. Someone once called this place 'the world's most beautiful thieves' den.'"

"Yeah, you *do* feel visually bombarded. You could spend weeks here, studying all the images. But of course we're here to look for a woman with a mask, and thank God Leonora told us where to look. Which way is the baptistery?"

"Over there, on the south side of the church." Sara led the way back down the central aisle to the atrium. At the end of it, however, a barricade covered the door and a uniformed man stood guard.

"It's closed to tourists, signora," he said.

"We aren't tourists. We have an authorization from the head of the History Department at the University of Venice." Joanna unfolded the letter and held it in front of him.

The guard perused the letter indifferently and handed it back. "That's a nice letter, signora, but the baptistery is locked and I don't have a key. Only the workmen do, and they don't come until six. You'll have to show this letter to Signor Niero."

"Niero? Who is he?"

"The foreman of the church repairs. He carries the key and is the one who admits the mosaic specialists. He comes at six, and they enter from outside, not from here."

Resigned, Joanna folded her letter. "Thank you for the information. We'll wait."

They wandered slowly from the baptistery entrance along the south atrium. "I have to remind myself that we're standing in the middle of countless mementi of great historical events, half-legendary names."

"You're right." Sara stopped and pointed toward the floor and remarked with feigned melodrama, "Here, for example, on this marble stone right in front of us, Friedrich Barbarossa knelt before..." She read the rest from the plaque. "'Before Pope Alexander III in 1177 and reconciled once again the so-called Holy Roman Empire with the papacy.' Jeez, just when you think you're *emperor*, along comes a guy in a mitre and one-ups you because he's got the God card."

Joanna linked arms with Sara and drew her toward the church portal. "With a baptismal credential like yours, you shouldn't be talking trash about the pope. Come on, let's get out of here and kill an hour outside. Any good ideas?"

"Yeah. How about another gelato?" Sara suggested.

Joanna glanced sideways at her. "I don't think so."

❖

At six in the evening the men were already sitting on the ground outside the baptistery smoking and talking among themselves. Joanna tried to engage them, but they replied to her with indifferent courtesy. Sara elicited a warmer response when she asked them in perfect Venetian, and with a Lauren Bacall voice, just what they did in the church.

"We're mosaic specialists," one of them said, staring at Sara's breasts.

"You take care of all that gold?" Sara's expression of admiration was exaggerated but at least partially genuine.

"No, another team does the walls and dome. We work on the floors."

"What's wrong with them?" Joanna asked.

"They're wavy." He made a wave gesture to illustrate. "Too much acqua alta."

A second man bent forward to get her attention. "This is just a little job. It's much worse in the crypt."

Sara sat down next to him. "There must be plenty of work in that church. Do you like your job?"

"Sure. But the tile's hard on the knees, and the church is cold."

"I'd be curious to see how you do it," Sara said.

"That's up to the foreman, and there he comes now." He pointed with the two fingers that held his cigarette.

A beefy, slightly balding man in a suit had just come around the corner from the main piazza. "What's going on here?"

"These ladies want to watch us repair marble in the church," the first man said.

"Out of the question. The church opens to the public at nine in the morning."

"We're not tourists, Signor Niero. Dr. Morosini, from the University of Venice, has, uh…sent us to look at the baptistery." She held out the letter, and he took it reluctantly. "We promise not to interfere with your workers in any way. We'll simply take a few pictures and leave."

Niero frowned and handed back the letter. "Dr. Morosini? Yeah, I know him. Why does he want pictures of our baptistery?"

Joanna left the misunderstanding uncorrected. "We're not sure exactly. He just wants some close-ups of one of the mosaics. We promise not to be long. You can keep an eye on us, if you want."

"I've got better things to do. Hey, Mario." He waved toward one of the three men. "You're responsible for these two. Make sure they don't touch anything, and that they leave after fifteen minutes."

"Thank you, Signor Niero," Joanna said to the foreman's back as he unlocked the baptistery door and strode away.

❖

Only the thinnest film of water remained on the baptistery floor, though the odor of mold revealed that the room had in fact flooded often.

Unlike the sanctuary, which had a walkway laid down for visitors, the baptistery had only its mosaic floor. It was warped in several places, just as the tile-setters had said.

The men laid out their mats and tools and went to work immediately around the baptismal font, carefully prying up the sections of mosaic tile and laying them on wooden trays. The one called Mario scraped away at the swollen plaster beneath with a scalpel-like instrument, but glanced up occasionally.

Sara smiled back at him, then joined Joanna in studying the mosaics overhead: an assortment of women, angels, saints, men seated at a table, and a woman in a long red dress.

Joanna turned a 360-degree circle and exhaled exasperation. "I don't see any masks."

"Nope, not a one," Sara said. "Unless that image over there could be construed as a mask." She pointed to the mosaic over the interior door of the baptistery, leading to the main church. They both studied it, heads tilted.

"It's Herod's daughter, isn't it? Only dancer in history to be paid with a decapitated head," Joanna remarked. "Though with the two-dimensionality, it does look a bit like she's carrying a mask over her head, not a platter."

"Is it possible that Leonora was referring to Salome in her letter?" Sara mused.

"Possibly, but she's not called Salome in the Bible, at least not in the King James version. She's simply called the daughter of Herod."

"You read the Bible?" Sara seemed surprised.

"It's part of the English Reformation. My area of expertise. Anyhow, the name comes from Flavius Josephus, a Jewish Roman historian, first century. He seems to have cobbled together a story of the lineage of the tetrarch Herod and declared that his stepdaughter was called Salome. The odd thing is that the Bible *does* name a Salome, but not the naughty dancing one. Bible Salome is one of the women who followed Jesus and appeared both on Calvary and at his tomb. For some reason, the popular imagination much prefers naughty Salome. In any case, she's the one in a lot of salacious paintings, and one great opera."

"Could they be the same person?"

"More like no person at all, just related legends. Who knows? I'm tending toward the view that Salome is just another beware-the-women tale, along with Eve and Delilah."

"Did you find what you wanted?" Mario called over to them from the floor on the other side of the baptismal font.

"Don't think so. We're looking for an image of a woman with a mask. Any ideas?"

"Sorry. I've been working in this church for years. I've never seen a mask. Of course, I haven't looked at the ones high up." He pried away another section of tile and placed it carefully on a tray next to its mate. The freshly exposed adhesive in the cavity was porous and crumbly.

"Will you take apart the entire floor?" Joanna asked.

"No, just the swells. Tomorrow the section by the outside door, the day after, the place where you're standing. Signor Niero has us on a tight schedule."

"Then we won't keep you. Do you work all night?"

"Nah, just until ten. Why? You looking for some male company this evening?"

Sara smiled, unperturbed. "Thank you, my husband would not be happy if I stayed out late."

"I know what you mean." He laughed. "My wife wouldn't like it either."

While the two bantered, Joanna snapped photos and, then, on an impulse, she asked, "How do you leave the church at night? Does the foreman come back and lock the door behind you?"

"No, it locks automatically when you leave. So once you're outside, there's no coming back in."

"Very efficient," Joanna replied, packing the camera into her rucksack. Next to her, Sara was rubbing her upper arms against the chill. The workmen were right; the church got very cold at night. "Ready to go?"

Sara nodded. "Have a good evening, Mario. Your colleagues too." They exited through the outside doors, which closed behind them with a loud click.

They left the basilica, then turned right on the piazza into the commercial streets in the direction of their apartment. After they had threaded their way through the crowds of people for a time, Sara felt a sudden chill that had nothing to do with the night air.

"I don't know why, it must be the guilt, but I feel like someone's watching us," she said, and quickened her pace.

❖

Shoeless and lethargic on the apartment sofa, Sara spoke to the ceiling. "No one with a mask in the baptistery. That's disappointing. Looks like we're at a dead end. Unless we go back and look at all the other mosaics. That should take about…um…two years."

"You shouldn't be so easily discouraged." At the dining table a few feet away, Joanna looked up from her notebook. "We'll find more information tomorrow. You'll see."

"Sorry. I'm a little bleak this evening. I have a headache again, though it'll go away once I'm asleep."

"Why don't you read something light? Or, no. Better something ponderous. That always knocks me right out."

Sara squinted, then rubbed her face. "Reading is the last thing I want to do. My eyes are already burning."

Joanna closed the book and stood up. "Maybe I can help. I'd intended to study the library booklet Tiziana gave us. How about I read it to you? Even if it doesn't make you sleep, we'll both learn something."

Sara shrugged. "That sounds dull. Soothing too, though. But if you're going to do bedtime reading, let me get ready for bed."

"Call me when you're ready, then, and I'll come in." Joanna went into the kitchen and poured milk into a saucepan. While she stirred absentmindedly, she thought of Sara in the next room changing identity. Like superwoman reverting to Clark Kent.

A few minutes later, Sara called from the bedroom and Joanna went in with the hot mug. Sara was tucked up in bed, propped against her pillows. She had obviously cold-creamed off the foundation makeup, but a thin line of mascara remained, feminizing already bright blue eyes. Joanna focused on them, trying not to look at the swelling of Sara's breasts under a sleep shirt. It always disconcerted her to think of Sara's breasts.

"My God, you've actually brought me cocoa."

"Yep, that and a chapter from *History of the Biblioteca Marciana* should be enough to get you dozing." Joanna pulled up a chair next to the bed.

Sara downed half the cocoa in three luxurious swallows and settled deep into the covers. "I haven't been read to since, gee, since I was a baby," she murmured.

"Let's see if this lives up to Rumpelstiltskin," Joanna said, leafing through the pamphlet. "Ah, here's where it gets exciting.

"'Biblioteca Marciana, known more commonly as the Library

of San Marco, founded under the patronage of Cardinal Bessarion of Trebizond, who in 1468 donated his collection consisting of some 750 codices, among these 250 manuscripts and a large number of printed works. Venice solemnly accepted these and thus was moved to order the construction of the Venetian Public Library that had already been proposed by Francesco Petrarca in 1362, without the power, however, to bring the project to a close. It was not until 1537 that Venice commissioned Jacopo Sansovino, a Florentine architect who had settled in Venice after the Sack of Rome, to create the library. Sansovino's building, constructed across from the Palazzo Ducale, brought the Roman Renaissance to Venice. All did not run smoothly, however, since the barrel-vault ceiling of the library collapsed shortly after construction and the architect was arrested. The artists Titian and Aretino, who were his friends, were able to prevail upon the Venetian authorities to release him.'"

Joanna paused.

Sara's eyes had closed, but when Joanna stopped reading, she murmured, "God, that really *is* boring."

❖

Frustrated that he couldn't see into their apartment, the stalker tried to circle around the building to approach it from the rear. Unfortunately, other buildings closed it off on all sides. A town map showed that they had a garden, but he would have had to break into one of the other buildings to enter it from outside. He hated not knowing what they were doing or talking about, how far they'd gotten in their investigation, and, more, what their private lives were like.

It had been a shock the first time he'd seen them; they were so different from everyone else, so obviously looking for more than they said they were. Soon it became an obsession to find out as much as possible about them. They knew something and he wanted to know it too, no matter at what cost.

It was remarkably easy to follow them; they were so preoccupied, and he knew every niche and alley to fade into. People rarely noticed him anyhow, though he was only bland, not ugly. But people seemed to feel a faint aversion toward him. People he passed seemed not to see him, and if they did, their gaze slipped right off him. Nobody he met for the second time ever seemed to remember meeting him the first time.

But now his anonymity was his greatest asset. He could remain in sight yet out of sight while he trailed the two women, filled with purpose. He wasn't sure what would come of it all or whether he even had the courage to go through with it. But he couldn't stop now. The two women wouldn't leave Venice until he had what he wanted from them.

CHAPTER FIFTEEN

R emind me again why we're going back to the Libreria Marciana," Sara said as they stepped out onto the street and locked the iron gate behind them. "It feels like we're backtracking."

"We have to find out more about the Arnoldi family. I think something's going on there that will lead us someplace."

"Are you sure you don't just want to see Tiziana again?"

"Don't be silly."

"You must find her attractive. I do. And you spent all that time with her during Alvise-the-rapist's masquerade party."

They walked over the footbridge at the corner leading to the row of mask and costume shops. The gondolier was there again, helping passengers into his gondola. He waved recognition and called, "You come today? I give you a beautiful ride."

Joanna waved back. "Sorry. Maybe tomorrow."

"I guess I'm losing my touch." Sara chuckled. "Usually it's me they flirt with. Except Tiziana."

Joanna halted directly in front of Sara. "Will you stop going on about Tiziana? She's married. She's religious. She likes men. I don't flirt with people I have to seduce out of their own worlds. They always end up going back when it's over, as if they were just trying you out like a sports car."

"You're talking from experience?"

"Bitter experience. So let's not go on about Tiziana any longer. She's knowledgeable and I'll accept any help she offers, but I don't think that will be much. She's already made it clear she won't be part of anything that undermines her faith."

"And you think Leonora's book—?"

"I think it absolutely."

❖

Joanna closed the last of the volumes she had read through and shoved it to the side with all the others. She let out a long breath and laid her head back, satisfied, but momentarily brain-fatigued, against her chair.

"Dead end, huh?" Sara asked, closing the two books she had been comparing. "From what I've read, Morosini was right. The family begins in the sixteenth century as a respected noble family, with a senator, prosperous merchants, clerics, sea captains, the cream of the Venetian upper class. But by the end of the century there are no clerics, no one in political office, no donations to the scuoli or charities. Instead, suspicions of embezzlement, family members in exile, accusations of conspiracy, and so on. By the next century, the family is invisible. I'm guessing you've found the same results."

"Well, yes and no," Joanna said provocatively. Morosini is right in one respect, that the dynasty did deteriorate right after the *Grazie Dei* voyage. But..." Joanna raised a forefinger dramatically. "But that's just the male line, the one that's easiest to trace."

"Yeeeessss?"

"Now the story gets interesting." Joanna leaned forward on her elbows, tapping with one finger on a page of scribbled notes. "Apparently Pietro Arnoldi had a daughter, named Eliana, who after the death of her father became associated with the Mocenigo family, possibly married and then widowed. In any case, in 1592, she met and married a man who had come to work as tutor to the Mocenigo family."

"You're killing me here with boredom. When does it get sexy?"

"That man was Giordano Bruno."

Sara's jaw dropped. "The most famous scientist-heretic of the Renaissance? The one who was burned to death in 1600 for teaching that the earth revolved around the sun?"

"That's the one."

"I thought he was a priest."

"He started off as a priest, but it looks like during his stay in Geneva, he sort of defrocked himself and started wearing the clothing of the Calvinists. In any case, he stopped being a priest and wandered around the courts of Europe, more or less as a scholar. He went to Venice in 1592, where he and Eliana apparently married shortly before the poor man was denounced as a heretic and dragged off to prison in Rome."

"Incredible. So the Arnoldi dynasty crumbled, and his daughter went off and married the devil himself."

"But hang on. There's more. Pietro's brother, the one who went to prison, also had a daughter, and she married into the Torricelli family. Her son was Evangelista Torricelli, physicist and mathematician of the 1600s. In case that isn't a household name for you, he was the first to describe the earth's atmosphere as an 'ocean' and he invented the barometer. He knew Gallileo and, in fact, succeeded him as professor of mathematics at the University of Pisa. He also built a number of telescopes and a microscope."

"You knew all of that already?"

"Eh, no. I read it just now. But don't distract me. I'm trying to make a case here that after the *Grazie Dei* voyage, the Arnoldi women seem to suddenly become prominent. I've found half a dozen Arnoldi women associated with the beginnings of European science. It's as if whatever broke the spirit of the Arnoldi men had just the opposite effect on the women."

Sara nodded, but hesitantly. "You might have a case. On the other hand, it could all be coincidental, couldn't it? I mean, we could simply be tracing a pattern where there is none."

"It's true. But it does seem that something momentous happened in 1560 that changed the Arnoldi family in a way—"

"How's the research going?" Tiziana stood suddenly at the end of the table. "Anything I can help you with?"

"Not really. We're coming along nicely, thank you," Sara replied. Joanna could almost hear the unexpressed thought: *so you can leave now*.

"Actually, we've done quite a bit more study on the Arnoldi family and found that your uncle's book tells only half the story."

Tiziana sat down on one of the empty chairs at the table and Sara shifted away a few inches. "Funny, I've been thinking about that family since the party the other night. It didn't seem important at the time, but since you're still studying them, I should mention that there are lots of Arnoldi around Venice. That in itself isn't especially interesting, but there's one Arnoldi whom you might want to talk to."

"Really? Who's that?" Sara asked with faint interest.

"A priest named Tomás. He was a brilliant historian and theologian but is quite old now, ninety-something, and no longer reads the mass. He lives in the care of the monks on the island of San Francesco del Deserto."

"And you think talking to him might give us some useful information?"

"It could give you some context. His memory fails him sometimes, but in his lucid moments he knows a lot about Church history too. Why don't you take a break from your reading? San Francesco del Deserto is a very pretty island, and it only takes fifteen minutes to get out there. I'll be glad to give the monastery a call and set up a meeting, if you'd like."

"It couldn't hurt to try. At the worst, it will still be a relief from combing through books in Old Italian," Joanna said. "Rewarding, but hard on the eyes."

"You'll enjoy a nice trip into the lagoon," Tiziana added.

Sara was silent.

❖

The early-morning vaporetto chugged across the rippling water of the Venetian lagoon, depositing most of its tourists at the better-known islands of Murano and Burano for their glassware and lace. Joanna let Sara take the lead in choosing where to stand on the boat. Sara seemed to weigh which location was less deadly: the outer deck of the vaporetto, where one might be swept off by the crowd, or inside the passenger cabin where, in the event of sinking, one would be trapped. She compromised by taking up position right at the doorway.

Joanna studied her Venetian guidebook and, as San Francesco del Deserto came into sight, she read out loud to Sara.

"According to legend, St Francis of Assisi rested on this tiny island on his way back from the Holy Land in the thirteenth century. The little church on the island dates from 1228, is surrounded by cypresses, and the atmosphere of the monastery and its grounds is serene."

"Serene, for sure. Now let's see if it's worth our taking off an afternoon," Sara said as they stepped off the vaporetto onto the dock.

❖

"Please take a seat, ladies," the young Franciscan said, gesturing toward a bench at the edge of an olive orchard. "I'll bring Father Arnoldi out in just a moment."

While he spoke, Joanna studied his habit. The dark brown robe was obviously cut from a modern, more washable fabric than its ancestor of pure wool, but the loose-sleeved gown belted at the waist by a white cord and seven-part rosary hadn't changed from the fifteenth century. A cowl hung around his neck and over his shoulders. His tonsure seemed less extreme than the portrayals she'd seen in her history books, and a thick ring of curly brown hair still circled his head like a crown. He wore sandals, of course, which Joanna recalled were mandatory. As he turned away, she noted the pointed hood of his cowl and couldn't help but think of Friar Tuck.

True to his word, the Franciscan returned in just a few moments holding the arm of a stooped man who was clearly of advanced age. Without introduction or comment, he deposited the old man on the path in front of them, nodded faintly, and walked away.

The old Franciscan stood there looking puzzled, his pale gray eyes watering, as if he waited for an explanation of why his sleep had been interrupted. He hunched over, both hands tucked under his long sleeves, and his habit, which looked so handsome on the younger man, hung like a brown blanket over a skeleton.

Joanna began the conversation. "Thank you for agreeing to meet with us, Father Arnoldi. Tiziana Morosini, the librarian at the Libreria Marciana, informs us you are an authority on Venetian and Church history, and she suggested we talk to you regarding certain events in the sixteenth century."

"Oh, my dears. I'm sure I can't tell you anything you can't find in Signora Morosini's library." Then he fell silent. They strolled for a while, admiring the grounds and the olive trees and the old man replying monosyllabically.

After some ten minutes of strolling, the monk finally spoke again. "If you don't mind, ladies…" He pointed toward a bench.

"You want to rest? Of course." Joanna was solicitous.

"No, no. I would like *you* to sit down. I have something to give to my friends, but they won't come if you stand too close." With that, he pulled a crumpled paper sack from inside his sleeve.

"Oh! The birds. Of course," Joanna said, and sat down while Arnoldi backed away a few paces and poured a small heap of bread crumbs into his palm.

Birds came almost immediately. Pigeons and sparrows first, then a pair of swallows swooped down and circled the monk. Many of them lit fearlessly on his hands and arms, apparently accustomed to a regular feeding. A few more timid ones hovered overhead before dropping to snatch a morsel of bread, then taking flight again. Joanna and Sara sat motionless, watching the spectacle. Like an illustration in a child's catechism, Joanna thought.

"Signora Morosini informs me you are interested in my family." He raised his voice to be heard across the distance between himself and the bench.

"Yes. The name Arnoldi shows up on some of our findings from 1560 and we thought you might—"

"Ah, the Counter-Reformation." He nodded. "A difficult time, when Rome put great pressure on the Republic. The city was full of printers and suddenly the Church gave them an index of forbidden books." His birds fluttered away momentarily while he poured out another handful of crumbs from his sack, but then they returned.

"Yes, the Church's reaction to Lutheranism…" Joanna let her voice trail off.

"Well, above all, the pope called for the final session of the Council of Trent." He stared into the air and seemed to be talking to himself. "Yes, yes. Right about 1560 it was. Dangerous ideas on the wind. Doubts, questions. Pius IV knew he had to nail them down."

"Nail down?" Sara asked. "Do you mean close some of the presses?

"No, no. The doctrines. The Church had to declare them again, make them absolute. There could be no room for uncertainties."

Sara smiled as one of the sparrows lit on her foot, found it breadless, and flew off in avian disappointment. "All because of Luther?"

"Luther, yes. But even more dangerous heresies were abroad. The Holy See knew it had to renew its dogmas and its sole authority to interpret Scripture, regardless of any artifacts that might arise thereafter."

"I think it also affirmed the seven sacraments," Sara said, "if I recall my Early Renaissance studies."

"Yes, the sacraments, of course, and the absolute necessity of the Church to mediate them." The old monk shrugged, sending sparrows off in all directions. "And all the rest too, the definition of original sin, the mass, the communion, purgatory, the use of prayer, veneration of Jesus and Mary and the saints, the selling of indulgences, papal infallibility."

Joanna was impressed. The man was an encyclopedia.

"But why just then?" Joanna pressed him for more information. "Why, when Luther himself had been dead for fifteen years and

Lutheranism had been spreading over Europe for thirty years already, did the pope call the Council of Trent in 1560?"

The breadcrumbs were gone now and only a few pigeons followed the monk as he came to join them on the bench. "A new threat, perhaps."

"What threat was that?" Joanna's heart quickened and she caught Sara's eye, but the old man didn't say any more.

Joanna took another tack. "We've come across some ancient letters written at sea in 1560. The vessel was the *Grazie Dei* and the ship's scribe was a certain Pietro Arnoldi. He wrote in his log that a man was murdered because of books that he was carrying, copies of a translation that was declared heretical. It appears that Pietro Arnoldi obtained a copy of it. Do you know anything about that?"

The old monk closed his eyes for nearly half a minute. Was he praying, considering his answer, or just dozing off? Finally they opened again. "How did you find out about this book?"

"From the State Archives. Your ancestor's account confirms our other documents that tell of a book so heretical that the man transporting copies was murdered and the books thrown into the sea."

"I learned that as a child. Pietro Arnoldi broke off his voyage on the *Grazie Dei* when a heretic gave him a book that turned him away from the Faith. Worse, he returned home and spread the heresy to others. As the story goes, someone denounced him and he was arrested, though because of his service to Venice, he was not executed but exiled for the rest of his life."

"Do you have any idea of the contents of the book?"

"No, that has always been a mystery. The book was passed around to many people, but eventually the Church confiscated it and warned that there might be others. It was around that time that the pope convened a new sitting of the Council of Trent."

"Do you see a connection between the discovery of the book and the Council?" Joanna asked, excitement creeping into her voice. Had they, in fact, found a living source that could confirm their wildest suppositions?

"Perhaps. It had been years since the Council had met, and this session was rather hurried. The outcome was the affirmation of the Nicene Creed, particularly the *filioque* clause."

Joanna frowned. "'Filioque' is Latin for 'and the Son.' But what is the filioque clause?"

"Do you know what the Nicene Creed is?" he asked.

"A declaration of faith in the major assertions of the Catholic doctrine," Sara answered. "Doesn't it begin with *Credo in unum Deum?*"

"Yes, formed in the early fourth century. In the sixth century, the churches in the West added '*Sanctum...Qui ex Patre Filioque procedit,*' that is, 'The Holy Spirit that proceeds from the Father and the Son.'"

"Yeeesss?" Joanna sensed him going off on a tangent. The Nicene Creed could add nothing to the puzzle, and she hoped he would return to the subject at hand.

The monk puckered thin lips, formulating a summary. "Well, the Orthodox and the Roman churches had disagreed about whether the Holy Spirit proceeds from the Father *through* the Son, or whether the Son himself is a source of the Holy Spirit."

The hair-splitting of theologians, Joanna thought. "There is a difference?"

"Oh, yes. If the former, then the Son is only a human being through whom the Father flowed, a mere prophet and not part of the substance of the Father. But the Council affirmed that the spirit flowed from both the Father *and* the Son."

Sara also seemed to have lost interest in theological niceties. "Yes, the how-much-of-Christ-was-God issue," she said with barely concealed impatience. "What does that have to do with the book or with the Arnoldi family?"

He glanced away. "That is perhaps something you might investigate yourself." Then, abruptly, he changed the subject, looking directly into Joanna's eyes.

"Are you baptized, signorina?"

"Uh, no. Why?"

He laid a trembling hand on hers. "God is not mocked, my child. Leave off this pursuit and accept the first sacrament. Do not be afraid. Baptism is but a little drowning, the death of the selfish will. The purified self rises from the water to the love of God."

Joanna touched the old man's desiccated hand. "Thank you for your concern for my soul," she said gently, ignoring the admonition. "But, please, can you think of any other connection between the Council of Trent, your family, and the forbidden book?"

"There's nothing more I can tell you." He pulled his hand away and seemed to deflate, forming a curve as he drooped forward.

In fact, the young Franciscan with the curly tonsure had followed discreetly behind and not let them out of his sight. As Arnoldi began to slump, he appeared immediately. "Thank you for your visit, ladies. As you can see, Father Arnoldi needs to rest now," he said, gently guiding the old man away from them and back to the shelter of the monastery.

CHAPTER SIXTEEN

Joanna reviewed her collection of notes while Sara boiled water for the now ritual end-of-the-day tea. "Tomás Arnoldi, how old do you think he is?" Sara called from the kitchen.

"Didn't Tiziana say he was ninety?"

"Oh, right. Can you imagine being a monk for so many years in physical and mental isolation, never allowed to fall in love with anyone because you were supposed to love only God?"

"I don't imagine they look at it as deprivation. They make do with fraternity, I suppose. The ones who don't cheat and sneak off for nasty guilt-ridden sex, then repent. But I can understand choosing isolation and finding satisfaction in a discipline. Anyone who's written a doctoral dissertation has done that."

"I guess that explains why I never got the doctorate. If I can identify with anyone in our little cast of characters, it's Leonora. She was alone, but not emotionally, because Anne was in her mind all the time. That kind of isolation I can understand." Sara came from the kitchen and sat down at the table with steaming tea mugs. "You know, we haven't even read her last letter. We might find some last useful bit of information in it." She pushed one of the mugs toward Joanna.

"Giulio's summary says it's just a description of life on shipboard."

Sara snorted quietly. "We've seen how useful Giulio's summaries are. Respect for the dead and all that, but the man could really be obtuse."

"Well, let's look at it now and put the whole collection to rest." Joanna took up the leather wallet, which already lay near her elbow. "Here it is, the last of the pages." She slid the letter across the table and opened to a blank page in her notebook. "Whenever you're ready."

Sara took a long drink of the tea and began.

5 July 1560
Cara mia,

How did your fragile frame endure these hardships, e'en with a condottiere father to cosset you? We are scarcely past Majorca, with weeks at sea yet ahead, and I am wretched. The day is given to leaden contemplation of the horizon. The night to vexatious cold, filth, and scarcely space in which to turn around. 'Tis true I should be grateful, for at the least I have a door and a bed. The crew sleeps on straw on decks below, 'tween main and mizzen mast. Cargo is everywhere. The gun deck is covered only o'er the cannon, and rain blows in, soaking the men. The deck below is dryer but needs tallow lanterns lest the men fall on each other in the dark. The stench is worse there, from the men's bodies, from the livestock in their midst, and from the bilge. In truth, though I pity them their hardship, they are rough men, and I do so weary of seeing them urinate overboard at their whim. A relief not granted me, of course. When I decline the open air and relieve myself in the hollow-bottomed "head," on the fo'castle that empties o'er the waves, their ribald mockery meets me when I emerge.

But for all that, in these weeks at sea, something has slipped away and another thing invaded me. I no longer remember Leonora, only Lawrence Bolde, roughened, mute, and free. Can you love me in this guise?

In faith, I would I were a man, so that I may start life anew protecting you. But as I come sailing toward England, the poisonous book comes too, for the captain keeps it by him. I implored him to drown it in the sea with its last victim, but he is obdurate. If it is false, he pleads, God's majesty will prevail. But if it speaks true, then men must some day know of it.

"Will you spread this heresy?" I asked him. "No,"

he said. "I fear the Inquisitor as much as you, and
I have other sins to protect. I'll leave the revelation
for more courageous men."

Sara turned the page, then stopped reading and frowned. "Wait.
Something's strange here. Look at the difference in the writing between
the one page and the next. It's the same script, but it's suddenly all over
the place. I have an uneasy feeling about this." She resumed reading.

My darling, if by God's grace this letter comes to
you, know that the hand that writes it trembles with
the ague. I burn with fever, and an oozing wound,
and I fear my hour has come.

Corsairs attacked us off the coast of Algiers on
the hunt for hostages and slaves. Unbeknownst, their
galley followed in our wake all through the night, and
at the break of dawn, they hove beside us. I could see
them, ferocious on the riggings, bristling with sabers.
The Grazie Dei could not escape them, and it was
too late for cannon. But this captain in his wisdom
had laid in firearms for the men, not just pikes and
javelins, and so we offered strong resistance.

Armed though we were, the foe boarded us,
scimitars swinging, and clove the skulls of the first
men to oppose them. Scarcely was the battle begun,
when one of the heathens slashed my weskit, cutting
me across my ribs. Though on my knees and profusely
bleeding, I fired my single shot at the assailant's
chest, and some hand dragged me to safety.

I know not what occurred thereafter, for I was
in a stupor, but awakening, I learned the corsairs
were driven off, though at great cost. Twelve men
were lost and sixteen wounded. I am brought to my
cabin where I dare not seek mending by the ship's
physician, a man beholden to the Council of Ten.
Fanatic that he is, he would demand I be clapped in
irons for my deceit. Each day the fever worsens, and
I fear this is my punishment for bringing the book
into the world. If God should claim me before you
do, the captain will step in. He is the nearest thing

to kinsman, and he has pledged to put these letters in your hand.

Oh, my beloved Anne. Remember me this way, and know that I love you absolutely, as man or woman. I am beyond all that, as angels are, and I shall find you in this life or in the next, in whatever form is granted me. I lie here on rough boards in this rank cell, benumbed by the dull pounding of the waves. You are all that's left to comfort me. You are my velvet pillow, my perfume, my melody. And when my flickering candle sputters out, leaving me to night and thirst, you will be my sunrise and my wine.

Sara folded the four-hundred-year-old letter with tenderness and handed it back to Joanna.

"How depressing, to think she died that way, alone at sea, without reaching the woman she loved." Sara stared into the distance, as if trying to imagine the face of the dying woman. "I wish I could have been there to comfort her."

Joanna gave a tiny shrug. "People die alone all the time. Expiring in the arms of someone you love only happens in movies and operas. Real life just isn't that way."

"You're so cynical. You can't imagine surrendering to passion, of loving someone absolutely?"

"Why would I want to surrender to anything? My one experience with romance was an error in judgment. Besides, we have no idea what was going on with Anne in England. In all likelihood she was married again by then."

"I'm talking about love in general. I have mixed feelings about it being possible for me. I may never meet anyone in whose arms I'd like to die, but I do believe it happens to some people—that magical, irrational feeling that can make you crazy. Actually, longing for it can make you crazy too," Sara said wistfully. "Look at all the great art that passion inspired."

"Justification by art. That's the same bad argument Tiziana used to defend religion. It's argument by effect, and she should know better. A shame, really. She seems like the kind of woman who'd give passion a run for its money." Joanna gave a slight smile. "At least of the carnal variety."

"And you'd like to dabble a little in that 'carnal variety'?"

"I've told you, she's married. But even if I did 'dabble,' what would be wrong with that?"

"Nothing, of course. But it's just scratching an itch." Sara's voice dropped to a mutter. "It's what men do."

Joanna's expression darkened. "I find it ironic that you, of all people, are accusing me of acting like a man."

Sara looked away. "I didn't mean it as an accusation. Only that I would have thought you'd understand Leonora the way I do. And I don't appreciate your reminding me that I was a man when I've worked so hard to be a woman for you. It's cruel."

Joanna felt under attack and struck back. "It isn't cruel if it's true." She instantly regretted the barb, but it was too late. It seemed to almost echo in the room.

Sara regarded Joanna for a long moment. "You don't know what's in my mind, what makes up my identity. I thought we'd gotten past those prejudices and stereotypes, but obviously not." She stood up from the table.

"Where are you going?"

"To a concert. I'd rather spend the evening with Vivaldi." She snatched up a sweater in passing and marched from the living room to the apartment door.

Joanna remained sitting, confused by the sudden departure, and heard the apartment door close, a bit more loudly than usual. What the hell had just happened? Was that what people called a trannie fit? If so, it was unprofessional. The two of them had to work—and live— together on this project. They didn't have time for temper tantrums.

Well, it wasn't exactly a tantrum, she answered herself. More like a bit of static that hadn't quite become a quarrel. But what had they almost quarreled about? Joanna cringed inwardly, realizing it had been the most unprofessional thing of all. They'd quarreled about love.

Was it true, what Monique had said, that she was heartless? In the space of a week, two people had implied she was, and the accusation stung. Joanna brooded. She wasn't a "touchy-feely" type, she had to admit, and wouldn't recognize a cuddle if it crashed into her.

That came, she supposed, from being the only child of parents who treated her like a small adult from the time she could talk, and that was before she was two. Her precociousness made her impatient with other children, though she managed very well without them. She created a world of her own, populated first by fantastical beings, then by historical ones, Egyptians and Romans, knights and ladies, and finally, discovering more nuanced details of history, by the great names of Tudor England. While other high-school students barely recognized the name of Henry VIII, Joanna could list each of his wives along with their fates, and she read Marlowe and Shakespeare for pleasure. She fantasized sweeping along the corridors of Windsor Castle in doublet and hose and imagined herself in witty conversation with the queens of England.

"What an ass I've been," she said suddenly out loud, and actually held her forehead in her hand. "An ungrateful, insensitive ass." Sara had given her a gift without either of them recognizing it. She'd given life to language Joanna had only read or heard recited on stage in iambic pentameter. But Sara read neither sonnet nor fiction, only the real outpourings of an aching heart.

It was like listening to the lovesick Anne Boleyn.

She rummaged through the papers on the dining table and found the flyer. The Maria Formosa church. Only a short distance away, just off the Calle delle Bande. Joanna grabbed her shoulder bag and went out the door, letting it close as loudly as Sara had, the new sound canceling the old one.

❖

When Joanna arrived, she noticed how skillfully the little church had been adapted for chamber music. The performance space was a square of red carpet at the transept of the church, with chairs in a semicircle around it. The "orchestra" was in fact a sextet: five strings and a harpsichord. The audience space was full, so she couldn't possibly find Sara and sit next to her. Resigned to simply hearing the concert, Joanna found a seat at the far end of the back row.

The ensemble was already playing the Vivaldi, and from her position, Joanna could see both the musicians and most of the listeners. Through the remainder of the first movement, she peered through the mass of heads in front of her, sweeping her glance along the rows on the other side, looking for Sara.

There she sat, almost directly across the concert space in the second row, deeply engrossed in the music. She seemed to focus intently on the instruments as they came in, one after another, and answered each other in the familiar conversation of the sextet. Curious. Joanna had heard Vivaldi's *Four Seasons* a thousand times, but had never paid much attention. Now, as she watched Sara shift her gaze at each new passage, registering the way the themes leapt from instrument to instrument, Joanna became aware of the melodic dancing. It was an odd intimacy, though, to experience lovely and complex music through the sensibilities of another person,

Joanna fixed her own gaze on Sara's poignant blue eyes and tried to fathom what was going on in her mind. No way to know, but Joanna recalled her remark when she spoke of love. Mixed feelings, she'd said.

Joanna's feelings were not mixed. No, they wouldn't mix at all. They crashed against each other like waves surging from several directions.

First was her familiar attraction to a beautiful woman with just a hint of the masculine under the feminine allure, a woman who seemed to smolder with desire that had never been satisfied. That crashed immediately against the distaste at the thought of heterosex. Joanna recalled all too clearly the awkward boyfriends she'd had at university: their hard kisses, their unsubtle fondling, their penetration that quickly became a breathless pounding until it was over. No, she was done with heterosex. But from another direction came the fascination for a person who seemed utterly gentle and did not fit into any behavior category Joanna knew. And last, visualizing the trauma of Tadzio's childhood, she felt a deep tenderness for the abandoned boy who would never grow up to be a man.

Lulled away from her personal cares by the silvery staccato of the strings in Vivaldi's "Winter," Joanna began to relax. For this little hour, she could set aside whatever was happening in her life, for here was something wonderful and timeless. Here was a give-and-take as compelling as any philosopher's argument, that drew one in and satisfied the way reality rarely did. Melody and counterpoint rocked her gently, and the interplay of wordless harmonies taught her reconciliation.

Joanna was surprised when the concert ended. The audience of tourists, who had nothing to say to each other, stood up and began filing out of the church. In the thinning crowd Sara finally caught sight of her and waited at the church door.

Joanna approached with a conciliatory smile. "Nice idea, coming here. Who would have thought that something they played over and over for tourists could be so fine?"

"It *was* fine, wasn't it? I was surprised too. But let's not analyze it."

"No, you're right. Some things shouldn't be analyzed. By the way, I'm sorry if I was insensitive this evening. You've been invaluable to me, as a scholar, interpreter, and as a friend. A woman friend." She chuckled softly. "You certainly swept Alvise off his feet." In a rush of girlish solidarity, Joanna linked her arm in Sara's. "You're really a beautiful woman, you know. I'm sorry I haven't said it sooner."

Sara suppressed a smile. "Bet you say that to all the trannies."

"No, just the ones who convince me to take them to Venice."

"Mmm." Sara's smile became more visible. "Listen," she said, changing her tone. "I've been thinking all evening about Maffeo Foscari."

"Really? That's who you daydream about in concerts?"

"Yes. And somewhere between the andante and the allegro movements, I decided that he was probably a bit like you."

"Like me?"

"Yes, ambitious and tenacious."

"Ooookay. I guess I deserve that."

"It's not a reproach. Just let me get to my point. Even if he didn't have the courage to spread the message of the book, whatever it was, he *can't* have thrown it away. He was too smart, too *professional* for that. If you'd been in his place, you'd have recognized its value and held on to it."

"So what are you saying?"

"That I'm certain he kept his copy. It's in Venice someplace and we just have to find it."

"It's an exciting idea, but where would we even start? We're talking about a four-hundred-year-old book with no title that a lot of people in Venice were keen to destroy. The Ca' Foscari has no family artifacts, so we won't find it in the university library, if that's what you mean."

They were at the Ponte di Greci now and turned right along the canal, past the bridge lantern. The night had cooled and Joanna found the warmth emanating from Sara's side as comforting as her voice.

"That doesn't mean we should give up. We've discovered a ton of things already, and we have another whole week ahead of us. I think we should just sleep on it for a night and start fresh in the morning."

"Vivaldi has recharged you, hasn't he?" Joanna unlocked the iron grill that opened to the tiny courtyard of their apartment building.

"Yes, in a way. I remembered what we said at Alvise's party, that he left the church right after he was ordained. Do you suppose he read Leonora's book and secretly renounced his faith?"

"Who knows? Venice was a small city. If a copy of that book was circulating, Vivaldi would have read it. But I suppose we'll never know." Sara pulled the iron gate closed behind them with a satisfying clang.

❖

Joanna lay back against her pillow, letting the events of the day flicker through her mind. The strange visit with Arnoldi, the Vivaldi concert, the Council of Trent. She should be drawing conclusions from the information she already had, if only, as in a syllogism, she just put things in the right order. Well, no. The three-part syllogism comparison didn't really work. The puzzle trying to settle itself in her mind had half a dozen parts, and none of them fit. Were the book, Leonora's "crime," and the shipboard murder mere symptoms of the Counter-Reformation? Blow and counterblow in a centuries-long battle of ideas? Or did they signal something more pivotal? Maybe she was missing the forest for the trees.

With no hope of sleeping, she sat up and turned on the light. Her eye fell on the booklet that Tiziana had given her the first day at the library. She flipped idly through it. The usual touristy language, extolling the beauty of its interior, a brief summary in catchphrases of its history and of Cardinal Bessarion, which she knew already. Bored, she tossed it back onto the table, where it slid off and fell cover-side down. The back page, she could see, listed the contributors.

Annoyed at the disorder she'd caused, she got out of bed and picked up the pamphlet, bringing it back into the light. The back page was in small print, perfect for helping her fall asleep, she thought, and she forced herself to plow through it.

Venice's main library now contains approximately 750,000 volumes and around 13,500 manuscripts, most of them Greek. The main donors to the collection during the 16th and 17th centuries are 1589: Melchiorre Guilandino di Marienburg (2,200 printed books); 1595: Jacopo Contarini (175 manuscripts and 1500 printed works). In 1619 Girolamo Fabrici D'Acquapendente donated 13 volumes with precious anatomical illustrations; 1624: Giacomo Gallicio (20 Greek manuscripts); 1734: Gian Battista Recanati (216 manuscripts); 1790: Family Foscari (950 manuscripts and printed works); 1794: Amedeo Svajer (340 manuscripts, among them the diaries of Marco Polo). In the following century—

Joanna stopped and did a mental double take. *1790: Family Foscari.*

"Yessss," she muttered gleefully to herself.

She threw back the covers and went to the bedroom where the door was slightly ajar. The light was out but surely Sara wasn't yet asleep. Joanna tapped lightly on the door.

"Mmm? C'min?" Sara pulled herself up and clicked on the bedside lamp. "What's wrong?"

Joanna marched in and sat down on the edge of the mattress. "The Foscari library is at the Marciana," she said triumphantly, and dropped the pamphlet onto the bed covers.

Sara squinted at the booklet for a moment, as if trying to read it in the dim light. Then she seemed to waken fully. "Well done, Joanna. Oh, bravo! Aren't we just the hottest detectives in Venice?"

"We are." Joanna placed a sudden kiss on Sara's cheek. Then, grinning with satisfaction, she marched back to the doorway.

"Won't we need a title to find it?" Sara asked.

"One step at a time. We'll work on that one tomorrow," Joanna said over her shoulder, then padded back to her couch and relaxed slowly into the sweet slumber of victory.

She had just fallen asleep when she felt a hand on her shoulder. She struggled to consciousness and saw the moonlit form of Sara standing over her. "Something wrong?"

"The title. I think I can find it. Do you have the telephone number of the Ca' Foscari?"

"You want to call them? In the middle of the night?"

"Maybe the night watchman will answer. If he does, it could save us a trip over there tomorrow morning."

Joanna thumbed through her notebook until she found it. "I understand your enthusiasm, but this is really a wild shot, don't you think?"

Without replying, Sara dialed the number and held the phone to her ear, nodding faintly and whispering, "Answer. Aaanswer."

Wrapped in her blanket on her sofa, Joanna watched, skeptical. "What are you trying to accomplish by—"

"Hello?" Sara held up a hand to silence her. "Is that you, Rosso?" Brief pause. "Yes, I know what time it is. I'm sorry, but I hoped you'd be there. Do you remember me? Silvio Falier's daughter. We spoke in the entrance hall a few days ago." Another pause, more nodding.

"Oh, good, I'm glad. Look, I know this sounds strange, but can you do me a favor? You know the two paintings in the entry hall? I'm interested in the one of the man holding the book and the mask. I need to know what's written on the cover of the book in his hand. Yes, of course, I'll wait."

They looked at each other silently. Two minutes, three minutes. Joanna resisted tapping her fingers. Then Sara took up a pen and paper and began to write.

"M-a-t-t. Fourteen…six. That's perfect! Thank you, Rosso. You've been very helpful. I'll be sure to tell Signor Morosini what you've done for us. Good night now."

Even by the soft light of the night lamp Joanna could see how flushed with excitement Sara was. "Will you tell me now what that was all about?"

Sara held up the piece of paper with the letters and numbers. "Remember the portrait of Maffeo Foscari? He's holding a book. A Bible. I remembered that the cover had some ciphers. The painter took the trouble to indicate chapter and verse of what Foscari was reading. Why would he do that?"

"Maybe it was arbitrary, just to show it was a Bible."

"That makes no sense. He could simply have painted 'Bible.' But maybe…" She paused, as if letting the thought percolate up on its own strength. "Think about it. Why would he have wanted a Bible painted in his hands in the first place? We know from Leonora's letter that he was nearly an apostate by the end of that voyage. So, maybe, Foscari himself wanted to leave a message in the painting, a message for some 'courageous' person to discover. Maybe the Bible chapter and verse notations, which are *completely* superfluous in his portrait, are supposed to tell us something."

"I'm already ahead of you," Joanna said, as she threw back her blanket and started toward the bookshelf by the fireplace. "We have a Bible."

"Bring it here and let's see what we come up with." Joanna handed over the little leather-bound volume and Sara sat down on the sofa with it under the light. "Matthew, chapter 14, verse 6," she mumbled, thumbing through the leather-bound volume. "Here it is, Gospel of Matthew."

> But on Herod's birthday, the daughter of Herodias danced before them: and pleased Herod. Whereupon he promised, with an oath, to give her whatsoever she would ask of him. But she, being instructed before by her mother, said: Give me here on a charger the head of John the Baptist. And the king was struck sad: yet because of his oath, and for them that sat with him at table, he commanded it to be given. And he sent, and beheaded John in the prison. And his head was brought on a charger: and it was given to the damsel, and she brought it to her mother.

"The story of Salome," Joanna murmured, trying to puzzle things out. "The image that Leonora talked about. The mosaic in the baptistery. But what's the connection with the book? *Is* there a connection?"

"I bet there is. I bet Foscari couldn't bear to hide the heretical book completely. I think he wanted it to be found, and this was his way of telling people what it was called."

"What? 'The Gospel of Matthew'?"

"No. Salome. Something about Salome. The woman carrying the head."

Joanna looked over at the folder with Leonora's letters. "No, the woman carrying the mask. The Mask of Salome."

"Yes."

CHAPTER SEVENTEEN

Joanna checked her watch as they came out of the Calle Canonica onto the piazzetta. One minute to nine. They hurried along the façade of the San Marco Basilica, threading through the loose mass of early-morning tourists. Just then the chimes sounded from the bell tower behind them. In spite of their hurry, they both made an about-face and watched as the two verdigris copper Moors hammered out the hour on the five-hundred-year-old bell.

They smiled at each other. It seemed a good sign. But as they reached the entrance of the doge's palace, someone called, "Signorinas! How nice to see you both."

Joanna stopped, annoyed now at the second delay. Still waving, a plump red-haired man with a receding chin strolled toward them. "I hope I'm not disturbing you," he said, offering his hand. "Orazio Barbieri. We met at Signor Alvise's party a few nights ago. Perhaps you don't recognize me without a mask. I was Il Dottore, the Plague Doctor."

Joanna forced polite laughter. "Sorry. No, I didn't recognize you. Uh, good morning." She hoped he would sense that they were in a hurry and be brief in his small talk. Though, as she recalled, sensitivity had not been one of his virtues.

"So, are you sightseeing today?" He came around in front of them, blocking their way.

"In fact, no. We're on our way to work," Sara said.

"Oh, well, no one is ever in a hurry to go to work." He chuckled at his own witticism. "So, how's the research on Pietro Arnoldi going? Was Professor Morosini's book any help?"

"Yes, it was. Thank you for asking."

"Such a sad story, the Arnoldi family, isn't it? And to think that the Foscari family was involved as well. Isn't it amazing the things you find out with a little study?"

Joanna tried to be polite without actually engaging in conversation. "Yes, and each new bit of information leads to other avenues. We're just on our way to the library now." She looked at her watch as conspicuously as possible, then started walking slowly, drawing him along with them.

"What a pity. I was hoping to invite you for a morning coffee." He came around and stood in their path again. "I believe I might be able to contribute something to your investigation."

"Oh, really?" Joanna halted. "What would that be?"

"If you'll join me for some coffee, I will explain it to you." He extended one hand toward the café immediately in front of them on the piazzetta. Only a few of the tables had customers and waiters stood by prepared to offer instant service. Joanna hesitated.

Sara saved the situation. "Why don't you do that, Joanna? In the meantime, I'll look in the catalog for our titles. By the time you arrive, I'll be able to tell you if anything matches our…speculation."

Barbieri seemed unhappy about the proposed separation. "Oh, I am of course inviting both of you. Such lovely company, and I think what I have to say would interest you too, Signorina Falier."

"Ah, no. That's quite all right." Sara was already several paces away now. "Enjoy your coffee. I'll just be plugging along at our usual table." With a wave that left no room for argument, she hurried toward the library entrance.

Shrugging off his partial defeat, Barbieri pulled out a plastic chair from one of the tables and signaled the waiter. "Two coffees, please."

Joanna sat down without undoing her jacket, making it clear she didn't intend to stay long. "So, what exactly do you think would be of interest to our investigation, Signor Barbieri?"

He took out a pack of cigarettes, patted two of them through its corner opening, and offered one to Joanna. She signaled "No, thank you."

He lit one for himself, inhaled deeply, and blew smoke out to the side. "Let me first explain who I am." From the same pocket as he had drawn the cigarette pack, he brought up a business card and presented it to her.

"'Major Orazio Barbieri, Carabinieri, National Heritage

Command,'" Joanna read out loud. "Very impressive. I had no idea there was a special branch, but it makes sense. But how, may I ask, does this relate to our research project?"

"It's about the book, of course," he announced. "The heretical translation that was the cause of the entire…well…disaster, I suppose you would say." The coffee service arrived and, transferring his cigarette to his left hand, he dropped two sugar cubes into his cup and stirred them gently. "Frankly, I don't think it's worth all your efforts. It seems a woman as intelligent as you could be researching something of, let us say, nobler quality."

"I'm not sure what you mean by 'nobler quality.' Do you know something about the book that I don't know? Its title? Its content? Why didn't you mention this the other night at the party?"

"Forgive me, but I had quite forgotten about it. One doesn't walk around every day thinking about sixteenth-century events. Only after I returned home and mulled over what we discussed at the table did I recall something that I had heard my grandfather say."

"Your grandfather?" Joanna sipped her coffee, which was in fact quite good, or maybe it was the fresh morning air and the sunshine on their table where she, fortunately, sat upwind of his smoke stream. "He knew about the book too? That seems rather strange."

"Not at all. You know, these stories float around in a family, sometimes for generations, until they become legends. In any case, it never seemed important. But then you mentioned it and the story came back to me."

"And what is that story, Signor Barbieri?"

"According to my family, a woman named Leonora was arrested for printing an offensive book, but she escaped and fled Venice. But, you see, the book was mere pornography, of a blasphemic nature, but pornography nonetheless."

Joanna set down her cup. "Excuse me? Pornographic blasphemy?"

"To be sure. We discussed the other night the way Carnival brought out the basest natures in men. In the same way, some presses at that time catered to the most vile tastes imaginable. Oh, yes. Obscenity that rivals anything being printed today, but taking biblical themes and persons as their subjects."

"And the book we are looking for is such a thing? Can you tell me its title?"

"Alas, no. But you should know that the entire output of this press was apparently of the most perverse nature. When all is said and done, whatever its title, such a book is not worthy of your investigation. It would serve you much better to simply focus on the justifiable closing of the press and the escape of the offender by merchant ship as one of the more colorful events in Venetian history. The book itself no longer exists, and if it did, I'm certain it would disappoint you."

Finishing her coffee, Joanna weighed the revelation he had just presented. It weighed, she decided, rather little.

"I appreciate having your insight into the subject, but I suppose, given your position, I should also ask if there is a legal problem involved in our research. Are we transgressing in any way against Italian law, that is, as it relates to the National Heritage?"

Barbieri stubbed out his cigarette. "Uh, no. Of course not. Research is never prohibited, is welcome, in fact. Though any artifacts you might discover would of course be the property of the Italian state. My remarks here are of a personal nature, out of a concern that in your fervor to uncover historical scandals, that you might, uh, jeopardize yourselves professionally."

Joanna was silent, trying to make sense of their entire conversation. Was it a veiled threat, intended to keep them away from the primary object of their search? Or simply a cavalier gesture from someone who knew more than he was telling? All she knew was that she didn't trust the man or his message.

"Thank you, Signor Barbieri, for that information and for your concern. I'm sure it will help us see the larger picture." She stood up and offered her hand. "Thank you also for the coffee." The handshake was quick and she backed away before he could engage her any further. "I'm afraid Sara will wonder what's kept me, so I'd better be hurrying along. Thank you again."

With a wave as silencing as Sara's had been earlier, she left him standing, like a failed salesman, in front of his two empty coffee cups.

❖

Forty paces brought her into the main reading room of the Libreria Marciana. It seemed brighter today, the morning sunshine that came into the great hall seemed more intense than the last time, as if their new knowledge had added to the light. But Sara wasn't there. The half dozen heads that bent over books were all male. No sign of Tiziana either. Frustration heated Joanna's face.

The catalog room, then. Though if Sara was still searching for titles after forty-five minutes, it wasn't a good sign. Joanna stepped into the double chamber of catalog drawers which, in contrast to the reading room, was in deep shadow. It was also empty. Joanna's chest felt heavy, her senses deadened. Things couldn't be going well. The faint residue of coffee that she still tasted was suddenly sour.

At the sound of shuffled feet, she turned. Sara stood silhouetted in the doorway, backlit by the radiance of the reading room. Her very posture, one elbow raised and resting against the door frame, was cocky, pregnant with announcement like the angel Gabriel. In her left hand she held a small square of paper.

Joanna murmured, "You did it, didn't you?"

Instead of replying, Sara stepped closer, grasped Joanna's hand, and placed the piece of paper on her palm. It was an order slip. "This is the copy. Tiziana has the original."

Joanna read the title as if it were line of scripture. *La Maschera di Salome.*

With unaccustomed joy, she threw one arm around Sara's neck and embraced her tightly. "You were right, you sly dog."

"We both were right. Together, we make one hell of a scholar, don't we? Tiziana's bringing it from the other building right now."

"Does she know what it is?"

"I don't think so. *We* don't know what it is. Yet. Let's just stay calm, okay?"

"Calm. Right." Joanna paced in the small space between the Bessarion statue and the first table. "Did the card say what press or publisher?"

"No, just 'Foscari Collection' and a catalog number."

"Did she say it would take long?"

Sara stopped Joanna's on one of her trajectories. "Well, I gave it to her over half an hour ago. And, no, she didn't say how long. She might not even find it."

"Don't say that."

"Sorry, but things do get—"

"Here it is," a cheerful voice behind them said. Tiziana came through the narrow Staff Only door carrying a tiny book, no larger than the average business calendar. Joanna's first reaction was disappointment. This couldn't possibly be what they were looking for. A booklet that size couldn't spark mutinies, murders, inquisitions, Church councils. She held out her hand.

"Is this what you're looking for? Leonora's infamous book?" Tiziana asked.

"We don't know. Could just be another dead end," Joanna said noncommittally. "As soon as we've checked through it, we'll give you a report."

"Yes, do let me know," Tiziana said lightly, and returned to her office. As soon as she was out of the reading room, they sat down, side by side.

The book was bound in leather, and the spine held the same title as the catalog card, *La Maschera di Salome*. It was clear, however, that the person who had bound it had never intended for the book to be opened, for the inside page was different.

A sudden frisson went through Joanna as she read the title page.

Sarah, figlio di Dio.

"*Sarah, Son of God*," she translated unnecessarily, then turned the first page reverently. "We're like children with a forbidden book," she murmured.

"It *was* a forbidden book."

"Amazing. It's less than a hundred pages. No larger than a breviary. Here." Joanna slid the book toward Sara. "You're the one who knows about early Italian printing. What do you make of it?"

Sara held the book as delicately as Joanna had and turned back to the title page. "First of all, it's an *octavo*. That is, the press printed sixteen pages on a single large piece of paper, then folded it down into a section. That was pretty common in the creation of small books. This one's sort of odd, though. It's dated 1560, when books were pretty modern-looking, but this one has a lot of earlier features. It looks like the Tratti Audaci was a small press and still used many of the old techniques."

"Like what?"

"Well, for starters, they're still printing the entire text in Italic, while the big presses were already switching over to Roman. It's sharper and easier to read, so allows smaller type and more lines to a page. This one has only about twenty lines per page, requiring, of course, more paper. The chapter headings are printed in red, a mimicking of the old manuscripts. And look here at where the word is hyphenated from one line to the next. It's broken according to line length, instead of by syllable."

"The printer's device in the center of the title page looks modern, though," Joanna remarked. "A simple red triangle with the two letters intertwined. I like it."

Sara turned the fragile pages carefully, not fully opening the book, so as to protect the spine as she leafed through the volume. "Ah, I see now. About two-thirds of it is explanation of where the original codex was found, by whom, etc. The translation doesn't begin until…let's see, page seventy. The end is also a set of notes. The actual translated text is"—she compared beginning and ending pages—"only fifteen pages."

"Barbieri just informed me this morning it was a dirty book. Let's see what sixteenth-century pornographic heresy looks like. Can you do a superficial run-through and translate as you go?"

Holding the book open at a 45-degree angle, Sara glanced over the first page. "It'll be slow, but I think I can. Let's sit where no one can hear us."

They installed themselves in the farthest corner, and Sara studied the first few pages without speaking, nodding as she read.

"So? What does it say?"

"First of all, Hakim Yaakub definitely did this translation. It seems to be all his work. On these pages, he gives his own credentials as a scholar, how he came to know Aramaic, and so forth. Mmm. Wow, Leonora never mentioned that."

"Mentioned what? Stop thinking out loud and talk to *me*."

"Oh, sorry. According to this, he was a mathematician and a poet and apparently a teacher of geometry at the court of Suleiman the Magnificent."

"A revered scholar," Joanna said with soft amazement. "And the poor man was reduced to cringing in fear of the lowlife sailors on the Grazie Dei."

Sara moved on to the next chapter and read silently for a few moments. "Here he gives a detailed account of how workers came across the codex in a clay cylinder while they were repairing the marble floor in an ancient house in Caesarea. He seems keen to provide verifiable evidence of the work's authenticity. He gives the complete names of all the workmen and where each one came from. I can't imagine a fiction writer would ever bother to do that."

She turned a few pages past drawings and maps of the vicinity.

"Here's even an engraving here. That must have cost him time and money to have made. It's a floor plan of the house, showing where they found the cylinder. Oh, Joanna, this is definitely *not* a work of fiction."

"Any information about Salome?"

"Just wait, let me look. Ah, yes, here's a brief history of the Herodian dynasty, who married whom, who killed whom, etc. I wonder if he got any of this from Josephus, or whether he had other sources."

"What about Salome?"

"I'm looking. I'm looking. Okay, here's a rundown on the probable owner of the codex, that is, the original recipient."

"Recipient? You mean it was a letter?"

"Something like that. It seems to not be a journal or commentary, but a confession. From Salome to her mother, Herodias."

"A confession? Oh, right. Leonora mentioned that. Can you skip over the notes and read a little of the confession itself? What was she confessing to?"

"Okay, it begins here." Sara's voice changed, going up a note in pitch, as she began to read the text of the codex.

Dearest Mother,

A black disk passed over the face of the sun today, benighting the sky."Behold, the end cometh!" they cried, that saw it, and though no man knows its meaning, each one took it as a sign. For me it was a rebuke, that I had abandoned a mother, and so I am resolved to clear my conscience before heaven and before you.

I am in Rome, held captive with scores of other Christians. We are in a cage nigh unto the arena. The Romans lead some of us forth each day in chains before the multitude. They cast us before wild beasts, or burn us as torches for their amusement. I do confess it, I am sore afraid.

I felt a brief rejoicing when Menassah found me, even in these final hours. He cannot save me, nor will I forsake my brethren, but it was a gift to see him and to learn that you still live. He called out to me with my old name for he knew not that I am Sarah, but I saw at once it was my old teacher. I beseeched him to bring me ink and parchment, and straightway he did, and made generous payment to the Roman jailor to let me write to you.

I do not think you will shed a tear for me, nor do I seek for pity, only reconciliation, after lo these twenty years. You are my mother, who bore me, and though you did use me for your gain, I forgive you. I am without bitterness, and offer only love. Love is what I would have in my soul when my body shall be torn from it.

Behold, I will tell you a wondrous thing, of what you set in motion in a single fit of spite. You could not know, near a lifetime hence, that you flung a pebble and it brought forth a landslide. The earth still rumbles from it, and I know not how great it will yet swell.

All this that I tell came from your fury at John, he who was called "the Baptist." He was the cause, but I was ripe for it long before. For you tried to make me a woman when I was still a child. Do you remember? Scarcely had my tiny breasts begun to swell when you dressed me like a harlot, in transparent veils. I remember with repugnance the captains and courtiers you paraded me before, seeking a husband for me, offering up my virginity to whosoever gave you political advantage. Thus it was to be a woman, you said, and though I did wish to be a woman, I abhorred to become one in the bed of a stranger.

Herod cast his eyes on me as well, though that stirred no reproach from you. No, the problem in your marriage was not your husband's appetites, but the fact he was your first husband's brother, and it shamed you that John preached your marriage was an offense to Jewish law. Thus, the timid tetrarch, in dread of usurpation, arrested John for fear the Baptist, on those grounds, would stir unrest against him.

Bethink you still the day the soldiers brought him to the palace and cast him into the cistern

awaiting Herod's judgment? Nor did he beg for
mercy, nor receive it, but called out from the pit
his condemnation. I was but fourteen and though
I was tall and slender and looked for all the world
like a boy, I knew naught of men. So I cajoled the
guards to let me attend the "wild man" in his cell.
They had torn off his leather raiment and bound
him with chains against the wall, and saw no harm
to let the daughter of Herod affront him.

He was magnificent.

Yet while I feared him, I was bewitched, for
he was the first man I had ere beheld naked. He
was muscular and well formed. A line of hair grew
down the middle of him from his throat to his sex,
so large and threatening I could not take my eyes
from it. His voice, like unto the growl of a desert
lion, held me rapt as well.

"The Kingdom of God is at hand," he
proclaimed. "There comes one whose sandals I am
not worthy to unlace."

"But you call the people unto you to baptize
them," I said. "Why press them into water? Is it
not enough to prophesy?" Forthwith he answered,
"That their wickedness be drowned as in the
Flood, and they might rise anew, for him that
follows me."

I bade him look upon me, but he would not.
And when I approached him, he cried out, "Hast
thou not heard the fluttering of the wings of
the Angel of Death?" Calling me "Daughter of
Babylon," he demanded the guards take me from
him.

Recall that Herod's birthday followed on the
morrow, and you enjoined me to dance before
him. I did so, obedient, turning and leaping in the
manner of the slaves who entertained him. He was
well pleased, as were his lords and captains who
celebrated with him.

Would that the night had been over then
and I had gone back to the women's quarters.

But Herod stood up, and with great show, in the presence of men, he offered me anything in his kingdom. Surely he bethought him that a young girl's desires would be meager. But he had not reckoned with your ambition.

There was retribution in your heart ere I danced, was there not? For, seeing Herod's hungry eyes, you had a demand ready for me to carry to him. And I did carry it, speaking the monstrous words.

"Give us the head of John the Baptist."

Straightway I repented of it, but it was too late. The slave went into the courtyard and descended into the black cistern with sword and lantern. In the silence that followed, there was no fluttering of angels' wings, only of the feathers of my dancing fan, for I was the Angel of Death. Anon, the bronze doors opened and Herod's slave marched solemnly into the dining hall with the silver charger held out before him. Thereon lay the head of John the Baptist.

Sara looked up from the page. "Well, there's a teen confession you don't read every day."

Joanna stared, incredulous, at the page. "Do you suppose it's true? And why did it constitute heresy?"

Sara shrugged. "I don't know. Maybe the heretical stuff comes later. As for being true, why shouldn't it be? Who would bother to make up something like that? It's not like people were writing historical fiction in those days."

"It should be easy enough to find out if it's authentic. Renaissance scientists knew what eclipses were, but they couldn't calculate them backward in time. If we can verify that an eclipse actually happened and was visible over Italy, the year Salome said it had been, that would at least prove that the confession originates in the first century."

Sara persisted. "But if it *is* a sixteenth-century fiction, couldn't Hakim—or whoever else—have known about the eclipse from ancient sources? One of the Roman historians, for example?"

"Then he would have to have read Pliny's *Natural History*. As far as I know, Pliny is the only Roman historian who recorded natural events like that. It seems far-fetched, though. Why would he bother?"

Sara thought for a moment. "There must be a book here that will give us the dates of past eclipses. An atlas or physics book or something."

Joanna stood up from the table. "I'll ask Tiziana."

While she waited, Sara reread the last several pages, to make sure she hadn't mistranslated anything. No. The Italian was clear. It was still possible there were errors in the translation. Hakim could have misunderstood the Aramaic. Or even perpetrated the fraud himself. But only if he knew about an eclipse during Nero's reign twenty-some years after the Crucifixion.

"That was easier than I thought." Joanna was back with a ponderous atlas and a smaller book, bound in linen. "There's a table of eclipses in the back of this one. Don't ask me how the scientists figure them out, but they can."

She leafed through the pages to the tables at the end. "Here's the list of the first-century eclipses. Look, they even indicate their paths. Amazing." She ran her finger down a column of dates. "February, 44 AD—North Atlantic and British Isles; August, 45 AD—Central Africa; July, 46 AD—Northern Siberia; April, 55 AD—Southern Italy."

"That's the one." Sara peered over her shoulder. "AD 55. During the reign of Nero. That's got to be the one she is writing about. Fantastic. Now we just have to find out if the writer read Pliny."

"My thought exactly, and that's why I brought his book." Joanna held it up. "The *Naturalis Historia*, by Pliny the Elder. It describes the eclipse of AD 55. That's what scholars in Renaissance Italy would have referred to."

Sara looked suddenly defeated. "So the writer of the confession *could* have taken the eclipse information from Pliny."

Joanna smiled. "No. He couldn't. We have an exact date for Leonora's printing, 1560. According to the preface here, Pliny's work wasn't printed until 1669. So whoever wrote the confession can only have known about the eclipse by seeing it firsthand."

"Well done! All right, then. Let's see what our Salome has to say that was so terrible that the Council of Trent had to reaffirm the entire

Church doctrine." Sara shoved aside the two reference books and took up the tiny translation of Salome's confession.

"That looks promising. Is it the book you've been looking for?" someone asked from behind them.

"Tiziana." Joanna glanced up, curiously guilt-ridden, and nodded cautiously. "We think so."

"Oh, that's wonderful. You've found your grail. I'm so happy for you. But if the book is so rare and precious, you really should be working with a photocopy rather than the original. I'm sure you'll want to study it on your own time, and you know I can't release the original to you."

"Yes, of course. You're quite right. We were about to do that."

Tiziana held out her hand. "I'll take it over there for you and tell them to do a rush job. Then you can have your copies in an hour. I know this is important to you."

"Ah, yes. Fine." Joanna handed over the small volume with only the faintest shadow of anxiety as it slid from her grasp. "Shall we wait here?"

"There's really no point. Why don't you go have lunch and it will be ready when you come back."

"Yes. Well, that's a good idea." Joanna didn't know what to do with her hands that were suddenly bookless. "We'll come back in an hour," she said, wishing it could have been fifteen minutes or ten, or none. Maybe they could stay and monitor the photocopying.

"Go on," Tiziana said cheerfully. "Go celebrate with wine and something good. You deserve it."

Joanna felt a bit foolish for her anxieties. "Yes, a glass of wine is in order," she said as Tiziana herded them from the reading room.

❖

"That may have been the longest hour of my life," Sara said as they reentered the library fifty minutes later. "If the copying isn't done, I'm just going to stand there and watch until it is."

"That's odd." Joanna checked her watch. "The copy room is closed. Do you suppose the copyist is having lunch?"

Sara was already chewing her lip. "That's annoying. I don't want to seem bitchy, but we were promised our book in an hour. Where's Tiziana? She'll know what the delay is."

The librarian's office was also closed.

"Damn. This is frustrating," Joanna groused. "If they were all going to lunch, they should have told us. I hate just standing around not knowing what's going on."

"Maybe they're in one of the restaurants, eating. Do you think it would be rude to track them down and find out when they plan to come back?"

Joanna was past annoyance. "Let's go look. I'm feeling some rude coming on."

As they stepped through the door of the library they met Tiziana coming from the piazzetta. Joanna tried to remove all petulance from her voice. "Oh, hello. We…uh…noticed that the copy room was closed and were just wondering…"

Tiziana's expression was solemn. "I'm sorry."

Sorry? The single word sent a jolt of dread through Joanna. Sorry didn't belong in that scenario. "What do you mean?"

"The book. I can't let you have it." Tiziana avoided eye contact. "I've sent it by courier to Dr. Morosini, as he required."

"What?" Joanna stammered, with increasing anger and alarm. "Whatever for? Why should he be involved?"

"Those were Dr. Morosini's instructions. He was sure you would never find a copy of it, but if you did, I was to send it to him immediately. At this point it's out of my hands. You must talk to him, though I doubt it will do you any good." She looked away again. "I'm sorry," she repeated. "Really, I am."

Then she walked past them into the library, leaving them stupefied in the doorway.

Chapter Eighteen

"Come in, ladies. Sit down. There's no reason we can't be comfortable while we talk." Morosini pulled out two chairs with the unctuous chivalry of a victor.

Joanna wasted no time. "You know why we're here, of course."

"Yes, I do. And I congratulate you." He sat down at his desk and Joanna saw that he had set the precious book in front of him, as if to taunt them. Morosini laid his hand on it, asserting ownership. "Foolish of us not to imagine that Maffeo Foscari had hidden one of the copies in his own library. And it lay in our own Libreria Marciana all this time."

He caressed the cover with his thumb. "Do you know what this is, Dr. Valois?"

"Yes, a translation of a confession by the biblical Salome. We read the first few pages. Why have you confiscated it?"

"Ah, I see you did not read through to the end. To be sure, I have not read it either, but I know it is more than the scribbled regrets of a foolish runaway. It is a description of the Crucifixion."

"We thought it might be something like that. But that still doesn't explain why you took it."

Morosini held the book between thumb and forefinger, examining its size. "Ironic, isn't it? All that bloodshed on the *Grazie Dei* over such a little book."

"How do you know about the bloodshed? We never discussed bloodshed with you."

"I know a great many things about this work, Dr. Valois. You see, your interest and your little academic project are only recent perturbations in a long stream of events. The Morosini family, on the other hand, has been the book's guardian for four hundred years. My ancestor Vettor Morosini was present on the *Grazie Dei* when the books were seized from the heretic transporting them to Constantinople. We had our own copy for several centuries, until we surrendered it to the Holy Office for safekeeping during the wave of anticlericalism following Napoleon. A shame, because I've always had a great curiosity about it."

"Then you know about the murder of Hakim."

"Was that the Jew's real name? My family has recorded it merely as Leon. In any case, yes. In the confusion onboard, no one was really sure how many copies were saved, or by whom. Vettor Morosini had the foresight to take two copies, however, and, upon returning from Corfu, he presented one of them to the Bishop of Venice, along with a full report of the unfortunate incident at sea. It emerged soon after, that others had also obtained copies on the same occasion, and these persons were also summoned to the Vatican where they and their descendants were put under oath to be forever watchful for more copies."

"And you've kept it a secret all these centuries?"

"Yes, the Morosini have been faithful to their oath for these four hundred years. The others have proven to be of somewhat weaker character."

"If you're so obsessed with concealing it, you must believe it to be authentic."

"Authentic or not, it has the power to do great harm. For two thousand years Christians have died for the faith and fought crusades for it. Do you think for a moment we would allow you to discredit all that by publicizing this depravity?" He strode toward a wall safe on a low shelf behind his desk and deposited the volume into it. The key went into his pocket.

Joanna stood up. "Don't you think it's too late to simply hide the book? We know now that it exists, even if we don't know why you find it so dangerous. But the news of your hiding it could be embarrassing."

"Without evidence, your assertions will sound rather foolish. The ravings of two silly academics trying to make a heroine out of a pornographer. I suggest you save yourself a lot of trouble and simply consider your research finished. If you return home now with your letters and your tales of the *Grazie Dei*, you can have a nice book out by next year."

"You actually think you can brush off a discovery of this magnitude?" Sara asked.

"In fact, I do." Morosini looked past them to two burly students who had just come into the office from the corridor. "Carlo, Bruno, please escort these two ladies to the entrance. Don't let them stop for anything or come back into the building, regardless of what they tell you. They are foreign journalists trying to create a scandal."

"But—"

"Good day, ladies." Joanna felt a hand touch her elbow directing her toward the door.

❖

Vincent Morosini caressed the cover of the book, hesitating as if he were about to enter a pornographic movie theater, for he had been inculcated since childhood with the idea that the book was obscene. Though he knew it held a heresy disputing the divinity of Jesus, he had wondered what that could have been. Most of his relatives were dismissive of the family obligation, calling it a legend, but Vincent relished the idea of such a sacred mission. It smacked of Teutonic knights and Crusader kings and it befit a family as noble as his. The Morosini had given statesmen, generals, and admirals to the Venetian Republic and cardinals to the Church. Eight times a Morosini had served the Republic, four times as doge and four times, by marriage, as dogesse.

Vettor Morosini had taken the Oath of Guardianship, along with the Bracco and Barbieri families, but unlike them, he had marked the occasion by adding the crusader's helmet to the family crest and remained vigilant his entire life. A grandson had counseled Vivaldi after the musician's contamination by the book and destroyed the offending volume that had fallen into his hands.

Now it was Vincent's turn, and he had dutifully monitored journals of freethinkers to uncover anything new in their attacks on Christianity. In almost half a century of vigilance, he'd found no references to new biblical documentation, nothing to upset the four-hundred-year-old Council of Trent decree.

He had never married and felt no urge to do so. Rather, he consecrated his life, not to the priesthood, but to scholarship of the history of the most pious of cities. He was proud of every church and palazzo, of every song and prayer that had risen up from its citizens, its gondoliers, its musicians. For him, watching for the book was just another way of caring for his beloved, unfathomably blessed Venice, the Serenissima.

When Alvise informed him of the two Americans and their newly found letters, it was like a trumpet call, and he suspected, even hoped, that they referred to the heresy he was on guard against. He planned first to simply join forces with Bracco and Barbieri to thwart their plans, to remove all documents relating to the event and let their research quickly reach a dead end. Bracco immediately concealed the ship's log, and it would not have been difficult to throw up other obstacles.

But gradually he had reversed his position. Bracco and Barbieri might be content to prevent the discovery, but it seemed more in keeping with the holy task the pope had laid upon the Morosini to actually lay hands on the remaining copy and destroy it. He had also to admit to a morbid fascination with evil and the titillation at the thought of actually confronting it.

He knew full well that the Congregation for the Doctrine of the Faith was the modern descendant of the Inquisition and, by reporting to them, he was in effect a modern inquisitor. But even they had not taken him seriously. Well, they'd stop smirking now, for he had been successful. Miraculously successful. Surely God had guided events this way into his hands.

He stroked the book again, preparing to uncover the abomination, to expose himself to its corruption. Then, after announcing his victory to Bracco and Barbieri, he would present the book, with some grand gesture, to the Vatican. In return he would perhaps ask for an endowment to the university, under his name, of course.

He opened the cover with a slight frisson…of what? Shame? No. It was more a sense of heroic self-sacrifice.

CHAPTER NINETEEN

Joanna sat brooding at the dining table, playing out the events of the last few days in her mind's eye. How could they have misread Vincent Morosini so completely? How could they have not sensed him lying, monitoring their progress, biding his time? They had saved him every labor, even that of ensnaring them, for they had simply handed the book over. They had held it in their hands, then lost it. Failure, humiliation, ridicule, snatched from the mouth of success. Nauseous, she pressed her palms against her closed eyes.

Sara paced around the living room giving voice to their frustration. "The bastard. So smug. After all our work. We should have copied it right away, ourselves. Then he could have had his damned book and we'd have had it too."

Joanna stood up and went to stand in front of one of the library shelves. "If only we could steal it, just for an hour, to copy it. Then if we can prove that it's authentic—and given the eclipse reference, we can—maybe we could embarrass the city of Venice into releasing the original for study, or at least admitting that it exists."

"Copy it? How? Go to the archives and photocopy it?"

"That's one possibility. But we also have a perfectly good camera here. We can photograph every page in half an hour. The volume is only about a hundred pages long. We just need to get our hands on it before Morosini gets rid of it."

Sara stopped pacing. "How can we be sure he hasn't already destroyed it?"

Joanna shook her head. "A four-hundred-year-old Venetian book, and most likely the only one left of its kind? If a hundred generations of Morosini have been sworn to find it, then surely the Vatican is aware of it. So he'll probably contact the Curia first and either transfer the volume to Rome or get approval to destroy it. That gives us, well, at least tonight to get hold of it. The more time that passes, though, the more likely he'll have moved it."

Sara crossed her arms in resolution. "Then we have to act tonight."

"And do what?"

"Break into the Ca' Foscari and get the book back. For just an hour."

Now Joanna paced as well. "But how do we do that? We need an ally. Tiziana could probably get the key, but she's the one who betrayed us in the first place."

"What about Rosso? Would he help? I could try my charms on him again." Hope had reentered Sara's voice.

"Only if he decides he likes you better than his job. But even if he did help us get inside, that doesn't get us into the safe. People don't usually leave the key to their strongbox with the night janitor." Joanna tapped her knuckles against her lips, as if to prod her brain to come up with something.

"What about Alvise? He knows that office. It used to be his."

"Alvise?" Sara moaned. "I don't want anything to do with him."

"Of course the man's a fool and a sleaze. But consider the stakes. We might still be able to use him." She paused to let the thought gel. "Besides, can you think of anyone else?"

Sara covered her eyes, then uncovered them, paced, stopped, and ran her hand through already disheveled hair. "All right. Telephone him."

"Right. But let's figure out how to approach him. We can't call and say, 'Hello, we need help in a burglary. Wanna come along?' We need to be a little more subtle." She stared off into space for a beat. "What about inviting him for dinner this evening? Even after the Carnival fiasco, I bet he still likes you enough to agree. The worst that can happen is that we're back to square one."

Sara sighed. "All right. But give me time to put on a rubber suit in case he tries to put his sweaty hands on me again."

❖

Antonio Alvise entered the apartment with a bottle of champagne in one hand and a large bouquet in the other. With a frozen smile, Sara relieved him of both without touching his hand and she escaped to the kitchen. Alvise stood just inside the doorway holding his own somewhat ingratiating smile. In a charcoal-gray suit and light blue tie, he was, Joanna had to admit, movie-star handsome. If you liked 1950s movies and the smell of aftershave.

"Thank you for coming on such short notice, Dr. Alvise." Joanna took up the rest of the courtesies. "But as I hinted on the telephone, we'd like to discuss something important with you, and it's so much easier over dinner and wine, don't you think?"

"Well, it was rather short notice, but what gentleman would refuse to dine alone with two beautiful women," he replied in his best baritone.

Cringing inwardly, Joanna took him into the living room. "Would you like a glass of wine?" Joanna held up an open bottle of Merlot.

"Oh, yes. That would be very nice. You will join me, I hope. And Signorina Falier also?"

"Signorina Falier is cooking and will join us shortly." Joanna poured a full glass for him and half a glass for herself.

He tapped his glass against hers in a toast. "Salute. Now, please tell me what this important thing is that you need to discuss."

Joanna studied her glass, wondering if she should wait for Sara to add visual attraction to her proposal. "I don't quite know where to begin."

"Begin at the beginning, my dear," he said, falling back on the cliché. "As you Americans say, 'I'm all ears.'"

"Well, the 'beginning' is too many centuries back. Our problems begin near the end. You know the research Sara, uh, Signorina Falier and I have been conducting."

"Yes, of course. You were looking for information about a sixteenth-century woman fleeing Venice for heresy. Have you discovered anything new?"

"Yes, we've uncovered, well, everything. The critical item is the book that this woman published and which originally caused her to be condemned."

"Oh, you've found it. That's splendid. Is that what we're celebrating?"

"No. Unfortunately, we can't celebrate just yet. You see, Dr. Morosini has confiscated the book."

Alvise looked perplexed. "Confiscated it? Whatever for? Did he tell you his reason?"

Joanna studied his expression, looking for deceit. It occurred to her just then that he might be one of those lined up against them. Perhaps all of Venice was against them. But Alvise's expression remained one of polite consternation, and he didn't seem subtle enough to feign such confusion. She pressed on.

"Apparently the very existence of the book was a secret and he wants to keep it that way. You should know that some of the events surrounding the escape and the book cast a very bad light on an ancestor of his."

Alvise sipped his wine. "Ah, yes. He feels very strongly about his ancestors. As if none of the rest of us had any."

"Something like that. In any case, we need to see the book again. Please understand, we don't want to *steal* the book. We never considered that, even for a moment. We know it's the property of the City of Venice and we honor that. All we want to do is photograph some of the pages."

"The pages that slander his ancestor?" Alvise chortled.

"Uh, not specifically. His ancestor is not mentioned in the original text, though I suppose if the book were revealed to the public, its concealment would probably be an embarrassment to the Morosini family."

"An embarrassment, you say?" He squinted for a moment, conspiratorially. "In that case, I will be happy to assist you."

"You will? Even if it means, well, breaking into Dr. Morosini's office?"

"His office. You're planning a burglary?"

"Not in the sense of a theft. We just want to stand right there and photograph it. The whole procedure shouldn't take more than half an hour. You'd be right there watching us."

"That sounds innocent enough. I've always disliked the man, the way he goes on and on about his pedigree. So tiresome. Frankly, I'd love to take him down a peg. As long as you don't break the law. I'd have to draw the line there."

"No laws will be broken, none whatsoever. But the problem is, the book's in his safe."

"The one behind the desk on the bookshelf?"

"Yes, at least that's where we saw him put it."

"Oh, I used that one all the time when I had that office. If I'm not mistaken, I still have a key." He adjusted his tie, obviously pleased that the entire solution lay with him.

Overhearing the conversation, Sara went into the living room and sat down next to Alvise. Looking straight at him for the first time, she said, with sincerity, "If you could get into the safe, just for a few minutes, we'd be endlessly grateful."

Alvise shifted his position to face her directly. "It would be my pleasure. And, by the way, Signorina Falier, I've been wanting to apologize to you for my outrageous behavior last week. It was unconscionable and oafish. I hope my assistance in this little escapade will reestablish my good name with you." He tilted forward, as if he might take her hand, then apparently thought better of it.

Sara took note of the aborted gesture and smiled. "If we can manage this…escapade, as you call it, you may consider the episode forgotten. But how do you propose we proceed?"

"Oh, it shouldn't be too difficult. Once or twice I worked very late at the school, so I know that the night cleaning service leaves just before dawn. For about two hours, the building is completely empty. If I pick you up in my boat at, say, five in the morning, we will have plenty of time to do everything you need. Then we can return the book and no one will be the wiser."

Joanna regarded Alvise for the first time with warmth, then glanced over at Sara. She stifled a sudden urge to laugh as she saw Sara blinking with feminine gratitude.

"Shall we open the champagne, then?"

CHAPTER TWENTY

As the three of them motored into the Grand Canal, the icy breeze coming from the lagoon blew the last bit of drowsiness from Joanna and set her shivering. She'd left the fedora in the apartment, fearing to lose it in the wind, but now regretted it. The best she could do was button her heavy jacket up to the collar and slide her hands into the pockets.

In the last hours before dawn, the festive lights had been turned off at most of the palazzi, and the Grand Canal had a desolate air. The water of the canal was black, save for the reflection of one or two sad lights along the embankment. A few private boats were visible, dark forms in the far distance that were no cause for alarm.

Nonetheless, for added secrecy, Alvise took the boat past the main water entrance of the school on the Grand Canal and came around to the smaller gate on the Rio Foscari side. A lantern on the palazzo wall that jutted out over the water was their only light, but they saw no sign of activity other than their own. The iron gate to the palazzo courtyard was unlocked and they tied up just inside it, then stepped up into the court. The pale stone caught enough moonlight to allow them to move without a flashlight across the opening until they reached the doors of the college.

"If you would be so kind…" Alvise handed the flashlight to Joanna while he drew a large key ring from his pocket. The lock turned with a satisfying click.

Without speaking, they filed into the entry hall. Joanna still held the flashlight and couldn't resist sweeping the beam once over the portrait of Maffeo Foscari. She nodded a greeting toward the Anthony Quinn face as they hurried past it.

Alvise led them up the steps to the office of the Chairman of

History and the second key did its work. Finally they were inside and Joanna took a deep breath of nervous anticipation.

The three of them made a semicircle around the safe as Alvise tried one, then another and another of his numerous keys, and with each failure, Joanna's stomach tightened. Unbearable, if they failed here, at the last moment. She was already sick at the thought.

"Ah!" Alvise's grunt of satisfaction focused her attention and her heart pounded as he pulled open the little door. She shone the flashlight inside.

The pile of objects confused her at first. A manila envelope and other business envelopes, a jeweled rosary and, finally, behind it, the book. Joanna breathed relief.

Alvise slid it out and held it close to the light beam. "So this is what all your labor has been for? What is it, anyhow? *Il Maschera di Salome*," he read. "Sounds like an opera."

"In a way it is," Joanna said, and gently took the book from his hand. "I'll explain it all later, but now we want to be quick about this, don't we? We can photograph it right here on the table. Do you have the camera ready, Sara?"

Sara moved aside several piles of papers, freeing up workspace, then held up the camera. "Yes, I'm using flash, but you'll need to hold the light on it for a minute while I focus."

"Can you manage with the page at an angle? I don't want to break the binding."

"Yes, just let me do the cover first. Okay, here's the first one." A blinding flash lit up the room, casting sudden monster shadows on the walls and ceiling behind them.

"Try to keep your fingertips far to the edge so I don't get them in the frame." Another painful white flash signaled the photographing of the opening page.

"What's going on here?"

All three of them jumped away from the table as if something had exploded in their faces. With a click, the overhead lights came on in the room, forcing them to cover their eyes against the sudden glare.

"Rosso," Alvise said. "I thought your shift was over."

"What are you doing in Dr. Morosini's office in the middle of the night?"

"It's just some private business. Nothing to worry about. The ladies are with me." Alvise approached the maintenance man in a feeble effort to conceal what they were doing.

Rosso was not fooled. "What are you photographing?" He glanced over toward the safe, where the door still hung open, indicting them. "You're stealing something?"

"We're just doing some urgent work." Alvise continued bluffing. "Dr. Morosini knows we are here."

Rosso snorted. "Of course he does. I called him the minute I saw you go in. He's on his way."

Sara glanced at Joanna with panic in her eyes.

Joanna closed the book, held it in front of her for the briefest moment of indecision, then thrust it into her rucksack. Sara dropped her camera in on top of it.

"Dr. Alvise," Joanna said. "I'm taking the book to our apartment. We'll finish it in an hour, then bring it back here. You have our word of honor. But Dr. Morosini is not getting it until it's copied. You can tell him that."

Alvise stood nonplussed between them and the exit. "But ladies, I don't think—"

"Our word of honor," Joanna repeated as she swerved around him toward the door. Rosso still stood in the doorway, and as they passed him, he tried to snatch the knapsack from Joanna's shoulder. Sara immediately pinned him by the shoulders to the wall while Joanna pivoted, twisting out of his grasp. Together they ran down the still-dark stairs to the front entrance.

As they sprinted across the courtyard, an alarm sounded from the main hall of the university. They fled across the narrow footbridge over the Rio Foscari and saw with rising panic that a boat was just arriving. Morosini.

"Do you think he's called the police?" Sara asked.

"I don't know. We haven't really committed any crime."

"It's all how you look at it. We did take something from his safe."

"Oh, hell. Where can we run? Do we dare go back to the apartment?" Sara panted.

"I don't know. I'm not used to running from the law. Do they know where we live? I can't remember if we told anyone."

"Morosini knows we live near the Ponte dei Greci, but not the exact address. Maybe we can circle around and find another way into the building."

Joanna thought of the closed garden at the rear. It only led to other gardens. "There's no other way in. And the entrance is right next to the Ponte. That's the first place they'll look.

"What about going to the State Archives in the other direction? They know us already, the police won't think of them, and it's close. It won't be open yet, but we can wait."

Grateful for any suggestion, Sara nodded and they sprinted across *campi* and *passagios*, emerging finally at the Piazza dei Frari. Though the public wasn't yet in the streets, lights inside the café showed they were getting ready for morning business.

Joanna halted at the door to the State Archives. "Just as I thought. They don't open until ten today. There must be some place we can go. We just need somewhere quiet to wait for a couple of hours."

"Let's try the church," Sara suggested. "It also doesn't open for a while, but the sacristans always come in much earlier, so we might find an open service door."

It was a good guess; the inconspicuous sacristan's door was open. Once inside the church, they pulled the door closed behind them and stopped, catching their breath. "What's a sacristan, anyhow?" Joanna asked as they crept along the wall inside.

"A housekeeper, stage manager, janitor, someone to do all the setup and cleanup according to ritual."

"Let's hope we don't run into one," Joanna muttered as they reached the center of the basilica.

They stood for a moment and glanced up toward the vault, where the dawn light glowed through the high windows. On both sides of them, Joanna could just make out the outlines of the massive tombs. One of them was populated by white marble statues with black faces, that looked for all the world like the ghosts of African slaves.

"Creepy, isn't it?" she said.

"We don't have time for creepy. Let's get busy. I guess we could lay the book anywhere. It'll be hard to focus the lens with so little light."

"It's set on automatic, so we'll just have to hope for the best."

At what seemed the optimum spot, Joanna drew the precious book from her rucksack and laid it out flat on the marble floor. She grimaced as she heard the cracking of the ancient spine of the book and knew she was committing a terrible offense against an artifact. "Forgive me," she whispered to the book, though she knew it would soon be confiscated and, almost certainly, destroyed.

Sara knelt down beside her and began snapping pictures, one after another. One photo of the double opening page, recto and verso, then one close-up of each page. "I'm sorry, my hands are shaking a little. The cold, I guess."

"It's all right. No one's going to bother us here," Joanna said reassuringly. "Just keep snapping."

"Hey! You there!" A voice reverberated in the vast hollow of the sanctuary. "What do you think you're doing here? The church is closed."

A man in a black cassock hurried toward them from the choir. The sacristan, Joanna concluded bleakly. The reason they had found an open door. She looked helplessly toward Sara, who was a better actress, but was any explanation possible?

"I'm sorry, signore." As the man hurried toward them, Sara tried feminine self-effacement. It had worked before. "We haven't touched anything. We came to pray and found the church closed. And we've taken some photos." No good. The explanation sounded slightly insane, even to Joanna's ears. The sacristan didn't even bother to respond to it.

"You'll have to leave immediately, or I'll call for assistance."

"Yes, of course." Shoving the book deep into her rucksack, Joanna used her softest, most conciliatory voice, but there was no longer any point. They were being thrown out, though so far without any alarm being sounded. Sara added her camera to the bulky pack and Sara slid it onto Joanna's shoulders.

The sacristan ushered them toward the tourist entrance at the side of church where a clerk was just setting up the ticket and souvenir counters. His face frozen in anger and contempt, the sacristan pushed open the oak door and held it with one arm as they walked past him into the campo.

Once outside, Joanna halted so suddenly that Sara almost crashed into her. On their right, coming from the café that had just opened, they saw the archives librarian. He quickened his step toward them. "Signoras," he called, raising one arm.

"Bracco," she muttered, as if it were a curse. In an instant, it all made sense. That's how Morosini knew what they'd found in the archives. Tiziana or Bracco must have reported every step they took, every discovery they made, to him. And now they were trapped again.

Should they run? Why? What could he do? It was not like they were bank robbers. She held her ground, sensing Sara's fear. Or perhaps it was just her own. She willed herself to calmness.

"Signora." He was in front of them now. Joanna smiled, but he did not smile in return. "I believe you have something that belongs to us."

"No, we don't." Joanna could hear how tense her voice sounded. "We have nothing that belongs to the archives." She tried to walk away.

A hand landed on her shoulder. "I mean the book you've stolen from Dr. Morosini."

"What? How do you…?" No point in asking. Obviously someone had telephoned him. Someone who had seen the direction they were running.

"You're mistaken," she said, shrugging off his hand.

"I must ask you to hand it over. Don't make me summon the police."

Joanna's mind raced. They were already in trouble, and surrendering wouldn't improve things. They had half the pictures they needed, only another ten or so pages to go. If only people would leave them alone.

"To hell with your police," Joanna sputtered, surprising herself, and pushed him hard on the chest. Caught off guard, Bracco fell backward, landing heavily on one hip.

Assault, Joanna thought. Another crime. Shit.

It took him half a minute to get to his feet again, and in that time, they gained a slight head start. They ran full out along the tiny calli, managing to evade him for a few minutes. Finally they turned a corner into an alley, the only alternative, though they had no idea where it led. Disaster. It led to water. Thirty paces and they came to a standstill, trapped and panting. In front of them was the Grand Canal. Behind them, Bracco had just turned the corner. Seeing his prey caught, he paused, then strolled down the narrow alleyway, obviously savoring the pleasure of their entrapment.

"Shit." Joanna repeated. It was all over.

"Signorina!" Someone called to them from the canal.

"Oh my God!" Sara shouted. "It's our gondolier." She waved frantically. *"Aiuto! Presto, prago!"*

Bracco was slow to discern what was happening. But as the gondola slipped into sight directly in front of his prey, he rushed forward. He reached the end of the street just as Sara fell to her knees in the gondola and Joanna was in midair between stone and boat. He reached for her, clutched air, and twisted awkwardly to avoid falling into the canal. *"Streghe,"* he muttered as the gondolier shoved away from the bank and with one powerful stroke brought the gondola completely out of reach.

"Signorinas!" the gondolier exclaimed exuberantly. "Every day I look for you and today, finally, it is like a dream. Two beautiful women call for my help and I save them in my gondola from the villains. I am like James Bond, *non é?*" He rowed them with a few strong pulls to the center of the Grand Canal.

"Much better than James Bond," Joanna said, making room for Sara on the bench beside her.

"Here you are safe, but the Goldfinger who chased you almost had the Venetian baptism." He laughed at his own joke.

"*Mille grazie* for coming to our rescue, but we aren't just running away. We need a private place. Can you take us away from the Grand Canal to the smallest, quietest rio possible?"

"A quiet place. *Sì, sì.* We have many of those. But two lovely ladies, all alone." He clucked. "What a pity."

"We're not looking for romance. We need to take some pictures undisturbed. Just take us where we can't be seen for half an hour."

"Whatever you wish, signorina. Shall I sing?"

"Uh, thank you, no. Some other time, perhaps."

He sighed and resigned himself to quiet rowing. True to his word, he took them at a leisurely pace into the labyrinth of canal and rio. Joanna fished camera and book from her rucksack again, and in the bright morning sunlight, they finished photographing the entire volume.

"We've done it," Sara said quietly, dropping back against the black cushioned gondola seat, camera on her lap. "Finally, after all that Sturm und Drang, we've done it. Now his lordship can have his damned book back." She held up the camera. "These pictures are priceless. We can recreate the entire work with these photographs alone." She packed both book and camera back into the rucksack. "Teach him to underestimate *us*," she muttered.

Joanna stretched out her arms luxuriously over the cushions of the gondola and took a deep breath. Slightly dazed, she looked around. "Where are we now?"

"The Rio del Palazzo," the gondolier said. "Almost at the end."

"Oh, right. There's the Ponte dei Sospiri right in front of us." Joanna rubbed her shoulders, which were stiff from kneeling and holding the book for half an hour. The gondola glided beneath the Bridge of Sighs and a moment later under the Ponte della Paglia, the final bridge at the San Marco waterfront. An army of tourists swarmed over it, several of them taking snapshots of their gondola as it drew up to the Riva degli Schiavoni embankment.

"I have brought you the long way around, signorinas. I'm afraid it will cost a little extra, though, for all the time it took."

"That's fine. You're the best gondolier I've ever ridden with." Joanna peeled off a significant number of large lira notes and pressed it into his hand. "I assume this will be sufficient." The gondolier glanced down with an expert eye at the wad of notes and did not count them. "From such lovely ladies as you, I am sure it is more than enough. Grazie, signorina." He adroitly pocketed the money, held his oar, and managed to kiss Joanna's hand before helping both of them up onto the riva.

Joanna swung her rucksack onto both shoulders and tightened the straps in case they had to run again. She was elated. It was only late morning and they had pulled off the whole bizarre coup. They were almost done now; the prize was already in hand.

The Italian sun glittered off the water around the gondolas moored near the embankment, the tang of the lagoon air promised spring, the chatter of the crowds behind them was uplifting, and life had never seemed sweeter.

The aroma of fresh garlic wafted over from a nearby restaurant, and Joanna's sudden hunger pang reminded her that they had been up since five in the morning and hadn't eaten since the night before. She glanced toward Sara, whose baleful look showed she was having the same thought.

"Soon. I promise," Joanna said. "In less than an hour, when we've stopped being fugitives."

"So we go back to Ca' Foscari, eh? Back into the lion's mouth?"

"Yes. We walk into Vincent Morosini's office like nothing ever happened, thank him, and whoever else is around, for their help, and wash our hands of the lot of them. Crime undone. Problem solved. Breakfast."

"So we just have to make one more trip on the vaporetto and avoid arrest for another twenty minutes?"

"That's the plan."

"All right, then. Let's get it over with. Right now, the whole crowd is making me nervous. Not to mention those carabinieri over there. Look, the vaporetto is at the dock. Let's run for it."

Checking that the rucksack was sitting snugly on her back, Joanna took off across the riva behind Sara, zigzagging through clusters of tourists scattering birdseed. Once again, they disrupted a flock of plump pigeons, and Joanna wondered if it was the same flock they had waded through on the first day. The crow, who stood his ground and declined to fly, was surely the same one.

The boarding guard on the vaporetto was just about to hook the guard chain across the entryway when she saw them coming, and she held it up for them, smiling. They both leapt the few inches from the dock and joined the crowd amid ship.

The vaporetto was full now, of residents going to work and of tourists out for breakfast or morning sightseeing. Rush hour in Venice. The loud pounding of the motor, the splash as the wake of the boat washed up against the metal dock, the murmured cacophony of awestruck tourists talking in a dozen languages, all seemed a protective blanket. It was almost over.

A few moments later, the vaporetto curved into its next stop, and the throbbing motor went into low gear. The pilot edged the craft toward the dock at the Salute stop, and the boarding guard unhooked the chain again. Some twenty people who had obviously just come from the Salute basilica crowded onto the vaporetto, forcing Joanna and Sara to the far side. The chain went down again, and the vessel chugged back into the canal.

Joanna exhaled slowly. Each stop brought them closer. She faced the shore, with some twenty yards of canal in front of her now, and shifted her shoulders, feeling the rucksack with its precious cargo. She drummed her fingers on the railing, then felt a hand on her backpack. "Sara? What are you—"

"Hand it over," a male voice growled. Joanna twisted around to see a face with a bright red birthmark running from eye to chin.

"Rosso."

Joanna tried to twist away from his grasp, the way she'd done that morning, but his hold was tenacious. He couldn't pull off her knapsack and Joanna couldn't free herself from his grasp. She thrashed and felt the knapsack slipping off her shoulders and down her back, locking her elbows together.

The vaporetto lurched and Joanna was suddenly suspended over the water. She heard Sara call out her name, then the icy water of the canal covered her face.

She sank. Shock, then terror. Desperation. Joanna struggled to pull her arms free from the rucksack. Her jacket, now sodden, stopped all movement of the straps, and the weight pulled her ever deeper. She kicked, trying to bring herself to the surface, but she was leaden. She tried to open her eyes, but the filthy water burned and everything was greenish black, so she shut them again. The rucksack still locked her elbows, and all her thrashing neither loosened the straps nor brought her upward. Her brain screamed for oxygen. Her stomach lurched, once, twice, and she began to black out. Something pressed up against her chest, tugging on her arms. Her last sensation was of sudden cold lightness. Then she lost consciousness and her mouth opened, letting the cruel water down her throat.

Wrestling with all her strength, Sara ripped open Joanna's coat, feeling the buttons pop away. Fear and panic kept her working at a frenzy, forcing off one sleeve, then the other. Finally the whole shapeless weight dropped away. Joanna was limp, lifeless, when Sara grabbed the front of her shirt and kicked upward from the greenish darkness to the surface. Unable to swim, she held Joanna's face over her head and kept kicking, gasping for air each time a kick brought her own mouth to the surface. She was exhausted now and could barely break the surface.

Then one of the boat crew was in the water beside her with a wooden ring. She seized it, threading it over Joanna's limp head and one arm. A second ring landed next to it, and she took hold of it, finally able to stop kicking. With her eyes focused on Joanna being lifted out of the water ahead of her, she scarcely registered that she too was being pulled to safety. Then hands took hold of her on both sides and hauled her up onto the deck.

Seizing deep lungfuls of air, she coughed, waved away assistance, and crawled toward the flaccid white form of Joanna. Someone brought a tank of oxygen and laid a plastic mask over Joanna's face. Long, agonizing minutes passed before she gagged and sputtered and coughed back to life. Heavy gray blankets appeared from nowhere, and Sara laid one over Joanna before wrapping one around her own trembling shoulders. They were back at the Salute dock.

Breathless and with teeth chattering, she tried to see past the faces and legs all around her. Rosso had disappeared, but directly in front of her, flanked by a uniformed officer, was Orazio Barbieri.

CHAPTER TWENTY-ONE

A re you sure you don't want us to take you to the hospital, just to be safe?" the medic asked as the fire department's rescue boat pulled up alongside the Ponto dei Greci embankment.

Handing over their damp blankets, Joanna and Sara both shook their heads. "Thank you for your concern, Officer, but I'm sure we'll be all right," Sara said. "Right now, we just want to shower and get warm."

"I understand." He turned to Joanna. "You were extremely lucky, signorina. You were unconscious only for a few seconds before your friend pulled you to the surface, so you did not breathe water."

Joanna laid her head in her hands. "I don't know why not. The last thing I remember is swallowing water."

"A natural reflex. As soon as you try to breathe for the first time, the larynx collapses and directs water into your stomach. That lasts for only a very short time, though. Eventually it relaxes again and water enters your lungs."

"Thank you for that information." Joanna tried not to be ironic as she shook hands with the medic. "Thank you for everything."

Orazio Barbieri had sat across from them through the entire trip filling out a report and smoking. Now, however, as the medic helped them over the gunwale onto the embankment, he stood up and followed them.

While Sara fumbled with the key to the iron gate, Joanna forced herself to look at the carabiniere. He had waited until the three of them were alone, and so obviously had something to say that the rescuers weren't supposed to hear. Given that he had been silent so far, she assumed he didn't intend to arrest them.

Barbieri dropped the butt of his cigarette onto the ground and crushed it under his shoe. "I did warn you that pursuing this book was unhealthy."

Joanna would have preferred to dismiss him with an expletive, but couldn't let the lie pass. "You warned us it would be pornographic, which we discovered wasn't at all true. You did not say that if we found the book, someone would try to kill us." Sara had the gate open now, but Joanna remained standing, to keep him from entering with them.

"Nonsense. No one tried to kill you. All the passenger reports indicate it was an accident. But the fact that it happened while you were fleeing with a stolen article should serve as a lesson to you that it's best to leave some parts of history unexamined."

"How do you know that we had stolen anything? And why are you trying to hide it, anyhow?" She shivered again, and her teeth were beginning to chatter.

Barbieri buttoned up his own jacket against the wind. "The question is idle, now that the book is gone, and you should be glad it is, so that I do not have to charge you with burglary and theft of a precious artifact. I suggest you return now to New York and do whatever it is that lady professors do these days. Venice has nothing more to offer you."

His remark was cutting and condescending, but Joanna had no will left to reply or take offense. "Good day, Major Barbieri," she said, and stepped through the gateway into the courtyard of their building. Without speaking, Sara shut the iron gate in the policeman's face.

Joanna glanced back once, to see him light another cigarette. Then he crossed the embankment and stepped down into the rescue boat.

❖

Just inside the apartment, Joanna stopped. As if she had been keeping herself composed by force of will, she suddenly slumped. Her jaw began to tremble and she bit her lips, trying to hold back tears. Sara took her into her arms and, in the soft embrace, Joanna let herself cry.

"It's all right. It's over. You're safe now. *We're* safe now."

"I just can't stop shivering. I don't know why," Joanna said through chattering teeth. Sara's damp shoulder was cold and smelled of the canal. Only her neck where Joanna pressed her forehead was warm.

"It's the shock, and the fact that we're both soaking wet. You'll feel much better after a hot shower."

"Thank you for saving my life. I don't know how one says that with enough conviction. God, you can't even swim, and you jumped in right after me."

Grasping Joanna by her shoulders, Sara held her at arm's length, feigning alarm. "Oh my God, you're right. What was I thinking?"

Joanna managed a weak smile, but tears still pooled in her eyes. Sara embraced her again. "Listen, you'll catch your death of cold if you don't get out of those clothes. Go on, you take the first shower. I'll put water on for tea, all right?"

Numb and morose, Joanna nodded and shuffled toward the bathroom. After peeling off her sour-smelling clothes, she stepped into the shower and lathered herself thoroughly. Under the soothing hot water, she shampooed twice and, afterward, brushed her teeth to get the taste of dirty water out of her mouth. She toweled dry, but had no will to dress, so she threw on the bathrobe the apartment service furnished. It was the closest she could get to being wrapped in a blanket.

While Sara hurried to take her own shower, Joanna draped her drenched clothing over a chair in the garden, then curled up on the sofa and resumed brooding on the loss. To keep from recalling the terror of being underwater and dying, she forced herself to focus on the clothes she still had left in her suitcase and what could substitute for the jacket she'd lost.

In just a few minutes, Sara was back, toweling her blond- and gold-streaked hair. She had put on jeans, stylish ones, of course, and a soft white shirt. She dropped onto the sofa next to Joanna and drew up her knees. "Let's talk about damage control," she ordered. "I lost a nice pair of shoes, but that's all. What about you? Did you lose your wallet, credit cards, all that sort of thing?"

Joanna was sullen, but she stared into the air for a moment, taking inventory. "I don't carry a wallet, just cash. Credit cards are with my passport."

"And where's your passport?"

"In my suitcase. With my driver's license."

"Okay. Then the damage to normal functioning is apparently minimal. Let's move on to the project. What did we lose? Leonora's letters?"

"The letters are still here, on the table. But we lost the camera and of course the book. The whole damned purpose for the trip."

"Yeah. While I was showering, I was trying to think of a way to retrieve them. You know, just theoretically, wondering if we could send a scuba diver. But that would be a major undertaking, and the police wouldn't allow it."

"Too late now, anyhow," Joanna said, dully. "The tide comes in and out every night and washes through the canals. By tomorrow both book and camera will be nowhere near where they fell. And in a few hours, the book will have disintegrated."

"Do you think we should just gather up what we have, then, and leave Venice?"

Joanna nodded slowly. "What's the point of staying longer? It seems like we followed the thread as far as it went and this is where it got us. And, except for Alvise, it doesn't look like we have any allies here. Everybody we thought was our friend has betrayed us and chased us all over Venice." She chewed her lip. "It just *galls* me that we have to leave this way, beaten."

"On the brighter side, we do have a lot of good material," Sara said. "Along with the letters, we have the record of the Council of Ten, the ship's manifest of the *Grazie Dei*, the scribe's report, and the Arnoldi history. We certainly have enough for a book. And, if we want, we can trash the reputations of Morosini, Bracco, and Barbieri."

"I wouldn't bother. That all seems petty now. It's myself I'm furious with. We had a treasure in our hands. We had the gold." Joanna got up from the sofa again and walked to the garden door, fists clenched in her bathrobe pockets. "And I let it slip through our fingers by trusting Tiziana. The thought of it just chokes me."

Sara came behind her and rested a hand lightly on her shoulder. "Don't do this to yourself, please," she murmured. Joanna didn't reply, just stared grimly through the glass door at the midday garden. A year's work, wasted. Wiped out by the combined forces of fanatical faith. Rage, bitterness, heartbreak churned in her chest, paralyzing her.

The doorbell rang.

❖

They glanced at each other in alarm. Were things about to get even worse? Scowling, Sara went to the door.

"Tiziana?" Joanna heard Sara say. Sensing a target for her rage, Joanna went to the end of the corridor and stood behind Sara.

Still in the outside hallway, Tiziana clutched the strap of a shoulder bag with both hands, obviously agitated. "Thank God you're both all right. I was terrified one of you had drowned."

Sara didn't invite her inside. "I must say, it takes a lot of nerve to come here after what you've done. How do you even know about what happened?"

"Rosso reported everything to my uncle. He swears he didn't push anyone, that it was just a terrible accident, but I suppose that's irrelevant, isn't it? In any case, I came to offer an apology and an explanation."

Sara was unmoved. "Look, you've done enough damage. Why don't you just—"

"Let her in," Joanna said from behind her. "I want to hear it." She returned to the sofa, and the other two followed her into the living room. Sara pulled over one of the dining-room chairs for Tiziana, as for an interrogation. Then she joined Joanna on the sofa, a tribunal of two.

Tiziana's hands came up in front of her, as if she were handing over something large. "Look, I know you're furious. You have every right to be. What happened was, well, criminal. And I admit that I set it all in motion. But you must let me tell you the whole story and offer you something that might redeem me a little."

"We're listening," Sara said in a monotone.

Tiziana took a deep breath. "I suppose you know by now that the Morosini have been the primary guardians of the book since the return of the *Grazie Dei* to Venice."

"Yeah, we heard," Joanna said, numbly.

Wincing slightly, Tiziana continued her explanation. "Well, actually it was three families, the Morosini, Bracco, and Barbieri. I think you already know the names, from your letters, but you don't know the details. Two Jesuits, both named Bracco, were ancestors of Benito Bracco, who works in the archives, and a lay brother, named Barbieri, was the forefather of Orazio Barbieri. Though I suppose you've figured that out yourselves by now."

No one replied, but Tiziana soldiered on.

"In any case, after they were arrested, they apparently kept a copy of the forbidden work and used it as evidence to exonerate themselves for the murder of Leon Negri."

"His name was Hakim Yaakub," Joanna interrupted, hating that the murdered man had lost even his real identity. "He was a mathematician and an honored scholar in his own country, who left a wife and daughters."

"All right. Hakim," Tiziana said. "In any case, they surrendered the work to the Bishop of Venice, who passed it on to the Holy Office in

Rome. Subsequently, all of them, Vettor Morosini, the brothers Bracco, and Barbieri, took a holy oath of secrecy and 'guardianship' of the book, for themselves and their posterity. The two Jesuits swore it on behalf of their married brother. That is, they were to watch for any other copies that might emerge. Vettor Morosini, apparently, had seized two copies and surrendered only one to the pope. The other remained with the family until the Napoleonic period, when the family surrendered it to Rome."

"Do we need to know all of this?" Joanna said, still sullen.

"Yes, you do." Tiziana held her ground. "I want you to hear it all. Anyhow, being in the Morosini family, I was more or less part of the little 'army of God' that still watched for the book."

"The 'army of God.' Were those the people at the masquerade?" Sara asked, more out of curiosity than bitterness.

"A few of them, although Morosini, who mostly paid for the party, invited a lot of others as well. It was a real party, and Alvise would have thrown it in any case, just to get close to Sara. But they also wanted to let Bracco and Barbieri get a good look at both of you without your recognizing them. That turned out to be useless, though, since both men decided to reveal themselves to you anyhow."

"Morosini, Bracco, Barbieri, all monitoring us? What fools we were," Joanna grumbled. "We should have recognized the names right away from the letters."

"Go on with your story," Sara said. "What happened in the centuries after this great oath? Were there more copies?"

"Yes, over the centuries, three more emerged, the first one already when Vivaldi was alive, two others during the Napoleon years, and each one was destroyed. But for our generation, no one had discovered any copies in two hundred years, so we thought they were all gone."

Joanna stared into empty space. "Well, now they *are* all gone."

"But why, for God's sake?" Sara asked. "So many generations obsessed with one tiny book. We still don't know what the outrage is all about. The section we read was nothing but a revising of the Salome legend."

"I didn't know either, and I never asked. It all seemed like a family ritual, you know, like baptism or communion. I never imagined it would become so deadly, and—"

"How could someone as intelligent as you go along with that oath, or even agree to the destruction of a book on such dubious grounds?"

Joanna suddenly asked. "You, who spend your life with precious manuscripts."

"Because I was taught from childhood that we had to protect the faith."

"Didn't 'protecting the faith' get a little discredited by all those crusades, not to mention the persecution of Galileo and Bruno?"

"That's an unfair comparison," Tiziana said, without elaborating why.

"So, what changed that? The realization that two people you knew almost died?"

"No. What's different is that I held the book in my hands."

"You mean you read it?" Sara was suddenly intrigued.

"Portions of it, before I brought it to you. But it was enough to plant doubt in my mind. Serious doubt."

"Welcome to the Age of Enlightenment," Joanna said sarcastically. "In a couple more centuries you'll have caught up."

"So why did you hand the book over to your uncle?" Sara asked softly. "If you'd had your doubts a little sooner, we might not have needed to go through that car chase with Morosini and his gang."

"It was too big a decision to make in a single moment. I was struggling with a centuries-old imperative and a new idea. It took time for me to see the folly of the old interdict. Then my uncle called me an hour ago to say that Rosso had told him the book was in the canal and it looked like you both had gone in too. He said the matter was closed now, and he thanked me for helping with 'the mission.' I was appalled."

"So you came here to apologize," Joanna said. "Do you really think that's enough?"

"No, of course I don't. I was very nearly an accomplice to manslaughter. But I have something that might redeem me."

"And what would that be?"

"This." Tiziana drew a piece of paper out of her pocket. It was folded into three parts, slightly torn, and brown with age. "It was inserted just inside the cover, and I took it out before I turned the book over to you. I'm not sure why. Maybe because I sensed something very big was happening and I wanted to have a bargaining chip. I'm sorry." She handed the paper to Sara. "There's a signature at the bottom."

Sara's eyebrows went up. "It's from Maffeo Foscari." She studied the large, unadorned script. "He says he believes the book to be true and bitterly regrets his own cowardice in withholding it from the world."

"Really? Those are his exact words?" Joanna unfolded from where she had crouched.

"I'll translate him directly," Sara said, and raised her voice.

To whosoever shall come upon this codex, know that a coward has concealed it. For it tells a tale I cannot suffer. I fear to dwell in a world that is not guided by God, whose incarnation was His Son. Yet this is but the newest of the voices that haunt me, who are called blasphemers and heretics, and will not be silenced.

I am like unto a man whose ship creeps along a coast from port to port while braver captains venture oceanward. I have not the mettle to sail into the unknown, and so surrender these revelations to another age. This volume shall from this day forth be buried amongst my books under false cover. You, into whose hands fate has commended it, I pray you give it your fair judgment and do not shrink from it.

As for the testament in Aramaic from which this work arises, my beloved Lucca has laid it at the feet of Salome, Daughter of Herod, who has been cruelly slandered by legend. I beg her forgiveness.

Sara glanced up from the ancient letter, perplexed. "What does that mean, 'at Salome's feet'? Salome wasn't a living person, or even a dead one anywhere in Italy. He couldn't lay anything at her feet."

"I don't know what he means either, but I think it is significant. It tells you that even if most of the books were destroyed, the original codex was not." Tiziana stood up from her interrogation chair. "More importantly, the 'guardians' don't know about it."

Tiziana smoothed the front of her skirt, as if brushing away some of her guilt, and looked directly at Joanna. "It's another puzzle, I know, but you've both been quite good at solving them. And if you solve this one, the first one will become irrelevant."

Joanna took a deep breath, and it seemed as if it were the first fresh air she had breathed since being dragged from the canal. "Thank you for coming," she said, walking alongside Tiziana to the door. Was she imagining it, or was there sadness in Tiziana's eyes? "I'm sorry if I was so hard on you," she added. "I have the feeling that you're also creeping along a familiar coast, afraid of the ocean."

Tiziana did not reply to the remark, but in parting said, "Please let me know if you find anything. I'll help you any way I can."

Joanna closed the door behind her and returned to the living room where Sara was staring into the garden.

She touched Sara lightly on the back. "Do you think we can trust her?"

"She seemed sincere, and she had no other reason to come here. After all, Morosini basically got what he wanted, so why would she bother unless she meant what she said? Besides, the note from Foscari looks authentic."

"So, I guess the project is back on then, right?"

"Are you up to it? After all that's happened?"

Joanna thought for a moment. "If the alternative is to return home, beaten, then yes, I'm up to it. Or I will be after a good meal. Do you realize we haven't eaten for about sixteen hours?"

"Ah, that's why I feel so crappy."

"Well, then, let's go and have a big spaghetti dinner some place and talk about what to do next."

Sara took Joanna's hand and held it in both of hers. "Listen, I already have an idea about what to do. While you were talking to Tiziana, I was thinking. Just, you know, running all the pieces of the puzzle through my brain trying to match them up."

"And? Did you get any match-ups?" Joanna liked having her hand held and pressed to Sara's chest. The warmth of Sara's palm seemed to flow into her, filling her with hope.

"Yes. Salome's feet."

Joanna's stomach rumbled as she waited for an explanation.

Sara obliged. "As far as we know, there's only one Salome in Venice, the one we've already seen."

"In the baptistery."

"Yes, where they're just about to repair the broken tiles—"

"At Salome's feet." Joanna felt warm all over. With her free hand, she grasped Sara's head and pressed a sudden kiss on her lips. "Looks like we're going to church again. As soon as we've eaten and I've got a new rucksack."

CHAPTER TWENTY-TWO

Joanna pushed her empty plate away and leaned back in her chair. "Amazing what a little hope can do to your appetite."

"Yeah, it's like having a reason to live again." Sara laid her knife and fork across her plate and folded her napkin. "So, have you decided how we're going to get into the baptistery after the workers have left?"

"Actually, we'll get in while they're still there, but this will really test your charm. Whenever any of them glance up from their work, they need to be interested in you alone."

"The flirty thing, you mean?"

"Yes, but you have to turn off the laser beam and do it in broadcast mode. Everyone in the room has to be hypnotized."

"Broadcast mode," Sara repeated slowly, looking up through a slight frown.

"So, we go in pretending to do more work for Morosini. We still have his letter, plus the workers know us. Yeah, I know, our camera's at the bottom of the canal, but fortunately I brought along one of those trashy little Instamatics. All we need is for the flashbulbs to go off to look like we're taking pictures."

"Sounds good. And then?"

Joanna looked at her watch. "Six o'clock. It's time. I'll explain it to you on the way."

❖

They entered the baptistery easily, just as the first workers left. Sara greeted the remaining men, and for some fifteen minutes, they snapped pictures of random mosaics, more or less behind the heads of the workers.

As expected, the novelty of them being in the baptistery had worn off, and, although the one called Mario glanced up at Sara occasionally, the tile workers mainly focused on their work. When it appeared that all the men's heads were down, Joanna slipped unseen into the main church while Sara stepped through the exterior door and leaned back through the doorway into the baptistery.

"Good night, everyone. We're leaving now. Thanks for all your help."

The indifferent mutters of "ciao," "addio," and "salute" suggested that the ruse worked.

Inside the main church, Joanna waited in a corner of one of the chapels until all sounds of activity in the neighboring baptistery stopped. She was relieved to note that the church wasn't completely dark. At the front of the sanctuary, near the atrium, trays of votive candles were still burning. Their flickering flames, reflected back dully from the gold on almost every surface, illuminated the front end of the sanctuary in a smoldering orange glow. At the other end, however, around the presbytery, the bronze urns that hung on long chains with low-watt electric bulbs, gave no useful light.

When the church was entirely silent, she checked her watch. Ten o'clock. She crept back into the baptistery, now dark and empty, and lit her way to the portal with a pocket flashlight. Sara was waiting by the door, and as soon as Joanna opened it from inside, she slipped in.

"There she is, our Salome." Joanna directed the flashlight beam at the overheard archway where Herod's stepdaughter stood. "Strange to realize what a lie that image is, now that we've read her own account." She slid the beam to the bottom of the figure. "'Beneath her feet.' What does that mean, precisely? You don't suppose it's walled up behind the mosaic."

"I doubt it. You can't just take apart a mosaic like that and put it back together again. Not with all those tiny gold tiles. I think it's the floor."

"I'm counting on your being right." Joanna traced a vertical line with the flashlight beam, bringing it down to a spot just to the side of the entryway under the arch. The workers hadn't pulled up the warped section of tiles there yet. She knelt at the side of the largest swell. "We don't have to do much. Just lift a few tiles and put them right back. The workmen will have to lift them out anyhow."

"That'll be difficult, I think," Sara remarked.

Joanna lifted out a section of tile with two fingers.

"Oh, I guess not."

"The mortar was already crumbling away. From the acqua alta, I suppose. And look at this." Joanna pointed to a pipe-like object visible in the newly exposed hole. Half of it jutted out and half of it extended back under the remaining tiles.

"Here, take the flashlight," Joanna said, and reached into the hole. She grasped the cylinder and, with tiny, nerve-wracking tugs, slowly urged it out.

Under the light beam, she held up a cylinder of fired clay some four inches in diameter and about a foot long. Like an enormous cigar holder, one end was rounded and the other was sealed with what appeared to be wax.

"That looks like what we're searching for," Sara noted.

"Whatever it is, we're taking it." Joanna handed the object to Sara and laid the original tiles back in place over the opening. "Now let's get out of here. If it's not what we're looking for, we'll send it back to them."

They were already on their feet, brushing dust off their knees, when they heard the sound of the key. Someone was returning to the baptistery through the outside door.

"Oh, hell. Just what we need," Joanna hissed. She clicked off the flashlight and they scurried into the church.

A voice called out from just inside the baptistery doorway. "Hello? Signorina? Are you there?"

"It's Niero," Joanna whispered. "Damn. The workers must have told him I didn't leave." They slipped farther into the semidarkness.

"Is anyone there?" he called again, moving from the baptistery into the main part of the church. "No one's allowed to stay here at night. If anyone's here, you have to leave."

Joanna and Sara crept from one corner to another, out of sight, and far enough away for their footfall not to be heard. The cat-and-mouse game continued for some ten minutes, with Niero's calls increasingly doubtful.

Finally, while they crouched at the entrance to the crypt, Niero made one more round near the presbytery. With no other place to evade him, they scurried down the stone steps. They cowered in the darkness at the bottom and Joanna fumed at herself for getting them both into trouble again. She braced for the humiliation of discovery, perhaps this time even of arrest. And how could they explain the cylinder?

But something worse happened.

At the top of the stairs, the door to the crypt clicked closed, leaving them in darkness. Instinctively, Joanna flicked on the tiny flashlight.

The crypt was enormous. Joanna knew from seeing the floor plan that it covered the ground beneath the presbytery and the side chapels with three naves and an apse, but all she could see with the tiny penlight were the short columns close by that supported a row of red brick arches.

The rest of the crypt was dim except for two flickering flames in the distance, candles that faintly illuminated a brass cross between them on an altar. "It looks like we may have to wait until someone comes in the morning," Joanna said. "Could it get any worse?"

"I'm afraid it could. Look over there," Sara said, and Joanna slid the beam along the floor.

"Oh, no."

On the floor of the crypt, blackish water was pouring through drains at various corners of the church. As they watched, it spread and pooled first in one spot, then in another, until the pools joined in a wide, flat surface that flowed toward them. The water smelled of rotting algae and mold.

"Dear God. Acqua alta."

"Don't worry," Sara said reassuringly. "It happens whenever there's a very high tide. It'll cover the floor down here, then subside in an hour. We'll be fine. We'll just have to stay on the stairs."

Joanna wanted to ask how Sara could be so cavalier when she hadn't even known about the tide warning the night before, but it was better not to dwell on the subject.

Without speaking, they moved to the highest steps and sat with their backs against the door. Though it was reinforced glass, it offered no light or comfort. Behind them was the sanctuary, only faintly lit by distant votive candles. In front of them was purgatory.

"We should be all right. The sacristan comes early in the morning." Sara's reassurance sounded hollow.

"You think we'll hear him through the door? The glass is awfully thick."

"I'm sure we can. Beside, he'll open it anyhow, for the public. Can't be more than another few hours." Sara was vague about the exact time.

Joanna forced calmness on herself. "We need to conserve the

flashlight battery. I'll turn it off and use it only when we need to." She shivered in the darkness.

"Come here. Sit on the step in front of me," Sara said. "I'll keep you warm."

Joanna shifted into the space between Sara's knees. Though she couldn't see her, she felt the immediate warmth of Sara's arms around her shoulders, Sara's cheek pressed against the side of her head. "I'm sorry. I've risked both our lives for this project."

"Only twice." Sara chuckled, tightening her embrace. Her breath tickled Joanna's ear. "I almost don't mind. Uh, let me rephrase that. When we're finally out of here, I won't mind. This has been the most exciting week of my life."

"The curse of interesting times. Yes, it's been that. I could do with a little less excitement, for a while." Joanna stopped shivering but the quiet darkness was too ominous. "Talk to me, Sara. About anything."

"About warm and fuzzy things? How about a kitten story? My neighbor Tony Foscari, remember I told you about him? Well, he had a cat who had six kittens. Once he let me lie on his couch with the mother cat on my chest. Then one by one, he put the kittens on to suckle till all six were squirming around on top of me in my arms. It was incredible to be part of that archetypal act of mothering. I almost cried."

"You are the most tender person I've ever met, you know," Joanna murmured. "I wish I had known you when you were a child. When we both were children. I'd have given you my best girl clothes to wear."

"Really?"

"Of course. But you might not have liked most of them. I usually wore cowboy shirts and jeans. I even had a little jungle jacket. I fought for weeks to get my parents to buy it for me."

"You'd have loved the boy stuff from my military school, then. We could have traded. In secret, of course."

Joanna began to relax. Obscurity bound them together and isolated them from outside judgment. It was liberating, in a way; she could say anything. "Do you like being Sara? All the time, I mean?"

"Oh, yes. It's not a façade. Or, rather, it's a *real* façade, if that makes any sense."

"It does. The way that Venice makes sense."

"What do you mean?"

"Venice is almost completely façade. It has a history of Carnival masks and regalia. Even now, gondoliers, concert peddlers, musicians—

everybody's in costume. Most of the buildings were erected in one century and their interiors remodeled in another. This basilica has small inside domes and big flashy domes over them. But Venice's 'façade' is absolutely not fake. It's the city's *raison d'être*."

"Yeah?" Sara said tentatively, drawing the word out, waiting for more explanation.

"The outside of you is this serene femininity of Sara, which I love. It's colorful, beautiful, captivating, like Venice, the Serenissima. But underneath is something more complicated, a bit sadder, more endangered, but adaptive, and I love that too. Both of them are terribly courageous."

"I never thought of myself as courageous, and if I am, it's only for you, Joanna. I want to take care of you and make you happy. What do women do for each other? Should I offer you a kitten or build you a bookshelf?"

Joanna rested her cheek against one of the arms that encircled her. "I can't really tell you. I don't take care of women all that well myself. Just ask Monique what an oaf I was."

"Monique was obviously not the right person for you."

"Maybe, but… Oh, God!" Joanna gasped.

"What? What is it? Put the light on!"

Joanna flicked the torch on and recoiled in terror. Black water from the floor of the crypt had risen toward them in the darkness and reached Joanna's foot. The pitiless sea had found them again but this time, brick finality was above their heads. They were going to drown, slowly, struggling for the last inches of air under the ceiling.

Drawing her feet up out of the frigid water, Joanna felt it again— the terrifying certainty of death. She fought off panic. "I love you, Sara," she whispered. "I've never said that to anyone before."

"You'll make me cry. I've never *heard* that from anyone." Sara tightened her embrace and her rapid breathing told Joanna that Sara was panicking too. She herself was almost hysterical.

A metallic clank sounded somewhere and they suddenly fell backward as the door behind them was yanked open. A spotlight shone in their faces and, momentarily blinded, they clambered toward it.

Outside the door, they scrambled up the steps to the ground level of the church and stood panting, well away from the maw of the crypt. Only then did Joanna finally focus on their liberator.

"Marco? From the archives?"

The young librarian pushed his glasses higher on his nose. "Uh-huh. So, are you all right? I'm sorry I took so long. I had to go home and get my father's key."

"How did you know we were here?"

"I...I followed you." He seemed to just then notice Joanna clutching the cylinder to her chest and, without speaking, he took off his jacket and laid it over her shoulders.

"Followed us? From where?" Sara was incredulous.

"From your house. I watched as Signorina Falier emerged alone from the baptistery and then, later, went back inside. I knew you both were in the church when my father went in to check, but he didn't know I was hiding outside. When he came out, I heard him telling one of the workmen that you were in the crypt but that he was going to leave you there overnight to teach you a lesson."

"By letting us drown?" Joanna was aghast.

"I guess he assumed the water wouldn't get that high. It usually doesn't. But to let you out, I had to follow him home, wait until he and my mother went to bed, and then steal the keys. That's why it took so long."

Then the secondary realization struck. "Your father is Signor Niero? The foreman?"

"Yes. He's usually pretty reasonable, but it really angered him to know you'd broken into the church. I was a little surprised myself when I followed you here."

"But I don't understand. You were following us tonight? Why?" Sara asked.

"I've been trailing you since you came to the archives. But not to do you any harm. I mean, I wasn't trying to see anything private. I'm not a pervert."

"Then why in God's name did you do it?" Sara tried to urge him forward, toward the door of the basilica, but he sat down on the steps leading to the chancel.

Joanna too wanted nothing more than to be out of the cold and still-flooding church, but it was clear that Marco had something on his chest, and he'd just saved their lives. She leaned against the wall beside him, slowly warming inside of his jacket while he spoke his piece.

"Um...Please don't misunderstand, Signorina Falier. It's just that, when I saw you the first day, I knew."

"You knew what?" Sara stopped.

"That you were like me," Marco said, drawing his knees up. "I mean, that you had *been* like me but that you had changed. I…I want to change too, but I don't know how."

"You spotted me?" Sara's face was obscured, but her voice revealed that she was appalled.

"Yes, though, don't worry. I'm sure no one else did. No one else knew what to look for."

"And you did?"

"Yes, I've been studying 'changing' for years, in every book I could find. When you walked into the archives, so beautiful and successful, I saw how it looked for real. I was so excited; I wanted to be like you. I thought if I followed you, I might find out more about how I could get there. You seemed happy, complete, and I just wanted to be in the same place as you." He took a breath. "I'm sorry if I acted like a criminal."

Sara sat down next to him on his step. "I don't know what to say. I'm glad you happened to be following us *tonight*, but it's also rather horrifying to think that you've been stalking us, whatever the reason. Maybe you could stop doing that now?"

"Yes, I'll stop. I will, if you'll help me, or at least talk to me about it. I mean, about changing."

Sara laid her hand gently on Marco's shoulder. "I promise you that. I'll tell you all the things you need to know, and who you could contact for help. But not tonight, okay? We're dealing with a sort of emergency."

"Did you find what you're looking for?"

"I think so." Joanna still held the cylinder, but now it was tucked inside Marco's jacket, and Sara avoided drawing attention to it. "But we won't know for a while. We have to take it back to New York for closer examination, and that may take a couple of weeks. But I give you my word, anything that belongs to Venice will be returned to Venice. You're the only person who knows that we did find something, and you could report us at any time, so that should be your guarantee. Besides, we'll stay in regular contact with you. Do we have an agreement?"

"You didn't take anything valuable from the church, did you? I'm on your side, but I can't let you steal from San Marco."

"You mean holy objects? No. I can swear to you, we took nothing sacred that belongs to this Church."

"What is it, then? Am I allowed to know?"

"A document that has nothing to do with this church, that nobody in Venice knows about, that Mr. Bracco didn't want us to ever see, and that we nearly died trying to find."

"Oh, yes. I heard about the accident on the vaporetto. And come to think of it, Mr. Bracco started acting very creepy right after you came to the library. Well, I'm glad you got around him."

"And I'm glad you're glad. So maybe now we should be leaving, don't you think?" Joanna succeeded in urging him along to the baptistery and through the exterior doors. Outside, on the piazzetta, the three quarter moon reflected off the water that had overflowed the embankment.

Sara laid her hand on his shoulder again. "Marco, listen. Don't let people convince you that you're sick. You aren't alone in the world. There are thousands of people like us. You'll find that out." Sara embraced him gently and kissed his cheek.

Obviously deeply affected, Marco stammered his thanks. Then to Joanna he said, "Go ahead and keep my jacket. I'll pick it up tomorrow? Maybe we can talk for a little while."

"Thank you. We'll be packing to leave, but we'll have some time together then."

He quickly embraced both of them again and sprinted across the piazza, skirting the wide pools of water that were still expanding.

❖

Scarcely fifteen minutes later, they were back in their apartment. Joanna secured the precious cylinder in her new rucksack, but after that, bone-weary, they simply took off their wet shoes and staggered toward their respective beds.

The doorbell rang.

They looked at each other, alarmed. No visit at that hour was good news. They both considered escape, then realized there was none. Even if they ran into the garden, they would only reach the center of a ring of apartments. Once again, they were trapped.

Joanna shoved the clay cylinder deeper under the clothes and shoved her rucksack behind the sofa. Also useless. The police would search her first, then the apartment. Would it never end? Or was *this* the end?

Sara was already at the door, peering through the tiny viewing bubble. "What?" was all she exclaimed before yanking open the door. To Joanna's vast relief, it was Tiziana.

"Thank God, I reached you. I've been calling you for the last half hour. My uncle is talking to Bracco and Barbieri right now.

He's summoning his troops again because he thinks you've found something."

"We have. We were in San Marco and pulled something out from under the tiles the workmen were already removing. Don't worry. We didn't break anything. We just reached into a hole that was already there. But if the workmen had found it, they'd have passed it on and it would have ended up with Morosini." Joanna suddenly realized she was talking at a speed that made her sound hysterical. "Oh, sorry, come in and sit down." She backed into the living room.

"I'm sure it's the cylinder that Leonora described in her letter," Sara said. "We don't dare open it, but I'm assuming papyrus or goatskin is rolled up inside. The original codex—"

"Brava. But how did you get in?"

"Long story. We tricked the workmen, or thought we did, but obviously their foreman Niero found out. He locked us in the crypt, but Niero's son got us out."

Tiziana's voice became more urgent. "Ah, that explains why they're up in arms again. Listen, if Niero knew you were in the church, you can be sure he told Morosini. Venice is a small city, and all those guys know each other. By now they've figured out you have something, and even if they don't know what it is, they'll be after you, especially once they find out you've escaped from San Marco. You have to leave Venice right away. Don't worry about the small stuff. Just take the codex and get out." She drew Sara into the living room with her and pointed to the open suitcase on the floor. "I mean tonight. I mean now."

A chill ran down Joanna's back. "Run away? How can we do that? I'm sure we can't get a flight to New York on such short notice."

"Don't even try to do that. They'll expect you to fly and will watch for you at the airport bus stop on the Piazzale Roma and at the water-taxi dock at the airport. Remember, Barbieri and the carabinieri are involved now. So go to Santa Lucia and take a train someplace—Rome, Milan, Geneva—and fly home from there. Just get away from Venice. In a few hours they'll have a better picture of things and they'll mobilize. By then, you won't be able to leave Italy."

"But they don't even know the codex exists."

"Yes, but they know you've been rummaging around in San Marco, and they'll bring you in for questioning. If you're still in Venice, they can lock you up for simple trespassing, or for damage to their repair work in the baptistery. But if you're out of the country, you're safe. They can file for extradition only if they have a specific felony to charge you with, which they don't. So go, for God's sake. For all I know, they're already on their way here." Tiziana gathered up loose clothing from the armchair and threw it into the suitcase.

Clearly persuaded, Sara rushed to the bedroom to dress and pack. Joanna tore off her pajamas and slid into blue jeans and a warm shirt. Then she crammed the remainder of her clothing and papers into her suitcase while Tiziana telephoned for a water taxi.

With astonishing speed, Sara also reappeared in black denims and a waist-length velveteen jacket. Fashionable, even on the run, Joanna noted. Sara had, however, made a significant concession to the emergency, for she wore no makeup. She hefted her fully packed suitcase. "I'm leaving the cosmetics in the bathroom. It'll take too long to pack them all."

"Very wise." Joanna did one last check out loud. "Passport, notes, articles, clothes, money." She pointed to the rucksack. "And the codex. Let's get the hell out of here."

Seizing Marco's jacket from the back of a chair, she made a mental note to mail it to him at the archives. He would surely understand. Finally, she put on her fedora, hoping the spirit of Nigel would speed them along. Then they hurried down the hallway of the apartment building and the external corridor to the iron gateway. The water taxi was waiting.

Sara dropped her suitcase over the side into the boat. A few steps behind her, Joanna turned quickly to Tiziana. "Thank you for all your help. You changed everything for us, you know." She pressed a quick kiss on Tiziana's cheek and was about to join Sara.

Tiziana took hold of her arm, halting her. "You changed everything for me too, and I've betrayed you more than once. Please forgive me." With that, she withdrew a fat envelope from her coat pocket and pressed it into Joanna's hand.

"What's this?"

"I thought, if you didn't find the codex, then I would throw this away. No one would believe you anyway. But you did find it, so you should have this too. You've earned it. Call me when you're safe." She returned Joanna's kiss and said, "I think you make a beautiful couple."

"What?" Joanna tried to ask, but Tiziana was already hurrying away.

CHAPTER TWENTY-THREE

Joanna and Sara leapt from the water taxi onto the embankment in front of Santa Lucia station. In the gray predawn light, the three widely spaced street lanterns gave a desolate illumination to the plaza. With no time to reflect on the incongruence of a modern concrete building at the doorstep of Venice, they sprinted up the steps into the station.

The departure schedule overhead showed a train at 5:14 to Verona, Porta Nuova. Track 6. Joanna checked her watch. "Come on, we can just make it."

"Ufff. It seems like we've been running for days," Joanna muttered, as they broke into a fast jog. They arrived at Track 6 just as the uniformed railmen were slamming the first few carriage doors shut. "Wait!" they called, and clambered onto the last car, hearing the final whistle for departure.

Mere moments behind them, two carabinieri had also entered the station at a run and had halted beneath the departure schedule as the train rolled down the tracks.

Bags bumping awkwardly against their legs, Joanna and Sara made their way down the corridor of the coach. Unsurprisingly, given the hour, there were plenty of seats, and they dropped gratefully into the closest ones.

Scarcely had their fear begun to ebb when the ticket taker appeared in the aisle.

Joanna pulled herself up from her exhausted slouch and reached for her wallet. "We have to buy our tickets from you. Is that all right?"

"Certainly. There is a small surcharge." He named an insignificant sum and in a moment the transaction was done.

"Do you happen to know what trains leave early from Verona to, um, Switzerland?" Joanna asked.

The ticket taker pulled a battered schedule from his back pocket and thumbed through it. "Train to Geneva at noon."

"Um, what about Germany?"

He thumbed again. "At 7:05. Train to Munich. It's a short connecting time, though. You'll have to hurry."

"Thanks, we're good at that."

The ticket taker slid his schedule book back into his pocket and moved down the aisle.

"How much time do we have?" Sara asked.

"About an hour. Not long enough to do anything, really. Not even sleep."

"We'll see about that." Sara crossed her arms and tilted sideways against the train window, closing her eyes.

Joanna withdrew Tiziana's mysterious envelope from the pocket of her oversized jacket. Lethargically, she tore it open, wondering what it could be. It was too thick to be a letter of apology, which by that time was unnecessary anyhow. She unfolded some dozen sheets of paper and gazed wearily at the first page.

She sat up abruptly. "Oh, my God."

Sara's eyes flew open. "What is it?"

"She photocopied it after all!"

"It? What?"

"The confession! From Tiziana. She copied some of the book before she gave it to us. Not the notes or the historical information, just the confession. She must have been able to read it well enough to spot where the translation began." Joanna riffled through the pages. "Look, she scribbled a note on the back."

Dear Joanna,

I should have given this to you at the very beginning. When you read it, you will discover why I feared to surrender it. It changes everything. Another regret, that I couldn't copy the whole volume.

Joanna looked up, stunned.

Sara was radiant. "She must have done it before she sent it off to Morosini. So? Are you going to read the thing?"

"No, you are. It has to be in your voice."

Sara glanced through the pages, looking for where she had stopped reading the day before. "Ah, here it is, 'the Angel of Death.'" She settled back against the cushioned seat. "All right. You liked me channeling a cross-dressing Venetian lesbian. Let's see how well I do as a Judean runaway."

...for I was the Angel of Death. Anon, the bronze doors opened and Herod's slave marched solemnly into the dining hall with the silver charger held out before him. Thereon lay the head of John the Baptist.

Straightway I repented and fled to my chamber. And yet, so little did you care, you did not even visit me that night, though I was undone. Had you come, or shown remorse, or tarried with me in any wise, you might have saved me.

On the morrow, while you wallowed in your bath and in your victory, I cast off my maiden's garments and clothed me as a boy, the more to travel unaccosted through the streets. Thus it was that I wandered through every quarter and sought them, the followers of the Baptist.

At last I found the one named Judas. Although I did not tell my crime, I besought him to take me into their fellowship and teach me about the Messiah. He first chided me for my dress, for offending the law that "the woman shall not wear that which pertaineth unto a man." Yet he list as I told of the fervor of my interest, that I had heard the Baptist's message and desired at all costs to know more of it. Judas said, "My master befriends publicans and fallen women; wherefore should I not befriend a maid hidden behind a boy?" He invited me then into his house, and I feared not, and followed after him.

"Speak to me of your master," I entreated. A light came into his face and, with the selfsame fire in his glance as I had seen in John, he told me of the Nazarene named Jesus. Some said he was

John the Baptist, risen from the dead, and that he was the Messiah. But his teachings, as Judas told them to me, were as cool water on my face. For he preached a new covenant that would bring peace to all nations, that the high would be made low and the poor man raised up. And so my eyes were opened.

For the rest of my fifteenth year I was by day your obedient daughter, and by night a rebellious boy. I escaped often, eluding Menassah, to worship in secret with Thomas and Judas and a woman named Mary Magdalene. I learned there were ten others who were the companions of Jesus.

In that time, Judas was as a brother and the Magdalena and I were like unto his sisters. Mary, for her part, had been much misused by men until she had met Jesus. He had raised her up from disgrace and welcomed her into the company of his followers. As the only woman at the gatherings, she lent a pleasant touch, serving wine and sometimes supper to the men.

Once, of an evening, when the three of us sat together, Judas revealed that Jesus, whom he loved beyond measure, foresaw his crucifixion, indeed its necessity, for it would reveal him as the Messiah. Truly, Jesus seemed set upon forcing the hand of the tyrant so that the prophecy of the Scriptures would be fulfilled.

Though I sorrowed to learn that the House of Herod - and you, whom I did love - must fall, Judas was certain of the coming of the Messiah and, truly, I could feel it in the air. I heard the stories of the Nazarene's miracles: walking on water on the Sea of Galilee, healing the sick at Capernaum, casting out devils, stilling the wind and waves. So enraptured was I that I almost wished to be lame so that he could heal me, and make a revelation of me.

Then it came to pass that the Nazarene entered into Jerusalem.

Mother, bethink you still the day the multitude
gathered outside the walls to welcome him? From
the roof of our palace, I could see him in the
distance, on a donkey. And as he neared, the palm
fronds the people waved were as grass blown by
the wind, that brought their cries of hosannah to
our ears.

Anon, we learned that he would preach on the
Mount of Olives, and when the hour came, I made
as if to take me to my sickbed. Once closeted,
I changed my garment and fled the palace and
Menassah's vigilance. How I ran with joy through
the city past the temple and through the Sheep's
Gate to the Mount where I saw the gathering
multitude.

At first I tarried at the rear, but then, little
by little, I crept through the rings of listeners.
What wondrous words fell upon my ears as I drew
close, things I had never heard from a rabbi or
Pharisee. That God would give the world to men
of peace, to the poor in spirit, the mourners, and
the meek. Jesus blessed the ones who hungered
for justice, the merciful, the pure in heart, the
peacemakers, the persecuted. I could not but think
of John, whose blood was on my hands, and I was
sore ashamed.

When his sermon was ended, the multitude sat
down to eat. A crowd surrounded him, but they
suffered me to pass through them unto him. At
last he turned his gaze on me and I knelt before
him, mindful only then of my false garment.

"Forgive me, Lord, for my lawless clothing.
I longed to see you, and a maid dare not go alone
in the streets of Jerusalem." He smiled and said
unto me, "Come to me as thou wouldst be, and
let thy garment not accuse thee. I love thee in this
guise too." I besought him for his blessing, which
he spoke, then others fell down before him and
supplanted me.

I departed, grateful for my moment, and

made haste to return to the palace ere Menassah discovered my empty chamber. Even as I hastened through the streets of Jerusalem, the Nazarene's words that had echoed down from the Mount were burned into my heart. Blessed are the meek.

❖

A tap on the glass of the compartment door drew their attention. The coffee cart had arrived, wheeled by a scarecrow of a man who would have done well to consume more of his own wares.

For all her fascination with Salome's tale, the thought of food seized Joanna's interest. Sara's apparently as well, for she immediately set aside the stapled pages and opened the compartment door.

They purchased two coffees and the attendant pastries and consumed them hungrily. Joanna swallowed the last of the coffee and sighed with shallow contentment. "Amazing how good really bad coffee can taste when you're starving."

"Yeah, and we even ate that pastry in plastic, which I'm sure was made in a factory long ago and far away." Sara wiped her mouth with a handkerchief that somehow had appeared from her jacket pocket. "So, what do you think about the confession so far?"

"I find it fascinating to get to know the real Salome. In the traditional view, she's a 'wanton woman,' almost a cartoon, but here she's complex and human, and serious. Not a spoiled teenager at all. But above all, I'm stunned—if the work is authentic—that we're reading the words of someone who actually *heard* the Sermon on the Mount and spoke with Jesus, someone who was a witness to arguably the most important event in the history of the Western world."

Sara took up the pages again. "I'm sure that's why it's so threatening. Whatever she has to say about any of those people—Herod, John the Baptist, Pilate, Jesus himself, and whatever she says about what *happened*—that trumps anything in the gospels, *and* in Paul's letters, all of which are second- or even thirdhand reports. No wonder the Church was threatened."

"Well, as far as we've read, there's nothing really shocking. It still sort of unfolds the way we expect it to." Joanna tried to recall the details of her own religious education. "I mean, the Sermon on the Mount sounds about the way I remember it."

Sara chuckled. "Except for that 'Let thy garment be thyself' thing that Jesus said. Imagine, cross-dressing was okay with Jesus. Now there's a Messiah I can relate to."

"Leonora too, I bet. Just remember, as the book's publisher, she must have read this too. Of course by the time she was cross-dressing, I suppose she'd long forgotten about the Sermon on the Mount. A shame."

"I also feel a little sorry for old Herodias, though. Okay, so she did ask for the head, but anyone can commit a little social blunder like that. After all, John was a threat to the legitimacy of her marriage. She had to protect the tetrarch from slander, after all."

Joanna crumpled up the plastic cups and pastry wrappers and crammed them into the miniscule trash container that was already full of the previous passenger's trash. "Everyone had something to protect, I suppose. Herod, Pilate, even creepy Caiaphas. Those were brutal times, and failure could mean a nasty death. Anyhow, I'm dying to find out what happens next. Are up to reading some more?"

"Sure. As long as my voice holds out." Sara folded back the pages to where they'd left off and began again.

The Nazarene drew the multitudes wheresoever he went, for each man or woman, having witnessed him, proclaimed him to others. The air was joyous with the message and with the promises of peace and, above all, of justice that was to come.

Yet even then there was strife around him. Though the Nazarene said he came not to overturn the Law but to fulfill it, the Pharisees list with sharp ears to his preaching and were offended. Caiaphas, before all others, was wroth.

You were there, Mother, when the high priest appeared before the tetrarch. I attended from the corridor, but you throned beside your husband while the old man ranted. The high priest's plaint, that the crowds around the Nazarene would surely bring down the iron hand of the Romans, seemed hysterical. But Herod was ever craven, and when Caiaphas conjured specters of Roman soldiers descending upon the Jews, Herod gave way to the doomsayer.

Caiaphas's foreboding might have gone

unfulfilled were it not for the conflict at the Temple, when Jesus drove out the merchants and the money changers. The air of jubilation was gone, and they that hated Jesus at last had a charge to bring against him.

For Herod could not be seen to suffer an attack on the temple, so he did give command that Jesus be arrested. Straightway, Caiaphas and the other priests sent their men to apprehend him, but so inept were they, they could not locate him until Jesus himself sent Judas to lead them back to Gethsemane. And so it was done, and the high priest's men did seize him, and poured scorn on him, and delivered him unto Pilate.

Pilate heard the prophet but, to our wonderment, he found him innocent, declaring that Jesus's preaching gave no offense to Rome. But the Pharisees reasoned among themselves and, desiring his condemnation, prevailed upon Pilate to remand Jesus to the court of Herod.

You knew how flattered Herod was to be granted this authority, and how ardent he was to see a miracle. The Pharisees already waited like hyenas at the doorway, and Herod made a show of calling them all before him.

Did you not see my feverish eyes as we stood together nigh to Herod's throne? I could scarce control the trembling in my knees when I saw him face-to-face again, the prophet whom Judas had begun to call the Savior.

He was of modest proportions, slender and soft-spoken. As John had been virile and hirsute, so Jesus was smooth, his long hair hung silken and straight, and his bearing was mild to submission. The tetrarch stood up and towered over him asking, "Jesus of Nazareth, men call you the Messiah. What say you to this?"

We all waited for the prisoner's answer, but he gave none, only gazed softly upward and spoke, as were he himself not sure. "Is that how men see me? It is thou who hast said this."

Displeased, the tetrarch sought to flatter the Nazarene and ordered a robe of purple brought to lay across his shoulders. "It suits you, Jesus," he said. "You see, we are prepared to honor you. If you are the Son of God, pray, give us a sign. We beseech you, to set all our minds at rest, give us the smallest of miracles."

But Jesus turned his face away and spoke, "I've done with miracles."

His refusal was an affront to Herod, who saw there was no profit from the hearing. With growing agitation, Herod accused him of being "as those men raving in the market square." Then, raising his scepter as was his wont, Herod commanded his guards to lay their hands on Jesus and confine him in the cistern.

That night, while you slept, I slipped away to the courtyard. The guards had consigned him to the selfsame dismal pit where John the Baptist had been slain. I was beset with guilt and shame, knowing that John's blood was surely still on the floor. Herod had given no interdict so, on the pretense of taking him a pitcher of water, I took a lantern and descended the ladder into the darkness. My eyes were troubled first, but then I saw him by the lantern light.

"Lord," I whispered, and he replied, "Come unto me, my child."

Barefoot and in chains, he was even smaller than in the court, scarcely more in height than I, and with the same long hair. But for his sparse beard, he could have been a girl. Could a man so delicate be the Messiah?

Strangely, he knew me still from our meeting on the Mount and remarked that I was comely, both as boy and maid. He seemed pleased to talk to me, and list when I replied, and there was no dominance in his bearing. Unlike John, whose pronouncements rang like bronze, the Nazarene was as one perplexed. He said, most plaintively, "I brought God's simplest commandments, that men make peace, love the slave, abjure greed and anger. Wherefore do they demand miracles before they accept this?"

"Herod simply craved a sign, like Moses gave to Pharaoh. You could have done a little one."

"The Son of God does not do magic tricks."

"But Lord, you walked on water, raised the dead, changed water into wine."

The Nazarene's reply was wondrous strange. "Misunderstandings, things seen from afar. Stories among the people are exaggerated. Everywhere, they are like children, seeking holy signs."

"And when you caused the lame to walk and the blind to see?"

"Some men need only to believe they are healed, and it is so," he replied.

"Even if the Messiah does not heal, he is prophesied to bring men justice. Can you not make it so, that the wicked cease to prosper?"

Jesus seemed troubled by the question and was silent for a time. Then he said, to my wonderment, "Thou hast spoken true. He makes the sun to rise on the evil and the good and sends rain on the just and the unjust."

"But how shall we suffer that? Wherefore does God not smite the wicked as he did in ancient times, at Samaria and Hebron?"

Jesus seemed to look into his heart, then became solemn, as one who had a sudden bitter knowledge. "It seems...that justice comes not from God, but from thee. From thine own hand. Thou must raise up the poor, comfort the mournful, defend the persecuted and the reviled."

"But how shall we do that without the help of God?"

"If thou learnest nothing else from me, know

that thou hast justice in thee, and mercy. Thou
doest not need God's command to bring forth the
good that dwells within thee." He looked aside, as
if in sorrow. "But men are weak and they want
miracles to reassure them. Verily, the world could
change in a day if all men gave voice to their own
virtue. There need only be a few to prepare the
way, as John did."

The mention of John sparked remorse and
shame in me. "Had I but known, Lord, I would have
been baptized by John," I lamented. "Yet, it was I
who murdered him. Can I ever be forgiven?"

Jesus took my hand, and I felt his love suffuse
me, like sunlight in that dark pit. "Thy repentance
frees thee of this guilt," he said. "And if it will
comfort thee, I will baptize thee now on John's
behalf. Come here, daughter of Herod, and receive
another name."

I knelt before him on the stone floor - perhaps
on stains of John's innocent blood - while Jesus
took the pitcher I had brought. "Raise thy face
to me," he said, and poured water slowly on my
forehead, saying that truly, I belonged to him and
to the Father. Salome was drowned and her sins
with her.

And I felt it, Mother. I felt my old self wash
away with the water.

Then, calling me by my new name, he bade me
rise again as Sarah.

"Lord, I will be with you until Judgment," I
pledged, "for you are the Messiah."

"My dearest Sarah," he said. "The people who
walk in darkness have seen a great light. A Son
is given to them and they will call him wondrous
names, Counselor, Almighty God, and Prince of
Peace." His words should have comforted me,
but he recited the names indifferently, and I was
scarcely reassured.

"And yet, the government shall be upon his
shoulder," he murmured. I thought I saw sudden

fear in his eyes, but it might have been the flickering light of the lantern.

"Government? You mean Herod? I will go before him and beg him to spare you. He has no charge against you."

"No, Sarah. Let the prophecy be fulfilled. Judas hath done his part and now thou must do thine. Like him, thou needst be strong for me."

He took my hand and raised it to his lips. His kiss on my fingers was the tenderest touch I ever knew. I laid my head upon his chest and he embraced me. And in his arms, I was as one transformed, my spirit swelled and yearned toward his and he welcomed me. It was joy and exaltation and humility, all at once. I understood his message of perfect love, the flowing together of our two lights into one. I would want no other man's love for the rest of my life and, as Sarah, would bear witness to his message, until my final breath.

On the morrow I went to Herod, and though he sat with Caiaphas and the other Pharisees, I threw myself before his feet. I besought him to spare Jesus, who had done no harm to anyone. He raised my chin and said however great my supplication, the matter had passed to Rome, and Pontius Pilate.

I fled the chamber, but Caiaphas followed after me and drew me to a quiet place and he upbraided me. The Nazarene, he said, was a danger to the Jews. It was malicious of me to interfere for I knew not the affairs of men.

Emboldened by the touch of Jesus - for it was Sarah now who spoke - I replied without fear. "And if he is the Chosen One, who is resurrected, after all? Will you not blush for shame? Then your name will be like a snake's hiss, when men tell the story."

Amazed and affronted, Caiaphas railed at me. I was a viper in my own house, a wanton who had danced naked and seduced my father for the head of John the Baptist. He would spread the tale and the world would ever after call me an abomination.

I fled him then, withdrawing to my quarters to await the Roman judgment.

Yet even Pilate would not play the tyrant, for like Herod, he feared an insurrection. In truth, it being Passover, he sought to soothe all factions in the quarrel by offering to free the prisoner. A clever move, to let the accusation stand, yet, out of mercy, to free the accused. Surely the Jews would be satisfied, for it was but a week before that they had gathered around Jesus on the Mount of Olives.

Yet, it was for naught. I watched from the palace wall while the prefect addressed the crowd bidding them choose between Jesus and the thief Barrabas. I could see Caiaphas and his men mingling amongst the people, crying out hither and yon, "Barrabas! Give us Barrabas!" Some of the people cried out for Jesus, but the priests called out with greater voice, and so sheeplike was the mob that they fell to chanting with Caiaphas.

Pilate seemed perplexed, but surely also relieved for he could now appear to fulfill the will of the Jews. With a gesture of contempt, he charged Barrabas to be freed forthwith and Jesus to be crucified.

Sore of heart, I descended into the city and sought out the disciples, but most had fled. I found only Judas in the crowd, and together we beheld the dreadful scourging. We wept together to see the gentle arms so cruelly cut by the whip, and cringed at every lash. Finally, unable to endure the horror, we betook us to a quiet place. Then, through his tears, Judas told his sorrowful tale.

Before the Passover supper, Jesus had called Judas aside and asked, "What wouldst thou do for me?" In his devotion, Judas had answered, "Anything, Lord."

Then Jesus said unto him, "Whosoever shall accuse me, whether it be Pharisees or Romans, you must deliver me unto them."

Judas was aghast. What a cruel demand to make of one who loved him so. And yet, Judas would serve the beloved at all costs, even unto death, even unto forced betrayal, though it would break his heart. His consolation would be the Resurrection.

But most ominous of all, Judas said, was that Jesus himself was testing God. Thus he had forced the hand both of his persecutors and of God himself, to see if he would fulfill the prophecy of Isaiah.

We fervently believed he would, and we wondered only what would happen then. Would men rush to be converted, seeing Jesus rise again? Would the Pharisees and Romans repent of killing him? Would the angel of God appear above the cross on Calvary and rend the sky with lightning, and smite the killers of God's prophet and Son? What was God's plan and what was our part in it? Save that we prayed for guidance, we were paralyzed with uncertainty.

When the hour came, we followed Jesus and two others as they bore their crossbeams along the streets of Jerusalem toward the Place of Skulls. The multitude, that only a week before had cried hosannah at Jesus, now jeered at him each time he faltered or fell. The condemned men labored most sorely on the rocky ground outside the city and up the slope of Mount Calvary. Finally, breathless and broken, they reached the top, and though they finally laid their burdens down, their greatest suffering had just begun.

The two Marys found us and we four stood together in the circle of the execution ground. We watched the Romans lay the condemned on the beams and heard the sickening sound of nails being pounded into their flesh, fixing them to the wood.

The soldiers set up their ladders aside the poles imbedded in the hillside, and the crowd went still as they hoisted the crossbeams up upon them. The crucified men cried out as the full weight of their bodies tore open their wrists. It was awkward for the Romans to fit the crossbeams, and while they struggled on their ladders, the crucified men dangled, screaming in their pain. When anon, all three beams were in place, the condemned men cried out yet again as nails were driven through their feet. At the sight of it, Mary, Mother of Jesus suddenly bent forward and was sick.

We tarried by the cross, thinking to lighten Jesus's suffering by our presence, and waited, praying, hour after hour, wondering if God would intervene.

The enemies of Jesus had the selfsame thought, for one of the priests did mock him, saying, "Let Christ, the King of Israel, now descend from the cross that we may see and believe."

Yet he suffered as the others suffered, and groaned even as they did. More and more we doubted. More and more we felt we had been fools. And at the end, Jesus doubted too, for with failing breath he cried out asking why God had forsaken him.

The train compartment door suddenly slid open with a thud, and Joanna and Sara were jolted away from Calvary. Both gazed around, a bit confused, and saw the train had stopped. Vicenza, the sign in the station said, and lines of people were crowding into the train.

The first to invade their compartment was a large, fleshy man, in a not-too-clean army fatigue jacket and knit hat. He held the hand of a little girl, about three years old, who sucked her thumb under a runny nose. Directly behind him was a woman, bland and exhausted-looking, who held a boy of about two in one arm and an infant in the other.

Sara hurriedly shifted their baggage up onto the overhead shelves, and the family distributed itself over the newly empty seats.

Resigned to the end of their solitude, Joanna folded the photocopy back into its envelope and slid it into the inside pocket of her jacket.

Obviously, reading out loud was now out of the question. She waited for things to settle down so she could read the remainder quietly to herself.

It soon became clear that a private reading was out of the question as well, since the two toddlers suddenly took an interest in their surroundings.

The three-year-old especially was enchanted by Joanna's fedora. She took her fingers out of her mouth and pointed to it. "Like my daddy," she said in what Sara recognized as local Italian. The younger boy, for his part, seemed content to stand in front of Sara and pat her knees with flat pudgy hands and constant laughter.

Their mother chided them halfheartedly for bothering the signorinas but also seemed relieved to be able to focus on the fretting infant. Indifferent to everyone, she pulled a sagging breast out from under her shirt and slid the nipple into the baby's mouth to quiet it.

The father remained silent and studied what appeared to be a small train schedule.

Sara and Joanna looked at each other and shrugged, acknowledging that they would spend the remaining part of the trip entertaining children.

As the train slowly pulled out of the Vicenza station, Joanna glanced through the window and saw with alarm that four carabinieri were stopping women and questioning them. That could mean only one thing.

"They're watching for us," she said in English to Sara. "Barbieri must have telephoned ahead."

"Oh, hell," Sara replied in English. "Then he'll have men in Verona too. They must have a description of us and are checking at every station. How will we get across the platform to the Munich train?"

Joanna brushed her knuckles against her lips. "We have half an hour to figure out something," she said, as the little girl reached up to take hold of her fedora. "Me try," she said in her baby Italian. Joanna put the hat on the child's head, where it dropped to her nose and covered her eyes completely. The little girl giggled and lifted it off again with pudgy hands and arms.

"You going to Verona?" the mother suddenly asked, perhaps relieved that the strangers were tolerating her children.

"No," Joanna answered. "We transfer to Munich."

"We do too. We're going to there to look for work. My husband is a bricklayer, and there's a lot of building in Munich," she announced.

The husband glanced sideways at his wife, but declined to join the conversation.

Watching the interplay between Joanna and the child, Sara seemed to have an idea and she spoke again in English. "Your fedora. Has anyone in Venice seen you in it?"

"I don't think so. I only wore it when we went to the museum with Alvise. I didn't want to lose it, so I mostly left it in the apartment."

"Good, then Morosini and his pack don't know about it. You can put your hair up inside your hat. In those jeans and with Marco's jacket, you look enough like a boy to slip past them, especially if you can stay in the middle of a group."

"What about you?"

"I don't know. Maybe I'll just run for it. In any case, we'll be harder to spot if we go separately." By now the little boy seemed completely smitten with Sara and had climbed onto her lap. Smiling up at her, he began to play with the gold buttons on her jacket, twirling them, then trying to put them into his mouth. Sara didn't seem to notice.

"Wait," Sara suddenly said. "How much cash are you carrying?"

"I don't know. A few thousand lira. Enough for supper and a night in a hotel for both of us, if we need it. After that, it's traveler's checks."

They were pulling into the Verona train station, and Joanna saw with alarm that carabinieri stood all along the platform. "Quick, give me about a quarter of it," Sara commanded. "Just peel off a wad of notes."

Joanna looked into her inside jacket pocket and fingered off a thick layer of bills. She did a quick calculation of the amount. Though the number of zeros seemed appallingly high, she knew it amounted to only about two hundred dollars. She handed the wad to Sara.

Without bothering to count it, Sara spread out the bills like a hand of cards in front of the man and said, "I want to buy your jacket and hat for this." She closed up the wad again and laid it into his hand.

He frowned in obvious suspicion. "No, I'm not interested," he answered spontaneously, obviously unwilling to undertake such a sudden and bizarre transaction with a stranger. The train had stopped and people were already in the corridor dragging their luggage. The man brushed away the bills and stood up.

Joanna looked at Sara, grasping what the plan was, then to the mother of the children. "Signora, the offer is serious. So much money for one old jacket." She repeated the amount.

The man hauled down the family suitcase from the luggage rack and started to shove it through the door of the compartment. Only the crowd in the corridor prevented him from moving forward.

Meanwhile, behind him, the woman was collecting her children, but never took her eyes off the wad of money that Sara still held out in front of her. Finally she tugged her husband's sleeve. "Don't be a fool, Guido. Look at how much money they're offering. You can buy two new coats in Munich for that, and clothes for the children too. Take it!"

Brushing her hand off his sleeve, he scowled and looked back and forth at Joanna and Sara. Then, as the crowd thinned and he could shove his suitcase into the train corridor, he cursed and snatched the money. He pulled off his jacket, grabbing various coins and wads of paper from the side pockets, and handed it to Sara. He also pulled off his wool cap, exposing greasy black hair, and slapped it into her hand. Then, pushing the suitcase along in front of him, he seized the wrist of his daughter and pulled her with him.

Without comment, Sara slipped the jacket over her own and zipped it. Then, though it clearly repulsed her, she stuffed her gold-blond hair up under the foul-smelling woolen cap. Joanna meanwhile had tucked her own hair up under her fedora and buttoned Marco's coat up to the neck.

At the same moment, the Italian woman shifted the fretting infant onto one shoulder and struggled to drape a large canvas bag on the other, while the two-year-old tugged on her skirt. In a single smooth gesture, Sara lifted the boy. "I'll carry him, signora. I'm going to the Munich train too." With her other hand, she reached for her own luggage.

Stepping into the corridor, the young mother nodded reluctant agreement, although she kept looking back to assure herself that the strange creature in her husband's coat was not a kidnapper.

Sara said over her shoulder in English, "Leave from the other end of the car and keep away from us if you can. I'll meet you at the back of the Munich train."

"What if one of us doesn't make it?"

"We'll make it," Sara said, with solemn certainty, her lovely jaw now rather masculine between the wool cap and the military jacket. It was a troubling image and Joanna was happy not to have to dwell on it.

Joanna drew on her rucksack and hauled her own suitcase from the rack. By the time she had everything in hand, the corridor was empty and she seemed to be the last one leaving the car. She made her way to the vestibule and the exit door and dropped down the metal steps onto the platform. Without looking up, she started off with a determined gait, trying to catch up with the main mass of passengers. She could see Sara's newly adopted "family" just ahead of her. Two men, one without a coat, a woman, and three children. They looked unassailable, and the police seemed to think so too as they passed them without interest.

Then, to Joanna's alarm, one of the officers marched toward her. Her mouth went dry. Disguise or no, she knew he would immediately hear her American accent and she would be caught. She cursed herself for not giving Sara the precious documents. She took a deep breath and wondered if she could outrun him. No, not in a million years.

He stepped up to her, then passed her, and through the roaring of her blood in her ears she discerned the baffling word "signorinas." Why was he speaking in the plural?

She pressed on for another ten paces, waiting for the hand on her shoulder, and when it never came, she dared to look quickly behind her. The carabiniere was confronting two nuns who must have descended from the train after her. She fought not to laugh out loud. Obviously, the policemen of Verona had seen too many escape farces.

Sara's "family" had already checked the departure schedule for the Munich train, and Joanna followed a short distance behind them to the last track. She was relieved to see them all boarding the coach just ahead of her. Sara glanced in her direction and acknowledged her as they both stepped up into the new train.

CHAPTER TWENTY-FOUR

The train was quite full, but Joanna found a compartment at the rear that still had seats and claimed two of them, dropping her suitcase onto the empty one as the train pulled out of the station.

She watched the corridor nervously, wondering when Sara would finally come. It shouldn't have been difficult to detach herself from the family that hadn't especially welcomed her. Five minutes passed, then ten. Had she misunderstood? Had the police taken her off the train after all? Joanna drummed her fingers on her luggage.

Finally she could stand it no longer. She leaned toward the elderly ladies who sat opposite her in the compartment. "Signoras. I am worried that my friend has not come as she promised. Can I leave my luggage here on these two seats and ask you to guard them? I should be back in just a few minutes."

"Sì, sì, go ahead," they said with grandmotherly solicitation, and Joanna slipped out of the compartment. In the passageway between the two coaches, she found Sara and the man arguing. Sara, clutching the malodorous cap in her fist, was obviously relieved to finally have support.

"He wants more money," Sara said simply.

The man who'd been so taciturn suddenly had much to say. "I see now you're running from the police. If you want me to be quiet, it'll cost you more." He named a sum similar to what he had already gotten.

"Don't try to reason with him, Sara," Joanna said. "Just give him his jacket back and tell him to forget the whole thing."

While Sara slipped off the field jacket, and thrust the woolen cap in the pocket, Joanna confronted the blackmailer. "Signor, you can tell your story to anyone you want on this train. No one will believe you." She took the jacket from Sara's hand and threw it at the stranger, who caught it in midair. "Here. You've got your money *and* your filthy clothes. I suggest you take both and consider yourself a lucky man today." Joanna was taking a chance, she knew, but was counting on the fact that the greasy blackmailer looked disreputable and his story of "she bought my coat" would sound insane, especially since he had it in his possession. The conductor, moreover, would have no idea of the police dragnet and would be too busy to want to interrogate a couple of attractive women on the basis of such a bizarre claim. She hoped.

Ignoring the man's muttering "Perverts," she led Sara into the last coach. Wordlessly, they marched back to Joanna's compartment, arriving just as the conductor appeared. They purchased tickets standing in the corridor and sat down, the two elderly ladies smiling approval.

Once they settled in, the elderly ladies dozed off, while Joanna and Sara spoke in low voices in English.

"It's almost over now," Joanna said. "Just a few more hours to the border with Austria."

"I don't suppose we can read any more of Salome's confession, can we?" Sara asked rhetorically. "I'm dying to know the ending."

"You *know* the ending already. He gets crucified," Joanna muttered.

"Yeah, that's what they say."

"Let's finish it tonight. We can stay at one of the hotels near the airport and catch a morning flight to New York. It'll be a relief to stop running."

"Yeah, I suppose I can wait. I just don't want it to slip through our fingers again."

Joanna patted the side of her jacket where the envelope was tucked into an inside pocket. "It won't, I promise. No water to fall into this time."

Sara smiled agreement and stared out the window for a while, visibly relaxing. The tension dropped from her face as much from satisfaction as from fatigue. "So, we've done it, then. More than we ever expected, in fact. You can start writing your book as soon as we get back."

"Not me. *We*. You and me. You've been doing all the translation, so of course it's your project too."

"Oh, I was hoping you'd ask. I'll have to continue working at the theater at the same time. You know, rent and all that. But on the theater's dark days, I'll be at your disposal."

"The theater? Oh, right. You were assistant stage manager. Will you, uh, go back to being Tadzio?"

Sara shook her head. "No. Tadzio—the one they kicked around at Stonewall—he's gone now."

Joanna studied Sara's face, devoid of makeup, and tried to see Tadzio. But she saw only Sara. She was relieved. It would have been hard to lose her beautiful companion so quickly, to discover she'd been an illusion. But, just like Venice, the façade had become the reality. "A caterpillar metamorphosed into a butterfly," she said, affectionately. "You're committed to staying Sara, then?"

"Yes, some form of her. The crew at the theater are good people, broad-minded people. They'll accept Sara without blinking an eye. It is the Village, after all."

Joanna glanced over at the elderly ladies for a sign that they'd understood anything, but both seemed asleep.

"What does that mean, 'some form'?" Joanna murmured. "Do you intend to go the whole route and have the surgeries? Or is that question too personal?"

Sara leaned close. "With you, nothing's too personal. But I can't answer right now. I mean, completely aside from the astronomical cost, I just don't know."

"Isn't surgery the logical conclusion?"

"Not necessarily. I haven't ruled it out. But just as I don't believe that you're sick, or a mistake, or broken, I don't believe that I am either. This is the way nature made me."

"Like a rare, exotic bird that science hasn't named yet," Joanna said, smiling. "But for now, I suppose the important question is, are you happy?"

"I'm happy when people accept me and laugh at my jokes rather than at me. I'm happy when I'm with you. I've laughed a lot with you this week."

"Yes, we have laughed together. But remind me not to eat raspberry gelato with you again. Ever."

❖

With the threat of capture now apparently gone, exhaustion caught up with both of them. Sara blinked slowly for a while and finally rested her head against the sidewall and closed her eyes.

Joanna also felt a heaviness come over her and a sweet syrupy feeling began behind her eyes. She too slouched sideways against the wall of the compartment, and after a minute of listening to the clacketing of the train wheels, she dropped into sleep.

She awakened with a jolt when someone prodded her knee. She opened her eyes to see a uniformed man in the doorway of the compartment. Behind him was a second man, also in military uniform. Both carried sidearms.

The two old ladies were gone. Only the policemen were there, and Joanna felt a surge of panic. Then the image came into focus. Red berets, uniforms of gray wool, the shoulder patch a shield of horizontal red-white-red, with an eagle landing on green foliage and above it the word *Grenzschutz*. Border Protection.

"Ausweiss, bitte," the soldier said, confirming that they had arrived at the Brenner Pass and Austrian Border Control was checking passports. They would have no knowledge of, or interest in, fugitives from Italian justice. Barbieri may have been able to mobilize the carabinieri, but not Interpol.

The officer compared her passport with her face and was satisfied, but with Sara he hesitated. The soldier peered at the passport photo, then at Sara. Her lack of makeup did facilitate comparison with the male photo, but her breasts obviously caused some confusion. The border guard seemed to have no idea what to do.

"Sie sind Tadzio Falier?" the guard asked, giving the name a curious Teutonic pronunciation.

Deducing the nature of the question, Sara replied, "Tadzio Falier, *ja.*" Then, as the guard persisted in studying her chest, she added, "Transexual." It was not quite true, but close enough.

The guard frowned, perplexed at a word he recognized but had probably never spoken in his entire life. Neither did the case fit into his inventory of official procedures. His confused pout suggested an inner conflict, whether to permit the entry of such a bizarre creature into his tranquil Catholic homeland or to prevent it and thus to initiate a lengthy process that would involve filing a report and giving testimony.

Uncertain, he simply handed the passport back over his shoulder to his partner. *"Was meinst du, Benno?"* He asked for his partner's opinion.

Benno, who was probably acutely aware that they had just begun the passport check and had an entire train to cover in twenty minutes, pushed the passport back to the other man. *"Ist gut, Marti. Kein Gesetz dagegen."* No law against that.

The one called Marti capitulated and handed the pass back to Sara, careful not to touch her well-manicured fingers.

The border control moved on to the next compartment and Joanna took Sara's hand. "I'm sorry about that little confrontation, but we're safe now. No one's chasing us any longer." She pointed toward the window. "And look what happened while we were sleeping. Isn't it gorgeous?"

They both stood up and lowered the upper train window to chin level. Cold air blew in at them but they ignored it, for the sight was breathtaking. Their coach was outside the station on an elevation that overlooked a plateau covered with houses. Snow coated all the surfaces and had piled up in a thick layer on the rooftops. Snow still fell or, rather, blew sideways, sometimes swirling in spirals with a burst of wind. Sounds outside were muffled, all but the high, piercing *pfweeet* of the conductor's whistle.

Joanna linked arms with Sara. "Somewhere out there, little kids in dirndls and lederhosen must be singing 'Silent Night.'"

"Yeah, and drinking cocoa by the fire. Wish I was," Sara answered. "How much farther now?"

"Hour, hour and a half. We'll pass through Innsbruck, cross the border into Germany, and then it's over. We'll go to one of the big hotels, and I'm betting we can get our airline tickets for the next day from there."

"You mean we get to have a night's sleep first? In a real bed? Hard to believe."

"Don't forget, we have a confession to finish reading. Don't you want to see how it ends?"

"Of course. But at this point, I'm running on sheer nerves. First, let's get some food and sleep. I don't mind delaying gratification, do you?"

Joanna looked sideways at her for a second, wondering, then responded, "I don't mind at all. It's better that way."

Chapter Twenty-five

Munich Four Seasons Hotel

Joanna dropped her bag onto the carpeted floor and let herself fall, drained and dizzy, onto one of the beds. "I've just calculated we haven't slept lying down for almost thirty hours and had a real meal for about fifteen. No wonder I feel like crap."

"I know. I'm battle-fatigued too, but I'm too wired to sleep. Plus, I need to eat something. Anything."

"We can order in. It's three in the afternoon, but in a classy hotel like this, we probably can still order breakfast. What do you think?"

"Sounds perfect. Just as long as I don't have to chew very much. I don't have enough strength to move my jaws."

Neither of them remarked on the fact that Joanna had booked one room rather than two. It would be the first time they'd shared a room since the sleeper on the train from Paris, a lifetime ago. But it was evident now that it could not be otherwise.

Twenty minutes later, after both had showered, the food cart arrived and they sat down, luxurious in the hotel's terry-cloth robes.

"Mmm. I never realized how incredibly delicious pancakes are. Especially with sour cream."

"Try the bacon and scrambled eggs. To die for." Joanna held up a slice of crisp bacon.

"I'll try the eggs, but hold the bacon. I don't eat anything that can suffer."

"You don't think the pancakes suffered?" Joanna asked rhetorically and with her mouth full.

"Carnivore logic," Sara remarked, scooping up some of the egg. They finished the meal in comfortable silence, in the serenity of a safe haven.

Finally sated, Joanna brushed her teeth and returned from the bathroom, limp with fatigue. "That's it. I've got about *this* much consciousness left." She held up thumb and index finger half an inch apart.

Sara stood in front of her. "I want us to sleep together."

"Please. This isn't the right time for sexual experimentation."

"I don't want sex. I just want to sleep. With you. We've almost died twice in the last forty-eight hours, both times in each other's arms. I think it's time we embraced just for the pleasure of being alive, don't you think?"

"You're right. I want that too. Come on." Joanna took off her bathrobe, revealing her T-shirt and sleep boxers. She drew back the blanket and slid into one of the beds. Drunk with encroaching sleep, she felt Sara climb into bed and embrace her, spoon fashion, from behind. She was vaguely aware that Sara wore a button shirt, though before she could wonder what was under it, she was unconscious.

❖

Joanna was the first to wake. The room was dark and the bedside clock said nine p.m. She'd slept for five hours. She slipped out from her side of the bed and drew open the curtains. Their room was high up and faced an open landscape of snow-covered fields and the low buildings of an industrial park. The sky was clear, and the nearly full moon cast everything in a soft blue-gray light. Stars were visible only near the horizon, far away from the bright disk. The only sound was the soft purr of the hotel heating system.

Joanna brooded. They'd come from colorful, frantic Venice to this frozen, dormant terrain, like traveling from spring suddenly to the dead of winter. Yet the frigid scene was deeply comforting, almost Christmasy. The winter bliss came, she decided, from the vivid contrast between the indifferent cold of the landscape and the hearth-warmth of the place from which she regarded it.

It was not just the warmth of the room. She realized, somewhat to her surprise, that Sara was her hearth. She glanced back at the bed where Sara still lay sleeping on her stomach, gold-blond hair in disarray, and she felt immeasurably rich. They had accomplished more than she ever expected, and Sara was in her life now, though whether she would remain was still unclear. But in her rucksack was a precious document they had found and saved against all odds. Together. And in her jacket pocket was its translation.

She'd delayed gratification long enough. Creeping across the carpet to the open luggage, she felt around on Marco's jacket and found the envelope in the inside pocket. Salome's confession. Now was the time to find out why the believing world had recoiled from it.

The sheets of the second bed in the room were cold, but it was better than disturbing Sara, who had worked heroically to save them both and deserved her peace. She felt for the bedside lamp on her side of the room and tilted the lamp shade away from her. Still, when she clicked it on, it illuminated the room far too brightly.

"Mmm. What are you doing?" a sleep-soaked voice asked.

"Oh, I'm sorry. I tried not to wake you. I just couldn't wait any longer. I wanted to see what happened to Salome."

Sara sat up and rubbed her face. "Oh, no. Don't read it without me. We have to do it together."

"I was just going to take a peek, but okay, if you're up to it, come on and we'll do it now. I can barely read Venetian anyhow."

"Wait, wait, wait, just let me…" Sara emerged from her blanket in a slightly rumpled nightshirt and climbed into the second, lamplit bed next to Joanna. "Oh, of course you had to pick the *cold* bed to do this in." She puffed the pillow behind her. "All right. Go ahead."

Joanna withdrew the photocopy from its envelope and leafed through the pages to where they'd left off reading. When she found the correct page she handed the bundle to Sara. "I'm sorry I even considered struggling through it alone. It has to be in your voice, of course. Please continue."

"I'll forgive you this one time," Sara said, taking the pages in hand. "Let's see…ah, here's where we stopped."

One of the priests did mock him, saying "Let Christ, the King of Israel now descend from the cross that we may see and believe."

Yet he suffered as the others suffered, and

groaned even as they did. More and more we
doubted. More and more we felt we had been
fools. And at the end, Jesus doubted too, for with
his failing breath he cried out asking why God had
forsaken him. After many long hours, his breath
grew short, and finally we saw by the sudden
dropping of his head that life had gone from him.
To be assured, the centurion pierced his side and
brought forth naught but a trickle of cadaver's
blood. The other two lingered until the centurions
broke their legs, and, anon, they expired as well.

When evening came, the centurions drove us
from Golgotha, and the mortal part of Jesus hung
there between the thieves throughout the night.

Some of the disciples had fled, fearing arrest.
But Peter stayed, even as Mary and Thomas, and
the faithful Judas, though it was clear to all he was
a broken man.

The five of us returned on the morrow to
stand watch, but vultures and crows had settled
on him. And as we topped the hill of Golgotha,
the flocks of carrion birds took flight, and the
fluttering of their wings was terrible to hear.

Heavy with dread, we came nigh to the
crucified Savior and were appalled. The crows had
pecked away his face.

Even as we had the same horror, we had
the selfsame question. How could he rise again in
the flesh if the flesh was eaten from him? It was
suddenly urgent that we protect his sacred body
from such debasement so we petitioned Pilate to
let us take him and entomb him. Pilate consented.

We brought a ladder and Judas mounted it.
He cried out see the ruined face of Jesus and
besought Mary to surrender up her veil to cover
it. Then, weeping still, Judas pried the nails from
Jesus's wrists and feet and lowered him into Peter's
arms.

A pious man named Joseph had offered his

tomb, and so we wrapped Jesus in a cloth and carried him hither. The sepulchre was of modest dimensions, with a stone bier at the center and a lamp of oil at its entrance. The men laid Jesus on the bier and covered him with a shroud. Some followed us, they who had been on the Mount of Olives, and others, waiting to know what would happen next. None of us knew.

The centurions rolled a stone against the entrance and set a guard beside it. We who loved him tarried awhile, then repaired to the House of Judas. Peter and Thomas sat brooding, and Mary and I prepared soup and Passover bread.

Thomas began to eat, then pushed his bowl away. "What if he is really dead? And if he does not rise again? What then?"

"Of course he'll rise again," Judas spat. "Shame on you for doubting the power of the Messiah. Haven't you seen enough of his miracles?" He set about eating as if the question was settled.

Thomas shook his head. "I watched him drive out demons once. But only that. I was not there when he walked on water. Peter was his witness."

Peter ate slowly as if without appetite. "I was there, but the Lord was some distance from our boat. Sunlight reflected on the water, blinding us a little, and I could not see whereon he stood. Yet truly, it seemed he was upon the water. I felt a great outpouring of love and faith and went to join him, but when I stepped beside the boat, I sank. He reproached me for my doubt, though at that moment I was never more certain of him. For all that, it happened very quickly. I didn't see him actually walk."

Judas grew angry and rose from the table. "How can you be of such little faith, and so soon? I'm ashamed of both of you. There were many miracles."

Peter chewed his bread. "I saw but few of them, when the lame threw off their crutches and fell into his arms. The people cheered and the cured men disappeared, I know not where."

"And Lazarus? Surely you bore witness to the raising of Lazarus?" I said from my side of the table.

Peter shook his head. "No, but there were many who did. You have but to listen to the stories the people tell."

I turned to the only other woman in the company. "And you, Mary? By what do you know him to be divine?"

She frowned, having for the first time to explain herself.

"He healed me. I was a sinner who had given myself to men, and carried a child of sin that was stillborn. Men misused me until my soul went out of me. I became as one possessed and could not eat nor sleep, or leave off weeping, for my wretchedness. Then Jesus laid his hands on me and drove the demons from me. I felt my spirit return, a glow within me that yearned toward him and felt his perfect love."

Her tale was eerily familiar and I wondered if I too had experienced a miracle. But one thing seemed to hang in the air, and it hung surely over the heads of all our brethren in hiding. Doubt.

Everything depended on the Resurrection. If Jesus rose, we would know he was the Messiah. If not... No one in the room dared utter the awful thought.

Mary's fear was more pious. "What if the Romans take the body and exchange it for another that is mortal?"

"Hush, woman," Peter said. "Do not speak foolishness."

"No, she speaks true," Thomas said. "They could do that. Caiaphas and his priests could too. None of them wants that miracle to take place."

Seeing the new sentiment, Peter took the lead. "Then we must watch over the body and be there when it happens."

"How can we?" Thomas asked. "The Romans will not suffer us nigh the sepulchre." It seemed the moment for me to speak.

"I can get a potion from Herod's physician," I announced. "I'll simply tell him it is for me. We can present it to the Romans in a gift of wine. Then, when they're asleep, we can carry away the Lord's body."

"And whither take it?" Thomas seemed vexed that I had intervened, but not so much that he wasn't interested.

"Why not here?" I said. "Then we'll all be witnesses to the Resurrection. We'll be the first to see the prophecy fulfilled."

Peter tugged on his beard, a sign he gave it thought. Finally he said, "Let it be so. Let Sarah bring a potion that the women shall give to the guards in wine, whilst we wait close by. If it fails, there is no harm."

Mary seized courage again and spoke. "Should we not involve the others?"

Peter shook his head. "No, there's no place where twelve can gather in Jerusalem without that we draw attention. If we succeed tonight, the Romans may look to question the disciples. Better to just let the nine assemble in another place, away from here."

Thomas also twisted his beard in thought. "Simon and Andrew are with Joseph of Arimathea at Emmaus. Since he's given up his sepulchre to the Christ, he opened his house for the vigil. Likely, the others will repair there as well."

Peter nodded. "Let them stay there until it is all over. Once the Lord is again among us, he will tell us what to do."

I returned to Herod's palace, lest I be missed at the evening meal. But after the common supper,

I sought out old Enoch, whom I could beguile. I complained of the woman's sickness and said I could not sleep for pain. Without hesitation, he mixed a potion from his flasks, saying I should be wary of it for its potency.

When the moon was halfway across the sky, I was with the three disciples and Mary again, and we took the wine to the place of tombs where two soldiers stood guard. They were already weary of their task and rather pleased to see two women. They whispered lewd remarks among themselves, but the night was hot and so they accepted the wine, expecting to have some amusement with us later. But shortly, they were fast asleep.

Our three men rolled the stone away, then Peter, the strongest among them, carried the precious body from the sepulchre. It was much corrupted from the heat, and the odor was difficult to bear. Though I had loved Jesus deeply and bethought me his embrace, I saw him not in the swollen cadaver. With two hearts, of horror and of mourning, I gathered up his shroud and the crown of thorns and followed the men down the path from the tomb.

We laid him under his shroud in the house of Judas, and then we waited. It was nigh unto dawn and I dared not be absent from the palace in the morning, so I ran home. It was prophesied that he would rise again the coming day which was the third, and I hoped to return on the morrow in time for the miracle.

I slept scarcely at all and breakfasted with you and the other women, though I doubt you will remember. One thing or another kept me in your sight, and it was not 'til midday that I escaped back to the house of Judas.

The mood was bleak. The body was turning black and the smell was sickening. Though the house was kept dark against the heat, I could see the others were as ghosts. Thomas sat unmoving. Peter paced, and poor Judas crouched in a corner, his face buried in his arms, a pile of silver coins at his feet. I sat down beside him.

"We watched all night," Mary said from her side of the room. "We saw no sign, no miracle, nothing."

Peter still paced, his fists closed tight, and he spoke into his beard. But any man could see he had ambition and that he could not suffer to be thwarted. "All our preaching, abandoning our livelihoods, our homes. No, we cannot walk away and say we were mistaken. We have to have a Resurrection."

"It's not yet the end of the third day." I said. "He enjoined us to be patient."

We all fell silent again, and I do not recall what was spoken between then and the sunset hour. I only remember the words of Judas, as all of us stood on the roof of the house and the last light of the sun flickered out on the horizon. "I would have given my life for him, but, instead, it was my task to help kill him," he whispered.

"I loved him too," Mary said. "If he was not the Messiah, he was the best of men, greater than the Baptist, and we must not suffer the people to forget him."

Judas was sullen. "They will forget him. Some disciples already talk of going home. Without the Resurrection, he was just a man that I loved."

"Stop brooding on your own loss, Judas," Thomas grumbled. "Think about the world that he sought to change."

"It will not change now." Peter brought his fist down on the wall. "Whither the spirit of Jesus has gone, we have not seen it go and no one will believe."

In deep sorrow, we descended to the room where the odor was nigh unbearable and Peter went to stand by the feet of Jesus, "This was to have been the greatest miracle of all. The miracle that men have longed for," he lamented.

"Then we must give it to them," I replied, beginning to form a thought that had hovered in my mind as a dark cloud, haunting me since Golgotha.

"What nonsense are you chattering, woman?" Peter said.

I was shocked at my own words as I spoke them. It had not been an idea, only the faintest glimmer of one, which terrified me when I examined it too closely. It was not until I uttered it that I knew what it was.

"One of us can appear in his place," I said.

All three disciples looked at me as one deranged, and Peter was contemptuous. "Impossible."

But a moment later, it was clear he had reflected on it too. "We're all too big," he said. "I'm twice his size, Judas is too tall, and Thomas has hands like lions' paws. The people would fall down laughing."

"I can do it." The words burst from me. "I am like unto him in stature."

"You?" Peter seemed dumbfounded.

Thomas was the first to come around. "Wherefore should we not? We would only have to cover her face." He stepped back to appraise me. "She is more slender, but he had hungered, so she could convince except..." I knew his thoughts; they were the same as mine. "Except for the wounds."

"Well, then. The ruse is futile," Thomas said, throwing up his hands. "No wounds, no crucifixion. We could not convince a goat."

Judas was appalled. "What? You would pretend to be the resurrected Christ? It is blasphemy! How can these words come from your mouth?" Judas's eyes were swollen and red from crying and from watching, sleepless, by the body. But there seemed a madness in them too.

"It is not blasphemy if Jesus is really dead," Thomas said.

Then Mary moved us all to resolution. "This morning I went with other women to the empty tomb and I proclaimed that he had risen. I was so certain it would happen."

"What?" Thomas and Judas spoke as one man, aghast.

But Peter proclaimed, "Then so he must. He need be seen but a single time. Then it's saved and we can go on preaching."

"Preaching what?" Judas asked, tearing at his hair. "He said he was the Messiah and, behold, he was not. How can you preach what you know is false?"

"If the messenger was false, the message was true," Mary said, and I was surprised to see she shared my judgment. "Don't you still believe in what he taught?"

Peter drew me aside. "What makes you think we can fool the people?" he asked in a low voice.

"Not all people. Only those who long to be fooled. The disciples yearn for the Messiah and will accept any sign. We have his shroud and the veil that covered his face."

"And we have this." Mary was suddenly beside us. With quiet solemnity, she held up the crown of thorns.

I took it carefully from her hands. "With this over the veil and the warning that my face is corrupted, no one will touch me. You can speak for me that I am about to cast away the flesh and go to my Father in heaven. If you wish, you can slaughter a goat and wipe my face with blood."

"What about the wounds? They will look for the wounds of the crucifixion."

I took a deep breath. It was the hardest thing

I ever had to say. "Pierce my hands. The blood of John the Baptist is on them anyhow. As you strike them with the wounds of Jesus, you will rid them of that guilt."

"And your feet?" Peter asked.

"My feet and my side also. But do it quickly, before I lose heart."

Peter made his decision and in the same instant took charge.

"Take hold of her," he commanded, and Judas and Thomas obeyed. "Speak now if you would change your mind," he said, taking up a long knife from the dinner table.

I shook my head and straightway they threw me onto the table. His free hand covering my screams, Peter plunged the blade into each of my wrists, turning it slightly to make the hole, as for a Roman nail. They pulled me to my feet again, and while Thomas pressed a cloth into my mouth, Peter plunged the blade again into my feet. Blood sprang from both my arms and feet, and I collapsed. I throbbed with pain, yet told myself, it was but a small portion of the suffering on the cross.

Only Judas would not join us, but gnashed his teeth and tore his garment. He cried out, "I cannot bear it," and fled from the house.

Peter paid no heed and bade Mary take the shroud from the cadaver. "Lift her up again," he ordered, and Thomas pulled me upright. I swayed on bloody aching feet, while Peter tore my smock and slid the tip of his blade along my ribs. Another bolt of pain added to the agony in my limbs.

Mary wrapped my feet with scraps torn from the edge of Jesus's shroud, mixing his mortal blood with mine, and thereupon Peter and Thomas bore the body of Jesus to the animal stall and covered it with straw.

Then they brought the donkey before the

door and carried me to him, laying the remaining piece of shroud over my head. It stank abominably, but the stench was the least of my woes. Mary, who was to remain behind in Jerusalem, reached me a final cup of water and we began the journey to the house of Joseph of Arimathea.

It took half a day to reach Emmaus, though it seemed an eternity, for I fainted often and Thomas had to hold me upright on the donkey's back. But at long last we reached the house of Joseph, and Peter helped me down. I hobbled, and with the shroud over my face, I could scarcely see whither they led me. My swollen feet all but crippled me, and so they left me standing against the wall in the upper room of Joseph's house.

A single candle in the corner gave but little light. In the main room below, where Joseph and the disciples sat, the oil lights gave forth an orange glow. Peter went before me to bring the tidings and made a great drama of it. He stood at the top of the steps, and I sensed all heads turning as he stretched out his arms in rejoicing. "My brothers, our vigil is over," he proclaimed. Then, softly, as if in awe, he whispered, "He is risen."

First there seemed an ominous silence, as of disbelief, and then the declaration was repeated, all around the room. Finally I heard the joyous cry, "Praise be to God!" and another voice asked, "Where is he, the Son of God? Where may we see him?"

"He is with us now and waits in the upper room," Peter said, and stood aside, to let them cast their eyes toward me in the near darkness. I breathed with difficulty and could see most poorly through the shroud, but I raised my still-bleeding hands in greeting as the disciples came up the steps unto me.

"Is it you, Lord?" one of them asked. "Are you truly risen?"

I nodded slowly. "It is fulfilled." It was all I dared to say, lest the ruse be discovered, and some were not convinced.

"Let us look upon your face, Lord," another one said.

Peter intervened, and his voice compelled obedience. "Fool, did you not hear what happened? The flesh is mortal, even the flesh of the Son of God. The face we kissed is corrupted and is cast off. Anon, the rest shall also be. Only the spirit and the Word remain."

I heard the murmurs of their uncertainty. Each one must have imagined resurrection differently. Then Peter chided them. "Ye of little faith. Not only did you forsake him in Gethsemane, but even now, while the wounds still bleed, you doubt him." He touched one of my hands and pointed at my feet.

"I saw him crucified and I know his wounds." It was Thomas, who had arrived with us, but had slipped in amongst the disciples, as if he had always been there. "I want to see the wounds before I believe."

Peter seized the moment. "How full of doubt you are, Thomas. Come hither and see for yourself. Put your finger in the nail holes and say if they are not real."

Thomas came close and I flinched in pain as he grasped my right hand and thrust his finger in the still-suppurating hole at my wrist. "The wound is real," he said, then lifted the folded cloth that hung from my shoulder to my waist and laid his hand on my side. He withdrew his bloodstained fingers and held them up and I could hear the men breathe "ahhh." Thomas the "doubter" had dispelled the doubts of all the others.

"Ah, Mary, mother of Jesus, you are here too," Peter said, and I feared suddenly that all might be lost. But, no. She must have wanted

more than all the others to know her child lived,
for she fell at my feet.

"My Jesus, my precious child, they have torn
out my heart," she said with trembling voice. "Tell
me it is you and that you are returned to me."

I whispered, "Fear not, Mother. I am with
my Father in heaven." Then she fell to weeping
greatly, holding the fabric of my robe to her face.
If there was any doubt remaining in the room, she
dispelled it then.

"A pity that Judas, who loved you most, is not
here to witness the moment of truth," someone
said.

"Judas?" I whispered again. I had been in so
much pain along the road, I had not thought to
ask if he followed us.

"He has hanged himself, Lord. On the road
to Emmaus. Remorse, the people say, for his
betraying you."

The news shook me. On the road we had
taken? Lord God. Had we passed the terrible fruit
hanging on the tree and never seen it, so intent
upon our deceit? My silent tears sprang forth.
Judas had been the most loving of the disciples
and the most true, yet nor his piety nor his love
could save him from this slander. Judas was not the
betrayer, but the one betrayed.

"What should we do now, Lord?" someone
asked.

Peter's voice rang with divine authority. "Go
forth now and preach the Word of God as the
Messiah has told you."

I added quietly, "I will be with you always."
Peter took up the theme and saw it as a way to
get me away. "The vigil is over. You know what
you must do. Go now and spread the news of the
Resurrection of the Savior, and proclaim to all men
that the day of reckoning is close at hand." There
was some foot-shuffling.

"Go now, the Savior has commanded it," Peter repeated, and slowly, one by one, the disciples slipped past me, some of them touching my shroud or the blood on my hands. Some fell down and kissed the hem of my robe. Finally only Joseph remained, whose house it was. Peter was adept here too.

"The Savior's spirit prepares to go to his Father, but with each hour, his mortal flesh fails him. We will take him now back to Gethsemane, where he will pray until God calls him to ascend into heaven."

"Lord, suffer me to carry you in my arms," Joseph offered, but Peter feared detection and said no, so I staggered on feet that could hardly bear me, into the courtyard. Thomas waited with the donkey and Peter lifted me onto its back. Joseph kissed one of my swollen feet, and I touched him on the head with a blessing ere we departed.

And so it was done. Word spread that the risen Christ had appeared both in Emmaus and in "another form" at the Sea of Galilee. I know not who was the "other form" in Galilee, but such is the power of imagination of men who long for a Messiah.

The two carried me back to Mary's house, where I collapsed and so was unaware when Peter and Thomas buried the remains of Jesus in a secret place. Mary tended me until I could recover from my wounds and from the fever that came over me. There was no talk of my returning to the House of Herod. If you did mourn for me, Mother, I am sorry.

It was nigh twenty days before I walked again, and then only with the limp that I have borne to this day. I asked to see the grave of Jesus, but it was among many others, all unmarked, and o'ergrown with thistle.

Soon thereafter I left Jerusalem with Mary and Thomas and some others, to preach the

New Covenant as we understood it. And people hearkened unto the Word, for they'd had their miracle, their Resurrection to prove it true.

Thus I have passed this score of years, in the company of Christians, though in the last year, the government has been on all our shoulders. Peter has just been executed; perhaps you know. He led our preaching, more or less, but while he was in Antioch a man named Paul began to have great influence. He is much concerned with rules and admonitions, and his opinion of women bears no resemblance to the love that Jesus offered us.

I am of the last of those who heard the voice of Jesus and knew his embrace, but for all that, I am silenced in the church. First, Paul required that I be veiled so as not to distract the men, and then he commanded the exclusion of women altogether, except for the teaching of children. You can imagine how this wounds me. Shame on Paul, for this injustice. For though I may no longer speak for Jesus, I will soon die for him, suffering even as the men.

I know you, Mother, and I hear you thinking that I was a fool to dedicate my life, and then to sacrifice it, to a lie. I do confess, there are two creatures in my heart, Faith and Doubt, but I think now that they dwelled in Jesus too.

Faith tells me that God waits outside, mysteriously, invisibly, and tests our obedience with suffering. Doubt whispers - in Jesus's voice - that rain falls upon the just and the unjust, that justice comes not from heaven, and that Jesus himself knew he had been forsaken.

And yet, Menassah's finding me, together with the eclipse of the sun, comfort me that all things happen as they must, and that darkness always passes. As the black disk slipped fully over the face of the sun, the halo that shone 'round it seemed to say, "Behold, even when darkness creeps o'er all things, the light is ne'er extinguished."

But in the end, it was Jesus that I loved, and not God. Jesus, who saw the natural virtue, the holiness in all men and women, that showed itself through forgiveness, even as I experienced it in his arms. While the old law taught us obedience to the God of the Jews, the new teaching is that Jew and gentile, slave and master, all of us are one. Perhaps this is the greater thing to die for, not for the hope for mercy, but for the godless mercy in ourselves.

I hear the Romans coming. We are the last to go, to the crushing jaws and to the flames. But Menassah stands at the cage door next to a well-bribed guard, and waits for this final page. Farewell, Mother. You, who would have sacrificed me to loveless servitude, remember this. In Jesus's name, I made the longing heart the core of the new faith. No one shall speak of Salome, save in derision, but you will know the truth. And when in Rome and Antioch and Corinth, ever growing Christian voices proclaim the Living God, know that Jesus did truly die for their timidity, but that a maid did save him. I am the virtue deep within their craven hearts. I am the mercy that needs no miracle.

I am the Resurrection.

CHAPTER TWENTY-SIX

Sara's voice had grown hoarse from the long reading, its weakness giving poignancy to the final pronouncement. Joanna leaned against the pillow and watched her, momentarily stunned, as if she were the daughter of Herod herself. It was dizzying to sense all three at once, each contained within the other like nesting dolls. She heard Tadzio who was Sara, and within her the love-sick Leonora who was Lawrence, and within her the fervent Sarah, who was the Son of God.

It was a blur of identities, a network of true deceits. A modern travesty had made the discovery possible, a travesty had brought the books out of Venice, and an ancient travesty had changed the course of the Western world.

Sara handed the pages back to her. "So that's it, then. The proof that there was no Son of God. It leaves one speechless."

Joanna folded the papers and set them aside. "Why should it? Biological science has long since proven that resurrection is impossible. That miracles are impossible. Nothing has changed, really."

"Not for unbelievers. But imagine spending your entire life believing that a divine trinity watched over your every act and thought. Then, suddenly, the foundation is removed and the whole thing collapses."

"Except it doesn't. Any high-school science book makes it clear that virgin birth and rising from the dead could never have happened, and the slightest study of Middle Eastern civilizations reveals that Christianity is a hodgepodge of earlier myths, of Osiris, Mithras, Dionysus. But for all that, Christianity persists. Religions persist. We have to accept that for millions, maybe billions of people, faith is stronger than fact."

Sara nodded reluctant agreement. "Strange, because the teachings of Jesus are so benign, so…in most cases…so reasonable—that we ourselves should raise up the poor, the mournful, the persecuted, the reviled." Sara half smiled at the irony. "You don't need God to do that."

"I think that was Sarah's point. Jesus as the first secular humanist." Joanna chuckled.

"Well, he does fall a bit short of that, even after concluding that God is not just. Strange, isn't it, to think that Jesus himself struggled with his faith, and sensed a deep moral problem with his divine Father. Nonetheless, he gave himself up to be crucified in the hope of fulfilling a prophecy. And then at the end, of course, the poor man must have grasped he wasn't the Messiah after all. Heartbreaking, isn't it?"

Joanna studied the genuine sorrow in Sara's eyes and found it endearing. "You know what I liked the best of his teachings?"

"What? The part about the reviled and the persecuted?"

"No. When he spoke to Salome on the Mount of Olives and said, 'Come to me as thou wouldst be, and let thy garment be thyself.'"

"I like that too, though that's only Sarah's recollection. It doesn't show up in Scripture. You think that was a coded message to transgendered people that got edited out?" Sara asked, half in jest.

"I'm sure it was. And a minute later, he said, 'I love you also in this guise.' Joanna touched Sara's hair. "I could have said it to you myself."

Sara looked down at herself, her breasts lightly covered by a rumpled shirt and a layer of sheet. "It's a strange 'guise,' I admit. Do you really love it?"

Joanna offered the first soft kiss just in front of Sara's ear. "You *are certainly* strange, but your 'strange' is exciting. You're complicated and deep and troubled, yet you're strong and brilliant. I want to take care of you and be taken care of by you."

"Oh, I do too." Sara drew Joanna close so they were breast to breast. They exchanged little kisses over each other's face. Innocent kisses, broken by quick smiles and lips brushing across fragrant skin. Sara's arms encircled Joanna and held her tightly. For a moment it remained a soft embrace, protective and desireless. Then the barriers fell away and they gave themselves over to their first amorous kiss. It was tender, not urgent, a simple affirmation of the inner journey they both had made and that now was finished. Though they were in an impersonal hotel room in a foreign city in a frigid landscape, they were home.

What was between them began as contentment, solace, the surrender of fear for playfulness. But comfort heated quickly to desire and to hunger, and the kiss took on breathless urgency.

Then Sara broke away. "I'm sorry if I'm clumsy. I've never done this before."

"You've never been with a woman?"

"I've never been with someone I loved."

Joanna kissed Sara's throat, past the faintest hint of Adam's apple, then, unbuttoning the sleep-wrinkled shirt, she pressed her lips into the notch between her collarbones. "I haven't either." Joanna inched her way down Sara's chest, then opened the shirt to gaze at girlish breasts. The nipples, a soft pink, hardened at Joanna's gentle teasing bite.

Sara threaded her fingers through chestnut hair as Joanna took a breast in her mouth. "Oh, God. So wonderful," she murmured.

Joanna sucked the other breast, then raked her teeth upward from breast to the pulsing throat and felt a thrilling urge to dominate, just a little, to erase the male-female divide. But how to force pleasure on a lover such as this? "I don't know how to make love to you," she whispered.

"You might take off your clothes to start." Sara pulled up Joanna's T-shirt and drew it over her head. "Everything. I want to touch everything," she insisted, and Joanna slipped off the little boxers. She was naked now, and arousal radiated out from her sex through her whole body. But she was uncertain. She hungered for Sara now, but not for Tadzio.

Then their mouths met again, open, giving and accepting, the fervent language of their tongues as if in a song. All became flesh, hot flesh, and nothing had a name. Joanna held the beloved in her arms and she was made of warmth, of moist skin and animal urge.

She felt Sara's weight, pressing her on her back, and she acquiesced, opening her eyes to the sweep of gold and blond hair sliding over her cheek. Her own nipples were hard before Sara took them, one by one, between gently torturing teeth.

Sara's hand moved from Joanna's breast slowly down her belly and came to rest on the mound between her legs. The hand began to stroke, not so much to arouse, it seemed, but to explore the unfamiliar place, yet every touch or pressure, every curve or hint of intrusion, sent electricity through her.

Then Sara ventured farther, sliding down the length of her, taking gentle bites along her belly, her pubis, her thighs. Pressure from warm fingers on both sides spread her thighs with gentle insistence. The thought of what was coming made Joanna dizzy, but only more torment followed. Teeth bit softly along the inside of her thighs, a tip of tongue flicked too quickly along her vulva. Joanna moaned for want.

Strong, kind hands that had saved her from death pulled her thighs farther apart, and she surrendered to the tiny hot invasion that darted wetly in and out and then in a circle, as if twirling rings of fire. Sara seemed to play an instrument, licking an intricate melody of light out of the glowing center of Joanna's sex.

Stroking the silken hair, Joanna felt as if she dissolved into a glowing spirit swelling toward another that welcomed her. She was joy and exaltation and humility, all at once. At that moment she understood perfection, the flowing together of their two lights into one.

Oh, don't let it stop, she begged silently, enduring ecstasy until the light exploded in a sudden fountain, once, twice, three, four times, then ebbed, pulsing in ever-smaller spurts. Finally, only the smoldering inside remained, and the floating as if in primal space, an infant star.

Sara was beside her again under the covers, and Joanna covered the sticky mouth, tasting herself still on the ardent lips. "I was on fire. You could have done anything you wanted with me just then."

"I *did* what I wanted, made love to you as a woman. Do I make a good lesbian?"

"Oh, God, yes. That was so much better than building me a bookshelf."

Sara embraced her again spoon fashion, brushing her face against Joanna's hair. "I don't want this to end. I want this to last forever."

"Are you asking me to marry you?" Joanna laughed.

Sara laughed with her. "No, I wasn't. But the irony of it is that we *could*. As bizarre a couple as we are, the law would allow it because one of us is only half a woman, so we're 'covered' legally and biblically. The implications are staggering."

"I don't want to think about the implications, legal or political, or to be an example, or a groundbreaker. I have no idea what the meaning of us is, or how we should define ourselves to the world. I don't even know what kind of sex we should be having. I mean, there's more to you, I know."

"There's more to both of us, and no rule book we have to follow. I'll do anything to please you."

Joanna traced a line around Sara's still-glistening mouth with her fingertip. "I was out of my head with 'pleased.' But I left men for a reason and thought I had the sexual-preference thing all worked out. Look, I *know* I love women. I have my lesbian license and little circles with fists embroidered onto my Levi's jacket. But then you come along and confuse the whole sexual landscape."

Sara nuzzled her again. "Confused? Welcome to my world. You know, I've always liked women. They're so much subtler than men. They negotiate for things while men bash you over the head and take them. That's the kind of man my father was and the kind I don't want to be—or be with."

"The hypermasculine male. We have a lot of them in the U.S.," Joanna murmured into Sara's embracing arm, drowsiness taking hold.

"He forced me to shoot guns and kill things," Sara said. "He even took me to a brothel when I was fifteen to try to 'teach' me to screw women. A grotesque experience for a boy who was already cross-dressing. It was not that I didn't want to be a man. I hated being forced to become one like him, and in the bed of a stranger."

"You sound like Salome, who didn't want to become a woman in the bed of a brute." Joanna was too sleepy to form the final consonant and muttered only 'bru…'"

"I don't know," Sara murmured into her ear. "Whatever I am, I'm whole, just as Leonora was, or Salome. I just live from day to day, and right now I'm in paradise in this room with you in my arms."

Joanna heard the declaration as a soft buzz as she drifted into sleep.

CHAPTER TWENTY-SEVEN

Seven days later

Its tires crunching on snow-covered gravel, the car pulled up the wooded hill to the rough patch of land that functioned as a parking spot. From inside the car, Joanna pointed farther up the slope through the winter trees, a mix of deciduous and evergreen. "There it is. Just up those stone steps. I left the lights on upstairs for us, but it looks like the downstairs neighbors came home too."

A light snow still fell and though only six thirty in the evening, it was almost night and the two-story wooden house radiated welcome from all windows. "Thanks for picking me up at the train station," Sara said. "I was ready to walk the distance, but I guess I'd have been pretty cold and wet by the time I got here. Is all of Port Jefferson like this?"

They lifted Sara's luggage out of the trunk and climbed the steps. "No, this is just the woodsy part. There's also a waterfront area, which is full of tourists in August, but this is where I prefer to be."

The downstairs doorway bypassed the neighbor's apartment and opened to an internal staircase that led to the upper floor. "Put your bag in the bedroom. I'll take you on a thirty-second tour before we settle in."

Joanna led Sara by the hand in a circle around the stairwell from living room to dining room to kitchen, to bedroom. "So, what do you think?"

"Oh, I love it. A house right at the edge of the woods. And up here you have a fantastic view." Sara wandered back to the dining room and looked through the window. "What sort of animals have you seen?"

"Come outside and get a better look." Joanna guided her through the kitchen door, which opened to a narrow porch and a wide panorama of the evening woods. "Squirrels, of course, raccoons, a fox or two, even deer."

"Marvelous. And I see you leave seeds for the birds." Sara pointed to a feeder jutting out from the wall.

"Yes, that's for the sparrows and finches and doves, but the squirrels get half of it." Just then a crow cawed directly overhead. The piercing *kaaaaa* resonated for a second and another second of delicious silence followed.

Sara searched the trees with her eyes. What a powerful sound. It's like he's up there announcing "I AM," just in case no one's noticed."

"Yeah, and I'm sure he's the same crow I saw in Paris and Venice."

"No doubt." Sara laughed and retreated to the warmth of the kitchen. "I'm going to love working here. I've arranged to be at the theater four days a week, so that'll give us a good three-day work period each time. And I'm looking forward to cooking for you. Do you like vegetarian?"

"For three days a week, I can eat vegetarian. And maybe you'll convert me. But no promises. I can't go cold turkey. So to speak."

"By the way," Sara said brightly, depositing her bag at the foot of the bed, "I telephoned Marco. He said thank you for express-mailing his jacket back to him. He's letting his hair grow long and has contacted a transvestite/transsexual organization in Rome called Circolo. It's an important first step, meeting other people and finding out what kind of help is available in Italy. There are so many steps, so many decisions all along the way, and so much hostility from the outside. At least Circolo will give him a base of support, especially if his family rejects him, which seems likely."

"That's the hard part, isn't it? To escape feeling like a pariah. Maybe we can invite him to visit next summer." Joanna turned toward the kitchen to set water on to boil, but Sara followed her to the stove and embraced her from behind. "I've missed you. And I've brought you a gift."

"Oh, yummy. What?"

Sara handed over a package slightly larger than a shoe box. "You'll think I'm crazy. I didn't have time to buy them in Venice, so I had to go to a special shop in Manhattan."

Joanna tore off the wrapping paper and opened the box. "Oh, they're beautiful." She held up two papier-mâché masks.

"Do you really like them? They're copies of the Bauta and Salome masks we wore. I know it was for a rather creepy party, but they'll also remind you of us, when you saved me from Alvise's clutches."

"Oh, I adore them. I'll hang them in the bedroom just like they were in Venice. But I've got a gift for you too." She made an about-face toward her desk. "This!" She held up a typescript of some dozen pages.

"The translation!" Sara was back at her side. "Forget making tea. Let's open a bottle of wine and read this."

"Go puff up the pillows on the sofa, and I'll bring in the wine. I've got some already open. Will rosé be all right?"

"Rosé's fine. Hey, what's this package?" Sara placed a finger on a carefully wrapped carton on the coffee table. The address was the Libreria Marciana, Venice.

"That's the codex." Joanna called back from the kitchen. "The university made excellent photographs of the entire scroll, so it's safe to release it back to Venice. I'll mail it express tomorrow. I've also made duplicates of Tiziana's photocopy, so we have more than one copy of Leonora's book. Actually, Hakim's book. Anyhow, I left a working photocopy there on the coffee table, right next to the package."

Joanna brought in two pink filled wineglasses while Sara studied the new typescript, comparing it page by page with the photocopy from Tiziana.

"Cheers, to us!" They toasted and sipped the wine, then turned back to the two documents that Sara had laid out side by side. "Did you show Dottie the photocopy of the Italian book?"

"No. First of all, she doesn't know any Italian, but I wouldn't have wanted to prejudice her anyhow. She worked only with the Aramaic codex. As I was reading it, though, I was struck by how almost identical the two versions were. Hakim's translation was first-rate."

"Good. I think we should highlight his role in the entire story. I'd like to think that by finally publishing his work, we might bring peace to his wandering spirit."

"And to Leonora's too. I hate thinking that she never made it to England, that she and Anne were never reunited."

"To Leonora, then," Joanna raised her glass again.

The phone rang.

"Damn, another call. It's been like that since I got back." Joanna got up to answer.

"Tiziana! What a nice surprise. It must be past midnight there. Is everything all right?" Joanna nodded through several *uh-huhs.* "Yes, we've just finished the photocopying and the translation, and the codex is already wrapped for express shipment tomorrow. Will you present it to Dr. Niero? I mean, it did come from the basilica, after all. No?" Joanna chuckled. "Oh, you're right, it would make a much bigger splash if you gave it to the mayor of Venice. No, I don't mind if you mention our names. They can't charge us with anything now." She chuckled again, but then her expression sobered and changed to one of intense listening.

"What? You discovered what?" She nodded silently for the next few minutes, her frown of concentration metamorphosing into open-mouthed joy. "Stupendous! Just a minute, let me get a pencil." She scribbled something down on a scrap of paper.

Sara peered over her shoulder to see what the excitement was about. The barely legible notations *1562. Bolde, Falke*, all made no sense.

"Will you be all right, Tiziana? You're sure you won't get in trouble when you hand over the codex? Good. Well, let us know when it arrives. Sara's going to *love* this news."

Joanna hung up, her face bright with a boy-have-I-got-a-surprise-for-you expression.

"What? What did she say?" Sara picked up the paper. "What's this all about?"

"It looks like our near drowning, *twice* in one day, may have been the best thing to have happened to us in Venice."

"What *are* you talking about? The best thing, how? Talk, will you?"

"The best thing *because* it made Tiziana feel very, very guilty."

"Guilty Tiziana is good. Go on."

"Sooo guilty that she spent the last week doing even more research for us."

"What more do we need?"

Joanna was still grinning, releasing the news in little droplets. "It turns out that our Tiziana, librarian extraordinaire, has contacts at the Bodleian Library at Oxford. You'll never guess what she found."

"Get to the point faster. Don't make me hook up the strappado."

"Well, she asked them to check the names of presses in late sixteenth-century London."

"And?"

"The records show that a license was granted to Lawrence Bolde and Anne Falke to establish a press in 1562."

Sara sighed in relief. "She made it."

"Yes, our Leonora made it to England and to Anne. That must have been the mysterious crate that Lucca brought her and that she carried with her the whole way: printers' stamps and dies. The makings of a new press."

"You're sure it's the same press?"

"Absolutely. They even called it Tratti Audaci."

"Oh, that's just wonderful. Let's drink to that too." Sara lifted her glass again.

"Aannd…" Joanna tapped glasses and took a swallow of wine. "In the same year, the London municipal records show a marriage by those same two people, Lawrence Bolde and Anne Falke. Imagine, Sara. They were legally married! Obviously Anne *did* like her Leonora dressed as a man, and she was convincing enough to pull off a wedding. Apparently they managed the printing press together as a married couple."

"Oh, that's the best news I've heard all day."

"No, it's not. Here's something even better."

"What could possibly be better than that? A cross-dressing disciple and a cross-dressing lesbian printer. That's just delicious."

"Then you'll love the taste of this. Tratti Audaci has a sort of 'descendant' press, located on the same premises. All modernized, of course, and Tiziana actually contacted its editor. Remember, as the head librarian at the Venetian State Library, she carries some weight. Anyhow, they talked for an hour about the work. She told them everything she knew, even gave them a list of the documentation we had. I mean, we have tons of stuff now: the letters, the photocopy of the Italian translation, the photos of the codex, Foscari's letter. So, get this. Tratti Audaci has their own set of artifacts relating to Lawrence Bolde and Anne Falke, and they want to print our study. They're *dying* to print it, in fact, not as an academic work, for an audience in the dozens, but as a commercial book. They think it'll be a major seller, and they're so sure of it they're offering a very large advance."

"I guess we'd better start working on it, then."

Joanna took Sara's face in her hand. "No, dear. Not just yet."

Postscript

If you've stayed with this story to the end, you will have noticed the liberties that the author has taken with the commonly accepted details of history. I hesitate to call them "facts," since all events are subject to "spin" and reporting omissions, and we can only assume that reportage of events four hundred years ago would be even more unreliable.

That said, my story—within a story—within a story—uses as much "factual" information as is available and colors it to suit both my whimsy and the "gay agenda."

Regarding the Counter-Reformation (last half of the sixteenth century) during which the novel begins, it is important to know that the Church was reeling from the spread of Protestantism in its several forms (i.e. from Luther, Melanchthon, Zwingli, Calvin, and Knox). It also had to contend with an ever-growing body of scientific information that seemed to contradict Catholic doctrine about the nature of the world. The iconic event of the Counter-Reformation was the revival of the medieval Inquisition. At its most benign, the Church founded new "intellectual" orders such as the Jesuits. At its most barbaric, it caused Giordano Bruno to be burned alive at the stake (1600) for declaring that the earth revolved around the sun.

This novel touches on these events and on the Council of Trent (1545–1563), which was the Church's way of "calling an emergency board meeting" to address the new heresy and to chisel in stone its doctrines, including the *Filioque* clause asserting the inherent divinity of Jesus. Readers are invited to Google any of these terms for more detailed (and fascinating) information about the period.

Rest assured, I *have* been faithful to Venice, a city one cannot talk about except in exuberant clichés. I made a research trip there while writing and used streets, churches, archives, apartments, and landmarks out of my own experience. There really is a torture room in the doge's palace, and San Marco Basilica regularly does get high water in its interior. The Ca' Foscari is the building housing the University of

Venice, and there really is a rather attractive librarian in the Libreria Marciana named Tiziana. (Say *"ciao bella"* from me, if you go there).

As for the transgendered character of Tadzio/Sara, I confess to having only a modest understanding of—but a strong sympathy for—the transgendered life. More relevant to the novel, I want to honor those troublemakers at the "trannie bar" called Stonewall, whose riots in 1969 fired the starting gun of gay liberation. I enjoy a comfortable friendship with several such brave people, but am not privy to their thoughts. Neither do I know what goes on in the mind of a Jesuit or a sea captain or a Renaissance printer. I have created all of these with goodwill out of my own inventory of personalities. However, the youthful, tousled-blond, gender-bending Eddie Izzard was a direct inspiration for the appearance of Tadzio/Sara Falier.

Most audacious, of course, is the novel's "take" on the New Testament. After a faithful reading of the gospels (Revised Standard Version), I created an interpretation, which will for the most part sound familiar, with only the ending being a smack in the face. Although Salome may seem a strange addition, the Bible, in fact, names her as one of the female followers of Jesus. The dancer of the seven veils, who purportedly demanded the head of John the Baptist, is not named in the Bible, but is simply called "Herod's Daughter." Whether the two are one person is anyone's guess. References to Pilate, Nero, Simon Peter, and Paul of Tarsus closely approximate the available historical evidence. I fudged a little on the eclipse, though only a little.

I also wanted to honor the printing press, both presses in general and one in particular. Without the printing press, we would all still likely believe that the earth is flat, that sickness comes from demons or sin, and that Barack Obama was born in Kenya. Sixteenth-century Venice was famous for its printing houses, though I have taken the liberty here of creating Tratti Audaci, a press that did not yet exist. I say "not yet" because it did come into existence—in New York, not Venice—under its English translation, Bold Strokes. You may use your imagination regarding the inspirations for Leonora and Anne.

About the Author

After years of "professing" at universities and writing for international literary journals, and a stint in opera management, Justine Saracen began writing fiction. Trips to the Middle East inspired the Ibis Prophecy books, which move from Ancient Egyptian theology to the Crusades. The playful first novel, *The 100th Generation*, was a finalist in the Queerlit Competition and the Ann Bannon Reader's Choice award. The sequel, *Vulture's Kiss*, focuses on the first crusade and vividly dramatizes the dangers of militant religion.

Justine then moved her literary spotlight up a few centuries, to the Renaissance, and a few kilometers to the north, to Rome. *Sistine Heresy*, winner of a 2009 Independent Publisher's Award, conjures up a thoroughly blasphemic backstory to Michelangelo's Sistine Chapel frescoes and immediately sold out at the 2009 Palm Springs Lesbian Book Festival.

Mephisto Aria, in contrast, deals with devilish things, in a WWII thriller that has one eye on the Faust story and the other on the world of opera. In Berlin, staggering toward recovery after WWII, a Russian soldier passes on his brilliance, but also his mortal guilt, to his opera singer daughter. The novel was a finalist in the EPIC award competition and won Rainbow Awards in two categories: Best Historical Novel and Best Writing Style.

Tyger, Tyger, Burning Bright, her work in progress, places us alongside Leni Riefenstahl, filmmaker of the Third Reich, and follows the desperate lives of collaborators, spies, and homosexual lovers in Nazi Germany.

Saracen lives in Brussels, a short flight or train ride to the great cities she loves to write about. Her favorite non-literary pursuits are parrot pampering, scuba diving, and listening to opera.

Books Available From Bold Strokes Books

Blood Hunt by LL Raand. In the second Midnight Hunters Novel, Detective Jody Gates, heir to a powerful Vampire clan, forges an uneasy alliance with Sylvan, the Wolf Were Alpha, to battle a shadow army of humans and rogue Weres, while fighting her growing hunger for human reporter Becca Land. (978-1-60282-209-2)

Loving Liz by Bobbi Marolt. When theater actor Marty Jamison turns diva and Liz Chandler walks out on her, Marty must confront a cheating lover from the past to understand why life is crumbling around her. (978-1-60282-210-8)

Kiss the Rain by Larkin Rose. How will successful fashion designer Eve Harris react when she discovers the new woman in her life, Jodi, and her secret fantasy phone date, Lexi, are one and the same? (978-1-60282-211-5)

Sarah, Son of God by Justine Saracen. In a story within a story within a story, a transgendered beauty takes us through Stonewall-rioting New York, Venice under the Inquisition, and Nero's Rome. (978-1-60282-212-2)

Sleeping Angel by Greg Herren. Eric Matthews survives a terrible car accident only to find out everyone in town thinks he's a murderer—and he has to clear his name even though he has no memories of what happened. (978-1-60282-214-6)

Dying to Live by Kim Baldwin & Xenia Alexiou. British socialite Zoe Anderson-Howe's pampered life is abruptly shattered when she's taken hostage by FARC guerrillas while on a business trip to Bogota, and Elite Operative Fetch must rescue her to complete her own harrowing mission. (978-1-60282-200-9)

Indigo Moon by Gill McKnight. Hope Glassy and Godfrey Meyers are on a mercy mission to save their friend Isabelle after she is attacked by a rogue werewolf—but does Isabelle want to be saved from the sexy wolf who claimed her as a mate? (978-1-60282-201-6)

Parties in Congress by Colette Moody. Bijal Rao, Indian-American moderate Independent, gets the break of her career when she's hired to work on the congressional campaign of Janet Denton—until she meets her remarkably attractive and charismatic opponent, Colleen O'Bannon. (978-1-60282-202-3)

Black Fire: Gay African-American Erotica, edited by Shane Allison. *Black Fire* celebrates the heat and power of sex between black men: the rude B-boys and gorgeous thugs, the worshippers of heavenly ass, and the devoutly religious in their forays through the subterranean grottoes of the down-low world. (978-1-60282-206-1)

The Collectors by Leslie Gowan. Laura owns what might be the world's most extensive collection of BDSM lesbian erotica, but that's as close as she's gotten to the world of her fantasies. Until, that is, her friend Adele introduces her to Adele's mistress Jeanne—art collector, heiress, and experienced dominant. With Jeanne's first command, Laura's life changes forever. (978-1-60282-208-5)

Breathless, edited by Radclyffe and Stacia Seaman. Bold Strokes Books romance authors give readers a glimpse into the lives of favorite couples celebrating special moments "after the honeymoon ends." Enjoy a new look at lesbians in love or revisit favorite characters from some of BSB's best-selling romances. (978-1-60282-207-8)

Breaker's Passion by Julie Cannon. Leaving a trail of broken hearts scattered across the Hawaiian Islands, surf instructor Colby Taylor is running full speed away from her selfish actions years earlier until she collides with Elizabeth Collins, a stuffy, judgmental college professor who changes everything. (978-1-60282-196-5)

Justifiable Risk by V.K. Powell. Work is the only thing that interests homicide detective Greer Ellis until internationally renowned journalist Eva Saldana comes to town looking for answers in her brother's death—then attraction threatens to override duty. (978-1-60282-197-2)

Nothing But the Truth by Carsen Taite. Sparks fly when two top-notch attorneys battle each other in the high-risk arena of the courtroom, but when a strange turn of events turns one of them from advocate to witness, prosecutor Ryan Foster and defense attorney Brett Logan join forces in their search for the truth. (978-1-60282-198-9)

Maye's Request by Clifford Henderson. When Brianna Bell promises her ailing mother she'll heal the rift between her "other two" parents, she discovers how little she knows about those closest to her and the impact family has on the fabric of our lives. (978-1-60282-199-6)

Chasing Love by Ronica Black. Adrian Edwards is looking for love—at girl bars, shady chat rooms, and women's sporting events—but love remains elusive until she looks closer to home. (978-1-60282-192-7)

Rum Spring by Yolanda Wallace. Rebecca Lapp is a devout follower of her Amish faith and a firm believer in the Ordnung, the set of rules that govern her life in the tiny Pennsylvania town she calls home. When she falls in love with a young "English" woman, however, the rules go out the window. (978-1-60282-193-4)

Indelible by Jove Belle. A single mother committed to shielding her son from the parade of transient relationships she endured as a child tries to resist the allure of a tattoo artist who already has a sometimes-girlfriend. (978-1-60282-194-1)

The Straight Shooter by Paul Faraday. With the help of his good pals Beso Tangelo and Jorge Ramirez, Nate Dainty tackles the Case of the Missing Porn Star, none other than his latest heartthrob—Myles Long! (978-1-60282-195-8)

Head Trip by D.L. Line. Shelby Hutchinson, a young computer professional, can't wait to take a virtual trip. She soon learns that chasing spies through Cold War Europe might be a great adventure, but nothing is ever as easy as it seems—especially love. (978-1-60282-187-3)

Desire by Starlight by Radclyffe. The only thing that might possibly save romance author Jenna Hardy from dying of boredom during a summer of forced R&R is a dalliance with Gardner Davis, the local vet—even if Gard is as unimpressed with Jenna's charms as she appears to be with Jenna's fame. (978-1-60282-188-0)

River Walker by Cate Culpepper. Grady Wrenn, a cultural anthropologist, and Elena Montalvo, a spiritual healer, must find a way to end the River Walker's murderous vendetta—and overcome a maze of cultural barriers to find each other. (978-1-60282-189-7)

Blood Sacraments, edited by Todd Gregory. In these tales of the gay vampire, some of today's top erotic writers explore the duality of blood lust coupled with passion and sensuality. (978-1-60282-190-3)

Mesmerized by David-Matthew Barnes. Through her close friendship with Brodie and Lance, Serena Albright learns about the many forms of love and finds comfort for the grief and guilt she feels over the brutal death of her older brother, the victim of a hate crime. (978-1-60282-191-0)

Whatever Gods May Be by Sophia Kell Hagin. Army sniper Jamie Gwynmorgan expects to fight hard for her country and her future. What she never expects is to find love. (978-1-60282-183-5)

nevermore by Nell Stark and Trinity Tam. In this sequel to *everafter*, Vampire Valentine Darrow and Were Alexa Newland confront a mysterious disease that ravages the shifter population of New York City. (978-1-60282-184-2)

Playing the Player by Lea Santos. Grace Obregon is beautiful, vulnerable, and exactly the kind of woman Madeira Pacias usually avoids, but when Madeira rescues Grace from a traffic accident, escape is impossible. (978-1-60282-185-9)